CROSSFIRE

Roman levered a round into the chamber of the Spencer carbine; the weapon was hot to the touch from the last firing. Then he slipped the long hot tubular magazine from the butt, replacing it with a full one from the wooden box that lay open on the sandy earth beside his shallow rifle pit, a tiny trench that had been scooped out with a mess tin less than twenty minutes before, when they had first ridden here, a headlong dash as the first Indian fire came at them from the high riverbanks, steep inclines no more than a pistol shot away on either side of their tiny island.

"You're seeing history made, boys," the lieutenant had said. "Nobody ever saw 'em fight like disciplined cavalry before this day!"

Roman would as soon not see such history being made, he thought, and wondered if, far out there to the east, beyond the heat-wave–wrinkled horizon, there was a single soul who gave a good damn about what was happening here on this strip of land in the bottom of a riverbed at the edge of the Colorado Territory.

Books by Douglas C. Jones

The Search for the Temperance Man
This Savage Race
Season of Yellow Leaf
Elkhorn Tavern
Roman Hasford

Published by HarperPaperbacks

ATTENTION: ORGANIZATIONS AND CORPORATIONS

Most HarperPaperbacks are available at special quantity discounts for
bulk purchases for sales promotions, premiums, or fund-raising.
For information, please call or write:
Special Markets Department, HarperCollins Publishers,
10 East 53rd Street, New York, N.Y. 10022.
Telephone: (212) 207-7528. Fax: (212) 207-7222.

ROMAN HASFORD

Formerly titled: *Roman*

DOUGLAS C. JONES

HarperPaperbacks
A Division of HarperCollins*Publishers*

This is a work of fiction. The characters, incidents, and dialogues are products of the author's imagination and are not to be construed as real. Any resemblance to actual events or persons, living or dead, is entirely coincidental.

HarperPaperbacks   *A Division of* HarperCollins*Publishers*
10 East 53rd Street, New York, N.Y. 10022

A hardcover edition of this work was originally published under the title *Roman* by Henry Holt and Co., Inc. It is reprinted here by arrangement with Henry Holt and Company, Inc.

Cover illustration by Harry Schaare

First HarperPaperbacks printing: March 1996

Printed in the United States of America

HarperPaperbacks and colophon are trademarks of HarperCollins*Publishers*

10 9 8 7 6 5 4 3 2 1

A great many people have asked, "What ever happened to Roman Hasford after Elkhorn Tavern burned?" What happened to him follows, and it's dedicated to all those who have seen sons come to manhood in troubled times.

Douglas C. Jones
Fayetteville, Arkansas

PART ONE

The old ones say that time's passage takes the harsh edges off the memory of disaster.

—from Roman's diary

The Cheyenne had come twice already, straight down the streambed toward the island, their charge splitting at the last moment to pass on either side. And he knew they would come again and in greater force because he could hear them out on the plain beyond the cutbanks and around the bend in the river, shouting, working up to it. He thought he could feel the earth tremble with the shock of the prancing pony hooves.

"One in the chamber and a full magazine," the commanding officer shouted from somewhere behind him. The commanding officer had been everywhere, moving as smart as on parade, a huge Army-model Colt revolver in his hand, now down with two wounds to the legs, still shouting instructions to the huddled troop of men. "And this time, don't shoot until I say!"

He levered a round into the chamber of the Spencer carbine; the weapon was hot to the touch from the last firing. Then he slipped the long, tubular magazine from the butt, replacing it with a full one from the wooden box that lay open on the sandy earth beside his shallow rifle pit, a tiny trench that had been scooped out with a mess tin less than twenty minutes before, when they had first ridden here, a headlong dash as the first Indian fire came at them from the high riverbanks, steep inclines no more than a pistol shot away on either side of their tiny island. Then the first horses had fallen with terrible screams and there had been the screeching curses, soldiers' curses, from men struck and bleeding.

He was at the far point of the island because he was a good marksman and had been placed there with others like him. He could see directly along the riverbed, dry now on this late-summer Thursday just a week short of the fall equinox. The sand and the low bluffs on either side reflected the sun in a blinding gray-white brilliance, as though the earth here were a mirror. The short grasses, gone brown and brittle from lack of rain, were bending with the movement of the wind. Behind him he could hear the soft rustle of leaves in the lone cottonwood tree and the wild plum and other scrub growing on the island.

But the wind was not strong enough to keep away biting September flies or the nasty little sand gnats that seemed intent on eating off his eyelids.

And not enough wind to blow away the smells, either. There was the stench of hot gun oil from the Spencer, and of sweating horse from his mount, which lay in front of the rifle pit with one hind leg pointing toward the pale sky. The big stallion had been hit twice on their dash to the island, but had stayed on his feet to this sandy beach where he fell, a barrier of flesh against bullets and arrows.

There was the scent of blood, too, something he could remember from the many times of hog-butchering on the farm. But there seemed to him a harsh difference between pigs' blood and that of horses. And of men.

Already he could hear the last gasping, incoherent babbles of men wounded to death, one of them their surgeon, shot through the head at the first rush of the hostiles. And the whistle of a crazed horse that finally broke away and ran across the narrow strip of sand on the south side of the island, scrambled up the cutbank in a cloud of dust, and disappeared. His last impression of that horse was a whipping tail and flapping, empty stirrups.

"How many did you tally?" he asked the man to his right.

"I heerd the major quote four hundred that first go. They'll be a sight more of the bastards this next round. Cheyenne mostly, but some Sioux and maybe some Arapaho."

"And us only fifty."

"Fifty, hell! They ain't even that many now."

Not far from where he lay, this drought-diminished streambed ran into the Republican River. It in turn flowed across Nebraska and then veered south into Kansas, and he wished he were anywhere along its course. Anywhere but here, with the gnats chewing and the flies biting and the sun making a dazzle on the land that caused his eyes to run water.

"You're seeing history made, boys," the lieutenant had said. "Nobody ever saw 'em fight like disciplined cavalry before this day!"

He'd as soon not see such history being made, he thought, and wondered if, far out there to the east, beyond the heat-wave–wrinkled horizon, there was a single soul who gave a good damn about what was happening on this strip of sand in the bottom of a riverbed at the edge of Colorado Territory.

Sweat was running into his eyes, attracting gnats in gigantic little swarms. Every gnat on the damned Arikaree River is biting me, he thought. The sun was hot, burning into his head through his wide-brim slouch hat. Beneath him, in the sandy depression, he could feel the seep of moisture, and it was warm as Mama's soup.

Mama's soup! Maybe that was what made him start remembering in little flashes, remembering all the women he had ever known. His mother, Ora Hasford, standing in her kitchen, arms whitened to the elbows with flour; his sister, Cal, married to a former Yankee army officer wounded at the battle of Pea Ridge; a whore in Ellsworth whose name he didn't even know and ashamed at the thought of her because her image came so close behind his sister's. And Katie Rose with her doughy kisses, and Victoria Cardin with her lovely face, and the sad cow eyes of Olivia Smith. And little Catrina Peel with a brutal black bruise across one cheek and her eyes with that deep melancholy you see only in the eyes of a child who knows the anguish and despair of a world peopled with cruel adults.

He struggled to get these faces out of his mind. This was not the time for idle daydreams. He wanted to concentrate on the front sight of the Spencer and the targets he knew would soon be there. But he only had to struggle for a little while. With Catrina's tiny face still shimmering among the heat waves of the Arikaree's sand, he saw them coming.

They were like clouds of prairie dust boiling down from the riverbanks and coming from beyond the far bend, fusing like quicksilver to form a solid mass that filled the riverbed from bank to bank, coming at a mad gallop toward the island, the ponies' hooves throwing up a sparkling spray of grit. And above it all, the high-voiced yipping and shouting, as though every wolf west of the Missouri had been set loose at once.

"God Almighty!" he said aloud, sighting the carbine and waiting for the major's command to shoot. "I ain't ever gonna see my next birthday!"

He was twenty-two and his name was Roman Hasford. He was not aware then of the little irony in any of this, but he had come all the way from Arkansas, by various routes, to find a Cheyenne chief who bore his name. Roman Nose.

On the day Roman Hasford's father came home from the war in June of 1865, it was raining. The new green of the Ozark hardwood timber was like washed lettuce, dripping clear crystals in the slow but steady fall of water from a pale sky that held the sun close above the clouds and was about to break through at any moment. It was not a bleak day. It was a pearl-gray day, shining and gentle, with even some of the birds ignoring the weather and making their sparkling calls that seemed, like the leaves, to be washed clean by the rain.

Roman was on the front porch, mending broken harness with strips of hog's-hide leather, obtained only the day before from the former slave who now ran the mill on Sugar Creek and did a little stock-raising and butchering on the side.

Roman saw his father coming back the same way he had gone, along Wire Road, which ran through the valley below the Hasford farm buildings. He was in tatters, only his slouch hat and the blanket that was rolled and looped over one shoulder having any semblance of utility. He wasn't carrying the rifle he'd had when he'd gone away almost four years before, and he was barefoot.

Roman watched him come, taking a long time to realize

that this was his father. Then he called softly, "Mama, I think we're about to have company."

She came onto the porch from the kitchen, wiping her hands on the half-apron she always wore. Her hands were fish-white and looked parboiled from washing dishes and pots, a sharp contrast to the dark tanned skin of her arms and face, long accustomed to the sun of the fields. Her graying hair was done in a tight bun at back, as it always was, and her square face was set in hard angles, as it always was when her mind was working. Yet now there was not the grim line of lip that had always been there over the past three years, when "having company" might mean a visit from one of the marauding partisan bands that had come periodically into these hills from Kansas or the Indian Territory. Even in her flimsy ankle-length calico dress, she looked indomitable. Which she was.

The forlorn figure in the rain had reached the bottom of the slope where the black locust trees stood in thick ranks, and there he turned toward the house, his face partly hidden under the flopping brim of his hat as he held his head down, watching his barefoot step through the fallen, thorny little limbs that always broke off old black locust at the first suggestion of wind and littered the ground until they were picked up to be used for kindling.

She recognized who it was from the first instant of seeing him, and Roman heard her make a small, gasping sound such as a chicken makes when a fist is closed on its neck. She moved quickly across the porch and to the first of the long steps that led down into the yard, and Roman thought she was going to run and meet his father and was somehow glad when she didn't. It had always embarrassed him a little to see his mother run, with her short legs and heavy body.

The elder Hasford stopped just short of the bottom step, Ora Hasford standing as still as midnight at the top. He took off his hat and raised his face, letting the rain fall on it and run down through his beard. He looked at them slowly, first one then the other and back again, and only after a long pause did a small smile struggle through the beard, and some of the water on his face might have been tears and not rain.

"It's been so long," he said, and then was up the steps quickly, dropping his hat on the ground and embracing his wife, both of them making choking noises. Although Roman had seldom seen his mother cry, he knew she was crying now.

It was a short, self-conscious embrace because these hill people had never been demonstrative, especially in full light of day and before a witness. So the witness, in this case Roman Hasford, saw nothing unusual about his mother and father making only a token show of their affection now, even after all the years apart.

Martin turned to his son, and Roman rose for the first time from his three-legged stool, letting the harness drop in a tangle at his feet, not knowing exactly what was expected of him. One thing he knew: if a man and wife hugged, it could be expected sometimes, but never such carryings-on between two grown men.

"Lord, boy," Martin Hasford said. "You've shot up like a weed!"

He thrust out his hand and Roman took it, feeling the hard flesh of his father's fingers, but somehow it was not so hard as his own, callused from four years at the plow.

"Come in and get your wet clothes off," Ora said in a voice tighter than Roman had ever heard it.

Hasford glanced down at his rags and then at Roman's neat homespun shirt and the duck trousers he wore, almost new, purchased only a week before from one of the mercantile drummers that had begun to come back into the county from Missouri once more now that the war was over.

"And there's hominy on the stove and some fresh eggs."

Hasford bobbed his head, making the drops of water shower off the end of his beard.

"It'll be good to eat some eggs I don't have to steal," he said. "If it hadn't been for the chicken coops between Virginia and here, I reckon I'd've starved to death on the walk home."

Then the mother hurried inside, the father close behind, and Roman sat back down on his stool and took up the harness. But he didn't work it for a while. He sat looking through the rain, seeing the shine of it along the black trunks of the locust trees. And he thought how small his father looked. And how this homecoming had been short and to the point, as though the elder Hasford had only been gone overnight. It wasn't what he'd expected it to be. He wasn't sure what he had expected—that maybe at least they'd kill the fatted calf, he thought, shaping in his mind words from Scripture, as his mother so often did. Only hers were always aloud, Roman's to himself.

Well, he thought, maybe not a fatted calf because we don't have one, fatted or otherwise. But he knew that before night his mother would be out by the barn, wringing the neck of some unfortunate chicken. Maybe that was just as good.

Then he thought about what his father had said about stealing eggs. He who before the war had often talked of going into the ministry of the Lord. Martin Hasford, his father, stealing! The thought twisted his long face, lips turning down, flesh tightening.

From inside the house he could hear the low mutter of their conversation. He felt a little left out because it had been a long time since his mother had held much conversation with anyone except him. Then her voice rose as she called to him.

"Roman, go down to the springhouse and get the crock of milk."

God Almighty, he thought. Goat's milk! She's gonna start him right off on that damned goat's millk, and him a Jersey cow man before the war!

He dropped the harness again, took down his yellow slicker from a whittled peg driven into the outside wall, pulled it on, and jumped off the end of the porch. He walked stoop-shouldered in the rain, past the barn and the pigsty and down through the white oaks of the little gully where the limestone springhouse stood over the sweet water that never ceased flowing from the depths of the land even in drought times.

Roman had been little aware of his having changed much during his father's absence. But he had. A tall, gangling boy when Martin Hasford walked away along Wire Road in 1861, now he was fleshed out and his muscles were hard and his blue eyes had lost their boyish innocence because of what he'd seen.

The battle of Pea Ridge had erupted practically in the Hasford farmyard, and Roman had watched men shot to pieces in the fight around Elkhorn Tavern. Later, when the bushwhackers and Jayhawkers came in the night, he had stood with his mother against their setting fire to any of the buildings, his mother with an old muzzle-loading shotgun, he with a Navy revolver that had come to him by way of a Confederate deserter after the battle. He and his mother had learned early that what the partisans wanted to steal, which was livestock to sell to the Federal depots in Missouri or to fill their own scrawny bellies, had to be hidden in the woods or else be lost.

As testament to the Hasford's ingenuity during those years, there were now hogs in the sty, offspring of an old sow that had escaped capture after she broke out of the pen, leaving two of her farrow behind; chickens in the coop; two horses and a new foal; and a milking goat that Roman hated with every fiber he could twitch for hating. But she gave rich milk and there was cheese from that, and she required little tending.

And now the fields across Wire Road were planted in Hasford corn, and Ora's garden beside the house was already sending up the first signs of turnips and onions and Irish potatoes and cabbages. Most of the latter were destined for kraut, because this was a family that could trace its lineage all the way back to Germany before the time that at least one of their men, maybe more, had gone off to join the Prussians to fight Napoleon.

Sweetest of all were the bees, given them by the former slave who ran the Sugar Creek mill, a man who was a particular friend of Roman, through what design nobody knew. The hives were hidden so well back in the woods that even Ora didn't know where they were.

All of this Roman considered his, as man of the household and because he had helped his mother intrigue and scheme to save and even increase it against all odds. But now, as he came back from the springhouse in the rain, there was the disquieting thought at the rear of his mind that it was no longer his but his father's. It was an ill-defined thought, but it was large. He knew that the war was finally over, and maybe a lot more besides.

It was difficult to remember afterward just when the notion of leaving home first came to Roman Hasford. Throughout the summer and toward harvest time, he and his father worked the fields and cut timber. These were the same fields and woodlands Roman had successfully tended for four years. Yet now he was simply his father's helper, taking orders about where to hoe, what to cut, how to plant late barley.

He could feel a little swell of hostility each time his father instructed him, which was often. And he was ashamed because this was his father and this land was his father's land. But the irritation and animosity were there each time, no matter how hard he fought them.

There was more on his mind than his father's having taken his place on the farm and with his mother. There was a lot more, more than he could manage. He was eighteen years old, and all he'd seen of the world had come to him—he had never gone to it. He had been born into the life of this valley and the hills around it, and had never been beyond that short horizon except once, when the family had gone to Springfield, Missouri. But Roman had been so young that he now had no memory of it.

Of course, he told himself, he'd seen great events, what with the battle fought in his valley and the partisan disturbances afterward. He and his mother had stood on their very own front porch and watched the orange flickering light when someone burned Elkhorn Tavern just north of the Hasford farm on Wire Road. He'd seen the night riders, been close enough to smell them and hear their rough language. But, somehow, none of that counted. It had all come to him. He hadn't gone out on his own and found it.

There was this other matter, too. He thought of it only occasionally, because it was something his upbringing had taught him not to dwell on because it wasn't exactly clean and would rot his brain. Getting together with some girl! That was it! And when he did think of it, there was a strange, intense heat that made a hard lump come up in his body.

The valley didn't offer much in the way of girls. There were a few scattered about who were beyond fifteen and still unmarried, but they were a sorry lot in his sight. Else why were they still maidens? He could imagine himself somewhere in the future marrying one of them because there was no one else available, and the thought of such a disaster made him a little sick.

One of the most confusing experiences he could recall was the time he'd taken their new sow to the mill on Sugar Creek to have her serviced by the boar there. He'd watched the whole process. It wasn't as if he didn't know about such things, having lived all his life on a farm. But that day with the boar and the sow, the contradictions suddenly welled up in his mind. On the one hand, it was an experience he wanted for himself with some girl. Any girl. On the other, his rearing told him a young man didn't go around like a boar doing it with anything that came to hand, just for the sake of doing it. It wasn't supposed to be all that pleasant, either, but just a thing any male animal was forced to do from time to time because of his baser instincts. That, too, came from his teachings.

He began to wonder about those teachings, subtle things his father had told him before going off to the war. How a man was supposed to act. How he was supposed to be decent, which meant that the only physical joy he had was in eating a good meal when he was hungry or drinking cool water when he was thirsty. How a man was supposed to lie with a woman only to beget. And there were some things that were not so discreet. Readings from the Bible, the Old Testament, about lust and carnal knowledge. And about how even a good man sometimes couldn't control bodily urges brought on by the devil.

Why, hell, he often thought, they can't tell me it's not fun, because Mama'd never put up with something that was just dirty and no pleasure in it.

But that was disquieting, too. Because he never enjoyed thinking about what his mother and father did in bed. He absolutely refused to speculate on how often anything happened, but he couldn't avoid the positive fact of two times, when he and his sister Calpurnia had been set on their courses.

When it entered his mind, he'd say aloud, Hell, I've gotta stop this thinking. There was always a little swearing in his thoughts, as a kind of rebellion against his father's long-standing objection to such words. He took some pleasure from the fact that his mother now and then was heard to explode with a few such terms, when she didn't know anyone was listening.

And there was something even more disquieting. He suspected that his mother knew what was happening in his mind and body. She'd look at him with sympathy written in her eyes as clearly as on a printed page. His father never seemed aware that Roman was anything more than a large child with a small child's appetites.

And another thing, he'd think. Papa's not the same man now. Something happened to him during that war. He's not the same.

Martin Hasford never said much about the war. He'd sit in the evenings with his big leatherbound Bible across his knees, much as Roman remembered him doing back when he and Calpurnia were still young enough to be playing with their homemade blocks, or pulling a batch of taffy after supper. Sometimes Martin would read aloud and sometimes he'd chuckle like a man happy with his lot and take the children on his lap and tousle their hair or maybe tell them stories of Germany, where the family came from, or about the Caesars according to Mr. Gibbon, throwing in a few Latin words for them to learn.

Now Cal was gone off to St. Louis with her Yankee husband, and according to her last letter she had delivered her firstborn, a son. And certainly Roman was too old to be told stories from books he himself had now read cover to cover.

Martin still sat with his Bible from time to time, but often he held the book open without looking at it. The only thing he ever seemed to read anymore was the long list of family names with dates of births and deaths, written in the front. And sometimes he would stare off across the room, or in daytime across the fields, as though his mind were a thousand miles away on some Virginia creek or mountain or woodland.

In fact, Roman thought, he never talks about the war or anything else. He says more to the horses than he does to me.

Some of his best memories were of long treks through the woods, his father pointing out the sign of various animals, like deer and fox and turkey and once even a wolf's pugs in the damp sand of a branch of Sugar Creek. He'd learned a lot about these hills from his father, and about raising things and about the magic of each season's coming and going. But now something had made all the words stop flowing, so that Roman was closed out from what was in his father's mind, as though some great and terrible barrier had been erected that his father had no power to bring down, even had he wanted to.

Besides, Roman thought, remembering the girls and his wanting but never having one, I feel like the family virgin around here, about to be sacrificed to the Jehovah of the Old Testament so next year's crops will come on good!

He knew his Bible well, having learned to read by studying it. Before the war, Martin had taught both him and Calpurnia, even before they'd had a few years of schooling in Leetown. All of which his mother had thought was a waste of time. Why did anyone need reading to know how to grow corn or bake cherry cobbler? she asked. But it was done nonetheless.

And by now, Roman knew a great deal more. There had been this old Jew who once ran the Sugar Creek mill, and his shack had housed a lode of books. Before the partisans killed him one terrible afternoon because he was so obstreperous, he'd encouraged Roman to read some of those books. It was wonderful, getting out of the valley through the printed word.

After the former slave took over the mill and that old Jew's house and other holdings, he'd given the books to Roman because although he was the best stock breeder and beekeeper in the county, he couldn't even read his own name.

But nowhere in any of those readings had Roman found the answer to his own problems. Why, hell, he thought, all I know how to do is plow and milk the damned goat and shoot squirrels with Mama's shotgun and load the Navy Colt that crazy Cherokee gave me before he lit out for the Indian Nations after the battle.

His decision was a long time coming, but when it came, Roman Hasford knew he'd follow the road he'd chosen, no matter what. And it wasn't going to be just the road that ran up and down this valley. But the thought of saying it out loud to his mother was terrifying. He knew the kind of reaction to unpleasantness of which she was capable. Everybody told the story of how once, when a hound turned on her in a fit of hunger, she'd killed the dog with her shotgun and would have continued to shoot the quivering carcass except that the gun only had two barrels.

Of course, he didn't expect his mother to shoot him. But she might give him a good clout on the head with her fist. She'd hit a cow once that had cornered her in a barn stall, square between the eyes. Even worse would be the look he'd get from her, sad and possessive and grieved that he wanted to leave her home. So he decided finally that the best way to go about it was through deviousness.

"Think I'll take a little trip up to St. Louis this fall and see Cal," he said. "Now the war's over."

The war's being over was a good excuse to do anything, he figured.

They had just finished supper. His mother and father were in rocking chairs on the front porch, and Roman sat below them on the steps. It was just short of bedtime, with the sun setting in a fiery red glow beyond the rough-edged foliage of the far hills. They could hear a mockingbird somewhere along Wire Road starting his evening serenade. There was the smell of summer evening about everything, and the smell of the kraut brewing in the two large cheesecloth-covered crocks in the shadows at one end of the porch. Though he'd just eaten, it made the saliva come thick into Roman's mouth, smelling that kraut of his mother's.

"After the crops are in would be the best time," Martin Hasford said.

"That's what I figured," said Roman.

"You could take one of the horses then."

"No, I reckoned on walking up to Missouri and then maybe take one of those coaches like used to run down through here when Mr. Butterfield was doing such things. Before the war."

Two of Ora's chickens had wandered into the front yard and were pecking at the sandy soil, getting nothing much but gravel. They walked slowly, lifting each foot as though they were wading in hot water. Roman had a handful of small pebbles and he tossed them, one by one, at the hens. They paid no attention to him until he hit one of them and she jumped and fluffed her feathers and sqawked, looking around with her crazy glass eyes.

"Leave the chickens alone, Roman," his mother said.

"You could take a little of that money we've made on fenceposts this summer," Martin said. "Been a good time for cutting posts, with people coming back onto the land, more livestock running loose. Good year for fenceposts."

"As long as the locust trees hold out, a man can make a living on fenceposts," Roman said, glad that it was going so easy, and Mama not saying a word about that St. Louis trip.

"Always be plenty of locusts," Martin said. "They sprout up like weeds, those locusts."

"After we cut the early barley," Roman said, "I guess I'll just go see Cal and her new baby."

"Lot of men on the road now," said his father. "Veterans. Mostly good men, I guess, but nowhere to go. Looking for something. Begging handouts."

Roman waited, but nothing else came. His father turned his head and gazed toward the west field and Roman knew nothing else would come. No advice. No details of what Martin knew about being on the road, and Roman knew he had to know a lot, having walked all the way home from Virginia after Appomattox. He could see only a steely hardness in his father's eyes, a complete disinterest in this whole affair because he had bigger things roiling about in his head.

Well, Roman thought, maybe he's telling me to act like I was a war veteran and beg food that way.

"Take the pistol," Ora said.

Martin came out of his reverie with a little start and sat there blinking, staring at his wife.

"The pistol? He won't need any pistol. He's going to St. Louis. He'd likely get arrested if he had a pistol in St. Louis."

"Take the pistol," Ora said very quietly, and there was the stone-hard finality in her voice that both men knew would brook no argument.

The night before Roman's departure, his mother was busy about her kitchen after supper, busier than he had ever seen her. In her kitchen she was always absolutely efficient, moving only what needed moving, making the fire huff in the woodburning cookstove, making the food appear at the appointed time without much effort, making the floors and all surfaces shine with cleanliness, without seeming ever to lay hand to them—an economy of effort that defied reason.

But on that night she fluttered like a wounded bird. Aimlessly. Doing the same thing twice, three times. Like a drone bee, Roman thought, working frantically around a new queen. He should have been out on the front porch with his father, but somehow he felt that in these last few hours he needed to stay close by his mother. Or maybe it was that she needed him close by her.

Then, in her half-frenzied make-work, she stopped dead in the center of the floor and looked squarely at him for the first time all day.

"You write me some letters," she said.

It was then that Roman knew his mother realized that this was more than a trip to St. Louis to visit his sister. It was escape, and maybe his never again coming back to this Hasford farm, where he had grown from a boy to a man. Never to taste the sweet cold water from the limestone spring or sit with her listening to the rustle of the new locusts each spring; never to turn the rich-smelling earth under the plow.

"I will, Mama," he said, and it was like an oath between them. "But I'll be back."

"You don't know what you'll find out there," she said. "But you remember, this is your land, it will be someday when your papa and me are gone from it. Don't ever forget, this is your land. You were born to it and you belong to it. Don't forget that."

"I won't, Mama," he said, and then she came to him quickly, surprising him as she always did that she could move so fast on those short legs. She threw her arms around him and held her face to his for just an instant, the first time in many years that she had touched him. It was finished quickly and she was back at her stove, turned from him.

"Now go fetch me some yellow onions from the root cellar. And see you don't take any sips from one of your father's jugs."

It was a brusque command, but it made the lump in his throat even harder than the brush of her lips against his cheek had done.

Later that night, he lay in his bunk in the loft over the kitchen and listened to the chorus of cicadas from the trees around the springhouse in the hollow. For the first time it came home to him that he was leaving, actually going from this place that had always been his life. It was an overwhelming thought, and there were a few tears that he furiously brushed away with the hard palms of his hands.

All right, Mama, he thought. I'll be back.

And he knew that it was a promise he had made secretly to himself a long time ago, when the first urgings to leave began to occupy his thinking.

When Roman Hasford first saw the city, it had already been a prospering community for over a century, its back to the Mississippi River and its face toward the great trans-Missouri frontier.

As with many established cities, there were in certain aspects of its character things hauntingly ancient, tied to an earlier and distinctly different culture. The impression was more apparent than real, even though the original fur-trading post had been named for Louis IX, who had conducted two militarily disastrous crusades in the direction of the Holy Land. The last one ended in Tunis, and Louis ended there, too, his body embalmed and shipped back to Paris. He had then been canonized by the Roman church, the only French king ever to be so honored; hence the name of the city that soon began to call itself the Gateway to the American West: St. Louis.

There was much in common between the city and the old king after whom it was named. He had been wildly hot-tempered and addicted to outrageous quantities of food, and many who came to his namesake town found it in at least these respects the same.

Other than giving it his name, that old French king never had any influence on the city. He was in his tomb in Notre

Dame for a long time before the Frenchmen came upriver from New Orleans and mapped out the first blockhouse above the muddy flow. In fact, no rulers anywhere ever had much influence on it, even though at various times the city had claimed allegiance to France twice, to Spain once, and finally to the United States of America, after Mr. Thomas Jefferson bought what was called the Louisiana Territory and made St. Louis its capital.

Regardless of flags, and even after Missouri attained statehood in 1821, St. Louis went its own way. It was a power unto itself from the beginning, owned, operated, and nurtured by the fur traders, then by combinations of rivermen, lumbermen, zinc miners, and, by the time Roman came, railroaders.

To those who knew its history, there was always the feeling that a heraldic fleur-de-lis might sprout magically from one of the gardens in back of a home on the elm-lined streets west of the business district; or that a mountain man with a hide shirt might walk up from the river and into the first saloon to announce the discovery of a new Indian tribe west of the Snake; or that a fresh wave of Mormon immigrants would forsake their Iowa route and cross the river from Illinois, heading for Zion and the Great Salt Lake; or that the old markets for beaver pelts would reopen; or that a new riot would break out along the waterfront between factions loyal to the South on one side, the Union on the other.

In the early fall of 1866, St. Louis was a little of all this and a lot more besides, like a cake built up by layers, year by year, each new tier flavored by the changes in the country all around it. But the river was still supreme. There were boats pulling away from the wharves with ten or twelve men each, going upstream to the mouth of the Missouri, using sweeps and poles, off on trading ventures. Long before, the original French *voyageurs* had set off on the same trip, even before Lewis and Clark set off from this point of departure to find out exactly what it was Mr. Jefferson had bought.

And the steamboats were very much still there, flat-bottomed shallow-draft little vessels that could crawl up a riverbed wetted only by a heavy dew, or so it was said. The early ones had traced the Missouri and all its tributaries, like the Kansas and the Platte and the Yellowstone, the latter all the way to what would become Fort Benton, Montana, head of navigation even for those sturdy little ships.

In St. Louis you could sense the presence of all the peoples from out along the water highways to the west; the Mandan and the Arikaree and the Sioux and the Crow and the Shoshone and the Blackfoot.

And you could feel the presence of the Western places, too: the Smoky Hill and the Tongue and the Rosebud rivers; the salt forks of almost every stream that ran through the country beyond the tall-grass prairies; the Grand Tetons and the Bitterroots and the Big Horns; and all the sky out there that everyone who had ever seen it claimed was so overpowering that it made everything else seem insignificant, and tiny as a speck. A vast space of dirt and wind and scrub, with buffalo and elk and pronghorn moving across it as though they were the only creatures on earth except for the red men who followed them for their meat and their hides and their bones and their hoof glue. It was a place the men in Congress had once called the Great American Desert.

The early white men who had seen it knew there was a lot more there than desert. In fact, compared to all else they found, there was very little desert at all. But they kept quiet about it because they wanted to keep a good thing to themselves. That wasn't possible, of course, once emigrants hungry for their own place and their own land began the long wagon journey to the Oregon country and California, and of necessity had to cross the Great Plains. Some of those trekkers had the audacity to claim that a man could grow wheat and corn and barley on those high, wind-seared expanses.

Whether they were going to the Northwest country or to the gold fields around Sacramento or to Santa Fe, these land voyagers mostly started from St. Louis. And a lot of them came back there, too. There was no better place than St. Louis to get information about the West.

When Roman Hasford arrived at what everyone considered the capital town of the whole Mississippi, discounting

New Orleans, but which had not really been a capital of anything since Mr. Jefferson's purchase, there was the taste of more than the ancient and the near past, because by then steel rails were moving out to the plains. Not just to the long-grass prairies, but to the high plains.

To the north, there was a dusty little town called Omaha where they were building the Union Pacific Railroad. St. Louis was not to be outdone. After all, its residents said, the first track laid west of the Mississippi had run right from the center of their city. That was before the war, when the metal road inched out toward Wyandotte and Leavenworth, like fingers groping in the dark. But now the war was over, turning loose unheard-of energy. The railroad era had begun, and everything seemed to be bursting at the seams. Already they were laying track beyond the western border of Missouri, out into the buffalo country along the Kansas River, heading straight for Denver.

St. Louis had always drawn people, and now more than ever. German immigrants had come all the way from the sugar-beet fields to America, where the railroads promised them cheap land and easy commerce. Irishmen and a few Poles and some French felt they were coming to their own city, and more than a few Welsh and English. Displaced Southerners were here, looking for anything and any way out of places that their families had called home for generations, but that were now under the heel of Federal army occupation. Eastern laborers came to work the lumber mills and the stockyards and the railroads. There were evangelists and temperance workers; former slaves and their forlorn children; the rich, looking to gain dominion over some of the Illinois farmland just across the river or in the cleared sections west of the city, where the corn and wheat and hogs grew; Union army veterans, set loose by war's end and having seen enough of new places during the conflict to create an appetite for seeing more; gamblers and whores and pickpockets and beggars and land speculators.

And of course there were those who had been there all along, the respectably established gentry and their families;

the bankers and the ship owners and the livery operators and the haberdashers and the doctors and the lawyers and the streetcar conductors and the dock foremen and the grain buyers and the copper and zinc brokers and the meatpackers. In other words, those who took their livelihood from the high-spirited proclivities of the adventurers and hence ended up with all the money.

It was, in short, a place to dismay a young man of considerable sophistication and travel and learning. And Roman Hasford was none of these, having lived all his life thus far within a world that, except at the flashing moment of the battle of Pea Ridge, contained fewer people than one could see along the St. Louis riverfront in the space of a single minute.

Roman Hasford came in late September, with the summer still hanging on along the river like a dank, hot gauze, suffocating and uncomfortable. But he hardly noticed the heat or the humidity or the cinders still lodged between his teeth from the train ride, or the sweat-soaked homespun shirt he wore, or the tight coat, one of his father's old ones, or the tendency of his damp duck trousers to creep up in the crotch with each step he took. He didn't notice any of that because the stunning, clamorous, impolite, and impersonal clatter of the city left him in a kind of shock he'd not known since the morning his favorite mule had been killed by artillery fire at Elkhorn Tavern.

He hadn't taken any horsedrawn coach from Cassville or anywhere else, as he said he would, and perhaps there was more involved than his pleasure in walking across the upper Ozarks in Missouri, where the hills were not so sharply defined as in Arkansas. Maybe part of it was getting away from home and doing whatever the hell he wanted, no matter what he said he'd do. For the first time in his life, he wasn't answerable to anybody.

He'd walked all the way to Jefferson City, carrying a small road poke, as his mama called it, across his shoulder. Therein were all the necessities of life: a clean shirt, a change of underwear and socks, some soap and a razor, a few baked Irish potatoes and some apples—and the Navy Colt revolver, along with bullets, caps, and powder. In his trousers pocket was a total of seventeen dollars, fencepost money. He spent almost nothing except twice in crossroad stores where he paused for a few hard crackers and rat cheese. Each time he ate that crumbling yellow cheese, he appreciated more the sweet, soft goat cheese his mother made, although he would never admit, even to himself, that something coming from that God damned goat was good for anything.

It was about two hundred miles from the Hasford front porch to Jefferson City, and Roman made it in just under ten days. He slept in the woods or in fields alongside the road, and the nights were warm and only once threatened rain. He ate his potatoes and apples, and a few more he took from orchards along the way, even though they were still pretty green. One night in the woods near Bolivar, he trapped and cooked a rabbit, and the smell of the roasting meat over his low fire was almost as nourishing as the eating of it. He was hungry most of the time, but he didn't mind. He'd been hungry before, after a raid on the farm by bushwhackers had stripped him and his mother of everything they had to eat.

In Jeff City, he saw a thing he'd never seen before—a steam locomotive with a string of cars stretched out behind. He spent a dollar of his money for a ride to St. Louis and blundered his way onto one of the cars and sat there staring at everything and clutching the road poke against his chest with both hands. There seemed to be a never-ending flow of people through the car.

Why, hell, he thought, these men are all Yankees, I guess.

They didn't look much different from most men Roman had ever seen, except that maybe they were better pressed and their beards more carefully trimmed. But the women were another thing.

Roman Hasford had never imagined such grandeur and flashing color. Some even had their faces tinted, giving them a perpetual blush. And the hats! To him, women's hats had always been wide-brimmed slouches like the one he wore, or else long-billed bonnets to ward off the sun. But these dainty little things he examined as each lady passed down the aisle between the seats were as fancy and feathered as pileated woodpecker crests.

He gaped too long and too often, of course, and one matron waddling along with her husband behind her glared at him, and her prim little mouth spat the words at him.

"What are you gawking at, young man?"

And her husband, moving her gently onward, said, "Never mind, Clara. It's just another one of these jake-leg rubbins."

What's a jake-leg rubbin? Roman wondered. He couldn't recall such a term from any of his father's classic literature that filled the scanty space along one shelf of the china closet, or from any of the books he'd acquired from the Sugar Creek mill and kept in his attic loft bedroom.

The way these people talk! he thought. Some sounded as though they might have been Roman's own cousins, but most had a rasping, abrupt sound in their language, and the words came so fast it was difficult to keep them separated. Maybe even worse than the strange people were the smells in the coach. The aroma of coal smoke and tobacco juice overwhelmed everything else, and though Roman was not new to tobacco juice, having started a few times to become a chewer himself, there was a great difference between fresh juice and that which had been splattered along the aisles of the car, left there to rot and pattern the floor with ugly patches of black and brown.

After the rebuff from the fat lady, Roman satisfied himself by looking out the open window, squinting against the smoke that roiled in from the puffing engine up ahead. He was more comfortable with the land passing the window than with the people passing inside. It wasn't exactly like home, even though he could recognize most of the hardwoods. He saw a lot of blood-red gum trees, and some of the sycamores were turning to yellow. Leaves change sooner up here than they do at home, he thought. It would be a long time before he would choose any point of reference except home.

All the amazement at riding the steam cars ended abruptly

in St. Louis, where the real wonder began. He gravitated toward the riverfront, gawking at the big buildings, brick and sandstone and a lot of window glass. And there were the horsedrawn streetcars clanging along among the buggies and hacks and all kinds of wheeled vehicles whose names Roman didn't know. There were shop windows displaying saddles and silk hats and firearms and quarters of beef and chains and crosscut saws and sledgehammers and boat anchors and velvet cloth and pots of ink and stacks of writing paper and cowhide shoes with mother-of-pearl buttons and medicine bottles with garish labels.

Why, hell, I guess you could get almost anything you wanted around here, he thought.

To him the river looked like an ocean, the far dim shore of Illinois showing flat and blue in the distance. The little boats moved up and down, resembling waterbugs belching black smoke, and more of them were tied to the piers like lines of shoes set just so under the bed at night. Everywhere church spires lifted to the blue sky, shining crosses on their domes and steeples. But the one thing he noticed the town had more of than churches was saloons.

It took Roman a while to remember why he'd come to this city, and he began to worry about how he'd ever find his sister in the puzzle of streets and people and big buildings. At first he thought he might ask a policeman. He'd seen a number of them, their silver badges shining on blue serge coats and their hats looking like beehives. But then he had a better idea.

At home, when anyone wanted to find out anything, he went to the taproom at Elkhorn Tavern. That was before the tavern burned, of course. But Roman figured if it worked in Arkansas, it might work here. So he found himself a little saloon where RYAN'S was printed in gilt letters across the window, and went inside, taking a deep breath first.

A fat bartender with a huge mustache and his hair greased down and parted in the middle eyed him suspiciously as Roman walked to the bar and lay the road poke before him and cupped it in his hands and nodded.

"Howdy," he said.

"What'll it be?"

There was an instant of panic then, but Roman suddenly recalled the label on a bottle his father had brought home once to make hot toddies when he and Calpurnia had the croup.

"Rye whiskey," he said, a little too loudly.

A man at the back of the room, leaning against the bar, turned his head slowly and stared at Roman, and Roman bobbed his head.

"Howdy," he said, but the man said nothing, turning back to the schooner of beer before him.

Roman watched the barkeep pour four ounces of dark liquid into what appeared to be a small water glass. The smell of it made Roman's throat pinch shut.

"That'll be a dime, mister," the barkeep said, his fat fingers still clutching the glass of rye until he saw the color of Roman's money.

The rye wasn't too bad against the tongue. Not so good as Papa's corn, Roman thought, but then everybody says Papa makes the best corn in the county. He ordered another. Soon he began to feel a little self-confidence creeping up from his belly. So he had another.

"Free lunch with drinks, mister," the bartender said, tweaking the pencil-point ends of his mustache.

The free-lunch table was at the end of the bar, and it held, among other things, pickled pig's feet, two kinds of sausage, white cheese, and hard-boiled eggs. Roman had some cold roast beef with black bread and a sour pickle. Then he took a slice of head cheese back to the bar to munch as he sipped another rye. The barkeep was watching him, but not suspiciously now. Some of these Yankees are all right, Roman thought.

"You ever heard of a lawyer named Pay?" he asked, bold enough now to ask Jefferson Davis the time of day.

"Why, the Pays got a firm as good as any in St. Louis, I suppose," the bartender said. "You got problems you need a lawyer?"

"No. But Allan Pay's my brother-in-law."

"Well, I'm damned," the barkeep said, his eyebrows lifting up to the center of his forehead, looking like twists of black yarn. It made Roman's chest swell to see how impressed the man was with his kinfolk. "Why, Allan Pay's a fine lawyer, they tell me. I never had no need of a lawyer myself."

"He married my sister during the war. After he lost his hand at the battle of Pea Ridge."

"The younger Pay's got a house out in the west section of town," the bartender said. "The old man, he lives in a boarding-house, now his old lady's gone."

"I don't know where my sister lives," Roman said. "So I figured I'd go find Allan and maybe get invited to supper."

Roman giggled at his little joke. The rye tasted better with each sip.

"That's right nice, coming to visit kin," the barkeep said. "You can find that office real easy. You go down to the river and turn right for two blocks. And there it is. You can't miss it. A big red brick bank building, law offices on the second floor. They's a brass sign at the bottom of the stairs. Says 'Pay and Pay, Attorneys-at-Law.'"

Thus Roman Hasford found his sister's husband, and presented himself with a large, crooked grin on his face, and his hat in hand. And more than a little drunk.

It didn't come to him until the next morning, waking in his sister's house on one of the streets west of the city, where the elm trees grew like soldiers standing in ranks along either side and where the passing horse-and-buggy traffic made a curiously muted drumbeat of sound on the cobblestones. His head hurt and his mouth was dry from all the rye at Ryan's saloon and the brandy he and Allan Pay had taken after their evening meal the night before. But he rose with the dawn, nonetheless, as was his habit, and staggered to the window and peered through the white lace curtains into the street below.

I don't know who she is, he thought.

There should be something, he supposed, to connect Calpurnia with all her life before, as Roman remembered it. She was part of that hill farm in Arkansas, wasn't she, a part of the walnut groves and limestone ridges and deer paths in the woods? A part of the family, cloistered among the valleys and maybe imprisoned by them, looking always inward and not knowing or caring what lay beyond?

But as hard as he looked, he couldn't find a thing that made her a Hasford, a part of Mama and Papa and himself. All of this was another world, another existence completely beyond anything that had gone before, and it disturbed him in some subtle way that was even more perplexing because he couldn't clearly define it. But he was sure of one thing: he had himself started along a path that would likely make him a stranger to his own mother someday, just as Cal was to him now.

But even though such a thought was sad and somehow made him feel guilty, he had no intention of tucking tail and running home while there was still time to keep things as they had always been. So he rationalized it as well as he could. Maybe with mothers it was different. Maybe with mothers it didn't matter when the cubs came back and were cubs no longer, because the memories of the young playing in the den were too strong to be overcome by anything that intervened.

St. Louis is farther from home than I ever figured, he thought. And it isn't just the people. It's the things, too.

He was afraid to sit on any of those straight chairs scattered about Calpurnia's house. They had dainty little legs, carved and curved, and seats patterned in pink and blue thread. He tried to recall whether he'd broken any of them the night before, simply by having lowered his butt to the needlepoint. The beds weren't anything to boost his self-confidence, either. There were no feather ticks, to which he was accustomed, but rather some kind of hard mattress, covered with combed cotton sheets. Better material than any shirt he'd ever had on his back.

And the gas-jet lamps on the walls, and the pumps with goose-neck handles. There must have been half a dozen of those, in the kitchen and in all the little rooms they called water closets, where there were big zinc-lined bathtubs, bigger than the Elkhorn Tavern horse trough. Flowered paper on the walls, the same colors as the thread in the bottoms of those straight chairs. And framed portraits of strange men with long mustaches, Allan Pay's kin, hanging along the stairwells, and there, too, a small brass medal bestowed on Allan for having served and lost a hand to the Yankee army.

Everything had started well. Allan was glad to see him, and Roman was surprised and pleased that the old resentment he'd always felt for this man who took his sister away from the farm was impossible to sustain. And Calpurnia went into a fit of delight at seeing her brother, kissing him square on the mouth twice, which made him stammer and go red-faced, and for the first hour she hovered about him with a pitcher of lemonade and a plate of oatmeal cookies. She was unable, it seemed, to keep her hands off him, as though she wanted to reassure herself that he was real.

There was some time spent in Roman's solemn assertions that everything in Benton County was just fine: Mama was just fine, Papa was just fine, the crops were just fine, and the two bluetick hounds, though growing old, were just fine.

Then they led him to the second-floor nursery, where he had his first look at Calpurnia's new baby, and Roman, who was unaccustomed to having squalling infants thrust into his arms, was visibly uncomfortable. The baby had a beet-red face, smoky blue eyes, and a thatch of corn-tassel hair over a large, round skull. The most impressive thing about him was the wide-open, toothless mouth that gave forth sounds more piercing to Roman's ears than a sawmill whistle.

"His name's Eben Pay," Calpurnia said, exploding with pride. "And someday he's going to be a fine lawyer, just like his father."

Roman wasn't accustomed to hearing "father" in his sister's mouth. It sounded so damned impersonal. But there was a lot more that had no place in his memories of her. She wasn't the bright-eyed girl with freckles sprinkled across her nose and hair falling loose all around her face. She was a full-grown woman now, a wife and mother. There were no freckles and her hair was done in some kind of roll around the back and sides of her head, and she kept her neck, which Roman had always admired, covered by the high collar of her dress. It wasn't an ordinary dress, either. Not one of those simple gingham things she always wore at home. It was expensive stuff the likes of which Roman had never seen before and was at a loss to name, with long sleeves that puffed at the elbows, and a full skirt falling away from a buttoned bodice all the way down to the tops of her high-heeled patent leather shoes.

The biggest shock was her hands. They were as soft as butter. He remembered when they were hard and browned by the sun, like Mama's, toughened by work in the fields and milking and slopping hogs.

Why, hell, he thought, she used to be as hard as the fender on an old saddle. Maybe all that softness is because of the maid.

It was astonishing, but they had a large, rather coarse-featured girl working for them who did most of the kitchen work and tending the baby, and who had difficulty with the English language.

"Miss Jabowski's a Polish girl," Allan said. "A fine one to have. We were lucky to find her."

Anytime she was in the same room with Roman, her big, vacant blue eyes followed him like tracking hounds. It made him uneasy. He had the impression that at the first opportunity she might try to grab him and press her big breasts against him. Such a thought had its pleasant aspects, but not in the house of his sister.

By suppertime he'd begun to sober up a little. Calpurnia called it dinner, and by then she was giving him the old fish-eyed look that Mama did when she knew he'd been tapping the root-cellar jug, her exuberance over the reunion giving way to a chilly indignation at the effects of Ryan's rye whiskey.

Miss Jabowski brought in a steaming tureen of a red, mushy-looking stew and Allan called it gumbo.

"They bring them up from New Orleans packed in barrels of ice," he said.

"They bring what up?"

"The oysters."

Swimming in the tomato sauce were what Roman thought looked like little grubs. He wasn't sure which was better, the oysters to kill the taste of the okra, or the other way round. At least he was still drunk enough to eat what was placed before him without gagging.

It probably wouldn't have mattered what happened at his sister's house. Anything would have gone a little sour. There had been some vague notion that the old spark would still be there between him and his sister, with Cal teasing and goading and encouraging him, and Roman losing his temper at least twice a day but still following her about adoringly, because she was the most wonderful, beautiful thing that had ever happened in his world. But she had become just another Mama, and although he would always love her, she had become another part of the same corral his mother had constructed around him—the fence he was trying to leap to be a man and not the family baby, to be something *different*.

There was no protest when he told them he wanted to go to Kansas, and the sooner the better before winter set in. It was spooky, he thought, the way Cal had always seemed to have the ability to see into his mind. She might bait him and make fun, but she'd always support him in his real needs. Maybe she knew his needs better than he did. So because there was no fuss about the idea of his leaving, and because, after all, this was Calpurnia, he said he'd spend a few days with them and see the sights of St. Louis.

"Stay out of the saloons," Cal said.

"So you want to see some buffalo?" Allan Pay asked. "And maybe a few red Indians besides? Kansas is good for all that, and the railroads are already building right into the buffalo country, up the Kansas and Smoky Hill rivers. You could ride in style, right from our own depot."

"I was thinking maybe a steamboat part way," Roman said.

"I thought you were in a hurry," Cal said.

"Boat ride would be nice," Allan said. "There won't be any steamboats left before long, with all the railroads. You can go from here all the way to St. Joseph on a quality boat. I've made the trip a few times myself when I had business in the district court there."

"He doesn't want to go all the way to St. Joseph," Cal said. "He wants to go to Independence or Leavenworth."

It made a little swell of pride grow in Roman's chest that she knew about the Kansas frontier, two hundred miles away, when not so long ago she'd been as ignorant as he was himself about any geography they hadn't covered on foot in a five-mile radius from the farm in Benton County.

"That's right," Allan said. "I'd say Leavenworth. There's a big army garrison there and a lot going on. You could get your prairie legs before striking out to the plains country. There's a branch line of the railroad that runs down from Leavenworth to connect with the main road at Lawrence."

That night Roman wrote his first letter home, telling his mother of his plans: "So I'll see some of the West and then be home in time for spring planting. Or maybe I'll find something that will keep me occupied there for a while."

He thought about scratching out that last line, but decided against it.

Later he recalled that his days in St. Louis were eventful, sometimes even exciting. They wanted him to see their city, except for the saloons. They toured the riverfront where the cotton was coming in again from downriver, the bales stacking up along the wharves to form great walls of burlap-wrapped gray fiber. They went to a Methodist church and had dinner one night with Allan's father in his favorite restaurant, and Roman had veal and pâté and cold chicken salad. There was a band concert in the park, the last one of the late summer, and a boat ride down the Mississippi to Ste. Genevieve, including dinner on the open deck with the boat's master, a close friend of Allan Pay's. They had ham and sweet potatoes, served by black boys in red jackets, and it was the best ham Roman had ever tasted.

"Virginia cured," Allan said.

"Maybe Papa had some of this when he was with Lee's army," said Roman.

"I doubt it."

Calpurnia insisted that the men go on a shopping spree, because Roman, as she put it, looked like a river tramp in his duck trousers and that old coat of Papa's. Roman knew that protesting a Calpurnia decision would be as fruitless as it had been back when they were growing up on the farm and playing all the games she wanted to play, picking in the blackberry patch where she wanted to pick, swimming in the hole of Little Sugar Creek where she wanted to swim. So he went without protest and came away from it with a pair of doeskin pants, new boots, a butt-length heavy broadcloth coat, and new shirts and socks, with a leather valise to carry them. He felt better-outfitted than any of those spiffy drummers he'd seen peddling their worm medicine and buggy whips along Wire Road before the war.

The last few moments came when Cal and Allan took him down to the wharf to catch his boat, all of them standing in the gray morning rain that had a cold September smell to it. Cal avoided his eyes and Roman suspected that as soon as he walked onto the gangway, she'd begin to cry. She looked almost as he recalled her looking when she'd been a little girl standing with the umbrella while Mama threw corn to the chickens.

"Now here's your ticket," Allan Pay said, handing Roman a fat envelope. "There's a letter of credit there, too, for a bank in either Leavenworth or Lawrence, in case you need funds. Don't hesitate to use it, or your sister and I will be very unhappy.

"Then there's this. Your mama gave us the last hard money she had that day during the war when Cal and I left the farm, and I know she'd never hear of me repaying it. But at least you can take this as a token for that kindness."

He placed a small leather pouch in Roman's hand, and Roman knew from the weight of it that there was a good deal of money inside. There was a long thong to loop around his neck so the bag could ride inside his new cotton shirt, bought on Fifth Street just the day before.

He shook Allan Pay's hand, and when he threw his arms around Calpurnia he could feel her shaking. Then he was away quickly and onto the gangway and the slippery deck of the sternwheeler.

Well, hell, he thought, I remember the day Mama gave him that double eagle, the last money we had, to send them off to Missouri and us not knowing where the next grub was coming from, so why not take whatever he wants to give? He's a rich son of a bitch anyway. But a pretty nice son of a bitch at that.

As he stood at the railing on the pilot deck, while the boat slowly inched back into the river's flow, he could see St. Louis spreading out before him, gray in the rain and the coal smoke. There was the smell of stagnant water and fish and wet timbers. As the boat drew farther from shore, his sister and her husband were still standing on the wharf, waving, looking very small and somehow forlorn in the rain.

He wondered where he was going, what lay ahead along this river and others like it, and for the first time since he'd started out on foot from Benton County, a vast and overwhelming loneliness came over him.

Later, as the little sternwheeler plowed upstream toward the mouth of the Missouri, he looked in the leather bag for the first time. There were five twenty-dollar gold pieces, more money than Roman had ever seen.

Captain Edwin Cardin, recently a major but now demoted, owing to the army's reorganization after the war, watched the heavy foliage of the countryside slip past as the little stern-wheeler made its way upriver. Leaves still clung to the web of branches, some a faded green, but most bright yellow or flaming scarlet. Now that the rain had stopped, the sun outlined each crown of oak and hickory and sycamore in blinding detail.

He wondered how often the great Osage had come down to these shores, moved along the banks, made their settlements in nearby groves. He knew something of the Osage, having spent a great deal of time at West Point, reading from the accounts of the early French traders who'd traveled along this very river.

The Missouri was a shining brown ribbon left lying across this multicolored carpet, twisted and coiled back on itself, with the towns alongside—Hermann and Jefferson City and New Franklin—pinpoints of activity in what otherwise appeared a wilderness. At each such point, the boat pulled in for a short pause, long enough for a passenger or two to disembark or else for others to scramble along the slippery gangway to the deck. Sometimes they docked overnight. There was little urgency in this river traffic now, already reduced to casual transport because of the railroads. The boat was in no great hurry, nor was Captain Edwin Cardin. In fact, he viewed each passing mile toward Fort Leavenworth with growing distaste.

Standing at the railing on the pilot's deck, where the sun's reflections on the passing water sent flashes of light across his lean face, he kept the visor of his French-style forage cap low across gray eyes that conveyed the impression of hard metal. He had given his daughter, Victoria, those same gray eyes. But little else. For it was known in all the officers' corps of the army that she, now in her seventeenth year, was the spit of her mother, with her sharp-boned cheeks, her dainty red mouth that invited kisses, and skin as fragile as Chinese rice paper. Some of the army's lieutenants, always interested in such things as distaff beauty, had actually seen Mrs. Captain Edwin Cardin, and each marveled in public and private at her comeliness. But she was gone now, having died of scarlet fever in the third year of the war.

Captain Cardin's face reflected the agony. It was etched in heavy lines on either side of a wide mouth that was only partially concealed by the drooping mustache, now turning gray in his forty-seventh year of life. His body was long and erect, and in his thigh-length blue coat with the shoulder boards showing the insignia of his rank, and the cape he wore to ward off stinging autumn breezes, he looked in all ways the soldier that he was. His face was stone-hard and weathered, not just from service in the field but from inner storms as well.

His wife's death was like a stone lying heavy in his mind, even when he wasn't thinking about it. Almost each day he thought of the anguish of James Longstreet, the Rebel general who had lost his children to the same disease at about the same time. And that added to his discomfort, for it always seemed that he had more in common with the Confederate officers than with the likes of McClellan and Halleck, both of whom he had served directly, and for neither of whom he had been able to generate much respect.

Although the death of his young and beautiful wife had

been the capstone of his distress, there had been a bounty of additional disasters that made him wonder if he had not been singled out for special consideration by the powers who devised the testing of one's faith. He had never before been much of a religious man, unlike most of his peers, who seldom hesitated to proclaim Divine Providence responsible for this or that event in life, especially on the battlefield. Yet now he was ready to admit that such might be the case. And it only added to his despondency to realize that not until she was gone had he come to at least some understanding of her devout New Testament creed. Whatever it was. He never came fully to grips with it. But it gave him some small comfort to think that perhaps there was an ordering of things, no matter how distasteful.

She had come from a good family of Poughkeepsie, and there he had courted her after his graduation from West Point, just downriver. He had finished seventeenth in the class of 1841 and remained for a time at the citadel above the Hudson, awaiting assignment as an officer of cavalry. He had given her gifts and sprays of violets, and written a few love poems for her, which her father, a High Church Episcopalian, detested almost as much as he did the young man who wrote them.

But the beautiful Delia had had a mind of her own. Her father's outrage notwithstanding, she had married the young officer the following year, just before he was posted to a dragoon regiment and just after he had published a book of his poetry. That publication was paid for by funds he had from his father, who was a land speculator along the shores of Lake Erie in western New York State. The book had sold a few copies among the Bohemians of various coastal cities south of Boston, but never enough to pay for itself.

The first bitterness came in 1846 with President Polk's war, which Cardin sat out in his native state, recruiting horse troopers. He would always believe that such a tour of duty was the result of his father-in-law's malicious meddling, of his having convinced powerful men in the War Department that Edwin Cardin was more intellectual than fighter. It never occurred to him that any such finagling might have come at Delia's insistence, in order to keep her man away from the dust and cactus of Mexico and near home, where she thought he belonged.

The disappointment of missing the action was softened somewhat by the delightful evenings he spent reading aloud to his wife. And then there were the nights in the bedroom of their Brooklyn Heights flat, memorable and, to him, constantly astonishing. He often teased her that one so devout and obedient to the high moral preachments of her family could be so wanton when the lights were out.

Victoria was born in the eighth year of their marriage, and shortly afterward he was posted to the United States Military Academy as an instructor of cavalry and English grammar. It was the best of times; the commandant of West Point often paused to chat with them as they strolled with the child on the high parade ground after evening drill, while the cadets were all in their quarters, bending over books.

The superintendent at the Point then was one Colonel Robert Edward Lee of Virginia, a man universally admired and obviously destined for large things in the army. He showed some interest in Edwin's poetry, and at one point took out two volumes of James Russell Lowell's verse from the library for recreational reading—on Edwin's recommendation, or so Delia always claimed. She and Colonel Lee struck it off nicely from the start, the Virginian displaying his lifelong penchant for the company of handsome women. Mostly they spoke of religion, both being Episcopalians, walking ahead while Edwin followed, pushing the baby's buggy, perfectly satisfied to stay out of any such discussion and always enjoying his isolation from the words, absorbed with the view of the Hudson where West Point's high bluffs cast late shadows across it.

The class of 1854 would always stand in his memory as a special group of cadets, soon split down the middle in their loyalty to either North or South. One he always recalled with great affection was J.E.B. Stuart, who was the ugliest man he had ever known, but who, even then, showed the spark of dashing courage that would make him a fine cavalry officer in the hard times ahead.

Even more fondly remembered was a young man named James A. Whistler. Like Cardin, Whistler craved creative endeavor, but he was never kindly disposed to learning the mysteries of field fortifications or the laying of artillery pieces. He was finally dismissed for failing grades and went off to Europe. On the evening of his departure, Whistler came to call at the Cardin quarters and said that he would make his home in Paris and London, study the great masters of the brush, and make himself a painter.

Then came Texas, the Second Cavalry, and chasing Comanches. It was a bittersweet time—bitter because he was so far removed from the beautiful Delia and the tender bedroom scenes, and from bouncing the laughing child Victoria on the toe of his riding boot. But sweet, too, because he was in the field with troops. Lee had preceded Cardin to Texas and was second-in-command of the unit. It was a joy to serve under the man who had helped make West Point such a pleasant place for him and his family. Albert Sidney Johnston and John Bell Hood were in the regiment as well, all of them, Lee included, destined to become his deadly enemies.

When the Civil War came, he jumped at the chance for promotion when he was offered a majority in the Sixteenth New York Infantry, even though it meant leaving the horse service behind. At Gaines Mill, he saw most of his regiment destroyed, rushing forward in a counterattack that failed, all wearing yellow straw hats only recently sent by the ladies of the regiment and other benefactors who knew such things would be wonderful in Virginia during the heat of June, but who had no idea of what visible targets they made.

It was an irony he often contemplated, having survived the hail of metal at Gaines Mill, only to fall with a shard in his leg at Malvern Hill, where all the advantage was with his side. It was not a casual shard. It left him senseless on the field. And his army left him for dead as they retreated down the James. The Confederates found him, nearly bled to death, and he spent the next year in Castle Thunder prison in Richmond.

It was there that a special messenger from his old comrade in the Second Cavalry in Texas, John Bell Hood, came with the news that Delia had died of scarlet fever. He was exchanged a week later, but not in time for her funeral.

Those first few months after he came home to Poughkeepsie, or at least to Delia's old home, were a nightmare he tried to avoid thinking about. His wounds still pained him and his future was uncertain. The family business in western New York had gone bust, and his father-in-law was like a great stormcloud, frowning about with hardly a smile even for the lovely Victoria, now quickly growing to young womanhood.

Because he was a regular, the army did not pension him out because of wounds. What they did might have been worse. They made him an officer of the quartermaster corps, a job he had detested then and still did now, as he traveled up the Missouri to become chief buyer and dispenser of horses and tentage and wagons and coal and axle grease for the Western regiments who stood against the Indians.

He had no choice in the matter, being destitute and with no talent for surviving in a civilian world. All he and Victoria had were the clothes on their backs. By now his early dreams of becoming a poet were as dead as old ashes. He was far too proud to prostrate himself before Victoria's grandfather and ask for help, so his dependence on the army paymaster was complete.

On to Leavenworth, then, there to deal like some ordinary merchant, keeping books and ledgers and counting money, which he had always hated, doing the inglorious things that were needed to sustain troops in the field. There was considerable campaigning now, what with people like Cump Sherman involved in putting down the frontier problem—Sioux and Cheyenne and other wild tribesmen kicking up dust, protesting the incursions of white men into the Great Plains hunting grounds. And those incursions were on a grand scale, now that the war was over.

There was one bright spot amid his dismal outlook. Seventeen-year-old Victoria was glorious to behold, he thought, and with him now in his position as Leavenworth quartermaster, there'd be little fear of his being sent off to some dusty post and leaving her behind with friendly army families. Now, as the little steamer coughed its way upstream, he looked at her, standing near the rail with that young man who had begun to hang about from the moment he saw her at their first meal in the dining cabin after leaving St. Louis. The lad was explaining to her, as Cardin could hear, the beauties of hill-country catfish, a foot long and no longer, blue as night sky and tender to the taste.

"But they're so ugly," she said, her pretty nose wrinkled with distaste under the stylish brim of her flowered sunbonnet. (More a hat for spring than for autumn, Cardin thought, but she had insisted on wearing it.) "I'd never eat such a thing."

He found himself smiling, as he often did when he watched his daughter, because her appearance was so soothing and her tiny voice so confident and firm.

But he was blinded, as some fathers are, and had never been able to perceive what a haughty, arrogant, self-centered young woman his little girl had become.

If Captain Edwin Cardin observed much of the riverbank as they made their way across Missouri, Roman Hasford did not. After that first meal of baked beans and fried river fish of undetermined species, which all the first-class passengers took in the cramped dining hall on the cabin deck, his eyes were only for Victoria.

From the start, she had not been unaware of his attention, and after deciding that this young man was too bashful to start a conversation, she did so herself, asking him where he'd served in the late war. When he said he wasn't old enough to have been a soldier, she laughed.

"My land," she said, "you certainly look old enough to be a veteran. You're as tall as my daddy. And besides, my daddy says there were a lot of men in the war younger than you."

"I reckon so," Roman mumbled, knowing his face was growing red. "But I stayed home to work the farm."

"I don't know anything about farms. Putting those little seeds in the ground and milking cows."

When it became apparent that no one else at the table was paying the slightest attention to this small talk, he found the courage to go on and said that his father had fought, but by her lights in the wrong army, he supposed. She laughed again, as though he'd made a great joke, and he felt his face growing even hotter.

The captain sat next to his daughter, intent on slathering soft butter on a chunk of coarse cornbread that was, they found, to be another staple of this voyage, along with the unidentified fish and cold baked beans. He seemed completely oblivious to everything around him, but Roman suspected the glint in his gray eyes indicated a silent attentiveness to every move his daughter made and every word that passed her lips.

Roman knew that most of Victoria's comments were teasing, but he had long experience of such things, having grown up in the same household with an older sister. And Calpurnia's tongue could be as sharp as that of any serpent in the Hasford Old Testament. But now there was a new spice to the thing, and he had no intention of losing his temper, as he usually did with Cal. He found to his amazement that with Victoria he was less tongue-tied than he had ever been before in the presence of a young woman. He surprised himself with the witty things he said, even though he realized that he might have made nothing more than unintelligible grunts and received the same response from the laughing girl.

All of it gave him the uneasy sensation that he was much like a prize hog on display for city folk. But he didn't care, so long as he held her attention. The urgency of his need to keep talking with Victoria, to have her realize that he existed, was overwhelming.

So the talk went on as the sternwheeler pushed upriver, and the measure of Roman's detachment from all else except the girl was his lack of interest in the passing landscape. Always until then he'd been keenly attuned to land and the things that grew on it and how the seasons affected it all. Now it didn't matter what she said. He was enraptured by her voice, as delicate and ladylike as her finely pointed little chin and gracefully sculpted lips. He was unaware that Victoria was enraptured by the same things, as though she were constantly holding a mirror up to admire her own image. But even though she might not hear all he said, at least she looked squarely at him, allowing him to see into the gray eyes with the longest black lashes he had ever seen.

She was enough to turn the gaze of all the other passengers, but they seemed satisfied to look and not engage her in small talk. She always wore brightly colored clothes, her dresses running to rather exaggerated full skirts that went down just far enough to conceal the tops of her felt-and-leather button shoes. On deck she wore the flowered bonnet with a ribbon that she pulled back tight to tie in a bow at the nape of her neck. She had long, shining black hair, and with the ribbon in place it was pulled back behind her ears, the most wondrous ears Roman had ever imagined could exist.

They strolled the decks, with Captain Cardin always near but seeming not to notice them at all. They watched the cook's helper fishing off the bow, but he never caught anything that they could see; at dockside, they leaned over the railing on the pilot deck and watched the passengers coming on board; they saw the crew loading wood at Jefferson City. It was all exciting to Roman, because he was sharing these things with Victoria.

She told him about her grandfather, a rich and influential man in Albany and even in Washington City, so she said. She told him her father had been a hero at Gaines Mill and Malvern Hill. And he told her about seeing the battle of Pea Ridge and then the partisans coming through the countryside, taking everything that wasn't effectively hidden. Her eyes widened and she made little gasping sounds and clutched her throat with one tiny hand and Roman wanted to put his arms around her and protect her from the whole world, to shield her from scoundrels and mountebanks and lechers.

Victoria embellished her father's war record somewhat and said he was a well-known man in all the cities of the

Northeast, as well known as General Phil Sheridan or George Armstrong Custer in New York. Roman responded that his father had been in Richmond a couple of times and that he had an uncle named Oscar who had gone off to Texas before the war to fight the Comanches. None of that brought the hand clutching at the throat or the little gasps, but rather a vacant stare from the wide gray eyes.

Victoria used words Roman had never heard before. When she exclaimed that her daddy was noted throughout the army for his "éclat," he had no notion what she meant, but assumed it was something good. Besides, her mouth fascinated him as it formed the word, the lips parted and still and the tip of a small pink tongue flicking behind the rows of even teeth.

"It's a French word," she said, seeing his confusion and capitalizing on it. "Don't you just love the French? This bonnet came from France."

"Well, some of my people didn't like them very much," he said. "They fought against Napoleon."

"Against Napoleon? Good land, Roman, why would anyone fight against Napoleon?"

Roman swallowed what he wanted to respond, that everything passed down through the generations of his family pegged the Corsican as a son of a bitch.

All of this was a little game, though Roman didn't know it. Victoria played the game well, and Roman was responding like a lapdog, awaiting each new instruction. He carried her umbrella to shield her fine skin from the sun on deck. He passed the butter at table before helping himself. He kept his head bared when they were together, holding his old slouch hat in both hands behind his back. He listened attentively as she spun tales of high society as it operated in Poughkeepsie: how young men would come to call and she would entertain them with lemonade and sometimes by playing the harpsichord. He knew what a harpsichord was, having seen the one in the parlor of Elkhorn Tavern before the place was burned by partisans, but he'd never heard anyone play the contraption.

The constant supply of beans that they were served from

the galley sometimes became an embarrassment. It seemed that more and more frequently as they stood together by the rail, he had a sudden and urgent need to relieve himself from gas pains. This always required a quick retreat, with one excuse or another, and he would move away quickly, preferably downwind, where he could self-consciously "explode his britches," as his father used to put it. It never occurred to him that these base functions were ever known to Victoria.

There were other tensions. One evening at the supper repast, he mentioned that he was going west to see some buffalo and maybe a few Cheyenne Indians, whom he'd heard Allan Pay mention as the great warriors of the Kansas plains. Victoria's reaction was shock.

"Indians? Why would anyone want to go looking for such creatures?"

Immediately the other diners broke into the conversation with stories of reported depredations and atrocities and how General Sherman was going to wipe out the red niggers, wipe them off the face of the earth. One gentleman had a two-week-old copy of the *Cincinnati Commercial* and he read an item that had attracted his attention to the effect that a few of the Indians should be spared so that they might be put in zoos and people could see them on Sundays before going to their picnic lunches at the lake shore.

Everyone laughed except Captain Cardin. And Roman. He could recall vividly a certain Cherokee who had brought deer and squirrels to the Hasford farm in the days when the partisans were stripping all the food from everyone. Victoria laughed loudest of all, and Roman was somehow pleased to see the scowl on her father's face deepen.

The whole episode left a sour spot at the pit of Roman's stomach, which added to the discomfort of the beans.

But if it was all confusing and sometimes painful, it was nonetheless a strange and heartbreaking rapture. Each night he lay on his bunk listening to his cabinmate snore. He was a little man who always wore striped pants and who was going to St. Joseph to sell patent medicine. In the resonant darkness, Roman lay and pictured Victoria's face and imagined the lilt of her voice and the way her fingers looked like the petals on some exotic alabaster flower when she held her hand just so.

He was sure this was the happiest time of his life, and yet the most dismal, because she made him feel inadequate and incapable of impressing her as much as she was impressing him. He was glad he was away from the family, and especially Calpurnia, who would take a single look at his face and exclaim that he was like a calf caught in the warm rain: enchanted with the soothing heat, yet uncomfortable with the dripping water and too dumb to walk away from it and into the shelter of the barn.

Then, finally, there was the kiss. It wasn't Roman's initiative. Such a thing was far from his mind—unattainable, like the Holy Grail King Arthur's men were always thrashing around trying to find in those books he'd gotten from the old Jew at the Sugar Creek mill. But on the last night of the voyage, just short of Leavenworth, before she went to her cabin, when they were standing at the rail watching the reflected light of kerosene torches on shore, she leaned to him and on tiptoe reached up her face to his, and he felt the hot brush of her parted lips on his mouth. Then she was gone, leaving him stunned and openmouthed.

He didn't sleep much that night, but lay there listening to the rasping breath of the medicine salesman and thinking that at last he had found one of life's great mysteries. And he'd only just started on his way to see the Cheyenne.

Two Mile Creek ran down into the Missouri from the heights east of the river to create a flat little valley that defined the boundary between Fort Leavenworth and the town of the same name. Here had been constructed the extensive holding pens for livestock where everything, from mules to Texas cattle to freight oxen to blooded horses, was marketed to the army and the emigrants who came upriver from Independence to fill out their wagon trains with animals before leaving the tall-grass prairies and launching out into the high plains beyond.

Those wagon trains had been coming since 1850, and the traffic had decreased only a little. The emigrant trace left the corrals and skirted the military reservation for a short distance and then turned west. Already, when Roman Hasford arrived, the ruts were cut deep into the hard ground and would be etched even deeper before it was finished, perhaps deep enough to stand for all time in testimony to the courage or maybe the foolhardiness of men who would challenge an unknown land of dust and storms and waterlessness and clouds of grasshoppers and hostile tribesmen, just for the satisfaction of claiming a quarter section somewhere beyond the place where the sun set, there to break their plows on rock-hard soil, learn to deliver their own offspring, and, with their wives, give the growing children the only education they would ever have.

Even though the railroads had come to eastern Kansas, the wagon people disdained them, usually because they couldn't afford to ride them. Besides, they needed to carry along such things as washtubs and feather beds and kids and milk cows and chickens and Aunt Nellie's leatherbound steamer trunk filled with all the clothes they owned that weren't on their backs, and guns and candle makers and bullet molds and plows and the family Bible and various other books and pamphlets detailing routes to the Golden West or else filled with recipes for baked prairie dog and instructions on curing scours in hogs and cattle.

And besides that, the railroads didn't go as far west as a lot of them wanted to go.

So they still came in the wagons covered with bowed canvas and pulled by teams of plodding oxen. In the wisdom passed back from those who had gone before, they knew that wagons pulled by oxen had a better chance out there than those drawn by mules, and certainly more chance than horse-drawn vehicles, which had almost no chance at all.

Even so, when Roman came, the big business in livestock at the Two Mile Creek corrals was no longer with emigrants but with the army. Fort Leavenworth had become the major quartermaster, ordnance, and commissary depot for all the troopers operating on the high plains. And there were a lot of them, all because of the emigrants, of course, who wanted protection and who were establishing towns and farmsteads along the westward route. The railroads were doing their fair share of sprouting towns, and besides, there were gold and silver strikes in some of the mountains beyond the short grass.

Everything out there drew more people, it seemed. They came like streams of termites into lands that really belonged to someone else, and when there was some dispute about who should have the right to stay, the army was put in motion to protect the interests of citizens who sprang from a nation with a biblically steadfast belief that it was destined to populate and rule the entire continent.

Hence, Fort Leavenworth, in this peak of real-estate hunger and frenzy, was like the tail following the dog into a wolves' den, trying to move material to soldiers fast enough so that the bite could be placed at the head end of the brute where it was needed. But always it was hard to catch up, because those emigrants with their nose for free land, and those speculators with their ear for profits that were not even a whisper yet, moved out as rapidly as the slugs from a quick-cranked Gatling gun, all without regard for the safety of women and children, but then screamed for help when they realized their peril and saw too late that their own teeth were not sharp enough to handle the wolf.

At least that was pretty much how the local politicians and businessmen who planned to make money from the whole thing explained it to themselves and to anyone else who wanted to listen. And the members of Congress, being politicians and perhaps even interested in making a few dollars themselves, wanted to listen. They could understand the reasoning because they, even more than the ones actually going west, understood the slogans about higher civilizations taming the wilderness. In fact, they had coined most of the slogans themselves.

So when some docile and hungry Delawares stole a cow one day, a great hue and cry went up from the locals and the politicos in Washington City to bolster the frontier army. Governors on the fringes of the action called state militia to service, and there were wild stories in various newspapers about uprisings and slaughter and massacre.

Sometimes there was justification for alarm, because most of the warlike tribes in the buffalo lands were getting damned tired of white men coming into their country without even a beg-your-pardon. And these bands were no sweet-potato grubbers, but were rather peoples who taught their young that there were only two ways for a man to demonstrate the courage and dignity passed down through the generations:

hunting and war. To protect the opportunity for the first, they had good reason for practicing the second.

The Two Mile Creek pens had been established ten years before the war by the enterprising partnership of Russell, Majors and Waddell, freighters to the army and other customers. Now the yard was operated by a Mr. Elisha Hankins, who still did a little freighting but whose best business was in beef for troop messes and in cavalry remounts for the growing number of horse units that General Sherman had out on the dusty high plains.

It was only natural for Roman Hasford to be drawn to the horse pens on his second day in town, the first having been spent finding lodgings at Mrs. Condon Murphy's house on Seventh Street, room and keep for four dollars a week, paid in advance. This included a narrow four-poster bed, which he would share with another of Mrs. Murphy's regular guests, and two meals a day—biscuits and hog meat for breakfast and roast beef with boiled potatoes for supper, all served in a room on the first floor, dominated by brass cuspidors in each corner, with windows overlooking the gravel street, and a huge sideboard along one wall, with a crock beer dispenser looking like a cold blue rain barrel with a spigot at the bottom for letting out the brew. On one wall was a framed woodcut portrait of General Grant that had been cut out of an old issue of *Harper's Weekly*.

"We're all a big family together," Mrs. Murphy said. "No female visitors on the upper floor."

Mrs. Murphy's was the second place Roman had sought lodging. He'd made up his mind to establish Leavenworth as his base so long as Victoria Cardin was close by at the military post, the gray stone and red brick buildings of which he could see on the high ground just north of town.

The first place had been the Garrison Hotel on Second Street, where a clerk with acne like a flash burn across his face had taken one look at Roman and decided that this tall, gangling youngster could not possibly be looking for a place to stay, the new St. Louis valise in his hand notwithstanding. So before Roman could inquire about quarters, the clerk offered Roman a job, and along with it a half-concealed sneer.

"We need a boy to empty pisspots each morning," he said. "You reckon you could handle that?"

Roman bridled. He was not in the best of moods, having just disembarked from the little river steamer and watched it nose along its short course upriver to the landing slip below the fort, thinking all the while that Victoria was on that boat going away from him. His despondency was such that he felt the need to visit the first saloon he found along First Street for a sip of rye whiskey, which was working hot in his belly now and making him a little belligerent.

"You reckon you could handle kissing my ass?" he asked.

Why, hell, Roman thought as he stalked out of the Garrison Hotel lobby, as startled by his comment as the clerk had been, these peckerwoods around here don't look any harder than men I've seen at home. So far, I haven't seen a single one carrying a pistol!

Disgruntled and brooding over his first contact with a Kansas citizen, he made sullen inquiries along Miami Street until finally someone told him the best bet in town was Mrs. Murphy's, where the grub was short on spice but long on plentiful.

Mrs. Murphy was as solidly built as Roman's mother and wore her hair in the same style, with a bun at the back. She had a lilting voice and a ready smile and a shine in her eyes that made Roman forget the smart-aleck hotel clerk. It seemed hardly noticeable at all that she usually held a pinch of snuff in her lower lip. She was delighted to have a young man who wore new doeskin pants and had no mud on his boots.

Roman was just in time for the evening beef and potatoes, and Mrs. Murphy quickly introduced him to the half-dozen men seated around the big table, already at their meal and with mouths too full to do much more than nod their heads and grunt.

Roman's sleeping companion was a wisp of a man named Moffet, who had a gray beard that came down to the second button on his nightshirt. He was the representative for a number of malt beverage outfits that brewed their five-cents-a-glass beer in various nearby Missouri towns like St. Joseph and Odessa. On the back of the dry sink, Mr. Moffet had a line of mason jars filled with the smoky liquid he merchandised, and he offered Roman a nightcap from one of these.

"Mrs. Murphy, bless her, cooks the kind of roast beef that needs a little wetting down," he explained.

As Roman lifted the jar to his mouth, the thick odor of the beer making his salivary glands contract, he could see the raised letters on the glass indicating that this particular container had been patented in 1858. It was the first one he'd ever seen, and he thought how happy his mother would be to have a few of them to line her kitchen shelves, all shiny and clean and showing the dried beans and apples and sassafras root inside. The idea of canning perishable food in the things never entered his mind.

It was a dreamless night, Roman willing himself to sleep all the quicker so he could get out to the fort early and find Victoria. And so, after the biscuits and hog meat in the gray of dawn, he was off along Seventh Street and came therefore straight into the old Russell, Majors and Waddell corrals. Even the thought of Victoria on this windy, cloudy October day could not take his attention away from the horses. And thus he came a step closer to the Cheyenne.

Elisha Hankins was shorthanded and having a devil of a time doing everything himself. At the moment, with Roman Hasford watching from outside the post-and-rail corral, he was trying to cull a few hammerhead ponies out from better-looking stock and move the best into an adjoining stone pen where he liked to show off animals to the army quartermaster officers when they came from Fort Leavenworth to contract for remounts.

The horses, half-wild and glassy-eyed, were having none of it, whistling and rushing around in thick clouds of dust, kicking and bucking and crashing into the sides of the corral. Even in the cool air, they had worked up a lather and had that smell horses get when they're spooked and unsure of what's expected of them.

They were bay and roan and calico, but all the colors flowed into a single, moving fabric of red and brown and buff when they bunched, running in circles and snorting, making the earth tremble with their pounding hooves. Then, without warning and as though a signal had been given, the mass would split into fragments; each pony charging off in its own direction, like puffs of dandelion seed running before the wind.

It was difficult to see what was happening because the dense cloud of dust turned the interior of the pen the same tint and texture as the gray autumn sky, where a thick bank of clouds completely obscured the sun. As the herd passed in a single thundering wave across the far side of the corral, only their heads were visible above the billowing grit.

And at the center of the enclosure was Mr. Hankins, running about futilely, from time to time dashing toward the horses and screaming obscenities, as wild-eyed as the ponies, all the while trying unsuccessfully to kick aside the little dog that darted about his legs like an oversized, black-and-white mouse. The dog appeared to believe this was all some kind of wonderful game and that the horses were just thrown in to add excitement. He was an off-breed rat terrier, the kind of dog Roman Hasford always reckoned to be useless for anything, and his voice had the piercing, staccato timbre of a saw being played by someone using a metal mallet.

"You jar-headed sonsabitches," Mr. Hankins screamed, holding a coil of rope in one hand, alternately slapping it against his leg or swinging it in the air like a kind of frantic semaphore, all of which the horses ignored while the dog took it as encouragement for his frenzied barking.

Somewhere in the melee, Mr. Hankins had lost his hat, and even in the dim light from leaden skies Roman could see the sweat glistening across his exposed forehead. It was a long forehead sloping back to graying hair that was so sparse it could hardly be recognized as hair at all, except around the ears and at the nape of the neck. The few strands that still sprouted from the top hung over Mr. Hankins's pate, plastered to the skin with perspiration. Roman was reminded of one of his mother's twine string mops hung out to dry on the back porch railing at home after she'd given the kitchen a good scrubbing.

It was all funny and a little tragic at the same time, and Roman laughed, loudly enough to attract Mr. Hankins's attention. The frustrated yardmaster stopped his gyrations and glared with large brown eyes that matched perfectly the color of his beard. He had abundant whiskers, and the fact that he could grow such imposing hair on his face but none on his head made Roman laugh again.

With Mr. Hankins momentarily stationary at the center of the corral, the horses came to a shuddering halt, all in a bunch at one corner of the pen, the dust slowly settling around them until at last their slender legs were visible. Their hooves shifted nervously, ready to take them off again in whatever direction they chose at the first threat from their tormentor.

The terrier stood motionless for the moment, tail up like a stiff buggy whip, head down between front paws, looking like a snake ready to strike. Mr. Hankins snorted and the dog leaped back, still poised to play some more of the game on cue from his master.

There were other spectators to the drama. On the top railing of a nearby pen perched half a dozen men dressed in duck trousers, flannel shirts, and flop-brimmed slouch hats, and wearing loose bandannas around their necks. They looked like blackbirds equally spaced along a wire fence, watching with no expression. They were gray-faced from the dust, and their hands hung listlessly between their knees. Their saddle horses were hitched to the corral railings beneath them, heads hanging, paying no attention to the spectacle of Mr. Hankins, his dog, and the wild herd.

Leaning against the rump of one saddle pony was yet another man, grinning. When he shouted, the six men on the corral railing turned their heads in unison to look at him.

"I told you them beauties was lively, Mr. Hankins!"

Slowly the man ambled over to stand beside Roman, shaking his head and still grinning. A tangled mass of straw-colored hair hung below his hat, stiff and dirty. His face was flat and hard-planed, like hickory worked for many hours with a steel rasp. Everything about him reminded Roman of wood. The backs of his long-fingered hands were as rough and dark as the bark on a honey locust, and even his teeth, showing large and crooked beneath a sparse mustache, had the appearance of pine chips left lying wherever they fell from the ax. He was the same height as Roman, but heavier, yet he carried his weight loosely, moving with fluid, unhurried grace.

Roman had heard one of the passengers on the boat out of St. Louis speaking about men on the frontier going heavily armed, calling them walking arsenals. Now Roman understood what it meant. Beneath this tawny-haired man's denim jacket under the left arm was the ugly butt of a Remington pistol. Hung over his right hip on a heavy, brass-studded belt was an Army-model Colt revolver in an open holster. And in his hands was a Henry repeating rifle, the stock showing the heads of tacks driven into the wood in the shape of an arrowhead.

"God damn it, Fawley!" Mr. Hankins shouted from the center of the corral. "Why the hell don't you and your boys come in here and help me get these wild beasts you sold me separated like I want 'em?"

Fawley's grin widened as he looped one elbow over the top rail of the pen and he glanced at Roman and winked.

"Why, Mr. Hankins, I just brang 'em in. I don't get paid to churn 'em after."

But he gently placed the butt of the Henry rifle on the ground, leaning the barrel against the corral railings, and Roman could hear him laughing, a gurgling sound deep in his chest, and there was a glint of light in his yellow-cast eyes. To Roman they looked like the eyes of a red fox kit he'd once taken from a den and put in a wire coop and kept there for a few days until his father told him to set the varmint loose before it got big enough to learn how to kill the chickens. Bright and brittle, alert not only to sight but to scent and sound as well.

"Sprout," the man said, looking at Roman with his fox eyes

and showing his pine-chip teeth, "let's you and me go in there and help that ole man get his horses calmed down."

At that moment, Roman wanted nothing more than to be in the pen with those horses. He'd been with horses all his life and had started riding them almost as soon as he could walk. Just like a damned Comanche sprout, the old Jew at Sugar Creek mill had said.

And that was another thing. This Fawley had called him "sprout," just as the old Jew had and just as his own father had, before the war. And there was even more. The sound of Fawley's voice, the way he moved, even the smell of sweat and tobacco and oiled leather, were like home in some remote corner of Roman's mind, faint and undefined, like the scent of blooming dogwood in the Ozark hills.

It's spooky, Roman thought, this man Fawley somehow knowing I want in there with those horses and to hell with wear and tear of new doeskin trousers.

So the three of them took on the task, the onlookers at the nearby fence neither offering their help nor being asked for it. They went about it slowly this time, methodically, doing a lot more standing still with their arms out and clucking softly than running in circles and screaming curses.

The terrier was ready. But Fawley was quicker of foot than Mr. Hankins, and with one swing of a booted foot he caught the dog full in the belly and sent him yipping to safety beyond the corral railings, where he sat watching, haunches down and tongue hanging out.

"You oughta get rid of that damned dog, Mr. Hankins," Fawley said. "He causes more trouble with your horses than a copperhead snake."

The ponies seemed to recognize something in Fawley, who had driven them into the Leavenworth pens in the first place. Roman could see the man had knowledge of horses. This was not the case with Mr. Hankins, who generally had hired help to take care of such chores. Roman reckoned Mr. Hankins with horses was like a hay salesman with hay, having no notion of how to plant the stuff or harvest it.

It took well into the morning to coerce the best stock into

the stone pen. When it was over, Fawley slapped Roman's shoulder and grinned.

"You act like a livestock man, sprout," he said, and it made Roman puff up a little with pride.

"I've worked horses some."

"Whereabouts?"

"On a farm in Arkansas. Benton County."

Fawley's eyes widened. "Well, I'm damned. Arkansas, huh? Me, too. Newton County. Ain't been there in a long spell. Left a long time ago to fight the war and never got back. I thought there was something about you that sounded like home in your talk. Want a chew?"

He took a black twist from his jacket pocket and offered it to Roman. It was the toughest tobacco Roman had ever had in his mouth, and as bitter as gall. He got the cud working in one cheek, like a lump of hemp rope, and Fawley did the same, winking as he gnawed off a huge bite from the plug.

"Tyne Fawley," and he offered his hand.

"Roman Hasford," Roman said, taking Fawley's hand and feeling the hard surface of the palm.

The terrier took that opportunity to gain its revenge, and made a try for Fawley's left heel with his sharp little teeth, but Fawley caught him again, this time with a spur, and the dog bolted off through the stockyard pens. The men still sitting on the corral railing laughed, but except for open mouths, Roman could see no change in their dusty expressions.

That's a mighty hard-looking bunch of men, he thought.

"Mr. Hankins ought to get rid of that damned dog," Fawley said. "Say, why don't you take care of my rifle while I go pay off my bushwackers over yonder, then me and you can go downtown and get us some dinner."

With Tyne Fawley off toward the blackbird men, already counting out greenbacks from a scarred wallet, Roman lifted the Henry from its place and hefted it. Repeating rifles that fired brass cartridges were not too plentiful in northwest Arkansas, and Roman marveled at the brass receiver and the tubular magazine that ran under the barrel.

Heavy as a fencepost, he thought.

He reckoned it was about a .44 caliber, and wondered if maybe Tyne Fawley had ever hunted buffalo with it. He imagined himself in the deep timber along Little Sugar Creek, stalking deer with the Henry, and was lifting it to his shoulder to squint along the sights when Mr. Hankins appeared beside him, glaring as though he were still pursuing wild horses around one of his pens.

"Son, my name's Elisha Hankins," he said. "I run this yard and I've had some dealings with Tyne Fawley. He's not the kind of man you want to consort with."

Sometimes good intentions were lost on Roman, who usually took them as nothing more than someone's suspicion that he lacked any judgment of his own. This was one of those times, and before he could control his mouth, he answered brusquely and was sorry as soon as the words had escaped his lips.

"Mr. Hankins, keep to your own affairs!"

Mr. Hankins blinked rapidly, his mouth open to respond, but then he clamped his jaw shut and shrugged.

"All right, son, it's not my business. You're old enough to know your own mind. But there's something that is my business."

He looked across the sprawl of corrals, some empty, some holding mules, and a few with horses inside, and across Seventh Street to where more corrals held rust-colored cattle.

"I like the way you worked in that pen a minute ago," he said. "I was pondering the possibility of hiring you on, if your plans don't call for anything better."

"Well, I don't really have any specific plans. I just came out here for a while to see things. Maybe some buffalo, and I'd like to see some Cheyenne Indians."

Mr. Hankins's eyes widened as he looked at Roman again, and now all his combativeness was gone. He looked ready to laugh.

"Cheyennes? Well, the army says there's plenty of those out west of here, but mostly they don't stand still long enough for the pilgrims to walk up and take a look at 'em. But about the buffalo, that's something else."

The yardmaster licked his lips and, being a good businessman able to quickly grasp the opportunities that passed his way, explained the kind of job he was offering.

"I could be help on those buffaloes—maybe as soon as the middle of next week. You could come in Monday, this being a Saturday and half gone anyway. You could learn this yard work right away from my other employees. That is, if they ever sober up and get back to work. One of the boys got married yesterday and they had him a big shivaree last night, shooting off guns and raising hell outside the bridal bedroom and getting drunker than Hooter Tom.

"Anyway, you impress me as a good, honest man and I need somebody to act as my agent to ride out to Abilene on the U.P.E.D. and bring back carloads of Texas cattle now and then. I buy 'em from the trail herds in carload lots and sell 'em to the army. Trail herds are about finished for this year, but the soldiers eat beef during the winter same as the summer, and I need to get me an agent out there, next week more than likely."

"What's that got to do with buffalo?" Roman asked, confused.

"The Union Pacific Eastern Division railroad runs a hunt train out across the prairie now and again. One goes out the middle of next week. I could get you on it."

"Hunt train?"

"That's right. The railroad takes these important people out to end-of-track so they can maybe see a few beasts and shoot some. One goes next week. It was in the newspaper just this morning."

"I don't know what an agent does," Roman said, thinking only about the buffalo.

"I can teach you that in fifteen minutes. There's not much to it. You just see that the cattle get loaded and headed east on the U.P.E.D."

"I have to buy the cattle?"

"That's no difficulty. They're all the same, those Texas cows, hide and horns. The army buys 'em no matter what."

Roman thought about it. He looked across the yard and

saw Tyne Fawley's men mounting up, having been paid off, and thought about what Fawley had called them. Bushwhackers. It crossed his mind that maybe some of these men, and maybe even Tyne Fawley himself, had been members of those partisan bands that had made life miserable for him and his mother.

Mr. Hankins had retrieved his hat from the horse corral and now set it gingerly on his bald head as though he might bruise the pale skin. He waited patiently, watching Roman's face.

There was a flurry of motion as Tyne Fawley's riders scrambled their ponies out of the yard and toward town, money in their pockets and plenty of saloons waiting for their business. Fawley himself was standing near his own mount, turned toward Roman and Mr. Hankins. Roman was suddenly afraid that Fawley might mount up and ride away, too.

"I can't talk anymore now, Mr. Hankins," he said. "I got a previous engagement."

"No need to talk. Just a yes or no for Monday morning. I'll pay you eight dollars a week and provide a saddle horse, gear included, for whatever riding you need to do in the business."

Perhaps it was the prospect of his own saddle horse, even if just for business. Or perhaps it was because Roman liked this Mr. Hankins, with his direct, steady brown eyes. Or perhaps it was the buffalo or maybe that it made him feel important to have a man such as Mr. Hankins offer his trust on first sight.

"I'll be here bright and early Monday morning," Roman said, and they shook hands.

Roman turned then and, strutting a little, moved toward Tyne Fawley, swinging the heavy rifle in one hand as though he'd carried such a thing all his life. Tyne Fawley was grinning at him, showing those long teeth, and Roman thought, Why, hell, he's no more a bushwhacker than I am.

Roman Hasford's first weekend in Kansas was like a great battle, or perhaps a tornado that blew the barn away—a time for him to remember through all his days.

At first he saw everything, sucking each scene into his consciousness like a sponge sucking in water, as though afraid even a single drop might escape. He noticed that Tyne Fawley seemed a little nervous inside buildings or even on the sidewalks, with all the people close around them. He noticed as the afternoon wore on that every man he saw appeared to be intent on drinking himself into complete oblivion, a consumption of liquor beyond all his imagination. He'd come from a society of men and women who took their gill of white whiskey, it was true, but usually in small doses and only after a hard day's work was finished or when there was a new baby in the family or when the right man had won a close election to office.

In Leavenworth during those October days of 1866, there seemed to him a contest of stomachs against distillers, like a foot race. It was his introduction into the uncloistered world away from Mama and Papa and Calpurnia and Allan Pay, out now in the company of a man who obviously knew every mahogany or planed-pine bar, every pool game and dance hall, every gambler and pimp and soldier and horse trader and river captain west of Independence. In that old world of his younger days, the feel of fiery liquid down the gullet was as infrequent as a good sermon on Sunday. But here he had his first look at what the tent-meeting preachers were always howling about—that the frontier was washing itself square to hell with riotous drink.

And he thought, midway through the afternoon, that he had seen more of the great world beyond Benton County, Arkansas, in the past three weeks than in all his life before. Yet he saw no single tree as large as the black oak on the ridge behind his father's farmhouse, where he and Cal had carved their initials when he was only just old enough to understand what initials were.

Roman Hasford's acute observations of the scene lasted only a little while after he and Tyne Fawley had gorged themselves at Rusty Randall's Café, paying four bits for two bowls brimful of beef hash heavy with sage, and double slabs of gooseberry pie. Coffee included. After that, it was the glass and boisterous companionship; liquor red as a bay horse, or beer golden in steins frosted from the icebox and topped with a head frothy and white as dry snow.

Soon, instead of precision of detail, there was little more than passing panels of color and sound and smell and the touch of rough fingers and, in one case, fingers soft and tender.

And although at the time, once it was finished, Roman Hasford wore guilt for a little while as though it were a heavy saddle, in later years he recalled it happily as one hell of a good weekend, when all kinds of things changed for him forever.

There were the dusty streets under the cold October sky, bordered sometimes by rough plank sidewalks, sometimes not, and inside the barrooms the soft, spongy feel of sawdust underfoot, and the sound of a drunken soldier trying to pick out the notes to "The Battle Hymn of the Republic" on an upright piano, the regular musician not being due until darkness when the bar girls came. And the smell of old beer, soaked and dried into the sawdust or, in the case of the billiard parlor, into the pine-board floor.

They tried a game of pocket pool until the proprietor, afraid that Roman in his condition would rip the green cloth cover, closed the game and gave them their money back. Tyne Fawley, fox eyes darting, not inclined to trouble, led Roman out, the latter protesting all the way.

Was that before or after the contraption that had a glass face and looked like a china closet and inside had hammers and chains and screws and metal bars, and when Roman slipped a nickel into the slot and wound the crank, it burst forth with a harsh, metallic rendition of "Sally Don't You Weep"? It seemed important to remember, later in the evening, when that had happened, that china-closet music box. But Roman couldn't even remember *where* it had happened, let alone how it fit into the sequence of things.

Then there was the barbershop where Tyne Fawley took

his fall bath, lying submerged in the soapy water in the back room with only his head showing and one hand hanging at the rim of the tub, holding a quart bottle of rye whiskey, half-empty, from which he took a jolt now and again to ease the pain of lye soap on his naked body. Roman, meanwhile, was getting his hair cut out front in the swivel barber chair, and getting besides that a dose of talcum powder in a cloud dense enough to make him cough and smell for the rest of the day, like one of the ladies in the Westerner Saloon and Dance Hall next door.

In their wavering passage from bar to bar, Roman paused frequently to amuse himself by reading aloud the various imprints in shop windows: LUMBER AND STOVES; GUNS AND PISTOLS REPAIRED; MR. LADD'S SHEEP DIP; FINE WATCHES SOLD OR TRADED; BOOTS AND SHOES MADE OR OLD ONES RESOLED; CANE CANDY AND LEMON DROPS 5 CENTS A POUND; GREEN-GROCER IN SEASON. And before a butcher shop, the most amusing sign of all: BEST CUTS OF FARM-RAISED BEEF. NO LONGHORNS.

A visit to the icehouse then, down by the river, and a little dark-skinned man with straight black hair and piercing black eyes who was a friend of Tyne Fawley from the days before Wilson Creek in Missouri and the days after, too, when the both of them, having had enough of the army and battle, deserted the Union and ran off to the Indian Nations, or so Roman thought they said. He wasn't sure. It all came to his ear in bubbly spurts. Cider? No, Crider. Crider Peel his name was, and he worked at the icehouse and at the tannery besides, just next door, doing double duty and doing it, Roman saw, with more than a little whiskey in his belly.

But though he was a deserter years ago from the real army, this Crider Peel was proud now of being in the Kansas state militia, drilling once every two weeks as a cavalry trooper and getting drunk afterward—and before, too, like as not. Maybe his real name wasn't Crider Peel or maybe that was his real name but he'd enlisted in the Yankee army under another, and so—the state of keeping records in that time and place being what it was—no one in the Kansas state militia was any the wiser for Crider Peel's having taken to shanks' mare after Wilson Creek, where he had his fill of Napoleon twelve-pounders spraying canister around his ass and Southern sharp-shooters putting holes in his hat.

"It's a heap sight easier fightin' red niggers than Rebel boys with rifled muskets," as Tyne Fawley, laughing, put it.

And there was Crider Peel's home, where they went so the two old soldier comrades and fellows-in-desertion could hash over favorite tales about Indian squaws and horse-stealing. Crider Peel's house had once been a mule shed. On the west end of town, it was almost out on the open prairie, surrounded mostly by empty buildings that had once been mule sheds, too, and the brown grass of autumn, as it moved in the wind, made a noise all around like women's stiff petticoats, and the whole place smelled of rotten potato peel and old mule sweat.

They ate there. At Crider Peel's home. Boiled beans, if Roman's memory later served him, but he wasn't sure. He sat at a battered oak table, staring glassily into the shine of a single coal-oil lamp, dripping pot liquor down his chin, trying to hear the tales being told, trying to understand the laughter, trying to comprehend which of the two was talking, the man with the hickory-planed face or the one with the dark, clean-shaven face who showed teeth as even and perfect as pearls set on a string. There was at least one jug of white whiskey, which made Roman feel a little more at home, although he couldn't tell if it was as good as the white whiskey his own father made, because by then his tongue and lips were numb. Along with everything else.

There was another thing at Crider Peel's, beyond the talking and the laughter and the beans and the white whiskey, and it haunted his thoughts afterward. He felt the presence of something in the room beyond the door that was hung with grain-sack burlap, a fleeting movement there, more than once, a pale passage like a bass moving quickly across a sun-lit patch of water and then gone under the deep purple shade of overhanging rock. And he was sure that once he felt a touch on his arm, the touch of a small hand, tentative and gone quickly.

He heard Crider Peel yelling. Angry, foam at the corners of his mouth.

"Gawd dammit, get your butt outa here. Go eat your beans."

But then he wasn't sure he'd heard anything but the wind. There was this ringing in his ears, this dizzy sensation that made him grip the edges of the table to keep from falling on the dirt floor.

The blast of cold air when they went outside revived him and they went back into town, back to the saloons where the piano players were playing and the dance girls dancing and the drunks getting drunker and everything now, even in the streets, was made up of patches of darkness and brilliant orange light from the lamps, and each room they came into smelled like coal oil and lilac water and bay rum and sometimes vomit.

Along the streets at midnight then, a bell ringing somewhere and a dog barking. Tyne Fawley yelling in the wind.

"That there's one of them newspaper presses."

Teetering against one another, they peered into a plateglass window and Roman saw there the massive iron machine with handles and levers and rollers, and beyond that, along a far wall, trays of type and stacks of old newspapers.

THE LEAVENWORTH CONSERVATIVE, gilt letters across the plate glass proclaimed. Daniel Anthony was the proprietor and editor, brother of Susan B., although Roman didn't know that, nor did he even know there was such a person as Susan B. Anthony.

Tyne Fawley's words: "Been shot at a few times, that son of a bitch, for the thangs he writes in his newspaper. And horsewhipped oncet."

They both found it outrageously funny and laughed out of control for a long time, clinging to one another to avoid falling in the street.

There was an outside stairway, up along the shiplap wall of a two-story building and turning on the second floor into a long porch across the back, the railing hardly strong enough to hold a whisper, much less a drunk man falling against it.

Roman could smell the river, and there were lights along the shore, where a late-arriving boat was being unloaded; Roman knew it was carrying lumber after hearing the slap of planks thrown down along the wharf. The steamboat whistle sounded and he recalled hazily the trip from St. Louis.

"Victoria," he mumbled.

"No, by Gawd, it's Katie Rose Rouse," Tyne Fawley said, banging on one of the doors that opened onto the narrow porch.

She was large. Not old-person large, but solid, mature large, with a painted mouth and cheeks as red as the sunward side of ripe peaches and a smell that made her small living room whirl with lavender. Before they'd taken off their hats, she was serving them a clear liquid in stem glasses, a liquid that tasted like licorice and turned smoky when water was added, and Tyne Fawley was slapping at the butt of Katie Rose Rouse each time it passed within his reach.

There was overstuffed furniture, and pillows embroidered with colorful thread, not like the seats of Calpurnia's straight-backed chairs, but as gaudy and harsh as Katie Rose's laughter, screaming out their colors like a voice. There were photographs on the walls, of old men with hanging mustaches and soldier boys with cocky French forage caps shading their eyes, and a framed Currier and Ives lithograph of two black horses pulling a surrey through snow. There was another room, where Tyne Fawley and Katie Rose Rouse disappeared for a long time, and at first Roman could hear their gentle laughter, but only for a little while before he went to sleep on the horsehair couch.

He dreamed of the face. Somewhere during this murky Saturday there had been that face—a tiny, heart-shaped face swimming through the blaze of yellow lamplight. And straight hair as black as a cold October night, tangled and unkempt. Eyes penetrating and black as well, or maybe brown. Along one cheek was a deep purple bruise, and the small, bow-shaped mouth was swollen at one corner and scabbed over. Where? Was it Crider Peel shouting? A name, with curses.

Catrina. A kitten's name for a kitten's face, terrified of the snarling dog.

It was Tyne Fawley's rough hand that shook him awake, and all the lights were out now, with the shine from night outside coming pale through the single window, and Fawley's dark form over him, his hat on his head, his voice harsh even in a whisper.

"Wake up, sprout. I'm outa here now. Maybe we'll run acrost one another again someday. Don't worry, my old love Katie Rose'll take good care of you."

There came a blast of cold air when the door was thrown open. There must be a stove in here, Roman thought, although he couldn't remember seeing one but now could smell coal dust and a coal fire. It didn't matter now, stove or not. Her hands were on his face, and he could hear her voice and make out the words.

"You let Katie Rose do it all."

Her fingers on him were as soft as hog fat, yet with the same firm foundation of solid flesh, and they seemed to know what they were doing, as though they had done it many times before.

"You come into Katie Rose a boy," she whispered. "But you'll go out a man."

It was a long time before he realized that what made it hard to breathe was her wide, soft mouth against his own.

It was the middle of Sunday afternoon before Roman came out of the gloom of Katie Rose Rouse's rooms. The skies had cleared and the wind laid, but still there was a sharp, autumn feel about everything. He stood on the high, narrow porch and gulped in the air. He'd slept all day, protesting each time Katie tried to wake him. So, listening to her in her back room, clanging pots and pans around on the stove or whatever it was she had in there, he dressed and slipped outside.

He could see the slanting October sun on the river, and there were boats there and once again he thought of Victoria, now with considerable shame as he recalled vaguely what had happened on that horsehair couch.

Well, hell, I'll go see her before long, he thought. A man sure gets caught up in things fast out here in the Wild West.

The walk along the street revived him a little, but he was thirsty and his head felt like a beer keg with large pebbles rolling about inside at each step. Sunday looked just like Saturday on these streets, and he could hear the voices from inside the saloons he passed, and the odors coming out made him gag.

He had to sit down on the edge of the sidewalk once, beside a cigar-store Indian that stood solid and fierce in the bright, lowering sun. He leaned against the carved wooden statue and groaned.

"God," he muttered aloud. "If I ever get back home, I'll never take another swallow of Papa's white whiskey."

The very thought of it made him think he might vomit. But after a little while, resting there before the tobacco shop, he felt better and went on to Mrs. Condon Murphy's boardinghouse.

He felt as though he'd betrayed somebody, but he didn't know whom. Maybe Mama or Calpurnia or maybe even himself. At least he couldn't put his finger on very much that had happened. But enough, with Katie Rose Rouse. He recalled that in a kind of smoky, dreamlike haze, and wondered if that was all this man-and-woman business amounted to. And thought that maybe there ought to be some love attached to it. Last night was about like scratching an itch and nothing more.

At Mrs. Murphy's, this being Sunday, most of the boarders were lounging about the parlor playing euchre, reading newspapers, and sipping beer from the blue crock barrel in the dining room. Mr. Moffet was there, and as Roman passed quickly toward the stairwell, the man lifted a dainty little blue-veined hand in greeting.

Roman sat on the edge of his bed for a long time, his hat still on his head. Suddenly it seemed very important to write his mother another letter, to get back in touch with home, if only for a few moments. Home. A place where he understood what was happening, a place that was simple and direct and there were no feelings of guilt about getting drunk and laying up all night in some painted woman's room above a newspaper shop.

It was a great effort. But at least he was proud to be able to explain his new position with Mr. Elisha Hankins's stockyards and to say further that he intended to stay in Kansas until he'd seen some buffalo and maybe a few native savages.

"From what I've been told," he wrote, "none of these Cheyennes are anything like the Indians Mr. James Fenimore Cooper wrote about."

From time to time he took a small sip from one of Mr. Moffet's fruit jars. The warm beer seemed to have a soothing effect on his stomach.

He started to tell his mother about Victoria Cardin, but decided against it. Hearing he had a responsible position with livestock was enough for her at one whack, he reckoned. He sat at the little desk below the window, his pad and quill before him, trying to frame Victoria's face in his mind. But all he could see was the little elfin face of the night before, with the penetrating, somehow tragic eyes that were too old for the rest of the face. Again he tried to recall more of the details, but couldn't. Maybe it was all a dream, he thought, but knew that wasn't true.

At last he signed off: "Your son, Roman Hasford. Postscript. Tell Papa I send greetings and that he would enjoy seeing some of the fine horses they have here."

Downstairs, Mrs. Murphy's little bell was ringing and he knew it was time for supper, and after Mr. Moffet's beer he was suddenly very hungry. As he rose, hearing the bell, it reminded him of Victoria Cardin's voice. But he still couldn't fix her features in his mind.

5

Going to the first real job he'd ever had, Roman Hasford felt not a twitch of apprehension because he knew livestock and how to work with horses, mules, and cattle. Arriving at the yard office even before Mr. Elisha Hankins did seemed to impress Roman's new employer yet further.

Although the behavior of most stockyard roustabouts gave Mr. Hankins an upset stomach, within the first hour of their association as boss and worker he recognized in Roman a young man who was both dependable and energetic. Hay and grain were distributed, manure cleaned out of the pens, horses graded and shifted from one corral to another with a minimum of fuss after Mr. Hankins issued only brief instructions.

Mr. Hankins sighed with pleasure a number of times that first morning, and enjoyed his ten o'clock coffee from the blue enamel pot on the office stove more than he had in a long time.

As for Roman, it was good that he could perform his tasks without much serious thinking, because his mind was not in the stockyards but farther north, on the high ground where Fort Leavenworth sprawled, a little city complete in itself.

Fort Leavenworth was mostly treeless except beyond the perimeter of the cluster of buildings and parade grounds and corrals that appeared to have been laid out with a surveyor's transit. The ordnance warehouses, two gray blocks with their second-story windows frowning out like rectangular caves in a limestone bluff, were bordered behind by oak and elm and mulberry and hop hornbeam, mostly leafless now, that stood in thick rows, apparently immune to the army's axes, along the high bluff that overlooked the Missouri River.

There was the usual collection of army post structures: headquarters and stables, barracks and officers' quarters, hospital and commissary store, gun sheds and ammunition magazines.

Plans had been made for running a trolley line from town to the fort, but it wasn't a reality yet, so on that Monday evening when Roman Hasford went looking for Victoria Cardin, he walked. Mr. Elisha Hankins had offered a horse, but Roman said he'd go afoot, seeing as how this was pleasure instead of stockyard business.

It turned out that there was damned little pleasure involved.

Roman wrote that comment himself, later. He'd heard his father say that during the war a lot of men, seeing new places and strange things and notable people, kept diaries to refresh their memories at a time when their adventures would be told. So Roman decided to keep a diary himself. It was a fine way to keep all this Wild West stuff together in his mind, he reckoned. Besides, for as long as he could remember, he'd gotten some kind of secret joy from writing words on paper. It was secret, insofar as he could keep it that way, because he had been afraid that if he advertised it his sister would tease him about it and his mother would dismiss it as a waste of time.

"If it's important enough to write down on a piece of paper, it ought to be important enough to stay in your head," she'd likely have said.

Roman had no trouble finding Captain Edwin Cardin's residence, having to ask directions only twice from passing soldiers just as they were leaving mess halls or else going there directly out of the stables, having finished late-day grooming and feeding of mules and horses. Some of these men wore fatigue uniforms and others were in off-duty blues. In either case, they made Roman a little nervous. They used words with which he was completely unfamiliar, army terms he supposed his father might understand but that he didn't. He decided the army was a world unto itself, where everybody was doing something important or had just finished something important or was rushing about looking for something important. And he heard more blasphemous and obscene expressions in ten minutes at Fort Leavenworth than he'd heard in ten years at home.

The Cardin quarters were in a long line of two-story, white- painted frame houses, a family living at either end of each building. There were wide covered verandas and neatly kept gravel walks that led to the banistered front steps, and kerosene lamps in wall brackets beside each door, already lit by enlisted orderlies. Roman had learned that these men who looked after the welfare of the officers and their families were called "dog robbers." He would soon learn that it was a term that in some regiments was applied to all enlisted men.

It almost took his breath away when Victoria herself answered to his knock. He stood staring at her, hat in hand, as her eyes widened and an expression of shock crossed her face, which Roman might have recognized had he not been so mesmerized by her beauty. In the well-lighted parlor behind her he could see other figures, in uniforms, and there was the sound of organ music and laughter. He hardly noticed. The sight of her and the scent of her perfume overwhelmed him.

He thought she would surely invite him inside, out of the west wind. Instead, she stepped onto the veranda and closed the door behind her, then stood facing him, hugging herself against the chill.

"Why, Mr. Hasford. What on earth are you doing here?"

Mr. Hasford? He gulped and mumbled something about how he was in the neighborhood on business and had thought he'd drop by to give his greetings to the captain.

"On business?" she asked, still hugging herself. In the

dim light, Roman couldn't make out the details of her flowing dress that flared out at the waist in the current "princess" style. But he wasn't interested in the dress, only in the face above the high-necked lace collar. "What kind of business?"

"I'm buying stock now," Roman said, a little too loudly, expecting to make a good impression and wanting her to understand that he was something more than a tourist.

"My goodness, the army's not selling any livestock," she said, and laughed. "And anyway, Father's engaged at the present. I'll tell him you called."

She turned toward the door.

"I thought I might tell you about the things I've seen in Leavenworth," he said desperately.

And then he thought, My God, what would I tell her about? Katie Rose Rouse?

"That sounds terribly interesting, Mr. Hasford, but I have to act as my father's hostess when he entertains. I know he'll be pleased that you called. Do you have a card?"

"A what?"

"A calling card, of course. My father always requires that visitors leave a calling card. Do you have one?"

"I guess not."

"I suppose I'll just have to tell him that you came."

"Well, give him my felicitations," Roman mumbled.

"Felicitations? What are you congratulating him for?" She giggled again and Roman shuffled his feet, twisting the hat in his hands, feeling the spray of hair fanning across his forehead in the wind.

"Well, I mean salutations," he said.

He wasn't even sure she'd heard that last. She was back inside, the door closed decisively behind her, leaving him standing there under the dim glare of the lamp, still hearing the organ music and the laughter from inside.

Roman had the uneasy feeling that someone had pulled aside the window curtains to peer at him from the brightly lighted room, so he jerked his hat onto his head, wheeled abruptly, and took his departure, stamping his boot heels across the planking of the veranda and the steps down to the gravel walk, hoping it all looked very nonchalant to whoever might be watching from the window.

"Shit!" he said aloud, using his father's favorite expression for times of utter exasperation.

As Roman Hasford walked back to Mrs. Condon Murphy's boardinghouse, he unaccountably thought of things his father had read aloud from the mythology of the Greeks. It had always seemed strange that his father, Martin Hasford, found such pleasure in the age of the civilized pagans, as he described them, as he had often suggested that his true calling might have been preaching the Gospel of Jesus. He had even given his children names that might have come directly out of those non-Christian times.

Of course, Martin Hasford had never revealed to his children the carnal acrobatics of the Greek gods, which had effectively eliminated many of their stories—which Roman caught up on when he learned to read himself—but there had been one tale his father told many times. Now, walking in the chill darkness along the road that led into Seventh Street, the cold wind whipping at his upturned coat collar, he remembered it vividly and gained some solace from it. He, Roman Hasford, living in the modern age of steam locomotives and the telegraph, was beneficiary of the one good thing in Pandora's box. Hope! Hope for another time, he thought, even though at the moment, after such a short and unsatisfactory reunion, hope seemed a frail reed to support something so important that he considered it an absolute requirement for his survival—that he kiss those red lips of Victoria Cardin once more. And more than once.

It was a bright spot in his misery, that he was able to view the whole business with some degree of detachment. This Wild West makes an old man out of you in a hurry, he thought. He didn't put it into exact words, but Victoria had given him something he had never been conscious of before—introspection, an ability he had always thought reserved for those far along in age. The old Jew at the Sugar Creek mill, the only real philosopher he'd ever known, had often said, "Don't fret, sprout, when you come to my number of years, you'll be as able as me to stand back and look at yourself and laugh."

Hell, he thought, I'm not *that* old yet, but it feels like it.

And he thought, It'll be all right when the guineas come home to roost. This was a thing he had often heard his mother say, and she was something of a philosopher in her own right.

It was a good time to ignore small and local defeats. In the morning he would be off on the Leavenworth spur line to catch the hunt train at Lawrence, his authorization in the coat pocket under his left arm, along with the letter of introduction from Mr. Elisha Hankins to a cattle buyer in Abilene.

The thought of the buffalo really saved his good temper that night as he settled beside the wheezing Mr. Moffet after a sip from the fruit-jar beer. He'd been a hunter since he was strong enough to carry a shotgun or a rifle—a woods hunter, stalking everything that roamed the hill timber country. Turkey and deer and coon and squirrel and quail. And like all good hunters, he'd always thrilled at the prospect of getting into the wilderness, not just to shoot those things for his mother's cooking pot, but just to see them, the untamed things, to watch them from hiding and marvel at their movements, their color, their alertness. Now he had a chance to see prairie game, big game, big as a Jersey bull. Even the memory of Victoria Cardin surrounded by a covey of laughing officers in their dress blue uniforms and polished brass couldn't completely dampen his anticipation.

It was the most impressive train Jared Dane had ever seen, and he'd seen a few, having been employed for some time as railroad detective, troubleshooter, and general get-things-done-in-a-hurry man—and, of course, wet nurse to the politicians and financiers who were largely responsible for building this line toward Denver and who were expecting to fleece taxpayers and emigrants and shippers and anybody else available along the right-of-way in order to further increase their bulging bank accounts and their safe boxes already stuffed with bonds and other negotiable securities. These characters held shares of stock in many companies involved with various forms of legal profit-taking that a lot of people were beginning to call highway robbery, from Baltimore to Cincinnati to this very Lawrence, Kansas, where the train waited on a siding less than a pistol shot from the main-line passenger depot, the engine sighing and coughing and smelling like grease and hot coal cinders.

Railroad roustabouts had cleaned the cars on this train, and it was ready to continue its journey to track's end as soon as the distinguished passengers decided they were ready to forgo the ladies and champagne of what little civilization could be found in Lawrence, Kansas, and come from their hotel to make the final trek into wilderness country where they might glimpse wild things such as American bison or perhaps even a hunting party of Cheyenne or Arapaho pausing in their search for food to shout unintelligible insults at the passing iron horse.

They'd started from Kansas City, Missouri, that old community called by various epithets since its founding in 1821 by François Chouteau, the Frenchman whose name had slipped south to the Cherokee Nation, where it somehow sounded more appropriate attached to a small crossroads village than it would have to the city that was growing at the confluence of the Missouri and Kaw rivers, already showing signs of becoming one of the biggest meat-packing centers in the world.

So from Kansas City they had come on their glorious train, these indomitable pioneers, roughing it far away from their paneled offices, yet each feeling in his heart of hearts that to lower such prosperous asses onto anything harder than mohair-upholstered chairs would be an affront to dignity and the ultimate insult to men who were making the frontier safe for lemon meringue pie and unchecked free enterprise.

So thought Jared Dane.

Host for the railroad was its major stockholder and the chairman of its board of directors, one August Bainbridge, a large man, always expensively outfitted, with a face clean-shaven except for muttonchop hair forward of each ear, like the unsheared fleece on an Angora goat, in the fashion of General John M. Schofield. The general was a friend of Mr. August Bainbridge and a personal hero as well, not so much for his successes in the Battle of Atlanta but because the general had suggested there might be a naval base established at a place called Pearl Harbor in the Hawaiian Islands, if the United States could ever come into possession of the place. Mr. Bainbridge could see so many possibilities for making money on such a project that it took his breath away. Making money was, indeed, his primary interest, whether it be made in Baltimore, Cincinnati, Kansas, or the far reaches of the Pacific Ocean. And if money could be made anywhere, Mr. August Bainbridge would know exactly how to go about it.

So also thought Jared Dane.

His cynicism was not ephemeral. It was a solid cornerstone of his character. There were adequate reasons for it; he had been closely associated with August Bainbridge for a long time. Not on a continuous basis, for once during the war and once immediately thereafter he had gone off on his own. But each time he had returned, though he was never able to explain to himself why. But Mr. August Bainbridge always took good care of him. Some said he even considered Jared a surrogate son, never having had a real one.

Bainbridge was as much a father to Jared Dane as any man had ever been. He had never known his real father, and his mother had died of consumption and overdoses of gin, making little effort to sustain herself. And so her son, at the age of ten or thereabouts, found himself on his own, which he had been pretty much all along, and he managed to survive on the waterfront of Baltimore by eating what he could steal and sleeping in warehouses until Bainbridge found him and took him to the big estate near Cheltenham, Prince Georges County, Maryland, to become a white slave, it seemed, serving alongside the black ones already there. His primary job at first was taking care of the Bainbridge collection of hunting rifles and shotguns and a few pistols, a duty the master always felt uncomfortable about entrusting to black hands.

By the time Jared reached twenty, Bainbridge had established a second home in Davenport, Iowa, and later still a third one in St. Louis, where he could become more intimately involved in building western railroads. Wherever he went, Jared went with him. By then, Jared had become a sort of bodyguard. Although he was not a large man, standing somewhat less than six feet tall, Jared did have considerable expertise with firearms, thanks to many hours of shooting at Cheltenham. And Bainbridge perceived a certain decisiveness of mind and hand in the young man that was eventually proved. Jared shot his first man in a Sioux City roundhouse when a distraught stockholder or some such malcontent made an attempt on Bainbridge's life with a large wrench normally used to tighten bolts on locomotive drive wheels.

That was a year before the war. When violence broke out in Missouri, Jared took his first leave of Mr. Bainbridge to become a Confederate spy, an occupation that appealed to his sense of free will. He had been under the tight discipline of the railroad tycoon for over a decade and wanted no part of regular army life, with bristle-faced noncommissioned officers telling him when he could spit and where.

But the spying profession was short-lived. He became disgusted with the work, primarily because Rebel generals were reluctant to take seriously any information he brought them about the activities of Union sympathizers or orders of battle of Federal units.

So he went back to Mr. August Bainbridge, who was so glad to see him that he invited Jared to sup with him under candlelight, where they dined on squab and French cherries with whipped cream for dessert. It was the only time the two of them had sat down at the same table.

When the war began to wind down, Jared's itch to leave again became irresistible, so he took a job as town constable in Baxter Springs, Kansas, where there were a great many rowdy lead miners and already the beginnings of the Texas cattle trade, with drovers getting drunk, terrorizing the town's women, and generally raising hell. The city fathers presented him with a .44 Army-model Colt pistol, its cylinder engraved in gold and its grips of solid ivory. This was a kind of bonus for his agreeing to take on a rather dangerous job for a wage of twenty dollars a week.

The Baxter Springs job lasted no longer than the spying had. During his tenure he shot two men, more or less in self-defense, and brained an unknown number with the barrel of the gift pistol. The townfolk decided Jared Dane was more perilous to them than miners and cowboys, and told him he had to leave. They demanded that he return the pistol, but he maintained it had been given and taken in good faith, and therefore, if they wanted it back, they would be required to take it by force. This was a thing none of them cared to attempt.

Now, as he stood on the siding in Lawrence, preparing to inspect the magnificent train, that same pistol was in a waist holster on his left side, butt forward for a cross-draw but well hidden beneath the coat of his black corduroy three-piece suit. The suit matched his black hat and black boots, and all of that stood in stark contrast to his white linen shirt. He was clean-shaven, his skin somewhat pasty, and his hair rust-colored. His eyebrows hardly showed at all, giving his face the appearance of having been plucked clean of all hair with tweezers. His eyes were blue, from what he supposed was a Scandinavian heritage, a cold blue. One of the men he had dispatched in Baxter Springs had said, just before he died, that those eyes were as lifeless and cold as glass marbles. His mouth was wide, thin-lipped, and turned down at the corners, reflecting his scorn for most of what he saw in the world.

When he appraised it fairly, he had to admit that his life with August Bainbridge had not been so bad. As he grew older, he had done a lot more than clean fowling pieces and revolvers. He had dealt cards at Bainbridge's frequent poker parties; he had carried messages to business competitors about the continuing good health they might enjoy by avoiding financial confrontations with the master; he had pimped; he had paid off debts better left from public view, most of these to young ladies who had been short-term acquaintances of Mr. Bainbridge; he had occasionally carried money and letters to Mrs. Bainbridge, who remained all the years in Maryland to be near other barren women who gathered in cozy Baltimore parlors to do needlepoint, sip port, and nibble candy mints; he had made surprise visits to various of Bainbridge's enterprises to check such things as employee management and money ledgers.

Most of all, he had received a very adequate education under Bainbridge's watchful eye, not only learning, from tutors in his young years, the magic of numbers on accounts current, but the beauty of literature and history and the manners of a gentleman in social discourse. What he had not learned was how to love any woman. He was a bachelor and intended to stay one, taking what physical pleasure he needed in quick night passages through the various bordellos he happened upon casually in his round of duties for the master.

Of course, he only called Bainbridge "the master" in his own thinking. Aloud, he called him Boss, a term he had picked up from the black slaves before the war at Cheltenham.

He was not a man to reflect on fond memories. But at scattered intervals he did recall with some pleasure the times when he was growing up in Maryland, and Bainbridge would seat him before a great fireplace and tell stories about Oliver Cromwell's revolution, or about the genius of Napoleon in the use of field artillery, or about the sweep of passion in the novels of Sir Walter Scott. At these times, as Jared Dane recalled, Bainbridge's face took on a gentle quality, completely foreign to its usual expression.

Jared's reverie was interrupted by the conductor who came up to him, tugging at the leather visor of his hat with its brass emblem, a wad of tobacco bulging his cheek beneath the beard. His blue serge suit was pressed and clean, a job performed each night on these guest trips by one of the black train attendants, because August Bainbridge insisted that his crew look their best for the gentlemen from whom could be expected investments, political favors, or free publicity in the newspapers.

"Turned out right nice," he said. "Not so cool today."

"Small difference to our bunch," said Jared Dane. "I don't expect any of them will alight from this train until we get 'em back to flowered wallpaper. One night in Lawrence will take away all their appetite for the rough life."

As they stood conversing alongside the locomotive tender, behind them they were aware of the engineer oiling piston rods and couplings and peering under the trucks. Inside the cab, the fireman was polishing brass tubing and checking the firebox and doing all the other things that firemen did before starting a run.

It was a Philadelphia Baldwin engine, one of the newest, a 4-4-0, meaning that it had four road wheels, two on either side of the truck just behind the massive cowcatcher, and four drive wheels, also two on a side. The wheels were painted cardinal red, rim and spokes, the drive shafts were silver, the cab butter yellow. There were gleaming brass fittings and railings alongside the boiler and above the treadway, polished bell and whistle and piston housings, and a kerosene headlamp just in front of the funnel-shaped smokestack; the lamp was housed in a square box with glass on the front, and on either side were porcelain panels painted in the style of fashionable china tableware—black-eyed Susans on a field of eggshell white. It was engine number 304, and its name, proclaimed in garish placards bolted to the cab just below the windows, was the *General Schofield*. This was a woodburner, and above the sides of the tender could be seen Missouri oak logs, stacked and ready for the fire.

Down the track, a tall, slender figure detached itself from the half-dozen loungers along the depot platform and started down the track toward August Bainbridge's train. Jared Dane saw him at once, because it was his job always to see such things, and he noted that this was a young man who walked with a certain air of self-confidence or perhaps even arrogance, which Jared thought could easily be a façade to hide uncertainty. He was wearing an obviously new bowler hat, shining in the sun, and an ankle-length yellow duster, and he carried a leather valise.

"That's not one of our people, but he's headed this way," Jared said.

The conductor squinted from beneath the leather bill of his cap and shook his head.

"No, but he acts like he knows where he's goin'."

"I hope he's not some jealous husband looking to shoot the Boss."

The conductor laughed and turned away to speak with the engineer about how this trip was going to be run. Jared, watching the young man approach, shifted his position so that his coat fell back to reveal the ivory grips of the revolver.

It never hurts to let strangers know where the authority lies, he thought.

When Roman Hasford walked up to the locomotive, he had the impression that the man standing there was not seeing him, that the man was looking through him. There seemed a quality about the pale eyes that made focusing unnecessary, seeing everything, no matter whether it was near or far, or seeing nothing at all, like the eyes of somebody who had just died.

"Howdy," Roman said, touching the brim of the bowler with the fingers of his free hand. "Is this the special to Abilene?"

"It is," the man said, his lips hardly moving.

"Well, I got a letter here," said Roman, setting down his valise in the cinders alongside the track and pulling the fat envelope from an inside pocket.

The man took the envelope with his left hand, and after a moment more of studying Roman's face, he lowered his head and took the sheaf of papers out and read what he needed to know.

"Elisha Hankins. Yes, we know him. We have an arrangement with him." He handed Roman his papers and lifted the pale eyes once more. "My name's Dane. You don't do anything on this train without asking me first. Come along. I'll show you your compartment."

Roman thought the corners of the wide mouth twitched upward a little, but not enough to call a smile.

"Thank you, Mr. Dane," he said, and followed as Dane turned toward the first car behind the tender.

The forward end of the car was a bunk area for the black attendants. As Dane led the way, four of them were standing back from the aisle, wide-eyed, as though they were expecting him to find something wrong. They were dressed in white jackets, white shirts with black string ties, and red pantaloons, like Zouave soldiers complete down to the gray spats and pointed-toed black shoes.

The other section of the car was a kitchen area, stove and sink and icebox, rows of canned vegetables, fruit, and milk. Those cans were the wonderful legacy of the war, when preserving foodstuffs had become such a great priority. Roman knew that because his father had told him about capturing Yankee grub in cans, one of the few things Martin Hasford ever mentioned about the war.

There was a sawdust pit with two three-hundred-pound blocks of burlap-covered ice, a hanging quarter of beef, tubs of lard and sacks of potatoes and tins of coffee beans. Jared Dane opened one of the icebox doors, as though proud to show off all these fancy victuals to a country bumpkin, revealing dressed chickens and squabs and butter and eggs. Then he paused beside an open barrel packed with chipped ice and oysters.

"We had to import one of those niggers all the way from where these came from, just to pop open the shells," Jared Dane said. "You won't get much of this fare. So don't expect any. What you'll get is a lot of fried beef between two chunks of that." And he waved toward a screened cabinet where there were loaves of bread stacked like the oak wood in the tender up ahead and looking to have about the same consistency.

As they crossed the platforms between cars, Dane spoke over his shoulder.

"Just be glad you can eat on this train. On usual trains, you eat whenever you get a chance to jump off when it stops and buy whatever some squaw might be selling."

"Cheyenne squaws?"

"Hell, no! Tame ones."

"Well, sandwiches are fine for me," Roman said.

He knew about sandwiches. Calpurnia had made some with a kind of gooey egg mixture inside, and Allan Pay had explained that the name came from an Englishman named John Montagu, Fourth Earl of Sandwich—a snack he had devised while engaged in a game of chance that lasted a long time back in the mid-eighteenth century.

But obviously Jared Dane hadn't expected him to know. He stopped and turned and stared at Roman for a moment before going on into the next car.

It was a combination dining and sleeping car, tables folded out from the wall and already covered with creamy linen cloths, set with heavy silver, bone chinaware, and shining crystal. Above, there were beds that hinged down for the sleepers after they'd finished their evening meal.

"Man in Illinois designed this car for us. You won't find any of these on usual trains, either. Maybe someday. His name's Pullman. I suppose you know all about him, too."

"No, I never heard of Mr. Pullman," Roman said, beginning to get irritated.

At the far end of the car was a smaller compartment, marked CONVENIENCE STATION. Inside were sinks and a booth containing a water pot with a walnut seat. There were mirrors on the walls and pipes running down to the sink faucets from water barrels bracketed to the ceiling. Small hand towels were suspended from brass racks, and each was monogrammed with the initials A.B.

"You won't see this again, either," said Jared Dane.

Next was the parlor car. It was more elaborate than Calpurnia's living room in St. Louis, with inlaid cherrywood panels between curtained windows, revolving plush chairs, and little tables for drinks and roasted chestnuts. There were cuspidors and metal-and-glass chandeliers. At one end of the car was a bar with rows of bottles lining shelves across the wall behind it, and stacks of cigar boxes and another sink. At the back side of the car was a rack holding about a dozen well-oiled large-caliber rifles above a row of cabinet drawers for ammunition.

Jared Dane waved one hand in the direction of the rifles.

"In case we see some buffalo."

"You think we might?"

"If we don't, Mr. Bainbridge is going to be almighty upset."

"I hope we see some," Roman couldn't help saying.

Dane turned once more to stare at him with those eyes that never seemed to focus.

"You a hunter, then?"

"Well, I've shot a few deer and turkeys and stuff like that. Back home in Arkansas."

"Your papers say your name's Hasford. That right?"

"Roman Hasford."

"All right, Roman Hasford, maybe we can show you a few buffalo. But it won't be much like hunting deer."

Then came the caboose. After the elegance of the other cars, it was drab and colorless, like the inside of a hickory woodbox, with splinters showing. There was a potbellied stove, a table and a rack of paper and a quill pen and inkwell, and bunks under the windows along the sides, covered with army blankets. There were seats at the rear end, the kind Roman had seen on his trip from Jeff City to St. Louis, hardwood and shining, on both sides of the aisle, two to the side facing one another.

"All right, Roman Hasford, this is your compartment," Dane said. Then he turned back along the car to the bunks. He waved a hand at one of them.

"Yours. Across the aisle, mine. The other two are for the brakeman and the conductor. All the niggers sleep up front in the kitchen car, so you can rest easy in case you've got some reluctance to bedding down near such people."

"I haven't," Roman said, his voice suddenly petulant. "And another thing, Mr. Dane. You've got a fine-looking train here and all that, but I don't want any of your oysters or your cigars and I don't want to use your God damned convenience station and you don't have to worry about having to shoot me with that pistol you've got under your coat because I'm not fixing to rob your Mr. Bainbridge. All I want is a way to get to Abilene and buy a few cattle!"

Now the eyes focused and a real smile came to the harsh mouth and Roman heard a low chuckle in Dane's throat.

"All right," he said. "You get settled down. Water cooler at the front of the car, with ice. All the way from Kansas City. Privy closet just across the aisle from that, but don't flush the water through the thing until we're out on the road. The Boss don't like dropping this train's shit close to the depots."

"Well, I didn't mean to speak disrespectful," Roman said, feeling his face going red.

"You don't have to worry about how you speak back here in the caboose," Dane said. "The rest of our guests will be along shortly, and then we'll be heading out. We'll spend the night on a siding in Topeka, but tomorrow maybe we can show you a few buffalo, if that's what you want to see."

He moved to the door but turned once more.

"You play dominoes?"

"Sure."

"We can have a few games."

After Jared Dane was gone, Roman thought, He's sure as hell a strange one.

Looking along the length of the caboose, he saw for the first time a large rifle hanging above the rear door. He judged it to be a Sharps Fifty, single-shot. He knew this weapon belonged to Jared Dane, and wondered what they might run into that would require such a cannon.

They saw buffalo the next day, just an hour out of Abilene. It was a small herd moving south in their feeding toward the lush grass country in the big bend of the Arkansas—Indian country, where there had been, until then, little intrusion by white men. The buffalo had been grazing along the Platte during the summer, and perhaps there they had seen railroad trains, what with the Union Pacific building along that route through Nebraska. But they showed no signs of recognizing danger.

The engineer stopped the train with no sounding of whistle or bell, but only a soft hammering of couplings, coming to rest directly in the path of the slow-moving herd, which was then about four hundred yards from the tracks. Although Roman Hasford had only limited experience with railroad trains, he voiced his concern, which was primarily about stopping on a main-line track and only secondarily about the buffalo.

"What if another train comes along?" he asked, peering from one of the caboose windows.

"No worry about that," said Jared Dane, beside him at the next window, his flat eyes a mirror of the glare of afternoon sun reflected from the tawny short grass of the land. "When a train with the Boss on it comes along, everything else moves onto sidings until we're clear."

Having no concept of what such a thing meant to freight and passenger schedules along the line, Roman was reassured and turned his whole attention to the buffalo, slowly drawing near. From the parlor car he could hear the exclamations of delight of the gentlemen who were guests of Mr. Bainbridge. Then there came a series of bumping sounds.

"What's that?"

"The gentlemen up ahead are opening their windows," said Jared Dane.

The buffalo were not so black as Roman had thought they would be. Rather, they were a mottled mixture of sienna and umber and gray—dust from their buffalo wallows and old hair burned pale by summer sun, and which they were shedding now to make place for new winter growth. Even at that distance they excited Roman, although they gave no impression of something wild like deer or hill-country turkey, fleet and slashing in their movements. They were, in fact, rather sluggish, like any other kind of cattle intent on their grazing.

To Roman's unpracticed eye they all seemed full grown, the calves of spring by now having come to some bulk and substance. There were huge bulls on the perimeter of the herd, yet they were not very good sentinels, because they, like the others, were head-down in the grass, apparently thinking the stopped train in their path was just another low ridge or rock outcrop.

"Don't they see us?" Roman asked.

"Bad eyesight," Jared Dane said. "And they don't smell us because we're downwind."

They were close enough now for Roman to hear their gentle snorting and puffing as they cropped the tough grass. He felt his heart beat faster as it had always done when he came in sight of wild game. Yet he could see no thrill in hunting such things. Where was the challenge that was always there with woodland creatures whose eyes and noses were so sensitive to intruders that even approaching them was a triumph of stealth?

Shooting these things would be like killing bulls in a pasture, he thought.

In the next car, the shouting and laughter had died out and there was an intense expectancy in the silence. Roman thought of those men there in the parlor car. He had watched them walking to the train in Lawrence, their silk hats and gold-headed walking canes shining in the sun. He knew now that they were all at their windows, watching, as he and Jared Dane were watching.

"All right," Dane said, rising. "It's about time."

He moved to the rear of the caboose and lifted down the Sharps rifle and took a handful of cartridges from a small cabinet built into the side of the car where Roman knew from the night before that the dominoes and checkerboard and decks of cards were kept. Dane dumped a handful of the brass sausages into each of his coat pockets and moved to the rear door. There he paused and looked back at Roman.

"You can see it better from outside," he said.

Roman scrambled up and out onto the caboose platform. He moved down the steep steps, stopping on the last and leaning out, holding himself in place with hands on the railings. Jared Dane was already on the ground, standing just to the rear of the caboose, levering open the Sharps and inserting one of the large cartridges.

Roman was about to ask a question, and later couldn't recall what it might have been, when the shooting broke out like the fusillade from a militia company. Looking alongside the cars, Roman could see the snouts of rifles at all the windows of the parlor car. Smoke billowed in the soft breeze and muzzle flashes made brilliant marks of color. The reports were hollow here on the plains, where there was nothing to echo back the sound. Immediately, he could smell the burned powder.

Among the herd, close now, there were sudden bursts of soil as slugs struck the ground, and puffs of dust from the hides of the buffalo where bullets went home, and a long, enraged, and frightful bellowing as the herd came to life and turned, running, showing their flanks to the shooters. A few staggered and coughed, tongues out, a few went to their knees and then struggled up to lumber after the rest, moving away now in a cloud of dust, away from the sounds of firing, uncertain, running to this side and that, leaving behind the ones that had been hit. Roman could see the glistening shine of blood along the humps and across the bellies, and he saw a small bull, cut through the spine, trying to drag himself after the others with only his forelegs and making a sound of high-pitched fury and pain such as Roman had never heard.

Then Jared Dane began to shoot. The first explosion, just beneath Roman's place on the platform, made him jump. And he saw one of the wounded buffalo seem to jerk and fold onto itself and collapse in a lump, and then another shot and another, each one bringing to ground an animal that had been wounded in the wild fire from the parlor car.

The herd had run out of range then, except for the disabled. There was another random shot from the parlor car. Then only Jared Dane's rifle continued, systematically putting down all the wounded. Between Jared's shots, Roman could hear the gentlemen up ahead shouting and laughing, congratulating one another, even though, as far as Roman could see, not a single buffalo had been killed by their volleys. Jared Dane's rifle went on, like a signal cannon, booming its message every ten seconds. The Sharps was beginning to smoke, and Roman could smell the hot oil.

Then it was over, except for the sound of Jared Dane levering out the last spent cartridge case, and the soft snick as he slid in a new round. He looked up at Roman.

"All right. Let's go have a closer look."

Jared walked toward the brown lumps that were the dead buffalo, and Roman leaped from the caboose and followed, hurrying to catch up.

"Stay back a step or so. In case one of them decides to get up and make a last stand."

Looking back along the train, a little apprehensive about coming into the field of fire of those parlor car windows, Roman could see that all the rifles had been withdrawn. Likely already at the whiskey, he thought, and knew that at this moment he could use a good jolt of the stuff himself.

At the other end of the train, two of the kitchen attendants had come out, their white jackets and red pantaloons bright in the afternoon sun, looking incongruous on the open prairie, knives shining in their hands, teeth shining in wide smiles.

Jared and Roman came to the first of the fallen animals. There was a musty, gamey smell about it, not unlike when a squirrel was skinned. Yet there was something different, an odor Roman had never encountered before, of wild things bleeding and of their excrement at the point of death. Jared Dane, ahead of him, was probing the carcasses with the muzzle of the rifle. Once he fired, a shot just behind the ear of an old bull, and the bull gave a mighty, convulsive jerk.

They're so God damned big, Roman thought. They looked larger lying there with the blood running out of them than they had when they were grazing.

After Dane had made sure all the buffalo were dead, he signaled the two kitchen attendants who had been waiting. They ran in among the buffalo and Roman watched, fascinated. They pulled the jaws open by placing one foot on the chin whiskers, the other pushing back the nose. Then they reached into the maw and pulled out the tongue with one hand, slicing it off with the other. The long, dripping chunks of meat went into a canvas bag that each wore suspended from his shoulder by a strap. Soon the bags were red and running blood.

Roman counted nineteen dead buffalo.

After the kitchen attendants had finished their work, Roman stood there beside the body of a small cow. He looked across the prairie, vacant of all game now, the survivors of the small herd having disappeared in some distant swale. He felt the wind on his face, and it was fresh and clean and better than that jolt of whiskey could have been. He was still standing there, looking away from the train, when Jared Dane called him.

"If you don't want to walk the rest of the way into Abilene, come on along."

Back in the caboose, Roman sat beside a window, looking at those lumps of hide and flesh, lying desolate and forlorn on the open plain of grass. He knew that soon the buzzards and perhaps a few wolves would arrive for the feast.

"Just the tongues?" he said aloud. "Just the tongues, and all that meat gone to waste?"

He could recall those days on the hill farm during the war, when a single rabbit would be enough to sustain him and his mother for two more days, and here were tons of meat left to rot. Each of those dark forms lying bloody and immobile would feed a large family for a month, he thought.

"Just the tongues?" he said again, and heard the grunt from behind him that indicated that Jared Dane had heard him, standing in the aisle now, hat off, wiping his brow with a white linen handkerchief, and looking at Roman with those dead eyes, which now seemed to show some sign of fire.

"Fried tongue for supper," Dane said. "Enough even for the caboose."

"I don't want any," Roman said.

"Suit yourself, Roman Hasford."

The engine up ahead gave a gentle lurch forward, closing the couplings between cars, and almost imperceptibly the train began to move again. Roman sat for a long time, facing the aisle, after Jared Dane had gone forward to compliment the railroad's guests on their marksmanship. But he couldn't resist one more look and he twisted in the seat and saw them disappearing in the distance, the nineteen lumps that looked now like old prairie dog burrows.

Somehow he felt that he was not alone in his repugnance at what had happened. Jared Dane didn't say much, but Roman had begun to get strong impressions from the way the thin-lipped mouth moved, the way the eyes sometimes slanted upward, the casual lift of a shoulder. And as he sat there, moving toward Abilene, he would have bet money that Dane had found the whole business distasteful, even though he generally gave the impression that not much of anything affected him one way or the other.

And Roman remembered the night before. On the Topeka siding before bedtime, they'd played dominoes. Dane had said little except to call out his scores. But midway through the evening he'd gone to the stove and brought back a cup of coffee for Roman, and from his pocket he'd produced a wax-paper-wrapped fried breast of chicken.

"I suspect the gentlemen up ahead won't miss this one piece," he'd said, sliding the chicken across the table. Then, even more surprising, he had continued in a voice that had suddenly lost its harsh abruptness, "If you have any trouble with the cattle jobbers in Abilene, just tell them you're a friend of Jared Dane. If that doesn't get the proper results, come see me. We'll be on a siding there for a couple of days while Mr. Bainbridge shows his gentlemen friends how railroads are built at the end of track."

This is a strange man, Roman thought.

But now he had little time for character study because the train was pulling into Abilene, a collection of tents, ramshackle buildings, sidings with stacks of rusty-looking iron rails and rough-cut crossties, stock pens only partly full of longhorn cattle, and dusty men with outlandishly wide hat brims. Saddle horses were hitched in rows along the streets he could see from the caboose windows. Lamps were lighted in the various business establishments, and Roman reckoned that at least fifty percent of these were saloons, judging from the crudely painted signs on the walls. One look was all it took to convince him that this was a town that hadn't yet taken on much of the polish of civilization.

After their evening meal, which one of the grinning kitchen attendants brought and which included a deep-dish dried-apple pie, Roman and Jared Dane had one short game of dominoes. This lamp-lit caboose had somehow taken on a comfortable atmosphere, and the scent of cinnamon from the pie still lingered. Roman's mind was occupied with the task ahead of him, going off this train tomorrow and doing his work for Mr. Elisha Hankins, so he went to bed early. The conductor and the brakeman came in and sat at the rear end of the car, talking in a low drone. Jared Dane had taken himself off to the fleshpots, as he called them.

Before he slept, the buffaloes came back to mind. And something else he recalled from a time when he was less than six years old.

One of the valley boys along Little Sugar Creek had found the nest of a brown thrasher, and brought it out to the middle of Wire Road so all his companions could admire it and the four baby birds inside. They were so new to life that the membrane was still over their eyes, and as the boys looked at them they yammered and squawked, holding knotty heads up on skinny necks, beaks open for the food they expected.

All the boys laughed. And then they took up rocks from beside the road and began to throw them into the nest. Roman ran for home, crying and hearing behind him the dismal croaking of the baby birds being stoned to death.

When his mother heard the story, after he burst into her kitchen with nose running and tears streaking his dusty cheeks, she held him close for a while. And his father came in from the back porch because he'd heard Roman's tale through the open door. His face was as hard and furious as Roman had ever seen it, and with his voice trembling in outrage, he told Roman that a man should never kill anything unless it was for eating.

Now, in the caboose bunk, the sounds of a boisterous Abilene coming to him through the windows only faintly because they were closed to October cold, he thought of those boys, some dead now in the war, and he thought of the shining silk hats and gold-headed canes of Mr. Bainbridge's gentlemen guests.

6

"It was easy as pie," Roman Hasford wrote in his diary.

In fact, it had been a little boring, finding one of the agents who bought Texas cattle, making Mr. Hankins's wishes known, going to the Abilene express office with the letter of authorization, making the necessary marks on the necessary papers so that four slat-sided stock cars could be loaded with the rust-colored longhorns, fifty cows to the car, making the arrangements with the railroad for transport, then riding in a caboose behind the cattle all the way back through Topeka and Lawrence and then along the Leavenworth spur, practically to the front gate of the stockyards.

"Any trouble?" Mr. Hankins asked.

"None. I used your papers and the name of a man I met, and between the two, everybody was happy to accommodate me," Roman said.

"What man?"

"Jared Dane."

Mr. Hankins's eyebrows lifted and his brown eyes bulged.

"My God, son, you do make friends with a wicked lot. Did you see your buffalo?"

"Yes," Roman said, but volunteered no details, and Mr.

Hankins had no time at the moment to make further inquiries.

Roman had thought about Victoria Cardin throughout the
trip back to Leavenworth. So, on the first Sunday after he returned, he went back to the fort for another try at seeing her.
This time he rode the horse Mr. Hankins offered, a big gray
stud that had come into the stockyards during the time
Roman was gone.

"He's got no name as I know of," Mr. Hankins said. "But
he looks good for your purposes."

"Excalibur," Roman said.

"Excalibur?"

"Yes. That's what we'll call him."

It was a name he liked the sound and essence of, and had
from the first time Calpurnia read aloud the tales of King
Arthur from Mr. Thomas Malory's writing in a book brought
to the Hasford farm by the old Jew at the Sugar Creek mill.
It had been pretty heavy stuff to Roman, who was seven
years old the first time he heard it, but he remembered the
part about pulling the sword from the rock, and he remembered the name of the sword. So the big gray stud became Excalibur.

"He's strong and bright, like polished metal," Roman
wrote in his diary.

It was one of those beautiful early-November days, with
the sun warm and the breeze down and only a few stubborn
leaves still clinging to the hardwoods, golden brown against
a sea-blue sky. Roman guided the horse along the banks of
the Missouri for a while before climbing to the ramparts of
Fort Leavenworth. In an eddy on the Missouri side of the
river he saw a flock of pintails that had apparently decided this
was far enough for their winter migration. Even at that distance, he knew what they were. He and his father had hunted
pintails along White River in the Ozarks during early autumn, when ducks and geese were flying south from places
like Hudson's Bay or the lakes of Saskatchewan or other distant waters. The sight of those ducks gave him a feeling of
warmth, of things familiar.

The warmth was short-lived.

At the Cardin quarters along officers' row, he noticed a sign he had missed on his last visit. It proclaimed that here lived the Quartermaster Officer for the Department of the Missouri. It sounded impressive when Roman said it to himself. Roman had heard about the Department of the Missouri, which included Kansas and Colorado and New Mexico and part of the Indian Territory. At least, that was Roman's understanding. And he wondered why they called it the Department of the Missouri, because the Missouri River didn't run through an inch of it, but instead marked only a part of its eastern boundary between Kansas City and the Nebraska line.

His concern with the army's naming of departments and the places where rivers flowed left his mind with a rush when a black woman, who he supposed was a maid or a cook or some such thing, answered to his knock and said that the captain was down at the stables with all the veterinarians he could lay hands on, because some of the army's horses had been dying of glanders, and that Miss Victoria was out riding west of the post with Lieutenant Thaddeus Archer, a member of the captain's staff.

And Roman thought, Well, if this Archer son of a bitch is the captain's man, why in hell isn't he down at the stables, too, where he belongs, and not out on the prairie showing off his polished brass and horsemanship to Victoria Cardin?

In a fit of pique, Roman kicked Excalibur into a dead run back to town, and all the way to the stockyards, where he unsaddled and left the horse in the little shed behind Mr. Hankins's office shack without bothering to give him much of a rubdown and after feeding him only two handfuls of corn. He stomped all the way down Seventh Street to Mrs. Condon Murphy's boardinghouse, ignored all the loungers in the parlor, and went on upstairs, still stomping, where he found Mr. Moffet in their room, reclining on the bed and reading the most recent edition of the *Kansas Weekly Herald*.

They had a few sips of Mr. Moffet's fruit-jar beer, but the gentle company of the malt-beverage salesman was not enough for Roman in his frustrated state of mind, so he soon left, seeking a few of the pleasures he had taken with Tyne Fawley less than two weeks before, even though he had trouble recalling exactly what they'd done that evening.

Having had a few bouts with the rye whiskey of First Street, he ended up, some hours later, at the door of Katie Rose Rouse. By the time he tapped on Katie Rose's door, the sun had gone and a cold wind had leaped up from the west, which did little to brighten Roman's spirits.

The place had a familiar look and smell, a cozy warmth emphasized somehow by the hanging bead curtains in the doorway between the rooms. The embroidered pillows seemed less garish than he remembered them. Because of that, or perhaps because of the rye, or perhaps because of a combination of both, Roman relaxed and poured out his vexations, damning the whole state of Kansas, the United States Army and all the lieutenants in it, the terrible quality of rye whiskey in Leavenworth saloons, and anything else he could think of. He had no idea if Katie Rose Rouse might have some inkling of his real problem. He'd heard that women were sometimes able to divine such things, especially about other women.

Katie Rose comforted and consoled him as a favorite aunt might do, with touches of her stubby fingers and generous quantities of clear liquid in one of her stemmed glasses. Soon, under the influence of such attention, Roman began to kiss her and hold her ample body close to his. His anger, along with the liquor, made him as bold as the hammer strokes on an anvil.

The next morning he left for the boardinghouse just in time to get into his work clothes. He felt as guilty as he had the first time, but at least now he was aware of exactly what he had done to cause it.

After taking Mrs. Murphy's standard Monday-morning breakfast of creamed beef on buttermilk biscuits, with a lot of black coffee, he returned to his room long enough to make a note in his diary.

"She has a very gentle face, once all the paint has been removed," he wrote. "And she is kind to me."

Walking along Seventh Street, he imagined what it would be like to marry Katie Rose Rouse and appear at the Cardin front door with her during one of those parties they always seemed to be having, and walking in and announcing the arrival of Mr. and Mrs. Roman Hasford!

Boy, that'd raise a few eyebrows, he thought.

And he also thought how different the kisses of Katie Rose were from the one he'd had from Victoria Cardin on the steamboat. But it was a difference difficult to define. They were all like ripe, juicy peaches, the second never tasting exactly like the first.

It was a busy November. At first, Mr. Elisha Hankins kept Roman close by his side, showing him how the business operated. He was aware that Roman was a cut or two above the other regular yard workers, who were usually either halfway or totally drunk or else getting over being in such a state. As time passed, more and more responsibilities were given to Roman. He became a kind of straw boss, and soon began to appreciate power as he ordered people around.

The day after Mr. Hankins outlined his new duties, Roman had an encounter with Elmer Scaggs, the biggest, meanest, dirtiest member of the yard crew. They were in the feed shed and Roman told the man to pick up a one-hundred-pound sack of oats and haul it out to the mule pen. Scaggs glared with red-rimmed eyes and said that if Roman wanted the God damned sack of oats moved, he could do it himself.

Roman lifted a hay hook off the wall rack. It had a vicious, question-mark shape, pointed at the end.

"Do what I tell you, or draw your pay," he said.

Scaggs picked up the sack and carried it out to the mule pen. For Roman, it was more intoxicating than three jolts of First Street rye.

It was obvious that Mr. Hankins valued Roman's ability, honesty, and diligence. There had been a bonus of twenty dollars after the trip to Abilene, and that, along with weekly wages, went into the small leather pouch where Allan Pay's five double eagles hid, and the pouch itself was stashed under the mattress in Mrs. Condon Murphy's boardinghouse.

As long as he didn't think of Victoria Cardin, it was a good time for Roman. There was the daily feeding of stock and the showing of some to prospective buyers; there was contracting each week for grain from one of the local feed merchants, and making tallies each morning in the cold November air to ensure that none of the horses had been stolen from the pens overnight; there were ledger books to be marked each day, and receipts to be carried to the local express office, where there was a potbellied safe in a small room behind a counter, and wire mesh on the windows. Outside the express office was a sign above the door indicating that this was an organization associated with the Kansas Railroad, a certain August Bainbridge being president of the company.

Roman was amazed to find that any private citizen could deposit his money with the express office and get paid interest—about three percent—and draw drafts on it anytime another express office could be found. And now there were express offices springing up all across Kansas, just behind the laying of the steel track.

Because he was familiar with the faces of those men who ran the express office, and not with those in the two banks of Leavenworth, the leather pouch containing his money came out from beneath Mrs. Murphy's mattress and went into the potbellied safe behind the wire-mesh windows.

Roman did not know Mr. Bainbridge personally, but he'd ridden on the same train and played dominoes with Jared Dane, which was almost as good. He had twinges of remorse about the buffalo killings, for which he held August Bainbridge personally responsible. But the Boss, as Jared Dane called him, was at least a known quantity. So Roman's money went into Mr. Bainbridge's express office safe, all receipted properly, and Roman being called "sir" in the bargain.

In the first week after his return from Abilene, Roman had the opportunity to see Lieutenant Thaddeus Archer at close range. The lieutenant came from the fort with Captain Edwin Cardin, both of them stiff and official, to buy the cattle Roman had brought.

Archer held himself as though Adjutant's Call had just sounded and he was ready to wheel into line on the parade ground. In his dress blue uniform, complete with saber, he cut a striking figure, straight as a rifle barrel and just as cold, eyeing Roman with ill-concealed contempt. Like Roman, he was clean-shaven. His hair, below an elaborate French kepi showing the piping of an officer of the quartermaster corps, was jet-black and his eyes were gray, a striking combination that Roman tried to ignore.

He's got a mouth just like a girl I used to know back home, Roman thought.

While they looked at the cattle in the corral on the west side of Seventh Street, Roman stood close by, as Mr. Hankins had asked him to do, listening and learning. Captain Cardin agreed to buy the lot of them at forty dollars a head, which surprised Roman because he knew it meant more than a hundred-percent profit on the critters. But any suspicions he might have had were obscured by his studied attempts to look knowledgeable and to avoid Lieutenant Archer's eyes.

I hope the son of a bitch steps in some horseshit with those fancy black boots, he thought.

After the deal was completed, Archer said he would send a detail of troopers the next day to drive the cattle to the army pens at the fort. Roman was delighted to hear that the lieutenant had a high, squeaky voice, completely out of keeping with the rugged lines of his jaw.

Captain Cardin relaxed then and spoke of the weather with Mr. Hankins. He took a cigar from his inside coat pocket, bit off the end, and allowed Lieutenant Archer to light it for him. Puffing blue smoke, he turned to Roman, giving him the first sign of recognition. He held out his hand and Roman shook it.

"I understand that on Sunday last you came to call," the captain said. "I'm sorry I missed you. You must come again."

"Yes, sir," Roman said, restraining himself from pointing

out that he had called twice. "I'm sorry to hear you're having all that trouble with glanders."

Cardin's face twisted with distress.

"Yes, it's a terrible thing to watch."

"Cedar smoke's pretty good for clearing up those lungs," Roman said, and he heard Archer snort.

Later, when he and Mr. Hankins were working the books for the day, Roman noticed that only half of the profit from those Texas cattle had been marked down. He didn't know what had happened to the other half, but he reckoned it was none of his business.

When the weather turned suddenly bitter in mid-November, Roman Hasford came down with his first Kansas cold. Mr. Elisha Hankins directed him to the only drugstore in town, and there Roman purchased a bottle of mandrake-root elixir, which made him dizzy and created strange shapes and colors in his mind. He gave that up and went to his mother's old remedy—hot lemonade, provided by Mrs. Condon Murphy, generously laced with sour-mash whiskey, provided by Mr. Moffett—and lay in bed under five blankets to sweat. The whole business was more uncomfortable than the cold, so he gave up the sweating part and concentrated only on the spiked lemonade for a few days. It crossed his mind that he was coming to depend on strong spirits.

But at least the trip to the druggist was not wasted. While there, Roman had seen a placard advertising a coming attraction at the Palace Theater on Third Street, something called a playhouse circus. He noted the date in his diary, and when the appointed night arrived, he bundled himself in the new overcoat with fur collar that Mr. Hankins had insisted he buy, and went to take his place among the other theatergoers, all sitting expectantly on hard folding chairs before a lamplit stage. The curtain appeared to be made of oilcloth or some such thing, and painted on it were the names of various Leavenworth enterprises. "Seeley's Lumber Yard." "Quackenbush for Harness and Leather Goods." "Elmo's

Barber Shop; Shave and a Haircut, Six Bits." "Doby McGuire's Public Baths."

The overture was played by three heavily mustachioed musicians on cornet, tuba, and alto horn—renditions of marching songs from the war, with the audience stamping their feet and clapping.

The show itself didn't amount to much. There was a fire-eater who also swallowed swords, an acrobat who also juggled, and a male quartet that sang such standards as "Lottie Lee" and "Don't You Go, Johnny." The best performance was the animal act, which consisted of a woman in sky-blue tights rolling out a cage in which there was a large, rather moth-eaten baboon. The beast seemed to enjoy facing away from the audience to expose his hairless and flame-red ass.

Then they brought out the sword-swallower again, and the people in the audience, predominantly men, began to hoot and throw Irish potatoes and rotten apples, it being past the season for fresh vegetables, and when the theater manager appeared, he was pelted as well, and there were shouts to bring out the lady in the blue underwear.

The jeering and good-humored harassment of the players on the stage inevitably degenerated into a few scattered fist-fights among members of the audience. This quickly spread as enthusiasm for it swept along the rows of seats. There were sounds of chairs splintering and of cloth ripping. Roman was shoved and kicked and struck across his sore nose, and somebody spilled a bucket of beer on one of his boots.

He was rescued by Elmer Scaggs, the reluctant grain-bag carrier from the stockyards, who grabbed Roman by one arm and pulled him through the milling throng toward the exit, bowling over a number of people who couldn't manage to get out of the way in time.

"You'd best be out of this place, boss man," said Scaggs, pushing Roman onto the sidewalk and displaying a horribly ugly smile. Then he turned back into the theater to join the free-for-all that was rapidly gaining destructive momentum.

The blow across his nose had not brought blood and it hardly hurt at all, and Roman moved into the chill night air, pulled on his new overcoat, and laughed for the first time since his recent attempt to see Victoria Gardin. As he started to turn away along the sidewalk, he felt a hand clutching his arm. Turning, he looked into the dark, smiling face of Crider Peel.

"I wondered if you was still in town," Peel said, his brilliant teeth flashing in the light of a streetlamp. He was wearing a little billed cap much like rivermen wore, and what Roman took to be a buffalo-robe coat, hair side out and looking as though it had been gnawed by a whole colony of rats. He smelled like the whiskey-soaked floor of a saloon. "Come on along to my place. We'll have a little drink and I want to show you something."

It was still early in the evening, and sitting in his room at Mrs. Condon Murphy's boardinghouse, sipping fruit-jar beer and discussing the infamy of a Roman Pope and the merits of Congregationalism with Mr. Moffet—very little of which he understood anyway and of what he did, disagreed with—was wearing a little thin. So Roman went. Crider Peel had to lead because Roman couldn't remember the way from the last time he made the same trip with Tyne Fawley.

It soon became apparent that there was more to this than showed on the surface. Crider Peel was extolling the virtues of becoming a Kansas state militiaman, and Roman realized he was being recruited. His first inclination was to turn about and forget the whole thing, but Crider Peel did seem genuinely happy to see him, and Roman was ready for any opportunity to spend a little time in his off-hours away from the boardinghouse.

Peel's converted mule-shed home was much as Roman recalled it, only now the images were more sharply defined, not swimming in an alcoholic fog. It was warm enough, too, after the chilly walk from the theater, a fire in the small iron stove at one end of the room giving off satisfied mumblings. The fleeting thought passed through Roman's mind that somebody had to have been here to stoke that fire while Crider was in town getting drunk, but he didn't dwell on it because Peel was bubbling with conversation as he shed his buffalo-robe coat, leaving it in a heap on the dirt floor. He brought a crock jug from some secret place in the room and poured an ample dose of clear whiskey into two tin cups.

"Mighty fine associations in the militia," Crider Peel was saying. "Why, you could join up and meet some good men and, if the governor calls us, earn a little extra money besides, little extra money never hurt anybody, did it? This corn whiskey, one of my militia friends makes it.

"Say, you got a bad cold, ain't you?

"Why, just drink up. That corn, good for colds."

It tasted like hell, and Roman wondered if this was part of the same batch he'd had here before. It hadn't seemed so bad then.

Crider Peel talked about the likelihood of the militia being called out, what with the Cheyenne kicking up trouble along the railroad line and rumors of more regulars coming and more rumors about a big campaign in the spring.

As Peel talked, Roman had the uncomfortable feeling that someone was watching him, the same sensation he'd had before in this mule shed. Only now he was sober and the effect was more disturbing. He was sitting at the table with his back toward the doorway that led into some other part of the place, and when Crider Peel turned to bring a stereoscope and a stack of photographs from the wooden boxes that served as a kitchen cabinet, Roman twisted in his chair and saw the burlap curtain that hung across the doorway swaying, as though somebody there had suddenly drawn back from it as soon as he turned.

"Now this here is what I wanted to show you," Peel said, placing the stereoscope and the photographs before Roman on the table. "I got it from a river captain. He says it's all the way from England and makes pictures look like real things."

"Yes, I saw one once at my sister's in St. Louis."

The photograph cards were lying face down, and Roman could read the printing on the backs: "Made in London with patent from Her Majesty. Viewed at the Crystal Palace, 1851."

Roman inserted one of the cards in the wire frame holder,

and lifting the stereoscope to his face, he peered through the little tunnel behind the two square pieces of magnifying glass. The scene was of the Houses of Parliament, leaping out in three-dimensional focus as he adjusted the card on the slide.

"Ever see anything like that?" Crider Peel asked, pouring himself another drink.

Making the expected murmurs of astonishment, Roman placed one after another of the cards in the device, viewing scenes from the Alps and from Paris and from places he had no way of identifying. About halfway through the stack of cards, he noted that the inscriptions on the backs had disappeared. The first of these he viewed gave him a start. It was of a naked woman standing before a dark drape, holding her hands above her head. To him, the patch of hair under one uplifted arm looked particularly obscene. Watching Roman's progress through the photographs, Crider Peel began to giggle.

"Ain't that the deuce?" he said, his voice becoming a little slurred and his bright black eyes a little out of focus.

Roman quickly went through the remainder of the cards. Each was that of a woman in various stages of undress and in strange positions. It was embarrassing, like being caught peeping through a keyhole. When he had finished, he placed the cards face down on the table along with the stereoscope.

"Very unusual," Roman said.

"Hell, I guess so. I'll bet it's the only such thing in Kansas. And I got it for a couple of cured hides I snuck out of the tannery. They'll never be missed." Crider Peel laughed, his lips wet with saliva. "Have another drink."

"No, I've got to get up early in the morning," Roman said. "And I need to get back to the boardinghouse and doctor this cold."

"Why, hell, you're drinking the best doctorin' there is for colds."

"Well, no more. Some other time," Roman said, and then his curiosity got the better of him, which happened often and which he considered a weakness in his character. "Mr. Peel. Do you live alone here?"

Crider Peel leaned far back in his chair, his eyes wide, as though bending close to Roman across the table didn't give him the proper perspective to answer such a question.

"Alone? Why, no. There's Catrina, my little girl."

"Your daughter?"

"Sure. My daughter," Peel said, leaning so far back in his chair that Roman thought he might fall over. Then he shouted, "Catrina! Come out here."

The child was abreast of Roman before he was aware of her entering the room, walking on bare feet. Only her shoulders and head came above the level of the table as she moved to her father's side. She was dressed in what looked to Roman like a flour sack, old and dirty, ripped in a number of places and roughly sewn together. She turned slowly, almost reluctantly, but her eyes were on Roman's face from the first, and there was no sign of timidity.

They were dark brown eyes, almost black in the lamplight, with a shine deep in them, and Roman was reminded of looking down a well and seeing the reflection of light on the water in the darkness far below. Her hair was matted and filthy and hung unevenly to her shoulders. It was as dark as her father's, as was her complexion. But whereas the hair was lusterless, her skin had a bright, translucent quality.

"This here's my monkey. Catrina," Crider Peel said, throwing one arm around the tiny shoulders and shaking the child back and forth roughly as he might a large dog. "She cooks for Daddy, and cleans up."

Catrina stared into Roman's face, her eyes almost unblinking, as though asking some silent question. Her face was much like some of the faintly tinted pixie pictures Roman had seen in illustrations from Calpurnia's childhood fairytale books, with a tiny, pointed chin, a delicately curved mouth, and eyes that seemed so large they could not possibly fit into the frame of hair that fell on either side. And along one cheek was the old bruise that Roman remembered from his night with Tyne Fawley in this place, purple and deep beneath the skin and looking as though it might never go away.

Roman first figured her to be six years old, but now, with

the eyes full on him, showing some childlike though worldly intensity, he decided she must be eight or maybe even nine, regardless of her diminutive size.

"This here's Mr. Hasford," Crider Peel was saying, shaking her again. "Say hello to Mr. Hasford."

Catrina's mouth opened to show rows of teeth that reminded Roman of the kernels in an ear of sweet corn, small and even and shining. But she didn't speak.

"Hello, Catrina," Roman said. "I'll bet you go to school, don't you?" But he knew even before he said it that she didn't, and that saying such a thing would likely infuriate Crider Peel. And it did.

"And burned Daddy's pork tonight, didn't she?" Peel shouted, and shoved the child violently away.

Catrina hardly seemed to stagger from the rough push, but kept her feet under her like a cat, and then, without taking her gaze away from Roman's face as she passed, she moved quickly and quietly back beyond the hanging burlap curtain, her expression never changing, her back straight and her shoulders squared. Roman reckoned that if he had ever seen defiance and resignation all tied up together, it was now.

"God damned young'uns," Crider Peel said, suddenly affable again. "Now, Mr. Hasford. I'd be willing to sell you this little device and all the pictures for three dollars. Only one in Kansas, I say."

He placed his hands over the stereoscope and the stack of cards, and Roman could see the crescents of black dirt under his fingernails.

"I don't believe so," Roman said. But then he thought, Maybe he needs money to buy food for that child. Or maybe it's just for more trips to the First Street saloons. I wonder what she eats in this place?

He got out as quickly as he could. Although Crider Peel was smiling, there was a sense of danger about him, and about this dismal place. Peel accompanied him to the door, pawing at his shoulder drunkenly, telling him he was always welcome because he was a friend of Tyne Fawley's.

All the way to Mrs. Condon Murphy's boardinghouse,

Roman thought about that little face, clear in his mind now. Somehow determined, somehow in despair, lost in something she could neither control nor understand.

Three days later, he wrote in his diary:

It may not be my affair, but this day I bought a half-dozen apples from one of the local grocers and took them to the house of Crider Peel. It was middle day, and Crider Peel was not there, as I had hoped he would not be. Catrina came to my knock after a long time. She stayed well back in the room but she knew who I was. She did not speak nor would she take the bag of fruit from my hands. I placed the bag on the sill and smiled at her and said goodbye. When I mounted Excalibur, I saw that she had taken the apples inside and closed the door. It is enough to turn the stomach of a strong man to think of what it must be like, a delicate creature like that living alone in a mule shed with Crider Peel.

The annual Fort Leavenworth turkey shoot was held on December 23, a Sunday. Twenty turkeys had been brought from various Kansas farms, each in its own woven locust-twig cage, to be offered as prizes for the best pistol and rifle marksmen who cared to compete.

People came from all around for these shoots, some even skiffing across the river from Missouri. Mostly they came to watch and converse with old friends and see who had gone to the grave over the past year. The shooters were almost an afterthought.

But these came as well, citizens who considered themselves crack shots in the pattern of the dime-novel heroes who were beginning to become so popular. Few of them were above average. Soldiers took part, too, and they were even worse than the civilians, because Congress appropriated only enough money for about a dozen rounds of ammunition per man for military rifle practice each year. Nonetheless, they all came in a festive mood, ready to pit their doubtful expertise against the few real experts who appeared—an occasional buffalo hunter or an old-line sergeant major—all of them laying down their dollar entry fee for each event, which went to pay for the birds.

For a whole week before the turkey shoot, troops of the garrison were on the ground, staking out white engineer's tape to mark the firing lines and nailing together the frames that would hold cardboard targets. All of this enterprise was under the hawklike eye of the post adjutant, and the soldiers went about their work cheerfully because it was a lot better duty than lifting heavy crates of ammunition or shoveling manure or any of the thousand other chores to which men at a depot fort fell heir.

Begun before the war, the shoot was held each year at the old smallpox hospital northwest of the post proper, just beyond Quarry Creek, where there were rolling hills and outcrops to act as backstops for all the flying metal. The place had been abandoned as a hospital long since, what with vaccinations cutting into the rate of smallpox among the troops, but there were a few of the old buildings remaining, in a dilapidated state. At least one of them was good enough for the Fort Leavenworth Officers' Wives' Benevolent Association to take refuge from the chill wind and dispense their black coffee in tin cups for a nickel, the receipts going into a fund that provided for such things as apple brown betty and ginger snaps and hot chocolate and writing paper for the soldiers confined to the regular Fort Leavenworth hospital, just off the main parade.

For those who wanted variety in their refreshments, the Town of Leavenworth Methodist Ladies' Aid Society always provided apple cider, spiced with cinnamon and heated in cast-iron pots under the tentative protection of an old brush arbor. This brush arbor had become a tradition of the shoot, and was refurbished each year by Methodist church youths, along with a contingent of extra-duty soldiers sent over by the post chaplain. No one ever complained that the church youths likely learned more from the soldiers about colorful language than they did about repairing brush arbors.

The "brush-arbor cider," as it came to be called, was very popular because it was homemade and rich and also free of charge. It had been observed that even some of the Leavenworth Baptists sipped a cup or two each year, although they were on about the same terms with Methodists as crows were with owls.

"Methodists and Baptists don't see eye to eye," said Mr. Elisha Hankins. "In fact, it appears to me to be a danger to public safety, having them mingle together in a place where there are so many loaded weapons handy."

No hard liquor was allowed on the grounds of the contest, the army's position being that a mixture of alcohol and firearms presented a possible danger both to shooters and to onlookers. But times being what they were, and thirst apparently a result of simply being on the frontier, some men brought their own supply of strong spirits. They had to be discreet enough to carry such supplies in pocket flasks tucked away in folds of their clothing. There were plenty of folds to tuck things away in, because late December in Kansas was not the most temperate of times, so almost everyone wore a long, heavy overcoat, ideal for secreting pints and quarts that could be quickly retrieved when opportunity presented itself, but never when one of the provost guards was looking.

This policy against hard liquor had been rather casually enforced by the army authorities until 1865, when a contestant in the large-bore rifle match laced his hot apple cider with too much First Street rye and shot two toes off his left foot.

After Mr. Hankins had told Roman that story, he wrote in his diary, "I have never seen people like these. What we would take at home for great misfortune, they laugh about and go on lighthearted to the next calamity!"

Roman Hasford had never entertained the thought of attending the Fort Leavenworth turkey shoot, as his boycott of the army post was still in effect. But he was persuaded by Mr. Hankins that he should enter the pistol contests after the two of them had gone along the river on a number of late-evening occasions, just before dark, to retrieve Mr. Hankins's trotlines and take a few potshots at old snags with the Navy Colt that Roman had brought from Arkansas.

Usually Mr. Hankins pulled at least half a dozen foot-long

blue catfish from the Missouri, and they would go in the gathering darkness to his home, where Mrs. Hankins, whom he called Spankin for some reason Roman could never discover, would kill and skin and gut the fish, roll them in cornmeal, fry them, and place them on the table along with boiled Irish potatoes, string beans cooked in salt pork, and a crock pitcher of cold buttermilk.

This was a fine little home not far from the stockyards, a three-room affair with curtains on the windows and a picket fence around a yard where two pin oaks and a hornbeam grew. It was as nice as any house in Leavenworth, although small, and that was worthy of note, since Leavenworth town and fort comprised a community of some twenty thousand souls.

On one such evening Mr. Hankins, while working his jaws furiously on a chunk of fish, observed that Roman was pretty good with that pistol.

"You ought to get into the turkey shoot," he said. "Most people around here couldn't hit a bull in the broad side with a handgun."

Spankin, who was tall and rawboned like her husband, but had a gentle face that showed the crow's-feet of habitual laughter at the corners of her eyes, shook her head and sighed.

"Mr. Hankins can't talk without making reference to some kind of livestock," she said, patting Roman's arm. "Eat some more fish, son. There's another whole skillet full on the stove."

Perhaps it was the warmth of this kitchen and the friendship there that made Roman waver in his firm decision not to set foot on army soil again. He had known for some time that he would stay in Kansas for Christmas. At first he had lied to himself and in his letters home, saying that come the holidays he would return to the place where he belonged. But perhaps he wasn't lying; perhaps he had just not yet realized that he was beginning to feel a part of this community. In any event, he knew now where he would be for that special season, and he was ready for a celebration. He knew from town talk that the shoot was a celebration. And he was sure Victoria Cardin would be there.

"This year there'll be a measure of sadness to it," Spankin was saying. "What with that dreadful news from Wyoming."

The newspapers had just reported that a detachment of soldiers had been wiped out by the Sioux near Fort Phil Kearny, during the continuing dispute caused by the passage of miners along the Bozeman Trail, which led to the Montana diggings.

"Yes, and the Cheyenne aren't too peaceful along the Kansas line," Mr. Hankins said. "Ever since Sand Creek, when that bunch of Colorado militia butchered their camp, they've been skittery as hell."

"Can't say I blame them," said Spankin. "Roman, have you heard those terrible stories about how the men who raided that camp cut off pieces of their victims to take back and show off in Denver?"

"Stories unfit for a woman's ears," Mr. Hankins shouted. "And likely not true."

"I think they're true," she said stubbornly.

"I read in the *Conservative* that Governor Crawford thinks there's going to be a general uprising," Roman said.

"Hell! Governor Crawford's always saying there's going to be a general uprising and asking the government to send more regulars and asking them to pay for calling out every Kansas militiaman in sight," said Mr. Hankins.

Spankin had begun to clear away dishes, making space for her gooseberry pan pie.

"You should be thankful, Mr. Hankins," she said. "The more army troops in Kansas, the more horses you sell and the more wagons you contract."

Mr. Hankins grunted. "That's exactly what Crawford knows. The more soldiers, the more money for his constituents."

"Yes, and you're one of his constituents."

She was laying out plates with thick slices of pie, the crust golden and the filling pale green and translucent. The spicy smell of the gooseberries made Roman's mouth water with anticipation.

"My business is good enough without stirring everybody up. And I never yet voted for that son of a bitch."

Spankin clucked at him, and Roman started on his pie.

"Poor Captain Fetterman and his men," Spankin said.

"Yes, Fetterman. Every officer on the frontier knows what a bragging, no-account son of a bitch he was," Mr. Hankins said, and Spankin clucked at him again. He stared across the table at Roman. "Your friend Crider Peel has been going up and down First Street telling everybody about it. The Fetterman Massacre."

"My friend?"

"You told me you'd been to his house."

"That pitiful child, what's her name?" asked Spankin.

"Catrina," Roman said, sorry that the subject had come up. With his mouth full of gooseberry pie as good as any he could recall his mother making, he wondered what Catrina might have had for her supper. A bacon rind? Suddenly the pie didn't taste so good.

"Crider passes himself off as the man who knows all about the frontier army," Mr. Hankins said. "Because he's in the state militia, you see, he knows all about it. But he ain't been on a hostile field since the war, so far as anybody knows. A Cheyenne with black paint on his face would scare him right out of his suspenders."

"He's a terrible man," Spankin said, picking at her pie, eating only the filling.

"He's a nice man when he's sober," said Mr. Hankins. "Only thing is, he's not sober too much. He's been boiled for two days now, getting a head start on his annual Christmas binge. Saved up his money for it, I suppose. Anyway, he's been spending a good deal. You stay away from him when he's been drinking, son. He's a mean son of a bitch when he's had a few."

Spankin clucked once more, and Mr. Hankins finished his pie in one mighty mouthful, the juice running from the corners of his mouth and into his whiskers.

Roman didn't stay for the usual game of checkers with his employer. The atmosphere had gone a little sour for him, what with all the talk of things that might spoil the good spirit of the turkey shoot. In addition to the Fetterman Massacre, there had been that little affair in Tecumseh a few days earlier, when parties unknown had broken into Mr. August Bainbridge's express office while the town slept and carted off the small safe in a wagon. But he couldn't seem to free himself from conversation that deepened his bad mood.

When he arrived at his room in Mrs. Condon Murphy's boardinghouse, he found Mr. Moffet in bed, covers pulled up to his chest and his nightcap low on his head. Roman could see that he was well along into the fruit-jar beer.

Roman decided to clean the Navy Colt, and while he did so, Mr. Moffet began a detailed discussion of the merits of lay preachers, and that somehow led into a rehash of what was being said around town about the robbery. Mr. Moffet's transitions always left Roman completely baffled.

A posse headed by Jared Dane had found the wagon, the horses that had pulled it, and the open and empty safe, blown with nitroglycerin, on the banks of the Neosho River. They also found the tracks of half a dozen horses headed straight for the Indian Territory, except for one set that doubled back to the north. This last set of tracks they lost on the stagecoach road between Lawrence and Topeka. The ones going south they didn't bother to follow.

"Too much head start," Jared Dane said. "None of those horses were shod. Indian Territory horses. And they won't slow down until they're back in Cherokee Nation."

The robbers left behind more than a shattered rear door at the express office. When the morning crew came in to discover the missing safe, they also found the night guard lying in a pool of blackened blood. The local marshal said he figured the guard had been killed with a large-caliber weapon, probably a .44, two rounds fired at close range.

Nobody was surprised that the gunfire went unnoticed. As chance would have it, a number of stray dogs had wandered into town two days previously, from the pack belonging to some Kaw Indians who were in the neighborhood, and a number of citizens had been dispatching them with shotguns whenever they had the opportunity. As a result, shooting at night was not unusual, so the pursuit was not begun until well after the discovery of the dead express man, and only then because Jared Dane happened to be nearby in Topeka, on railroad business.

Mr. Moffet, after a short sentence or two on the quality of hymns sung by the Congregationalists, swung back into the robbery, sipping beer from a mason jar as he went along.

"There are people in Kansas who take delight in Mr. Bainbridge being separated from his money. Of course, some of this money was likely the savings of trusting depositors. But there are people in Kansas who admire Mr. Bainbridge because he is helping to push civilization into the plains. After all," and he took a long sip of beer, "it is the Lord's intent that white Protestants go out and take the Bible and its teachings to the savage land. It's unfortunate that the express man was killed, but the Lord moves in mysterious ways." And so forth.

Having had his fill of religion and killing for one night, Roman returned the Colt pistol to its bag, undressed, and crawled under the covers, his back to Mr. Moffet, who was still talking, now about Robert E. Lee, who he had heard kept a pet snake when he served in Texas, but the snake died because it wouldn't eat the frogs brought to it by Lee's troopers.

"I suppose he was a good man, General Lee," Mr. Moffet said, leaning from the bed to blow out the lamp on the nightstand. "Even if he was an Episcopalian."

And a moment later, from the darkness, he said, "I wonder how long it takes a snake to die of starvation."

Before he slept, Roman thought about Crider Peel. Somebody had told Roman that Crider Peel got himself a horse just a day or so ago. One of those scrawny-looking things that came out of the Indian Territory, like the wild ponies Tyne Fawley sold Mr. Hankins that time.

His drowsy thinking took him no further along that path. But the next morning, before going down to Mrs. Condon Murphy's breakfast, he wrote in his diary: "It would be in-

teresting to know if Crider Peel saved enough money to buy
a horse and his Yule whiskey, and had enough left over to get
a Christmas present for his little girl."

It was all that Roman Hasford had expected, and much more.
He marked it in memory for years ahead as the single point
when his fortunes changed. Viewed in retrospect, it was exhilarating, terrible, and wonderful, all at the same time.

The sun was at its zenith when Roman guided Excalibur
across Quarry Creek and onto the old hospital grounds. There
was already a large crowd; soldiers were supervising the targets and firing line, and the first competition was about to
begin, men standing about in groups, some holding rifles or
pistols. There were stovepipe and slouch hats and a few
bowlers, like Roman's; ladies were wearing lavender and blue
and light gray, the bright brocades of collar and cuff peeking
from the confines of twill-weave brown broadcloth coats. Little clusters of people talked, standing in the bright sun or else
under the leafless oak and hornbeam, where the shadows cast
by the bare branches looked like black lace across the yellow
ground and the pink faces. There were parasols and bright,
fur-trimmed bonnets, and almost everyone had on a cape,
even the men; the capes hung in straight, dignified lines because on this day the wind had calmed. There was the sharp
feeling of frost in the air, just enough to be invigorating, and
the scent under some of the trees of overripe persimmons that
had somehow been missed by feeding possums and were left
on the branches to wither and turn black.

There was a place for distinguished persons, under two
giant elm trees, and folding chairs were set out there, along
with lap robes, all provided by the army. Central among this
group was General Winfield Scott Hancock, hero of the Federal center at Gettysburg and now commander of the Department of the Missouri, with headquarters at Fort
Leavenworth.

General Hancock was not seated on one of the army folding chairs. In fact, these were occupied exclusively by women

of his party. The general stood in his long overcoat, his hands clasped behind him, as he might have done that afternoon as he watched Pickett's men coming. He wore a narrow-brimmed hat, and in its shadow his face was handsome and romantic, though growing rather heavy about the jowls, the chin whiskers and mustache looking as fine as silk and freshly combed.

Conversing with Hancock were a number of portly, bearded men, cheeks pink in the cold, many carrying canes and showing at the winged collars of their white linen shirts expensive, boldly knotted neckties that had come from St. Louis or Chicago or Cincinnati. A few members of the general's staff were at hand to respond to any of his requests and most especially to attend the ladies of important guests.

Roman saw Lieutenant Colonel George Armstrong Custer for the first time. He had come to Fort Leavenworth from Fort Riley, where the Seventh Cavalry was stationed, to confer with his commanding general about possible coming operations, or so everybody said. He had brought his attractive wife, Elizabeth, who lavished on her husband attention that bordered on adulation, and shared with him the praise that came from his reputation in the war as a dashing leader of cavalry. She ignored those who said her Beau was a vainglorious, impetuous egomaniac.

Custer had also brought two of his huge hunting dogs, which he led on a pair of chain leashes, and he warned passing children to stay clear of their teeth and laughed the high, vibrant laugh that had so captivated women in high society, from Monroe, Michigan, to Hoffmann House and Delmonico's in the city of New York.

Custer was nominal commander of the Seventh Cavalry, one of those regiments brought to duty immediately after the war for service against the Indians. Nominal because the colonel of the regiment was always away on detached service. Apparently because of his Civil War record, Custer was already said to be a great Indian fighter, and his outfit the cream of the frontier army. Those who said such things, like Eastern newspaper reporters and editors, overlooked the fact that

Custer had yet to fight any Indians, and his outfit boasted the highest desertion rate of any regiment in the entire army.

Mr. Elisha Hankins was aware of this contradiction, even though the Eastern press ignored it, and had said to Roman, "He stutters and he puts perfume in his hair and I never heard of a good Indian fighter yet who did either."

Custer certainly played the part of the Indian fighter. On the day of the turkey shoot, he wore a uniform of his own design, which featured knee-length boots, a brilliant yellow bandanna, and a fringed buckskin jacket with the shoulder boards of a lieutenant colonel. There were those who observed that he would much prefer the insignia of a general, which he had been during the war.

His hat was remarkable. It was of fawn-colored felt, with one side of the wide brim turned up against the crown and a long feather plume that trailed behind him like the tail of a giant albino fox squirrel. His hair was yellow in the sunlight, falling in ringlets to his shoulders. His mustache and goatee were oiled and seemed to come to points here and there.

Custer was the only officer on the grounds who was armed, carrying one of his favorite pistols, a British Webley .455-caliber double-action rimfire revolver, sheathed in a snub-nosed flap holster riding on his left side.

Following him and Libbie, as he called her, were all the Custer relatives and in-laws, who were either commissioned officers in his regiment or else civilians hired by the regiment to perform services of some sort that nobody was ever completely able to comprehend. This entourage moved about the grounds of the turkey shoot as though they were a constellation in orbit, pausing only now and again to greet other officers and noticeably staying clear of General Hancock, because, everybody said, the Golden Cavalier did not wish the luster of his own fame dimmed by the close proximity of the hero of Cemetery Ridge.

The Hankinses were there, having driven out in a hack drawn by two of Mr. Hankins's prize dun-colored mules, and they waved to Roman from afar as he went to one of the folding tables where entry fees were being taken by a troop sergeant who issued each shooter a yellow card with his name printed on it. This process was accomplished with a large lead pencil, which the sergeant felt inclined to lick a few times before each writing.

And Mrs. Condon Murphy was there in company with Mr. Moffet, the two of them looking at a distance like a large Irish mother with her son, he in a much-used derby and a coat of blue-and-red plaid, making a splash of color equal to that of any lady's muffler or gay bonnet.

Standing in small, isolated groups well back from everybody else were a few blanket-wrapped Indians, a couple of them wearing white men's hats. They never seemed to move, but stood watching, a few of them smoking pipes. Roman thought they looked particularly forlorn. He knew these were Kaws, who never gave anybody trouble, and some of whom had been reduced to begging on the streets of Leavenworth.

At a greater distance still were three Delawares, more flamboyantly attired than the Kaws, and all three had beautifully roached hair held straight up in the shining sunlight, with rattlesnake skins, blue jay feathers, and mussel shells entwined in it. Roman knew these were men who sometimes scouted for the army, and in their spare time they managed to obtain enough whiskey from the soldiers to make them bleary-eyed.

And there was Elmer Scaggs, from the stockyard. He was hard to miss because Roman had no sooner arrived, dismounted, and hitched Excalibur to a rope picket line than Scaggs appeared, grinning and staying at a distance, his huge form stooped and his arms hanging far down his sides, reminding Roman of the drawing of a gorilla he had seen in one of Calpurnia's picture books a long time ago. Elmer Scaggs wore an overcoat that was black with dirt, and his hair thrust out from under a woolen stocking cap like reaching, thorny fingers.

It looks like I've got myself a bodyguard, Roman thought, whether I want one or not. I should have run him off completely with that hay hook.

He didn't speak to Scaggs, or Scaggs to him, but everywhere Roman went during the day, he was aware of the big man's hulking presence just a few steps behind.

Crider Peel was not there. But Roman saw the Cardins somewhat apart from the Hancock group, the captain in his overcoat and cape, Victoria beside him, looking slender and lovely in a winter hat that shaded her face. Even so, Roman could see the flash of her teeth as she smiled, and he hoped it was because she had seen and recognized him. Next to her, as rigid as a rail, was Lieutenant Thaddeus Archer, breasting the cold without a topcoat, his dress blues pressed and gleaming and his saber cased at his side.

And Roman thought, I reckon the son of a bitch wears that sword to bed.

Roman started toward them, framing in his mind how he would greet the captain, how he would seem aloof to Victoria until she acknowledged him, how he would ignore Archer with haughty disdain. But he was intercepted in his movement by a strong hand on his arm, and turning, he looked into the flat, cold eyes of Jared Dane.

"Roman Hasford, I believe," said Jared Dane.

"The same," said Roman, taking Dane's hand in his and surprised at how small and soft it felt.

Dane looked as he had that morning in Abilene when Roman left the caboose of Mr. August Bainbridge. He was clad in dark hues, a sharp contrast to the color of his face, where the skin stretched over high cheekbones had the appearance of pink wax paper.

"I understand you've entered the first pistol shoot," Dane said. "Too bad you've wasted your money."

"Wasted my money?"

"Yes. I've entered the same list."

It was a simple statement, made without expression or heat, and perhaps because of that, because of the casual way in which Dane passed off as futile any expectation of Roman's winning, Roman felt the bile coming to his throat as it had at least once before with this cold man. He felt his face flushing, and despite trying to will it not to happen, he answered, with an edge of hostility in his voice, "Maybe you've wasted *your* money."

Dane turned his gaze away from Roman's face, and that hint of a smile came to his thin lips. For a long time, without speaking, he looked at the various groups standing about the grounds, his eyes darting like nervous water bugs. But he paused for a time when he discovered Elmer Scaggs standing a few yards behind Roman.

"I see you have a friend following you," he said.

And Roman, without turning but knowing who Dane meant, and seeing in his mind the leering, bearded face, the stained teeth and the overlarge nose of Elmer Scaggs, and wanting at that moment to claim even the most unsavory thing so long as it was *his* thing, said, once more despite his best intentions, "Yes. He works for me."

"It's always good to have loyal men about you," Dane said, and once more fixed his dead stare on Roman's face. "But now. About this shoot. Perhaps a little wager on the side, you with that pistol in your cloth sack and me with a revolver that's seen its best days."

Roman had no notion of how Dane knew there was a weapon in the sack he carried.

"In what amount?" he asked, once more against his better judgment.

"Only a token. Say five silver dollars."

Roman laughed. "All my silver dollars are in your Mr. Bainbridge's express office. Where it turns out they may not be too safe, after what happened in Tecumseh."

There was a quick ripple of emotion across Dane's face, like wind across the surface of a still-water pool. But it was gone almost before it was there, and Dane's lips twisted in his inexplicable face.

"Well, then, your pistol against mine."

"Done," Roman said, sorry as soon as the words were out.

Already the post adjutant was calling competitors to their places for the first pistol shoot. And Roman was into it now, and thinking, as he walked beside Jared Dane toward the white engineer's tape that marked off the firing line in the front of the targets, that he was about to lose the Navy Colt he'd held so long and tenderly since those years when the night riders came to his mother's front porch.

Roman Hasford knew what his capabilities were, as much as anyone did. And they were considerable, his having come to young manhood in an environment of work and self-sufficiency, in a place where a man, or a woman for that matter, survived or failed to survive by the skill of hands and mind, by the contest of will against the elements and sometimes against other men, producing his own food, breeding his own stock, cutting his own wood, killing his own game, tanning his own hides, living with what came almost exclusively from his own labor.

But he felt his stomach twisting at the prospect of pitting his skill with a firearm against someone like Jared Dane. Roman was self-confident, but there was little foolish vanity in it.

Damn my bad temper, he thought. Because he knew the little flares of angry passion, however brief, were what always got him into trouble he couldn't wade out of gracefully. So, on the short journey to the firing line, he was thinking that Victoria Cardin would see him humiliated. And at the moment, nothing appeared to be worse than that.

He lost the Navy Colt, of course. It took only a series of three rounds, six shots each, to eliminate all the other pistoleers, then he and Dane stood side by side, blasting away at the white cardboard targets, smelling the sharp blackpowder odor, feeling the kick of the revolvers in their hands, and on the last series Jared Dane put six holes in the mark and Roman only four.

"Keep your pistol," Jared Dane said when Roman held out his tote bag with the Navy Colt and accoutrements inside. "There's another pistol shoot. We'll have a second go at it and see what happens. If I beat you twice, I get the Colt. Done?"

"Done."

And on the second competition Roman won his pistol back, on the last series putting in six shots to Jared Dane's five. When the troop sergeant, who was still licking his pencil, entered on their cards that they each had a turkey coming, Roman heard Jared Dane chuckle. It was a strange sound, like hens clucking in the distance. Roman wondered how much Dane had pulled off his aim intentionally.

But the exuberance at having won a turkey and keeping his Navy Colt besides set such thinking quickly aside. Who knows the difference? he thought. Only Jared Dane and me. On the short walk to the place where the turkey cages were stacked and where a corporal attached their tags to two of the cages, they spoke casually of the merits of Remington versus Colt revolvers, Dane in a professional monotone, Roman with high spirits. Because no matter if Jared Dane, who made his living at least partially with a handgun, had aimed wide, he, Roman Hasford, had put all of those last six shots into the black.

"Put Roman Hasford's name on my turkey, too," Dane said to the corporal. "I have no use for such a bird."

Roman started to protest, but Dane looked at him, and although there was no hint of his faint smile or yet any uncommon glint of hardness in his eyes, there was something in his expression that made Roman keep his mouth shut.

"Come on along," Dane said, taking Roman's arm. "It's time you met the Boss."

They moved directly to the Hancock group under the elms, the sounds of the first rifle competition breaking out behind them. The black-powder smoke rolled across the gently sloping ground as though a small battle had broken out nearby. There were shouts of delight and others of rage as the shooters hit the mark or missed it. Now and again the ladies in the Hancock group, sitting under lap robes on the army's folding chairs, applauded, although Roman could see no reason why. They were entirely too far away from the firing line to see the effect of the shots.

Roman wasn't sure what he'd been expecting in Mr. August Bainbridge, but whatever it was, he was pleasantly surprised. The man had an open, almost childlike face. He had the look, too, of a very well-fed and prosperous man. Plenty of flesh on his bones. There was about him the aura of one devoted to pleasure and luxury and making money. He had pale blue eyes, and with these he looked directly into Roman's face as they shook hands, as though August Bainbridge were seeing not a very young man but simply a man. Roman liked that.

"Jared tells me you accompanied us on the last buffalo hunt we made by rail," Bainbridge said. "I hope you enjoyed it. You must join us again when the tracks extend deeper into buffalo country. Perhaps next spring."

"Thank you, sir," said Roman.

"And we look forward to doing business with you when you have livestock to ship east from the pens along the tracks. I can assure you of special rates."

"Thank you, sir."

"No word of that to your competitors, of course." Mr. Bainbridge laughed, showing a great deal of gold in his rather small teeth.

General Hancock had taken note of this conversation and now he moved over and fixed Roman with his direct, penetrating stare. He also offered his hand, which Roman took tentatively, wondering all the while if perhaps some of the troops commanded by this man might have tried to kill his father at Gettysburg or some other place while Martin Hasford was serving in the old Third Arkansas Infantry.

"You're the new young man who works for Elisha Hankins," said the general. "It's a pleasure knowing you. We'll be expecting to do a great deal of business with you, come next spring."

Roman took that to mean that all the rumors he'd heard of a big campaign were true.

"Yes, sir," Roman said, wondering what he might be expected to say to these powerful and exalted men. The eyes of their women were on him, measuring him, making him squirm and hope he had not inadvertently sat in a cow pie at some forgotten time since the last brushing of his overcoat.

"Excuse us now, General," Jared Dane said, plucking at Roman's sleeve and guiding him away from the almighty without seeming to. Once beyond earshot of the Hancock group, he said softly, "Now you can introduce me to that lady of yours."

"Lady of mine? What lady?"

"Come now, Roman, the place where your eyes have wandered all afternoon. Do I look to you like a blind man? I'd like to meet that lady."

So they moved to Captain Cardin's group, Roman cursing himself for being so obvious, and as he presented them to each other, Victoria's eyes were intense on Jared Dane, who swept his hat off and made a slight bow, and Roman cursed himself again, for standing there like a country dolt with his bowler still firmly on his head. Dane was transformed, with a real smile on his face, exhibiting good teeth strong and white, and each of the remarks he directed at Victoria somehow made deference to her father as well.

"It is a pleasant day for December, don't you think, Miss Cardin?" he asked. "I hope this beastly gunfire has not been too disturbing. I'm sure you're accustomed to such things, Captain."

Lieutenant Thaddeus Archer was standing aloof, glaring. He had not offered his hand to Jared Dane, perhaps because Dane behaved as though the lieutenant were not there, as though Archer were nothing more significant than a chance fencepost stuck in the ground beside Victoria Cardin. Quick to perceive this little byplay, Roman began to enjoy himself.

Finally, Victoria spoke, using that teasing tone even now, with the notorious Jared Dane, and Roman found that refreshing as well, because it indicated that she had not necessarily singled him out for such treatment.

"Did you win a turkey, Mr. Dane?" she asked, smiling and fluttering her eyelashes in the manner of her generation of young ladies. To Roman she looked like an angel straight out of a print he had seen on Calpurnia's wall in St. Louis.

"As a matter of fact, I did," said Dane. "Of course, I gave it to my friend here because he looked somewhat hungry to me."

Everyone laughed, even Roman, though he knew he was blushing. By now, he didn't care.

That's the second time he's made himself to be my friend in front of other people, Roman thought.

"And you, Mr. Hasford?" Victoria asked, turning her eyes to Roman, the lashes still doing their little dance.

Before he could speak, Jared Dane did it for him.

"Of course he won a turkey, Miss Cardin. He's a true sharpshooter, you know. I'm sure he'd be glad to offer one of those birds he now owns for your Christmas table, Captain Cardin."

"That would be kind, I'm sure," the captain said. He seemed a little uncomfortable. "You must plan to come and have Christmas dinner with us."

"I'm sorry to say that I will be in St. Louis then. But I'm sure Roman is not engaged."

Why, hell, this son of a bitch, who's as cold as a woodyard wedge, is jerking and bowing and making a fool of himself but maybe making me the hero of all this, Roman thought.

Victoria, at least, was giving them her undivided attention, which was something, and even though Roman had been little more than an innocent spectator to the entire exchange, Jared Dane had included him in a most blunt and straightforward way, as though he would not be there himself if not for Roman. Which, of course, was true.

"It goes without saying," Captain Cardin said. "I'm sure we can offer better fare than Mrs. Murphy's boardinghouse. My cook, Melissa, is particularly adept with fowl. So we expect to see you on Christmas, Mr. Hasford. About midday. It's been a pleasure meeting you, Mr. Dane, and seeing you again, Mr. Hasford. And now, come, Victoria."

As the Cardins and Lieutenant Archer turned away and walked toward the main post, Victoria threw glances over her shoulder like small bouquets, and Roman wasn't sure whether they were for him or Jared Dane, who was still bowing and scraping. But soon now, the hat was back on his head and the face returned to the mask that Roman had come to expect.

"All right, Roman Hasford. A favor returned. You eat Christmas dinner with your lady."

"What the hell favor?" Roman asked, and Jared Dane actually chuckled again.

"For not telling the Boss what you really thought of that little buffalo slaughter of his," said Dane. "You have a certain tact about you that is rare on this border. I don't meet many civilized men. Now, goodbye."

And Jared Dane wheeled about abruptly and stalked off toward the General Hancock group. Watching him go, Roman knew that this man had made turkey-shoot day a success for him, something that would lead him to unexpected adventure. That was the word Roman thought of. *Adventure*.

I've met General Hancock and Mr. Bainbridge, he thought. And I'm going to have Christmas dinner with Victoria.

It was almost too much to bear, and he pondered his relationship with this strange railroad man. He had no idea what had passed between them during their short acquaintance, but something had. Despite Dane's hard, impersonal exterior, there always seemed to be a hidden warmth in his voice and eyes as he spoke to Roman. Or perhaps not warmth, but an ill-defined quality of affection.

Later, Roman would write in his diary, "Maybe he has no way of showing his feelings. I knew some people back home who had never been hugged by their papas or mamas after they'd passed the age of five or six. Maybe he's like that. Or maybe he's never had any requirement to show any feeling."

But for himself on that day of the turkey shoot, there was a quiet exaltation of soul for the things the day had brought.

Elmer Scaggs was still close by, grinning his filthy grin, his arms hanging like a pair of idle oars, the great hooks of his hands reaching almost to his knees.

"Scaggs! Come over here!" Roman shouted with all the authority he could muster, and Elmer Scaggs shuffled forward like a dog, his teeth showing.

"Yeah, boss."

That's what Dane calls Mr. Bainbridge, Roman thought, and he rather liked the sound of it.

"I want you to go claim two turkeys," Roman said, Scaggs

standing before him, nodding. "Take one to Captain Cardin's quarters on officers' row at the fort."

"I know where it's at."

"And the other . . ." Roman paused and thought of Mrs. Murphy's, and of the catfish he'd had at Spankin Hankins's table. "Take the other to that hack over there and wait for Mr. Hankins to come back, and tell him it's my Christmas gift to him and his wife."

"Yeah, boss."

"And remember, there's still one more working day till Christmas, so be at the yards bright and early tomorrow."

"Bright and early, boss."

"And on Christmas day, I want you to come and help me throw hay for the stock. Bright and early. It won't take long."

"Bright and early, boss."

Elmer Scaggs gave a little salute, his limp hand touching the hair that hung across his eyes, and as he ambled away toward the stacks of turkey crates guarded by the corporal trumpeter, Roman marveled at the strange people one met out here on the border.

As the day faded away, so did the people, going off in tight little groups as though to protect themselves from the wind that had come up from the west, and tugging coat collars tighter around their necks for the same purpose, laughing and talking in the quiet, subdued tones of evening. Some who thought they knew said they could smell snow.

Many paused at the main parade, where General Hancock had arranged a final little show for their benefit. Two companies of the garrison had fallen out in dress blue uniforms and capes, rifles gleaming, and the post band was there, a good one because this was a departmental headquarters and had some need from time to time for martial music on the grand scale to impress visitors, military and otherwise.

Adjutant's Call was sounded and the troops came on line before a small, raised reviewing stand where General Hancock and his staff took their posts, the band playing all the while. When everyone was in place, the musicians marched across the field and took position at the right of the line of troops, and there fell silent. The companies were accounted, company first sergeants calling out that all were present, and then the officers took their posts at the head of their soldiers and brought the formations to rest until a bugler played Colors, with everyone coming to attention. A single post cannon boomed from behind the warehouses and overlooking the river. The command "Present arms!" rang out, and the flag on the main parade staff came down, the bugler now sounding Retreat.

The band struck up a marching air, "Garry Owen," in honor of the Seventh Cavalry, whose song it was, and in honor of Custer, who was now beside General Hancock, Elizabeth directly behind him. At Carry Arms now, the troops, in columns of platoons on line, wheeled past the reviewing stand and off into the dusk toward their barracks.

Watching it, Roman felt a shiver go down his back, and not from the chill wind alone. As he turned Excalibur toward town, he heard the trumpeter blow Mess Call, and he'd been near an army post long enough to know that on Sunday night that meant cold baked beans and hard bread in the troop messes, and pickled tongue sliced and served with applesauce for the officers.

To the west there was a rising bank of dark cloud, the upper edges fringed with red lace from the hidden sun beyond the horizon. As the wind whipped against his cheeks, Roman thought of that country lying out there, beneath the clouds now, cold and maybe covered with snow, and of his Cheyennes in their hide houses, before fires made of buffalo chips. In his mind he had come to call them "my Cheyennes," because he knew that someday, somehow, he would see them.

It was the best turkey Roman Hasford had ever tasted. Melissa, the Cardins' black maid-cook-overseer, carried it out on a huge platter, golden and juicy, and the captain carved. There was white wine and sweet potatoes and cranberries, canned asparagus and pickled peaches and light bread dressing. Roman's mother had always made it with cornbread, but he liked this, especially the chestnuts in it, and with a generous splash of giblet gravy over it. Then there was coffee, ginger cake with raisins and candied cherries in it, covered with whipped cream, and a dark wine.

"White meat or dark, Mr. Hasford?" the captain had asked, knife and fork poised over the bird.

"Dark, please."

"I like the dark best, too," Victoria had said.

As hostess, she was at the foot of the table opposite her father at the head, with Roman and Lieutenant Thaddeus Archer on either side of her. Since Roman had walked into the house an hour earlier, she had been calling him by his first name and smiling and fluttering her eyelashes and creating a most stunning picture in a deep blue dress trimmed in white, of French "princess" design, with long sleeves and a winged collar and a skirt that billowed out behind so that Roman had no idea how she negotiated sitting in a dining room chair.

By the time they came to the table, Roman had become, to his amazement, the center of attention. It was something he had not intended, or imagined possible, but he found it exceedingly agreeable. They had been in the parlor when this process began, sipping port wine and standing in a wide circle around a large blaze in the fireplace, where a row of German porcelain figurines shone like gleaming little sentinels across the polished oak mantelpiece. The room was warm, and the odor of hot butter and fresh bread and sage came from the kitchen.

A Captain Ward and his wife were present, she a rather frumpy little woman with bright and darting eyes that signaled an inquisitive nature. When, in the casual conversation, she learned that Roman had been on one of Mr. August Bainbridge's buffalo hunts, she insisted on hearing all the bloody details, which seemed a little unladylike to Roman. So he told it in the gentlest terms possible, considering the subject matter, and everyone appeared to hang on his words—except for Lieutenant Archer, who stood somewhat apart in a corner of the room under an engraving showing a Civil War cavalry company drawn up into line.

"Father, Roman needs more port," Victoria kept saying.

She stood close to him and sometimes even touched his arm with her fingertips, and all the while Lieutenant Archer glared, his face as gray as the skies outside.

After almost an hour, the port seemed to oil Roman's diction and vocabulary, at least to his own way of thinking. The more he talked, the closer Victoria stood. So if he was slightly giddy by the time Melissa called them to table, it was as much from smelling Victoria's perfume as from the wine.

Captain Cardin himself had been sipping all morning, and by noon he was pink-cheeked and in a jocular mood, making little jokes about the valor of men who shot wild game from railroad-car windows. The wine had washed away the stern lines in his face, and Roman decided that perhaps he was not the flint-hearted son of a bitch he had seemed at first.

Even before the turkey, Roman was delighted that he had made the decision not to go home for Christmas.

Once seated and served, and after the first few bites, Roman expressed his delight with the various victuals. He told them a story of how, during the war, he and his mother had sometimes survived on baked acorns after the night riders came and took all their dried black-eyed peas and milled cornmeal. When the dinner was done, he complimented Melissa as she hovered about the guests with a coffeepot. She beamed, and so did Victoria, touching Roman on the sleeve. They were having a cup of eggnog after dessert when the captain explained that Melissa was the daughter born years before the war to a free Negro woman and a Seneca man in upstate New York, where the woman's family had been serving Victoria's for two generations.

Roman then explained that their turkey was the indirect gift of a Cherokee who had deserted the Confederate army at the battle of Pea Ridge and given Roman and his mother the very Navy Colt that had been used in winning the bird. The captain said it was appropriate that so many people native to America, which was also true of turkeys, had had a part in bringing them all together. Everyone laughed, except for Lieutenant Archer.

He doesn't seem to be enjoying this much, Roman thought, and it helped add to the pleasure of his day.

Roman was ready to talk more about Indians, but Mrs. Ward insisted that he explain the battle of Pea Ridge. Roman responded that he didn't know much except what he'd seen from behind a dead mule, where he and a friend of his had taken refuge moments before the Rebel charge through the yard of Elkhorn Tavern. But because Victoria seemed as intent on his words as everyone else, he expanded on the fight that had occurred practically on his mother's doorstep, leaving out the parts about seeing men dismembered by explosive shells and one decapitated by a solid shot. Remembering where he was, and in whose company, he did not refer to the Union soldiers as Yankees or bluebellies.

"That's all so exciting," Victoria said, touching his arm

again. "Thaddeus was never in a battle because he graduated after the war was over, and here you are, just a civilian."

Roman was kind enough not to look at Archer's face at that moment. But he tried to impress on his memory what Victoria had said, so that he could think about it once he was away from here and was recalling all the best parts of the day.

After the eggnog, Captain Cardin led the men back into the parlor for cigars while the women helped Melissa clear the table. They stood about the fireplace once more, drinking brandy from bellbottom snifters, with which Roman was not familiar. He kept bumping his nose with the rim of the glass as he tipped it to his mouth. But in his mood, it was not in the least embarrassing. The brandy made a fine, hot glow in his stomach and was so beneficial to his feeling of warmth that he cast friendly glances now and again in Lieutenant Archer's direction. They were not returned.

"Next year will be a bloody one, I'm afraid," Captain Cardin was saying. "I've heard the general tell his staff many times that when he goes out he will be ready to talk, but if the Cheyenne want a fight, he'll accommodate them."

"How can you talk with savages?" Archer asked.

"One way or another, they've got to be cooled down," Captain Ward said. "Hardly a day passes that some war party doesn't disrupt railroad construction or a stagecoach run or even destroy property."

"And kill women and children," Archer said.

"Mr. Hankins says it's the only way they know how to make war," Roman said. "The way they've always fought."

"And now our mule salesman is the resident expert on the savages," Archer said acidly.

"He's been out here a long time," Roman said.

"Well, it's true, the railroad's building right through their buffalo land," the captain said, pouring more brandy for all. "It's not like the Union Pacific, across Nebraska. That line goes a little too far south to bother the Sioux much, and a little too far north to affect the Smoky Hill grazing range, where so many of the Cheyennes hunt."

"That's true," Captain Ward said. "But which is better? A railroad or a bunch of wild animals?"

"Which are the wild animals to which you allude?" the captain asked, laughing. "The buffalo or the Cheyennes?"

"Both," Archer said.

"It really doesn't matter to us, does it?" said Captain Cardin. "We'll take orders and do what the politicians decide we should do, either slow or fast, either peacefully or with Gatling guns."

"I say the quicker the better, and the more metal we use against them the better," said Archer.

Roman started to retort, some of the genial feeling in him fading under the blunt, bitter remarks of Lieutenant Archer, but at that moment Victoria and Mrs. Ward came in with bowls of toasted walnuts, and the conversation turned immediately from the grim to the trivial. The captain remarked on a number of quaint characters he'd seen at the turkey shoot, and everyone laughed at each reference.

"Did you see that mountain man?" he asked. "With an old beaver top hat, the kind that went out of style during the War of 1812? Hide moccasins and leggings. The snow king, with his white beard. He looked as old as the rocks and as spry as a new kitten."

"Yes, Emil Durand," Ward said. "He's scouting for the army now. They say he speaks a dozen savage dialects."

"A damned Frenchman," Lieutenant Archer said, and then blushed and looked quickly at Victoria. "I beg your pardon."

"The French are all right," the captain said. "After all, Thaddeus, the forage cap you wore here today comes directly from the style in their army."

"I beg your pardon, sir," Archer said, and Roman actually felt sorry for him.

After a while, Victoria sat at the organ and played a few of the favorite Christmas carols, singing, too, in a clear, thin lead while Mrs. Ward added a rather scratchy alto. The men stood about, listening, nodding their approval and smiling. Except for Lieutenant Archer, who was by then back under his engraving of cavalrymen. Roman hardly listened, consumed as he was with drinking in Victoria's face, her small teeth gleaming as she smiled at him.

It had turned deep dusk outside when they began to take their departures. Captain and Mrs. Ward went first, Cardin standing at his door and shaking hands with the captain and inviting them back. Then Lieutenant Archer, glaring with nostrils flared, taking the captain's hand stiffly, back straight. At least, thought Roman, he didn't wear that sword.

At the door, Captain Cardin held Roman's hand for a long time, looking into his face.

"We enjoyed your company, Roman," he said. It was the first time the captain had called him by his first name. "You must come again. And you have no requirement for calling cards, as I understand Victoria mentioned once."

And then on the porch, Victoria came to the head of the steps with him, holding his arm, and then Melissa ran out with a small bundle, something wrapped in a blue-and-white-checkered dish towel.

"Mist' Roman, this here's a little piece of turkey left over, and a slab of my ginger cake. You take it, 'cause after a while you gonna get hongry."

When Roman thanked her and had taken the food and Melissa had moved back, he stood on the top step and turned to say goodbye to Victoria. She bent quickly, placing her hands lightly on his shoulders, and kissed him, her lips barely brushing his. Melissa laughed, as explosively as a cannon shot.

"Miss Victoria, you behave! Your papa see you kissin' on folks, he'll give you what-for!" she shouted, loud enough to be heard all the way to post headquarters. Victoria ran back inside, her great princess skirt flowing as though it needed no movement of limbs beneath, Melissa holding the door and her half-freedman, half-Seneca face glowing like a black sun.

As Roman swung up into Excalibur's saddle in front of the Cardin quarters, he looked back toward the house and was sure he saw a front window curtain fluttering. He smiled and lifted his slouch hat, the bowler having been assigned to storage for the winter, and reined Excalibur away toward town and felt the first icy snowflake fall against his cheek. It felt wonderful.

The wind was laid and the snow was coming in feathery flakes, straight down, and before Roman and Excalibur were near the outskirts of Leavenworth town, a blanket of white lay across the land, making the night bright. Roman rode with his head down, the brim of his slouch hat over his face, letting the horse pick his own way and his own gait along the road that would become Seventh Street just short of the stockyards.

Because of the season, he began to recall home. At Christmastime, the house was always heavy with the scent of roasting pork, one of the spring farrow always set aside specifically for the Yule dinner. And three days before Christmas, he and his father, once he was old enough to ride double, would take the mare and go back along the ridges above White River and find a small cedar and cut it and carry it back, lashed behind the saddle, to the house that stood only a short half-mile south of Elkhorn Tavern and along the wagon trace that would be called Wire Road once the poles and wires had been put in, and later still would become the route of the Butterfield stagecoach from St. Louis to San Francisco. Roman could recall standing in the locust grove alongside of the road, watching the horses and the bounding coach pass in a cloud of dust, and thinking, There's a thing going all the way to California, wherever that is.

They'd always set up the tree in the parlor, a room seldom used except for holidays, and decorate it with ribbons of looped colored paper and popcorn threaded on string with a needle, and little rag dolls of red and green and white. The tree filled the house with the smell of cedar, and the fireplace blaze made amber reflections along the clustered needles.

On Christmas Eve, there were always friends in for dinner, the pork ready by then and served with a thick sauce and sometimes rice, and always with the apple butter that Ora

Hasford had made herself in the autumn just past. After they ate, Martin Hasford would sing a few old German carols about Father Christmas and the glory of the season and of the *Tannenbaum*. And all in the language of his grandfathers who had come to the New World in the decade after Napoleon's final fall.

Then, before bedtime, the guests all departed now, Roman and Calpurnia would hang their stockings at either end of the fireplace mantelpiece and then climb up to their sleeping places under the windows beneath the eaves in the attic. Calpurnia usually came to Roman's bed, scampering along in her bare feet under the long flannel nightgown, to whisper and giggle far into Christmas Eve night and into Christmas morning about all manner of things and always about how wonderfully Papa sang in the old words that he had never bothered to teach his children. In fact, he had intentionally avoided teaching them, as though he wanted to break all ties between them and the generations of Hassfurts, as they spelled it in the Old Country, who had lived in the valley of the Rignitz. Yet for himself at least he had kept a few things, like those carols he sang in German.

On Christmas morning, at dawn, Roman and his sister would clamber down the steep steps from the loft into the parlor to see what Father Christmas had left them. Of course, from the earliest time he could remember, Roman had known there was no real Father Christmas, because Calpurnia had told him so. But gifts were gifts, no matter the source.

The most memorable time had been the Christmas when the old Jew at the Sugar Creek mill had left a little cast-iron wagon for Roman, with a movable tongue, and a pink porcelain kitten for Cal, with a slot in its back for dropping in coins, when coins were available. So far as Roman knew, no coins had ever entered the slot. The porcelain kitten sat on Calpurnia's windowsill above her bed in the loft until it was shattered by a stray bullet from the fighting during the first day of the battle of Pea Ridge.

Most of those Christmases had passed with little or nothing in the way of gifts. A rag doll for Cal, made by her mother from scrap quilt pieces and cotton batting. A whittled willow-stick whistle for Roman, made by his father. But it didn't matter. It had always been a special time.

Always on Christmas night Martin Hasford would take his children on his lap, until Calpurnia got too big and then she sat at his feet, and rocking before the fireplace, he would tell the story of the Star and the Wise Men and all the other things, getting so carried away that he was soon into the Child in the temple with the Jewish elders and then the Sermon on the Mount and all the way to the cross outside Jerusalem until finally Ora, the realist in the family, would cut in to point out that most of that was the Easter story and it was past time for the children to be in bed.

It had always been a very special time; thinking of it, Roman felt a large lump in his chest, wondering how it would be this year, his mother and father at home alone and likely no Yule tree. He hoped it was snowing in the Ozarks, because his mother had always liked snow, had liked going out in the hard crystal dawn to feed her chickens and, after Martin left for the war, to milk the cow. Thinking about the cow, Roman laughed, causing Excalibur to shy a little from the sudden sound. After the cow had been killed by artillery fire during the battle, and they got the goat from the old Jew at the Sugar Creek mill, his mother had lost interest in milking, so it fell to Roman's lot. And he thought that maybe it was because there was something about a goat's teat that was particularly obscene. But he knew that was absurd.

"Mama just didn't like the God damned goat," he said aloud. "No more than I did."

Deep in his reverie, Roman wasn't aware that they had arrived at the stockyard horse sheds until Excalibur stopped and began to snort, impatient for his nightly graining and rubdown. Roman sat for a moment, thinking still about this special day and what it had meant to him as a child. And without his having willed it, the image of Catrina Peel came to his mind like a dash of icy water.

For a long time he sat in the saddle, looking toward Leavenworth town, holding the dish-towel-wrapped package in one hand. Down there, beyond the veil of snow, he knew there would be a lot of men with no families, out celebrating Christmas as they celebrated every other day, in the saloons. Elmer Scaggs would be there, perhaps with a fistfight or two behind him by now. And Crider Peel, most likely. Not Mr. Moffet, of course, because he had gone to St. Joseph to visit his sister and her houseful of kids.

Excalibur protested a little when Roman reined him away from the horse shed, but with a gentle, coaxing voice he got the big stud started toward town. There was little activity along the streets where he rode, passing through the town from north to south. The snow hung like milled cotton along the eaves and window ledges, and any sound of merrymaking from the riverfront was completely muffled. Even Excalibur's hooves along the hard surface of the frozen street made little impression on the ears. It was a hushed and somber world that Roman rode through.

Finally he was beyond the street buildings and there were only occasional structures to either side, dark, silent blocks of darkness in the snow. When at last he came to the old mule barns, he could see them lying like crooked loaves of bread frosted across the top with melted confectioner's sugar.

When he drew rein before the home of Crider Peel, he could see a dim, faintly orange light in the single window. He dismounted and tied Excalibur to the well curbing and went to the door and knocked gently.

"Mr. Peel," he called.

The snow muffled his voice, so he called again, louder this time.

It was so quiet that Roman thought he could hear the hiss of snowflakes against the wide brim of his hat. He tried the latch on the door, and it gave and the door swung open.

When he stepped inside he saw immediately that Crider Peel was not on First Street, finishing out his Christmas binge. He was in the corner bunk, fully clothed, on his back, mouth open like a dead man. At first Roman thought he was dead, but then he heard deep, gurgling breathing. Moving over to the bunk, he could smell the sour fumes of whiskey along with sweat and onions and urine.

Roman moved back to the center of the room, to the table where the lamp burned, and placed the dish towel with the turkey and cake there beside a chipped plate containing a greasy mess of pinto beans and a crust of cornbread. There were two tin cups, one overturned, the other half full of brown whiskey. He looked toward the doorway that led to the back, and saw that the curtain hung motionless.

"Catrina," he said softly.

He could hear the huffing of the fire in the small stove at the far end of the room. There was a table there with a water bucket on it, and he went to it and saw that it was empty. He took it and quickly stepped back across the room and outside. At the well he drew up a fresh bucket of water. The pulley creaked dismally and the hemp rope was frost-crusted in his hands. He poured the water into the kitchen bucket and carried that back inside and placed it on the water stand.

"Catrina," he called again.

He could hear Crider Peel snoring from the corner, and the stove breathing, but there was no other sound.

"Catrina, I've got some Christmas supper for you. Some turkey and a piece of ginger cake."

He watched the curtain at the rear door, but there was no movement there. He knew beyond any doubt that she was watching him from behind that burlap screen. He started toward it but stopped after a step, somehow feeling that this was forbidden ground, beyond casual trespass, like his own father's mind when he was holding his Bible in his hands and staring across his fields.

"Catrina," he said.

By now there were little snakes rippling along the skin of his back. He shuddered and turned to the door, and there on a stool alongside the wall he saw a box, open and filled with the kind of thin white paper used for wrapping gifts. Lifting it, he saw a doll inside, porcelain face painted in brilliant colors, lips red, eyes sky blue. And real hair pasted to the little rounded skull.

He could tell it was new. It smelled new, the only thing in this place that did. And he knew that Crider Peel had somehow, even in his drunken stupor, taken time to buy his daughter a Christmas gift. He recalled thinking about the possibility of such a thing previously, and dismissing it as unlikely. But it had happened. He glanced once more toward the curtain and thought it moved. But perhaps it was only the wavering glow from the coal-oil lamp.

The saddle was cold when he mounted. Excalibur was in a hurry, so they went through town at a gallop, the stud running all the way to the stockyards, where he got his grain and rubdown. Walking back to Mrs. Murphy's, Roman's legs felt stiff and his head was as heavy as lead, what with the brandy and wine wearing off, and the image of that child hiding behind a burlap door.

In his room he undressed in the darkness, down to long underwear and woolen stockings, and sat at his desk under the window. He rubbed the ice crystals off the glass and could see that it had stopped snowing. There was a wide, bright panorama out there, all the way across the river and into Missouri.

He thought about that new doll. I've got a habit of misjudging people. Crider Peel may be a dyed-in-the-wool bastard, yet he bought that doll. But I wonder how many times this Yule season he's hit her in the face with his fist?

It had taken him a long time to arrive at the brutal truth about those marks on Catrina's face, his having come from a family where a child was never struck, except across the butt with a willow switch, and only then infrequently and when it was deserved. It was an absolute shuddering horror to imagine his own father ever striking Calpurnia with his hands.

"I'll box your ears," his mother used to say, to him and his sister both, but she never did. It was always the willow switch, and always applied by his mother, never by his father.

"God *damn!*" he said aloud.

It was cold in the room, the fire in the stove burned out. But he lighted his lamp and took out ink and quill and the diary from the desk drawer, because there were a few words he wanted to get down before he forgot them.

"It is amazing how quickly pleasant thoughts and surroundings can be pushed aside by bad. In the Cardins' house, it seemed that there could be no end of joy. Well, the year is almost gone. So Happy Yuletide should be the rule and hopes for nothing but laughter in the future."

He reread that twice, thinking some of his writing was beginning to sound more like Calpurnia than himself. He started to scratch the whole thing out, but didn't. He carefully placed the pen and ink and diary back in the desk drawer, blew out the lamp, and sat for a moment longer in darkness, staring out the window that had already begun to frost over again. He thought of Victoria's touch on his sleeve. And of the little Valentine face in the mule shed. And of Katie Rouse. And of home.

Finally he went to the bed and slipped under the heavy quilt, woolen stockings and all. He wondered if there was any fruit-jar beer at Mr. Moffet's sister's house.

"Merry Christmas, Mama," he said aloud. And tried to sleep. It took only a few seconds, and his dreams were of rabbits playing in the snow alongside Wire Road.

PART TWO

A man has to have a place that belongs to him where nobody else can come in. This diary is my place and sometimes it's a happy place and sometimes it's not. To be alone is necessary now and again. But to be lonely is not the same thing.

—from Roman's diary

Just before midnight the clouds had broken up and been driven away toward Missouri by a gentle west wind. Now the full January moon was standing out stark and milky just past zenith in the sky, turning the snow-covered land a cold, harsh white, all the leafless trees casting shadows from their limbs like black pencil marks on bleached linen. The wind had departed with the clouds, so it was still, the air clinging to the earth, and every frozen breath felt like shards of ice burning down into the lungs.

The Kansas River was black in the cold light of the moon, moving sluggishly, as though a single degree of lowering temperature would freeze it solid. It made no sound in the night as it twisted in the big northward bend toward the sleeping village of Bonner Springs, where it would finally turn east for the last short flow into the Missouri.

At the edge of a small stand of sycamores well back from the river were the saddle horses, their moon shadows fat across the snow beneath their bellies. They stood close together for warmth, and about their heads was a constant cloud of vapor from their breathing, which cast a shadow as well until it dissipated in the frigid air. Close to the horses but nearer the river were two men, one tall with a wide-brimmed hat, the other much shorter and wearing a billed cap of the kind rivermen wore. The tall man leaned against the trunk of a sandbar willow, and the shadows from its limbs were across the crown of his hat.

The tall man stood perfectly still, but the small man paced back and forth in the snow, smoking a short cigar, taking it from his mouth from time to time with a quick movement of his hand like a cat darting a blow at a ball of twine. Each time he spat explosively before replacing the cigar between clenched teeth.

"I wish there wasn't all this light," the small man said, glaring up at the moon and catching its light reflected in his eyes. "I wish the clouds had stayed."

"Quit your bellyachin'," the tall man said in a soft voice. "We ain't gonna be here long."

"I don't like all this."

"You like the money well enough."

"I mean you hitting that man. You hit him hard with the rifle."

"They ain't gonna find him till mornin'. By then, we'll be a long way off."

"I won't be. I'll be going back."

"Just do like the last time. Leave that horse you stole in the street and get on the train."

"It's like the last time, all right, you leaving a dead man. They hang a man for leaving dead men, you know."

"They hang men for stealin' horses, too. So what's the Gawd damned difference, so long as you got the money?"

Nearer the river was a wagon and team on a gravel bar, just short of the black water. A group of half a dozen men were bent over a dark, square object on the ground behind the wagon. If they spoke at all, the two men under the sandbar willows could not hear them. In the silence, a dog started to bark far to the east, the sound carrying across the hard frozen snow. Then there was a train whistle from the north, sounding very distant and cold.

The two under the willows watched, the tall one immobile against the tree trunk as though he were a part of the tree, the second one pacing, spitting, crunching the snow beneath his nervous feet.

Soon the men at the river's edge moved toward the willows, except for one of them who was still bending down. There was a spark of orange light as he struck a match, and then the trace of a red-burning fuse. The man who lit the fuse hurried back up the sloping riverbank, and behind him there was a muffled explosion that caused the horses hitched to the wagon to snort and jerk against the trace lines. But they had been hobbled and the wagon did not move. The dense cloud of the explosion drifted upward lazily, retaining its form for a long time in the still air of the night, and gleaming brilliant white in the moonlight.

The dark group ran back to the gravel bar and there bent over once more, a formless mass against the background of snow, and the two under the tree could hear them now, the voices excited and sharp. After a moment they moved up toward the men under the willows, the one in the lead carrying a burlap sack, the others trailing out behind. As they drew near, the tall man pushed himself away from the tree trunk and moved to meet them, and soon all were standing in the bright light away from the trees.

"You want the lantern?" one of the dark group asked.

"No. There's plenty of moon for this," said the tall man. "Gimme the poke."

He squatted, and with hands looking grotesquely large and flour-covered in the flat white light, he opened the sack and took out bundles of wrapped currency. He fingered the money for a long time and finally looked up at the short man with the billed cap.

"This ain't much payroll, is it?"

"It's not a payroll," the short man said. "I told you that. It's equipment money sent out to buy horses and such things for the militia if they're called up."

The tall man, still squatting, handed up a few bills and the short man in the river cap took them quickly, like a cat pawing, and shoved them inside his coat.

"I gotta get riding," he said. "I gotta make that early-morning train in Lawrence."

As the short man turned and ran for the saddle horses, the tall man rose, putting the rest of the money in the sack, tossing the sack back to the man who had brought it from the blown safe. Then he called to the short man, who was already near the saddle horses.

"I'll be sendin' one of these bushwhackers in two, three weeks. So you can tell him anything he needs to know and pass on to us."

"Don't send him to my house," the small man called, catching up his horse and mounting awkwardly.

"I ain't ever sent him to your house before, have I? He'll be around. You'll see him and he'll see you. Be careful who you talk to. Go on now, and let that horse loose in the street and get on that train."

The dark group watched as the small man wheeled his horse out from the sycamores and whipped him away toward the north. The tall man sighed and turned back to his group and looked beyond them to the river and beyond that to the flat white land where it sloped up to oak and hickory groves.

"That little son of a bitch. At least this time he was sober," the tall man said. "All right. Unhitch that team. I ain't gonna leave 'em here. We can get good money for 'em in the Territory."

"We could sell the wagon, too," one of the others said.

"No. Wagon'll hold us up. Makes too much trace anyway, in this Gawd damned snow. We'll just let the farmer we got it from find it, even if he ain't got no team now to pull it."

Everyone laughed, their breathing explosive and white.

Two men went to the wagon and unhitched the team. The others went to the saddle horses and led them down to the gravel bar at the stream's edge. No one spoke. They got lead ropes on the farmer's plow horses and then mounted and splashed into the cold water of the Kansas River, in no particular hurry, throwing up very little spray. Even at midstream the water was not belly deep to the horses.

On the far bank, the tall man reined about to look back

across the river. The wagon on the gravel bar was starkly clear in the silver light, and beyond that were the willows and the scattered sycamores, all deserted now and looking empty and cold, the bark on the sycamores gleaming. The tall man turned his horse sharply and trotted to catch up with the others.

"Hope we don't run acrost no Cheyenne war parties," one of them said.

"Yeah," the tall man said, laughing because he knew it was a joke but explaining it anyway because he knew it was his duty to explain things. "It's too Gawd damned cold for any bucks to be out, and besides, we're too far east for Cheyennes. And besides that, we're carryin' more iron than they got in the whole Gawd damned Cheyenne nation."

They all chuckled with him and rode on unhurriedly, knowing that one hundred forty miles ahead was the border of the Indian Nations. One of them began to hum a song, one they had all known when they rode with Quantrill during the war, when they had sacked Lawrence, Kansas, and raised hell in three states and taken what they wanted. The horses moved head-down, blowing great clouds of vapor before them, and the riders, who knew how to make long journeys in cold saddles, sat loosely, their weapons gleaming in the moonlight.

And the tall man, whose name was Tyne Fawley, was content because even though his toes in the snow-crusted boots were cold and he was hungry, there was a good horse between his legs and men he could trust around him, and all of this was something he had been doing for a long, long time.

9

It was a white beginning to the year that would see Roman Hasford into more projects than he had ever imagined possible, establishing himself as a premier stockyard man, wagonmaster, and entrepreneur of other business. It was the coldest winter of his life to that time, because in the Ozarks, even with long periods of bitter weather, there were never the strong winds that came off the high plains to glaze the snow cover with a hard crust of ice each night after the day's sun had created a minor thaw. But he thought it was the most wonderful period in memory because of Victoria.

Roman became a regular visitor to the Cardins', often taking supper with the captain and his daughter and talking politics in the parlor afterward, while Victoria and Melissa cleaned up dishes and pans in the kitchen. Mostly the talk was of Eastern politics, in which Roman had little interest, but when the captain started on the frontier, Roman became intensely interested, sitting on the edge of his chair and bumping his nose with the rim of his brandy snifter.

"General Sherman wants the army to have jurisdiction over all the tribes," Captain Cardin said one night, rocking in his chair and puffing a long-stemmed clay pipe between sips of after-dinner brandy. "But Congress says no. It stays with the Interior people. So General Sherman asks, How in hell can the army maintain peace when we don't have any control over the potential belligerents? And from that comes our role. We act like sentinels walking post until there's mischief, and then we're sent out, after it's too late to avoid trouble."

"From what I hear, I reckon there's some dishonest people dealing with the Indians," Roman said.

"Some of the agents are good, but some line their own pockets at the tribes' expense, mostly shorting them on food. And the army has to feed a few starving warriors every winter. If they're caught out, they simply resign. If an army officer were in the same situation, he'd be court-martialed."

"Well, Mr. Hankins has got three agents off in Missouri buying horses for the spring campaign."

"And you can bet we'll need every one of them before the end of summer."

After their talk, which the women never interrupted, there were always dainty desserts with Victoria joining them and Melissa standing in the kitchen doorway, grinning. Finally he'd say goodbye to Victoria on the front porch, sometimes with a good-night kiss to warm him in the blistering cold west wind, and sometimes no kiss at all, but in any case he'd be mounted on Excalibur and riding toward town before the post trumpeter blew Call to Quarters.

During January and February and well into March, when the Hancock campaign got under way, Roman usually ate only breakfast at Mrs. Condon Murphy's boardinghouse, taking his noon meal with Mr. Hankins in the stockyard office shack, where Spankin could usually be relied upon to have provided a generous portion of cold fried chicken or pickled pig's feet to go with the coffee always gurgling in its pot on the cast-iron stove. Suppers in the little house with the hornbeam in the front yard became almost daily affairs, as though he were going home to his mother's own kitchen, except for the times he was on the post at the Cardins'.

He found time during the week and always on Sundays to escort Victoria around the fort in the snow, trailing Excalibur behind because they were never sure when they might decide to ride double on the big stud to some outlying area, like Fort Sully, where somebody in his wisdom had installed a siege gun during the war. Or perhaps toward the north, where the high ground dropped off to a road that ran along the river toward an old Kickapoo village. Best of all were the times they walked along the ridge above the Missouri, behind the post buildings, where there were infrequent kisses over the snow-covered barrel of a twelve-pounder that looked menacingly upriver toward St. Joseph, their noses cold against one another's faces and always afterward Victoria laughing as though she were surprised and shocked, showing her tiny, perfect teeth.

Victoria was never again so attentive as she had been on Christmas Day, and Roman decided the little performance at the Cardin quarters had been to irritate Lieutenant Thaddeus Archer. As to what her motive might have been, he had no idea and didn't really care. The times were too good even to contemplate it, being near her without that ramrod officer and his polished brass standing by like a provost guard protecting Victoria's virtue, and ready to snatch it himself if the opportunity arose.

Sometimes Victoria made a great to-do over Excalibur, petting him and talking to him, and Roman didn't mind. After all, he reasoned, it was *his* horse. And those riding-double jogs to outlying areas of the post were almost unbearably wonderful, with her behind the saddle and both her arms around his waist and his feeling the whole length of her body against his back, even through heavy winter clothing. It was enough to set his heart thumping.

He wrote in his diary, "It's good in courting time to have a nice animal around."

He could recall the summer along Wire Road when a Sugar Creek valley girl had come often to the Hasford farm, saying she was there to bring huckleberries from her mama to Roman's mother, but she was really there mostly to moon around Roman, all the while never looking at him directly, but instead petting one of the bluetick hounds that Roman's father kept for treeing coons and hunting bears, and exclaiming about how big they were compared to the little multicolored foxhounds her own pa kept. Roman remembered that she had red hair, like Jared Dane's, only she was uglier than Jared Dane, which made her very ugly indeed. But at least she was a girl, provoking all the strange chemistry that developed in most twelve-year-old boys, even though he never got close enough to her to touch her, and wouldn't have known what to do if he had.

"That was a good time, before the war," he wrote. "But nothing to compare with Leavenworth in these early months of the Year of Our Lord 1867."

At first Captain Cardin had insisted that Melissa accompany Roman and Victoria on their little excursions, a kind of benevolent black chaperone, but Melissa complained so bitterly about being out in the cold and getting her shoes full of snow that the enterprise was short-lived.

"Besides," Melissa said, "them two got the whole garrison of this fort all around them, watchin' what they do."

Cardin acquiesced because he had become more and more favorably impressed with the young man so obviously paying court to his daughter. Roman wasn't very well educated from the standpoint of formal schooling, but he was clearly well read and a gentleman in whose hands the captain felt that Victoria was perfectly safe. He thought he sensed that Roman was so much in love with her that even if he had the opportunity, he would falter at taking unseemly advantage; that to Roman's school of thought, taking base physical pleasure from a girl he loved was unthinkable. The captain knew there were many such young men because he'd seen a few, and he prided himself in evaluating suitors. It made looking after Victoria's chastity a lot easier.

So they went on their little journeys alone, often extending them well into the evening, when the snow-covered ground made everything bright as daylight, passing soldiers who sometimes politely touched the bills of their caps because they knew who she was, or helping the children of other officers construct snowmen, or laughing when they saw the troops engaged in furious snowball fights after Retreat had sounded. Going about the post at that time of day, they heard all the bugle calls and Victoria identified them until finally Roman knew them all himself.

Sometimes they watched the Sunday-afternoon parades, when the troops marched for the officers and ladies of the garrison. And once they went with Victoria's father to an officers' ball, and Roman spoke to General Hancock, and the handsome general remembered him from the turkey shoot.

Roman wasn't much for dancing, although he and Calpurnia had done a few jigs together when they were children. But Victoria was as good at teaching the two-step as she was at recognizing bugle calls, and before the evening was finished, Roman was sweating happily as he stamped across the floor with his hand on Victoria's tiny waist, glad that he'd just the day before bought himself a new woolen suit and low quarter shoes, bad for snow, but good for dancing.

The best times were those above the river when they weren't going anywhere in particular, just leaning on one of the cannons and watching the river below or the far, flat fields of Missouri. It was during one of these times that Roman collected all his courage and blurted out the thing that had been weighing on his mind like a heavy lead sinker on a fishline.

"Victoria, you have grown very large in my affections!"

It came from his reading sometime in the dim past, that formal declaration, and Victoria laughed and patted his arm and he almost lost his temper for the first time that winter.

"You're a sweet boy, Roman."

She had the capacity to make him feel like a fool. Just like Cal when we were growing up, he thought. And in both cases he had to credit himself with playing into their hands.

Why, hell, he thought, that's the dumbest thing I ever said.

Victoria seemed most fascinated with him when he told stories of adventure, things he'd heard his father tell about the family coming from Germany and eventually ending up in the Ozarks, when the Osages still roamed that timbered country, or things he'd seen during the battle of Pea Ridge, or how his sister had married a wounded Yankee officer, or how his Uncle Oscar was killed by Comanches in New Mexico Territory. Of course, he had known nothing about Uncle Oscar's death until mid-January, when the army scout Emil Durand came looking for him at the stockyard.

It was the first day of Elmer Scaggs's rebirth, as Roman came to think of it. A week before, he'd become so disgusted with the way Scaggs dressed, and the obvious lack of soap and water put to good use on his body, that he'd railed at the big man for almost ten minutes, telling Scaggs he was a representative of Mr. Hankins and the stockyards and that he ought to at least wash his face now and again.

"You're a damned disgrace," Roman had shouted. "For God's sake, why don't you get some clean clothes? You smell worse than my mama's milking goat after a heavy rain."

Scaggs had grinned and bobbed his head and blinked, and after two days he'd appeared in new duck trousers and jacket and with his face clean-shaven, pink from scrubbing. Had it not been for the crooked grin and the dangling arms, Roman might not have recognized him.

"Well," Roman had said. "Maybe I ought to ask Mr. Hankins if he might consider a raise in your pay, now that you look like a human being."

"That's fine, boss. Whatever you say, boss."

Following the shock of seeing a whistle-clean Scaggs, and after he'd finished feeding the cattle in the pen across Seventh Street that day, Roman repaired quickly to the stockyard office and stood before the little cast-iron stove, warming his fingers. He had just begun to feel some warmth returning to his toes when the door swung open and Emil Durand walked in, followed by a small Indian woman whose face was barely visible in a cowl-type blanket coat, like an oval of polished walnut in a red-and-blue-striped frame.

Although Roman could not recall seeing Durand at the turkey shoot, he recognized the man from Captain Cardin's description. There was the old beaver hat with what appeared to be buzzard feathers trailing out behind, a coat of hides worn hair-side out and with various-sized pieces sewn together by leather thongs, the whole conglomeration hanging just above the tops of heavily fringed leggings that led in turn to filthy moccasins with beads across the toes.

"Emil Durand, army scout," he shouted. He held out his hand and Roman took it, feeling the scaly texture of old skin and hard muscle beneath. "This here's my wife, Min. She's a Crow."

Min's tiny face was sharp-featured and her eyes were as bright as black porcelain chips, altogether attractive and unlike some of the Indian women Roman had seen about Leavenworth with their drunken husbands.

Durand had a shock of white hair that hung beneath the beaver hat in three plaits, one along either side of his face and the third down his back and all tied at the ends with red flannel cloth. He was clean shaven and his face had the same texture Roman had felt in the skin of his hands, leathery and wrinkled but with hard flesh beneath. The light brown eyes glared out from beneath eyebrows that matched the hair, and they had the brilliance of youth, although Roman knew this was an old man, old enough to be the Crow woman's grandfather.

"I understand your name's Hasford," Durand said, opening his great coat to reveal an old, tattered woolen jacket fastened across the middle with a garish metal chain from which were suspended a half-dozen polished bear claws. The tops of his trousers were stuffed into the leggings, rumpled and slapdash, as though this had been done in a hurry when the old man was still half asleep.

"That's right. I'm Roman Hasford."

The Crow woman had closed the door soundlessly behind her and moved to the side, leaning against the wall of the shack office with her eyes on Roman's face, boldly and without blinking, as though she were inspecting a horse.

"I knew a Hasford once," said Durand. "And I know where he's buried at. So I thought I'd better come by and give my greetings. Besides, I seen you shoot at the contest they had out at the fort, and I've always admired any man who can hit a bull in the ass with a pistol."

Roman couldn't help recalling Mr. Hankins's metaphor along the same lines.

"Well, you and your wife have a seat."

Durand pulled one of the straight chairs scattered about the office close to the stove and sat down, but the Crow woman remained where she was, motionless, her eyes on Roman's face. It was beginning to be unsettling, those black eyes staring at him.

"Don't pay no attention to my wife," Durand said. "She ain't nothin' but a wild heathen and so ain't got no manners to speak of. But as fine a woman as ever crawled between my blankets."

He pulled a small crock bottle from somewhere beneath the great coat and took a long sip and laughed, showing teeth amazingly white and even for a man of his years. He gasped and gagged after his drink, still laughing, his eyes watering, and offered the bottle to Roman, but Roman shook his head.

"I seen you lookin' at my teeth," Durand said. "Got 'em in St. Louis a long time ago. Come in from rendezvous with some company men one spring so I could have a good, hot-weather drunk in the big town. But it wasn't no fun a-tall because my old snags was about to kill me, so I went to this dentist and he pulled all of 'em out with one of them pairs of pliers they use for such things, and he had this set of nice teeth he'd made for some gambler who had died of something or other, and they fit pretty good. So I had me new teeth."

He slipped the two plates from his mouth and held them out in his hand, his face now with a sunken, hollow look.

"You like to see a good set of china teeth?"

Roman shook his head and Durand laughed again, his old gums showing, before he slipped the plates back into place with a loud clack.

"Hell, I don't blame you," he said, wiggling his lower jaw to position the teeth. "I never much liked the idea of handlin' another man's teeth, either.

"Now, what I come for. You see, I'm an old trappin' man. I was young when I was out in the great rock mountains takin' beaver before all the markets fell dead on us. Hell of a life.

Knew Jim Bridger and Colter and a lot more good sons-abitches. I got to know more about beaver and red niggers than I did about myself. All except Blackfeet. Always had a little trouble with them. But I can speak their talk, like I can the Crow and Arapaho and Cheyenne. And a little Ute.

"Wintered once with the Utes. They was Gawd damned stingy with their women, too."

He glanced back at the Crow woman, then turned to Roman once more.

"Have to watch her," he said. "She'll steal anything she can lay her hands on. It's kind of a game with them people. Steal stuff they don't need, but do it just to see if they're smart enough to get away with it. Don't take no offense at it.

"I was married to an Arikaree once. Worst thief I ever seen. And she never done it for fun, like this Crow will. She done it because she was mean, mean as a snake, that woman. She had two of my sons, that Arikaree, but they both died. Smallpox.

"Anyway, after the fur trade fizzled on us, I started doin' other things. Did some mule-draggin' along the trail to Santa Fe. There was this time a while before the war, I don't recollect just when, and me and three others was comin' from Santa Fe with a string of horses. Gonna sell 'em at Bent's Fort on the Arkansas. We was just clear of Raton Pass, just takin' it easy, shootin' a little game along the way and smellin' the country.

"So one afternoon a bunch of young Comanche bucks jumped us. After the horses, of course. We drove the Comanches off without much trouble, well armed like we was. I still had my old Hawken rifle then, best damned piece I ever saw. Lost it one summer on the Flat Head, same time I almost lost my hair. Never knew who it was done it. I was drunker than sin when it happened and my memory ain't clear on it."

Durand took out his crock bottle and had another drink and continued, after an elaborate smacking of lips and clicking of teeth.

"Anyway, before we run off them Comanches, they put an arrow into one of our boys, right in the middle. One of them

Comanche arrows with the black grooves cut in it and vaned with owl feathers. Killed him dead. So we buried him on a little hogback and covered him all over with slab rock and we set around that grave all night, keepin' him company and waitin' for the Comanches to come back. But they never did. I guess maybe we barked a few of 'em when they made their run at our horses.

"So the name of that man we buried just north of Raton Pass was Oscar Hasford. Soon as I seen you out at the fort that day of the turkey shoot I figured maybe I'd seen you before. Then when I heerd your name I knew what I seen was family resemblance. So was this Oscar Hasford some of your kin?"

Roman backed away until his butt was against Mr. Hankins's desk and he settled on it, looking at this strange old mountain man with the name of his Uncle Oscar on his lips.

"My God," he said. "Uncle Oscar."

"What'd he look like, this Uncle Oscar?"

"I don't know. I never saw him. He left the farm before I was born, went to Texas. He was my papa's brother. He almost married my mama."

"Who? Your papa?"

"No, Uncle Oscar. Him and Papa flipped a coin to see who'd marry her. Mama told me all about it years later, after Uncle Oscar had been in Texas a long time. They never heard from him after he left."

"Never heerd of a man gettin' a wife with a coin flip. I got one once by outdrinkin' this Gawd damned old Englishman who'd started in the beaver trade with the Hudson's Bay Company. That was someplace in the Wind River country, I think. She was a Shoshone. Good wife, but she run off the next spring. And took one of my best horses with her.

"Anyway, it appears that I helped bury your uncle. And I thought you ought to know. It's always nice to find out what's happened to your kin. I wanted you to know we set around his grave all night, keepin' him company until the sun come up. A nice place, too, with yucca all around, them petals pale yeller. Just like the skin on a Chinese whore I knew once in Virginia City."

"Uncle Oscar," Roman said, only half listening to the old man's ramblings.

He was already thinking that he'd have to write his father now, not his mother. After all, Uncle Oscar was his father's brother and he suddenly felt guilty that thus far he'd never addressed anything to his father, even though he knew that what he sent to his mother would become family property as soon as delivered.

"I hear you wanta see some Cheyennes," Durand was saying. "All I can show you now is a female Crow. But maybe later sometime you come out to Fort Hays or thereabouts and I'll show you plenty of 'em. I'll be out there somewheres next summer, with the army. Now, just in remembrance of a good man, your Uncle Oscar, I got a little gift for you."

Durand turned to his wife and said something in a language that sounded to Roman like gentle hen's clucking. The Crow woman took a small leather pouch from beneath her clothing and from that pulled forth what looked like a necklace, a leather thong with red and yellow and blue beads spaced at regular intervals and in the center a brown pendant about three inches long.

"Here now," Durand said. "You take this as a gift from me and them other fellas who set around your uncle's grave. He was a good man. You take it."

Roman, hardly looking at the necklace, took it in his hand. There was a strange lightness to it, as though he were holding cotton floss. The old man was rising, pulling his hide coat together across his flat belly. He smiled, showing off his bought teeth.

"I'll be expectin' you next summer, or maybe the next. Maybe I'll even see you around here again before me and General Hancock goes out. But someday I'll show you some Cheyennes. Good-lookin' people. But not as good-lookin' as Crows."

He wheeled about, leaving a whiff of snuff and whiskey behind, like a faint cloud of dust kicked up by suddenly turning wild horses. He spun the Crow woman toward the door and slapped her across the butt as she opened it. Roman

stood for a long time after they were gone, trying to understand that some complete stranger had come out of nowhere
to tell him what had happened to an uncle he had never seen.

Then he looked at the necklace in his hand. He felt the
long pendant, and it was like touching a piece of hard beef
jerky, weightless and with the texture of wrinkled silk. And
he saw the shining, horny end and realized for the first time
that it was two joints of a dried human finger.

Mr. Moffet was visibly upset when Roman hung his finger-
pendant necklace on the wall of their room at Mrs. Condon
Murphy's boardinghouse. But then Mr. Moffet was upset for
other reasons.

He'd come back from his Christmas visit with his sister in
St. Joseph with terrible news. A cousin who lived in Liberty,
Missouri, as he explained in great detail, had a young daughter who had taken up with a man named Jesse Woodson
James who had ridden with Quantrill, so it was said, and there
were a lot of people in Clay County who suspected he'd had
something to do with the robbery of the Liberty bank just before the holidays.

Roman wrote in his diary: "I can't become too excited
over a robbery now and again over in Missouri. We've got our
share here. Somebody made off with another of Mr. Bainbridge's safes from an express office in Bonner Springs this
month, and they left behind a dead man, beat to death with
something heavy. It looks like being an employee for August
Bainbridge isn't a safe occupation in Kansas."

So Roman ignored Mr. Moffet's complaints about the
finger-pendant necklace and his ranting about Jesse Woodson James, whom Roman had never heard of and never
expected to hear of again. Besides, he was preoccupied with
the letter to his father.

The most perplexing aspect was whether to mention the
dried finger. Roman had no way of knowing to whom it belonged. As he sat at his desk, the dry end of his pen between
his teeth, staring at the necklace hanging on its nail in the wall

beside the window, and hearing Mr. Moffet's continued grumbling about outlawry, like the drone of September flies, Roman couldn't help wondering if perhaps this was his Uncle Oscar's digit. Or had Emil Durand taken it from some savage warrior after killing him, or as a present from some friendly chief? The mummified skin was dark brown, but Roman had no notion what a white man's skin looked like after being dried and suspended from somebody's neck for years.

He finally put it from his mind, deciding against mentioning the thing at all, and simply wrote the facts as Emil Durand had told them, adding his own touch that somebody had read the Scriptures over Uncle Oscar's grave, which he knew had not happened but would nonetheless make his father feel a little better about the whole thing.

He thought for a time about penning some personal thought. "I miss seeing you very much." Or perhaps "I often think of the things you taught me and the stories you read to Cal and me when we were growing up." But he decided against that, too, because somehow, ever since the war, there was a wall standing between them in Roman's mind. It was as though he were writing not to the father he had known in the good days, but to a stranger.

His feet were getting cold, but he sat for a while longer, thinking of home. He recalled how well his mother managed mules and horses, and how she rode boldly but always sidesaddle. A lady never rode astride, she always said, and Roman thought of Victoria, climbing up behind the saddle pommel when they took Excalibur off to some far corner of the post, her legs pressed along either flank of the big stud and her skirt pulled up tight to reveal button shoes and silk stockings. It troubled him a little, that image of Victoria and what his mother had always said about a woman riding astride.

"I've had a hard day, Roman," Mr. Moffet said from the bed where he sat with covers to the chin and his nightcap down across his eyebrows. "How much longer are you going to be at that business?"

Roman signed the letter, "Your affectionate son, Roman Hasford," and blew out the lamp.

10

Katie Rose Rouse could hardly read or write anything beyond her own name, and her ability with numbers was only slightly better. Yet she was highly successful in her trade, a fact that was evident from her having been for many years an independent whore, outside the confines of an organized house where a madam could control her waking and sleeping, her eating and bathing, her list of clients.

Others were amazed that Katie Rose was unable to decipher the details of what was contained in a mortgage or a quickclaim or a deed, but in each instance she seemed able to grasp immediately what such documents represented. And those who had known her for a long time said she could measure a man as quickly and surely as she could assess the value of a piece of paper in the circuit clerk's office at the courthouse.

Coming out of southern Illinois as what appeared to be an ignorant farm girl in the decade before the war, and taking up her chosen profession in East St. Louis, she quickly found that she had a feel for her trade and everything associated with it, including the ability to take care of herself without assistance and establish a solvent independent business that was envied by other ladies in the trade. She had no head for figures, the other ladies said, but she had a talent for survival.

Because of this penchant for operating more on intuition than on logic, she saw Roman Hasford for much more than the sum of his visible parts. Somehow, Roman sensed this and knew he could go to her rooms and have friendly discussions over a few sips of her clear liquid spirits without worrying about pretense. He was convinced that she knew of his guilt from the first two visits, but it didn't matter. It probably even promoted the atmosphere of good fellowship, because she never implied or mentioned shame in any form, and certainly never proposed any kind of recreation other than the sipping and discussing.

They enjoyed each other's company, as long as nothing was expected except the talking. She knew his intentions as he knew his own. And after those first two educational trips into Aphrodite's country, about which he knew a great deal from his secret reading back on the hill farm, he considered all of the visits to her as strictly honorable.

Roman often went to the rooms above and behind the newspaper shop. It was always warm and comfortable there, and it somehow filled a hunger in his new life that nothing else quite satisfied. He made no excuses to himself, nor did he try to hide the visits from others, often going up the outside stairs from the street in broad daylight on those Sunday afternoons when Victoria had other plans, such as sitting with the ladies of the garrison at quilting parties, or participating in cake bakes with the Fort Leavenworth Officers' Wives' Benevolent Association, or attending teas given by the wives of the general staff.

In a corner of his mind, he liked to think that Victoria would know where he went during those times she could not see him. But if she ever learned, she said nothing about it.

These were not troubled times for Roman, but unsettled ones. There were more and more images in his head that tried to tell him things he couldn't understand because there were no words to define them. He had always been eloquent enough in describing scenes from his memory, but there were thoughts hidden for lack of ways to express them, and Katie Rose Rouse, above anyone else he had ever known, seemed to have an appreciation of it, seemed to be able to read behind his face.

With Victoria, such a thing was almost unthinkable. She was like a shield, deflecting everything. With Calpurnia there had always been the bright spirit encouraging him or causing him to lose his temper, yet she couldn't plumb his mind. His mother had always been the gentle yet unbending matriarch who was above understanding. She was simply the one who made everything work. Before the war, his father had come close sometimes, but afterward he seemed to be in the same situation as his son, with shapes in his mind too terrible to expose even to himself.

From the first memory of childhood, Roman had always imagined that he knew things his family didn't know and never could.

And so the two of them, Roman Hasford and Katie Rose Rouse, effected a strange but highly compatible relationship. She had waited a long time for the right man to appear, and now she was sure she'd found him. She would say later that it was a union not made in heaven but one that nonetheless eventually made a hell of a lot of money.

It was a cold Saturday evening a short time after Emil Durand had come to Roman with the news of Uncle Oscar's demise, and Roman and Katie Rose were sitting in the pillow-stuffed room, discreetly on either side of it, two glasses of the clear liquor between them as well, when she brought up the subject that had been whirling about in her mind for a long time, like a mass of dreamlike clouds that revealed distinguishable shapes only occasionally, but shapes that were sharp-edged when they came.

"The army eats a lot of beef, don't it?" she asked.

"Yes. We sell a lot to them, and so do other stockmen."

"Well, men like to eat a little pork now and then, too, don't they?"

"I suppose they do."

"It's been my experience," she said, bending to her decanter to refill their glasses. As she moved, her breasts swayed like cantaloupes under the dressing gown, and Roman was a little embarrassed—not with her but with himself, because he always thought about cantaloupes at such times.

"Somebody around here oughta think about pork," she said. "There's a good market for it, fresh or cured, right here in Leavenworth. But nobody seems to give a damn about it. Dollars passin' right under their noses. The closest curing plant is in Kansas City, and that one ain't much to speak of, everybody down there so interested in Texas cows. You ever think about that?"

"I can't say as I have."

"Well, I have. You know anything about hogs?"

"A lot more than I do about cows. The only beef we ever saw was the milk cow. But we bred pigs every year."

"Roman, I think you and me oughta come to a little situation I've had on my mind," Katie Rose said, leaning back against a half-dozen of her pillows with a great sigh and enveloping her aperitif glass with full lips. Roman could see the glint in her eyes, like the shine he'd seen in a good bluetick's eyes when he'd just come onto the scent of a fat possum.

After Katie Rose Rouse outlined the venture, it took Roman a while to organize it. Well after Mr. Moffet had gone off into a grumbling sleep, he sat with his cold feet wrapped in a yarn throw rug, frowning and wiping his nose with the back of his hand and placing all the figures on the pages of a lined school tablet, trying to recall the information he had gathered during the day.

Elmer Scaggs was Roman's willing accomplice in this little conspiracy, which involved doing everything that had to be done without Mr. Elisha Hankins knowing about it before Roman was ready. It was good to note that the big man's eyes were clear each morning and his breath sweet, so Roman knew he was staying clear of the First Street saloons at night.

Getting everything on paper was not a particularly difficult task, because he had watched every year, from the time he was big enough, while his father spent winter evenings at the kitchen table under a coal-oil lamp, making the tabulations for the coming year: how many fenceposts had to be cut and sold at what expected price; how much land would be allocated to corn, and how much to hay; how much extra milk from Ora Hasford's cow and how many eggs from her hens and guineas could be sold at Elkhorn Tavern; how many of the brood sow's farrow need be retained for the family, and how many would be left to sell to the butcher in Leetown.

And in opposing columns he would write down the cost of new wire or lumber or harness or plowshares, or cloth for making shirts; ready-made coats and shoes would have to be bought as well, at the general mercantile in Bentonville; how much a year's supply of salt and pepper and sugar and coffee would take in hard cash, and if no hard cash was available, what would be there to barter in crops.

Even with that experience, a lot of pages from the lined tablet had to be redone, and sometimes by two in the morning, as he was sitting there in the cold, the floor around him would be covered with wads of discarded paper.

Finally he was ready, but he waited for the right moment. As he had anticipated, it didn't take long before there was an evening supper at the Hankinses', featuring bacon. It was delicious, as was everything that came from Spankin's stove, and what better time, Roman reckoned, to bring up the subject of pork.

They'd cleaned their plates of the last of meat and brown beans and fried potatoes and cornbread and lemon pie—this last having been made from the real fruit, brought upriver on rare occasion and costing seventy cents a pound.

"I was in town today," Roman said. "I noticed that bacon has gone up to twenty cents."

"It's hard to pay such a terrible price for meat," Spankin said.

Roman let that sit for a while so it could rise like good yeast bread. They talked about the coming army campaign against the Cheyenne, although none of them knew much about it except they had strong signals from the fort that there would be a lot of cavalry remounts required. At last Roman eased into his proposition, concluding, "I see it as a three-way partnership."

"Well, I knew you'd been up to something the last few days, involving heavy thinking," said Mr. Elisha Hankins.

"He told me that," Spankin said. "He said you'd been preoccupied."

They were sitting around the kitchen table, the best place in the house, bent forward over cups of steaming coffee, caressing the cups with their hands and listening to the sweep of wind around the eaves. A fine time for talk, Roman thought, with bellies full of good grub and the tart taste of lemon still under the tongue, and all through the house the scent of cooked bacon.

"Before you go any further," said Mr. Hankins, "just tell me who this third partner is. Not Elmer Scaggs, I hope."

"No. It's Katie Rose Rouse."

Might as well get it out at the first, Roman thought, because if that part doesn't work, none of it will.

Mr. Hankins's eyes widened and he blinked rapidly and sucked his pipe. Spankin became suddenly interested in the coffee cup before her, peering intently into the black brew as though she'd discovered something there that required close scrutiny.

"I assume she'd be a silent partner," Mr. Hankins said.

"That's what she'd want."

"Me as well." Mr. Hankins glanced at his wife; she was still studying the coffee cup. "Well, it's said she knows how to use money. What's the rest of it?"

So Roman told him.

"Katie Rose Rouse owns forty acres about a quarter-mile out that old road that runs past the mule pens where Crider Peel lives. I've seen the deed in the courthouse and I've studied her abstract. All legal, bought with cash about five years ago. It doesn't amount to much. Some scrub timber on land that slopes down to a little creek that flows southwest. But there's water close underground, Elmer Scaggs says."

"So now Elmer's a water witch, is he?"

"He's done a lot of well-digging in his day. He did a lot of things before the bottle started taking hold of him. Do you know how old he is? Almost sixty."

Mr. Hankins and Spankin exchanged a quick glance; she hid a small smile behind her hand because both of them were past that age.

"So she provides the land," Roman said, "and five hundred dollars cash money. I supply the management and a hundred dollars. What we need for your share is a wagon and team and another five hundred dollars. And Elmer Scaggs to run it."

"Well, son, you know how to get my curiosity at a gallop. Just what the hell is it you're about to build down there among the scrub timber?"

"Hog pens," Roman said. "And a curing plant. Actually, a big smokehouse. I know about smokehouses, and so does Elmer Scaggs. There's a big market for pork around here. We're close to an army post and a good-sized town besides. We wouldn't have much transport cost, getting the meat to buyers. We'd be a head up on Kansas City."

Mr. Hankins shook his head, and slowly took the pipe from his mouth and lay it on the table beside his coffee cup.

"Tell me the details."

Roman had his lined tablet paper with him, the figures running neatly along both sides of the page, and he took it now from his inside coat pocket and unfolded it on the table.

The initial expense, he explained, would be primarily for lumber to build the pens and smokehouse, but enough money would be left over to pay temporary hired help for the construction, and the wages of Elmer Scaggs, who would supervise the whole thing.

"If I decided you knew what you were doing," Mr. Hankins said, "and wanted to get into this thing, then why couldn't we just keep Elmer on the stockyard payroll like he is now?"

Roman thought, I've got him! But he spoke as calmly as he could. "I hadn't figured on that. It'd mean we'd have more capital through the first year or so."

"How about the stock?"

"We'd need to buy a string of good brood sows and at least a couple of young boars."

"How many sows?"

"I'd say fifty. With that, in a little over a year's time we could have better than two hundred and fifty hogs to market and plenty more for breeding left over, and that's just reckoning on five pigs to the farrow, which is fewer than we'd likely get. Elmer can go over to Missouri and buy the brood stock."

"And how do you aim to feed all these critters?"

"We'll need to buy a little grain. We can get it from our own agents at the stockyard, at wholesale. Some corn, I reckon. And after a while, maybe after the first year, when we've got the pens and the curing house in, we can plant the rest of that land in corn and we'd have a lot of our needs taken care of for grain and roughage, too.

"But the best part is this. I've talked to Captain Cardin out at the fort. I can have all the slops from the army messes there. For nothing. They're glad to have somebody get rid of it for them. And if that works, we might think about getting some more wagons and see if maybe we can collect garbage from all over Leavenworth town. And charge a price to do it. And Mr. Moffet at the boardinghouse says we can have the discarded mash from a couple of breweries around here, free for hauling it off."

"You after drunk pigs?"

"I don't care if they're drunk or sober, so long as they make bacon."

Mr. Hankins snorted a short laugh, and Roman could see the prospect of profits making his eyes shine.

"By God, son, let's have a look at some of those numbers you got on the paper."

"Well, before we do that—we could do this thing two ways. We could sign a contract, the three of us, so the money we made would go in percentage according to investment. Or else we can go in a three-way split from the first, and I'd bond myself to paying the both of you off to your share from my own part of it."

Mr. Hankins reached across the table and slapped Roman's arm.

"Hell, son, I don't need no contract with you. If you say a thing, it's good enough. And a three-way split at the first. How does our silent partner feel about it?"

"The same."

As Spankin rose to bring more coffee, the two men bent over the lined tablet paper, Roman going down the columns with his finger, item by item. Cure hams and bacon and shoulders, render lard, pickle the feet and make head cheese, sell fresh loins and chops as well as livers, then take what's left and grind strong sage-and-black-pepper sausage. Anything the army wouldn't buy, the townspeople would.

"By God, it took this to make Elmer Scaggs a sober man," Mr. Hankins said.

"It took Roman," Spankin said, pouring them fresh coffee.

It was the most exhilarating feeling Roman had ever had, except maybe for those times when he was able to steal kisses from Victoria over the barrel of a snow-covered Fort Leavenworth cannon. And this was perhaps better because now he wasn't braced to retreat in the face of stormy opposition. He was attacking.

"We'll need a lot of hickory and sassafras for the smoke-curing," Roman said.

"We can get some right here in eastern Kansas and what else we need from Missouri," said Mr. Hankins, and Roman didn't miss the fact that he was saying "we."

"And why don't we start with two wagons and get that garbage collection thing in town going right now? And why don't we start with a hundred brood sows instead of fifty?"

"We'd need another full-time employee besides Elmer Scaggs."

"Then hire one. Hell, son, let's help make that old whore rich!"

"Mr. Hankins," Spankin said sharply. "No need to talk dirty just because Roman's showed you how to make some money."

"I haven't enjoyed myself so much in years," Mr. Hankins said. "Roman, let's have another cup of coffee."

That was how the Hasford Meat and Lard Company and the Hasford Garbage Collection Agency began. Mr. Hankins insisted on the name and he also insisted that he be as much a silent partner as Katie Rose Rouse. Roman didn't understand why, and Mr. Hankins didn't explain his motives, and it would be a long time before Roman learned them.

But there was too much to do for such small details to bother him, and the next day he sent Elmer Scaggs to buy posthole diggers and shovels, contract for a few loads of two-by-four and shiplap lumber, and hire some help for the coming spring.

"Hell," Elmer Scaggs said. "Let's get it started. That ground's not so frozen we can't get a well or two started. And, boss, I'm gonna lay in rock-and-mortar flooring for a lot of those pens. It's hell on pigs' feet, but they ain't gonna be around long enough to hurt much. And hard-surface pens are easy to clean and keep down the smell. Folks don't take too kindly to a hog-pen smell when it gets rare."

So the two of them, Roman on Excalibur and Elmer Scaggs on a stockyard mule, rode out almost every day to plan and plot and stake out ground, and they made the design of a small living-quarters shack with a stove and two bunks, where Elmer and the other permanent hired man could live.

"It'll be good havin' men here at night," Elmer said. "You don't hear much about hog rustlin' around here, but you can't ever tell when some town jaypop might sneak out here to steal a little piglet. I got an ole single-barrel shotgun and fill that girl with rock salt. Stings like hell but there ain't no mess of blood after, and no laws nosin' around askin' about your business because you killed somebody."

Because of the proximity of the hog ranch, as Elmer Scaggs called it, to the Crider Peel mule-barn home, Roman found many opportunities as the winter ran out to take little presents of food to Catrina Peel. Apples or pears, and once a sack of oranges. He never saw her, and only once during that time did he find Crider Peel at home, passed out drunk in his bunk. He always called out so he wouldn't startle the child just by bursting in, and when there was no response, which there never was, he would ease the door open and place his fruit and sometimes stick candy just inside. He knew she was there. In his mind was a strong sense of her presence, an image of her face. And he came to think of her as a small, frightened animal, staying hidden even from a proven friend.

"It makes my heart ache," he wrote in his diary. He wanted to do more for her but he didn't know how. So he satisfied himself with taking the small presents to her, each time with the hope that Crider Peel wouldn't eat all of it himself. "Maybe not. Maybe he cares for her. He bought her that doll for Christmas."

Before General Hancock's spring campaign got under way, Roman placed an advertisement in the *Leavenworth Conservative* informing all interested citizens that their town now had a garbage-disposal outfit, and that for a small fee their slops would be picked up twice a week in winter and every day in summer, except Saturdays and Sundays.

He and Elmer were astonished at the response. It seemed that from the beginning things were working their way, because only that same winter the town fathers of Leavenworth had begun making noises about ironclad ordinances against people throwing their garbage into the streets. Of course, until the pens were completed and the hogs arrived, this refuse had to be hauled out onto the prairie and dumped on the ground. But it was a good beginning.

"Boss, me and this man I've hired, Tracy Benson, we'll do all this slops collection," Elmer Scaggs said. "Hell, you being the big man in this operation, we can't have you ridin' up and down the streets on a garbage wagon. You got to have some dignity, like that Mr. August Bainbridge. Me and Tracy— why, hell, most of the popjays in this town figure that's where we belong. Riding a load of stuff the sober citizens has throwed away."

But Elmer Scaggs was staying sober himself now, and shaved every day. Except that sometimes on Saturday nights, especially when the weather began to break for the better, he couldn't resist the First Street saloons and a few friendly fist-fights. Roman didn't mind. He wrote in his diary, "Maybe it's the whiskey and the rioting that in some way makes Elmer Scaggs's ugliness so beautiful."

11

It wasn't called Kansas when Francisco Coronado came with his friars to convert the heathen in 1541. That was a long time before it was called much of anything. Actually, Coronado came not to convert the heathen but to look for wealth, which to the Spaniards meant gold, and when he didn't find any, he went away.

If there were any Cheyennes along the Smoky Hill River then, they were afoot, because the same horses that people like Coronado brought to the New World had not yet had time to spread out across the grasslands and become a part of the buffalo culture. The Cheyennes along the Smoky Hill then, if there were any, didn't even know what a horse was.

The soldiers of fortune rode under the flag of Charles I, a Hapsburg on the throne of Castile. The people who were already in Kansas, and who were under no flag at all, knew nothing of Hapsburgs and wars of succession; they had been there for perhaps as long as ten thousand years and saw the high plains as they would remain until the English-speaking white man arrived much later, bringing his iron plows and steel railroad tracks as well as his family and his European ideas of God and profit and property ownership and eminent domain.

Little more than a pistol shot west of the Missouri River

began a high, flat, almost treeless plain marked by foliage only along the stream lines where the cottonwood and Chickasaw plum and hackberry made their signature in what many men would later call the Sea of Grass.

There were herds of humpbacked bison, followed by flocks of crows wherever they grazed, and prairie falcons giving their piercing little cries, and at night the barking of coyotes and often the songs of mating wolves. Lizards slithered across scab rock, and prairie mice played—when the falcons weren't around—and there was long-stemmed grass in the east and short grass in the west, and sometimes the land would burst into orange and purple and pink blossoms after a rain, making it known to yellowjackets and ground bees that here was an abundant supply of sweet nectar.

There were winds that came from the North Pole in winter and from the southwest desert in summer, alternately freezing or baking the flat ground. And tornadoes in spring and autumn that came with such power they could twist a tree up by its roots. There were snows that blanketed the surface with two feet of white in a single hour, and rains that turned the little dry washes into raging torrents within minutes. Then the black clouds would march off toward the east and the sun would come back, brittle and shining through the ice shards in winter, or lifting heat waves in summer that looked from a distance like ruffled lace above a hell-hot fire.

After Coronado decided he didn't want it, Robert Cavelier, whom everyone knew as Sieur de La Salle, decided he did, and so it went on as it had for eons, only now under the colors of France, until finally there was that purchase by Mr. Jefferson, the same one that brought St. Louis and a lot of other places into the new United States of America.

Everyone knew that Coronado came from Spain and La Salle from France and Mr. Jefferson from some unknown holy chamber after he wrote the Declaration of Independence. But nobody had the vaguest notion from whence came the Cheyenne or the Arapaho or the Pawnee or the Kaw or the Missouri or the Kiowa or any of the other peoples who used the great Kansas tableland as their own hunting preserve. Nobody even thought much about where they came from. They were just there, like lice on a summer dog, and equally as irritating.

The buffalo were there as well, and nobody knew where they'd come from, either, but they moved in great gray waves across the land, like low clouds, fording the Saline and the Solomon and the Republican and the Smoky Hill and the Kaw and the big bend of the Arkansas, as they had before any of those rivers had such names, moving south to north, north to south as the seasons dictated, for a long time providing the meat and the hides and the mystic gift of the gods for all the people who ranged after them, even when those people were on foot.

But after the Spanish horse arrived, the people became formidable nomads, with no comprehension of the white man's gods, or of ownership of land, or of eminent domain. And least of all of Manifest Destiny.

Nothing much changed that before the Civil War, at least not on the far western reaches of the plains, and the red man watched as the struggle began between groups of white men over the issue of how Kansas would finally enter the Union, as a free-soil or a slavery state. The Kansas-Nebraska Act that Congress passed in 1854 stated that the area would have statehood on the basis of a referendum to decide whether the state would be free-soil or slave, and this shortsighted plan made in Washington City touched off a rush of people to Kansas, wanting to be there for the vote, most of them carrying guns. Soon the newspapers were calling it Bleeding Kansas. A lot of free-soilers were shooting pro-slavery people and a lot of pro-slavery people were shooting free-soilers, so the bleeding was prolonged and agonizing and sometimes came in hot flashes of hatred and fury at places like Pottawatamie and Lawrence, where whole populations were put to the bullet and the torch. The red men had little understanding of what was happening and likely cared not at all, so long as they were left alone to hunt their buffalo.

But they weren't left alone, because too many of their high-spirited young men saw in all the disorder among the whites a golden opportunity for raiding here and there, which caused the whites to forget their own problems long enough to strike back.

One incident was so terrible that it left a scar on the Cheyennes that they remembered for years. At Sand Creek, in the last year of the Civil War, a unit of Colorado militia attacked a Cheyenne village that may or may not have sheltered summertime raiders.

It was said that afterward some of the militiamen involved returned to Denver to get drunk, brag about their exploits, and display various trophies such as scalps and noses and ears and female breasts and male genitals crudely severed from victims with hatchet or skinning knife.

There was an outcry led by churches, a few newspapers, and abolitionists who had run out of anything else to do since the Thirteenth Amendment outlawing slavery was a sure bet to become a part of the United States Constitution soon. The regular army joined in the protest, which couldn't have impressed the Cheyenne very much, because to them a white man in a blue uniform was dangerous whether he was paid by some state or by the Federal government.

After Kansas became a free state, the Cheyenne still held Sand Creek hot in their memory, but when the white man's war with himself was finished, there was even more to be concerned about. Everything seemed to be rushing out from the eastern prairie onto the buffalo-grass country and even toward the loop of the big bend of the Arkansas, where the Kiowas often came up from the Indian Territory in summer to hold their annual Sun Dance. Iron roads began to creep out into the short grass, and towns sprouted like dog fennel along the Kaw and the Smoky Hill, and the Texas herds of rust-colored cattle with wide horns were being driven north to the railheads, and the rutted stagecoach roads ran all the way to Denver and began to create over the entire area a dusty spiderweb of white man's passage across the land.

That route of the railroad along the Smoky Hill ran directly through the heart of the best buffalo land in the country, with the possible exception of the high plains of west Texas. The white man liked it, but the Cheyenne didn't like it at all, even though there were many old chiefs among them who wanted peace at almost any price. There were always those young men, their blood running hot and remembering Sand Creek and remembering, without even knowing it, the traditions of their grandfathers that had to do with good medicine and strong ponies and war lances and black paint on their faces.

Everyone began to see, if they hadn't before, that railroads and free-roaming buffalo herds didn't work too well together. That suited the whites just fine, because they knew the rails would prevail. After all, steel rails are not mortal; they lie there forever without any life in them. The Cheyenne knew that as well, and they also knew that a man couldn't feed his children on steel rails.

So the Cheyenne began to resist more and more, breaking their old custom of being kind to passing strangers, because they had finally come to realize that these were not passing strangers. These were a people come to put down roots, and to hell with the buffalo and anybody who hunted free-ranging across the plains. And the white man retaliated, marching under the flag of Manifest Destiny just as old Francisco Coronado had marched under the flag of Charles I of Castile.

Everybody, from Andrew Johnson, the President, through Edwin Stanton, the Secretary of War, through Sam Grant, General of the Army, through Cump Sherman, Commanding General of the Division of Missouri, to Winfield Scott Hancock at Leavenworth, decided that the best thing to bring peace was a show of force. But what it brought was a larger war, because they apparently forgot what their experience in the Civil War should have taught them: in an alley fight, if you don't deliver a brutal, overpowering blow at the beginning, you do little more than make the other party furious.

And through it all there was the constant wind over that land, blowing the soil from the roots of scrub growth and pushing the clumps of resulting unanchored brush along the ground like giant spiny balls. It was the same wind that had touched the cheeks of the red man from the beginning, and then the Spaniards and the French and then the saintly or demonic John Brown at Pottawatamie and the soldier or scavenger William Clark Quantrill at Lawrence and at last the cheeks of Winfield Scott Hancock and George Armstrong Custer and Roman Hasford in the spring of 1867.

In March it snowed again, and after a short respite and thaw the rains came, and that turned to sleet, and then the spongy ground froze solid. Elmer Scaggs and his crew were trying to sink two wells at the hog pens, but having little success, because when the ice-hard land didn't resist, the underlying scab rock did. Elmer finally resorted to black powder, drilling holes into the ground with a long-shanked wood auger to set the charges. The resounding explosions shook windows in Leavenworth, and at first a few people thought the Hancock campaign had already started right at their doorstep.

At last the temperature moderated, but the rain continued on and off for two more weeks. At the fort, Hancock the Superb, as the newspapers still called him as a result of his stand at Gettysburg, was going nearly mad with impatience, so everyone said, cursing the weather as he hadn't done since July 5, 1863, when the Confederate army slipped away and escaped from Pennsylvania in the rain.

It was a miserable start to what would become a miserable year for the hero of Cemetery Ridge. It wasn't much better for Roman Hasford, who had been looking forward to great adventure and excitement, but in later years would recall it as a time of bits and pieces hung precariously together by events that were neither adventurous nor exciting. All of 1867 seemed the edge of something, but without any hint of what was beyond, like standing on the rim of an Ozark bluff in summer and wondering what lay under the dense foliage below.

There was a flash of what Roman thought must be real passion, which made him a little ashamed of himself, when Victoria Cardin kissed him hard on the mouth as they stood under the lamp on her father's porch, and pressed herself against him, feeling like a steel spring suddenly releasing its energy against his body.

Then she said, "Roman, you're the nice man in my life."

And then she was gone, back inside, leaving him groping at thin air with eager hands and almost bursting inside with the glory of it. He felt at that moment as though the embrace were affirmation not only of his own longing, but of Victoria's as well.

Less than an hour later, in his room at Mrs. Condon Murphy's boardinghouse, listening to Mr. Moffet's monologue on how the Catholic Pope was trying to rule the world through communion using real wine instead of grape juice, Roman began to realize his mind had put more into the little episode than was really there. It was bitter to contemplate, but not nearly so bitter as the information he had the next day to the effect that Victoria had taken Melissa and gone on a packet boat to St. Louis, en route to visit her grandfather in Poughkeepsie, and wouldn't return until fall.

Why, hell, he thought, it's not even spring yet!

The whole thing left him in a snit. He was harsh with Elmer Scaggs and sullen with Mr. Hankins, and for a long time he even refused to come to the little house with the trees in the front yard for Spankin's hot evening grub. It was so bad that Mr. Hankins asked him if he was developing the piles, because he'd seen the same symptoms in other people who had. This so infuriated Roman that he took Excalibur out of the shed and rode into town and got a little drunk in the First Street saloons.

He ended up at Katie Rose Rouse's place and leveled off on her clear liquor while she scolded him for getting what she called the sweet ass for somebody that didn't amount to a hill of beans. Somehow, her saying it made Roman feel better and he led Excalibur back to the stockyards in the rain and slept in the shed with the big stud. The next morning he felt a little better. Mr. Hankins didn't say any more about the piles.

At least there was a lot of hard work to be done in preparation for the summer march against the Cheyenne, buying horses and seeing they were all well shod at Orvile Tucker's blacksmith shop, immediately adjacent to the stockyards, and inventorying the dwindling supply of grain on hand and making contracts for more with the merchants in town. Life for Roman was not completely unbearable, because there was always the shining prospect that he might see some of those tall plains warriors. It had become something of an obsession with him, and he felt it even more strongly now with Victoria gone and nothing to do with his evenings but picture in his mind half-naked bronze men riding around on scrubby little ponies that had their tails clubbed and bright paint smeared across their flanks.

It was March 22 before Hancock got his columns into motion. There were eleven troops of cavalry (which most people still called companies), seven companies of infantry, and a battery of artillery. Nobody could imagine Hancock the Superb going anywhere without artillery, although most of the old veterans on the plains said an Indian with any sense at all wouldn't come within five miles of guns mounted on wheels. Before this impressive formation was on the move, Roman had already arrived at Fort Riley, where the Seventh Cavalry was stationed.

The army had contracted with Mr. Hankins for fifty horses, and these were loaded on boxcars and dispatched to Junction City, Roman going along in the caboose behind them in order to supervise their handling and unloading in the Fort Riley pens. Mr. Hankins sent an extra carload of horses, which he called the reserve, horses that still belonged to him but that he suspected the army would need before the summer was out. The army apparently agreed with him, because they allowed these remounts to be billeted in a Fort Riley corral as well.

After he had all the horses safely behind the high plank enclosures that bordered the red brick stable buildings at the fort, Roman rode across the Republican River to Junction City. He'd had the foresight to bring a saddle and other gear, and he used one of the reserve horses for the trip, which wasn't far, only a little over three miles. He took a room at the River Hotel and waited for further instructions from Mr. Hankins, who had told him to stand pat at Riley and see what developed. He saw the sights of the little plains town, which didn't take more than the shank of an afternoon. Junction City was Leavenworth in miniature, a town catering to the army post nearby and not to cattle drovers, as did Abilene and Ellsworth and some of the others.

Roman didn't have long to wait, but the instructions came from an unexpected quarter. He was having a breakfast of eggs and beefsteak in the hotel dining room, and the eggs were as hard as saddle leather and the beefsteak even worse, and he was thinking that maybe he ought to get some coal oil to rub himself with because his hard straw mattress upstairs was populated with a vicious type of bedbug that had left the mark of its passage with little drops of blood along his thighs during the night just spent.

The cavalry courier who came looking for him was wearing a pair of galluses shining like mustard stripes against a dusty blue shirt, and he had a great deal of difficulty with the English language. Roman reckoned him as German but he wasn't sure because his father had never bothered to instruct him in the speech of the Old Country.

But at last it was made clear that the acting commander of the regiment wanted Roman Hasford at the fort for important conversation. After he'd retrieved his horse from the only livery stable in town, Roman and the courier went to the fort, the ironshod hooves of their mounts making a loud, echoing thunder as they rode across the wooden bridge that arched the Republican, and never a word between them as they passed the time together.

All the way Roman was thinking that perhaps this meant that somehow he would be included with the cavalry when it went out. He was sure he could keep up, because he'd heard from various quarters that half the men in the regiment had never been on a horse until they enlisted, and these men of the Seventh Cavalry were mostly new men, with the exception of noncommissioned officers. A bartender at the Salamander Saloon in Junction City had told him that if he wanted to have some fun, he should go to the fort on any afternoon and watch the recruits trying to stay on a McClellan saddle.

"And they shoot worse than they ride," the bartender had snorted.

The courier left him beside the reserve herd corral, which puzzled Roman, and he sat there for a long time until finally a small cavalcade came from the rows of sandstone buildings to the north of the stable area. Leading this group of horsemen was a man with flowing blond hair and a well-clipped mustache and beard, a hat with one side of the brim pinned up to the crown, a bright new buckskin jacket with a lot of long fringes, and the shoulder boards of a lieutenant colonel. Although he had seen this man only once, and then with other things on his mind, Roman recognized him as George Armstrong Custer.

Why, hell, Roman thought, he's got more officers following his ass than General Hancock ever has.

Upon arriving at the corral, Custer and his party dismounted smartly, as though they were all on the same string. As Custer approached Roman, the others were two steps behind, and each of them was like the commander, stern-faced and businesslike. The European-style knee-length boots that Custer affected looked a little outlandish. Roman dismounted to meet them, and as Custer walked up stiffly to stand before him, Roman touched the brim of his sweaty slouch hat with two fingers.

"How do, General," he said, although he knew that Custer was no longer a general. He also knew from Leavenworth talk that Custer still considered himself one.

"Sir," Custer said, his voice sharp and high, with a slight stammer in it, "I've called you here to protest your attempt to deliver faulted stock to my regiment!"

Roman didn't like his tone of voice or his manner or the glare of his pale blue eyes. And even less the implication in his words. Why, hell, he thought, I'm not one of his God damned soldiers.

"Well, these horses in this pen aren't your regiment's

horses. They belong to Mr. Elisha Hankins of Leavenworth, Kansas."

"But you brought them here to sell the army later in the year if that becomes necessary," said Custer, and he turned abruptly and gave a hand signal to a pair of enlisted soldiers who had walked up behind the staff group, one carrying a halter. The soldiers bent quickly through the parallel planking of the pen and began to move the horses about until they had a small bay mare isolated from the rest. They pulled the halter over her head and led her to the fence where Custer was standing.

"That horse," Custer said, pointing his finger like a pistol, "is lame."

Roman couldn't believe what he was hearing. He'd been assured by Mr. Hankins that all of these horses had been thoroughly checked before they were loaded on the cars at Leavenworth.

"That can't be," Roman said, but now his anger was punctured and all the air going out of it.

"See for yourself."

By the time Roman got into the corral, the two enlisted men, one of them a troop sergeant, were close on either side of the mare as though they thought she might bolt, although in fact she was standing calm and motionless, her eyes on the saddled cavalry mounts outside the pen.

She was a Morgan, standing about fourteen hands, not nearly as large as Excalibur. She had strong, solid lines and Roman liked the shape of her head, with its large eyes and open, protruding nostrils. He knelt and felt her forelegs, down from the forearm and elbow to the pastern and fetlock. He was frowning, aware that Custer and all of his staff were watching, judging him as he was judging the horse. Custer stood with his arms folded across his chest.

Perfumed son of a bitch, Roman thought.

He led the mare around in small circles, holding the halter in one hand close to her muzzle and crooning to her softly to keep her calm, watching her front hooves in the dust of the corral. It was a rare day of clear skies in that season of rain, and the sun played across the mare's hips like lamplight across good red wine.

Satisfied, he turned the reins over to the troop sergeant and moved back to the corral fence facing Custer.

"I don't know what could have happened," he said. "It's not too plain, but it's there. I think she's got the start of windgalls. That's a good-looking horse to have windgalls."

"Ah," said Custer, his head bobbing. "Then we'll just take her out of here and destroy her."

Roman gave a start, and his anger returned in a rush of color to his face.

"No, you won't destroy her. She's not yours to destroy. I'll take her out of here and lead her to town and ship her back to Leavenworth."

"To sell her off to some quartermaster clerk who wouldn't know a windgall from a healthy fetlock, I suppose?"

Roman bristled, his fists clenching, but he held his temper in check after a few deep breaths, he and the commander of the Seventh Cavalry glaring into one another's eyes.

"All right. That's a fair question. But I can give you my word it won't happen."

"Then to what purpose, sir?"

Roman turned back to look at the mare. He was thinking that Custer was only doing what he was supposed to do, looking to the welfare of his regiment.

"She looks like good Morgan stock," Roman said, still watching the mare. "I think I'll breed her to a stallion I've got."

"And then?"

"Well, we sure as hell won't destroy her." He turned back to Custer, and when he clamped his jaw tight there were little ridges of muscle that stood out along either side of his mouth. "We'll put her to pasture and let her live as long as we can."

"Very well," said Custer, arms still folded across the front of the new buckskin jacket. "See it's done in that manner. I'll be watching your remounts very closely, these horses that come from Mr. Elisha Hankins's pens. The trouble with Mr. Elisha Hankins is that he has become too close to headquarters people who can be taken advantage of. But he must be made aware that he cannot take advantage of me."

Roman's fury boiled up in his throat then, but before he could retort, Custer wheeled to his horse, buckskin fringes flying, and mounted. His staff, still on a single string, did the same, and without a backward look the Golden Cavalier, as the newspapers called him, reined away and galloped off toward the far sandstone buildings from whence he had come, his retinue charging along but falling behind as though it were planned that way.

"Why, that horse's-ass son of a bitch," Roman said aloud, and the troop sergeant, just bending to come between the corral slats, heard him and laughed.

"They's them that say so," he said. "And they's them that don't. But if ole Horse Killer rides like he mostly does, you're gonna need a hell of a lot more horses than this before we're through with the heathen savages this summer."

Roman had hardly arrived back in his hotel room in Junction City after delivering the mare to the stock-shipping agent at the railroad depot when the same broken-English soldier appeared at his door, disturbing him as he paced back and forth muttering to himself and alternately wondering how he'd missed that lame horse and thinking up spicy replies to what Custer had said to him. Only this time there was no need for the trooper to make himself understood. He handed Roman an envelope sealed with red wax and clattered back along the hallway to the stairs, his boot heels making small cannonshot sounds on the bare oak floor.

Inside the envelope was a small card, snow white and inscribed in india ink by the hand of someone who had practiced a lot of penmanship.

Mr. Roman Hasford, Esquire:
You are cordially invited to attend a small social gathering and informal supper at the quarters of General George A. Custer, Fort Riley, Kansas, on the evening

of Saturday, March 16, following the regimental review on the main parade.

It was signed "Mrs. G. A. Custer."
"Well, I'll be damned," Roman said.

By the time Roman Hasford had managed to ship the Morgan mare back to Leavenworth, Mr. Elisha Hankins and Elmer Scaggs had already been instructed in his Western Union telegraph message about what was expected of them. Mr. Hankins was somewhat skeptical, but Elmer Scaggs was as enthusiastic about the project as he always seemed to be about anything his young boss wanted done.

"Hell, Mr. Hankins," Elmer said, "just because that mare's got a touch of windgall don't mean any of her foals is gonna have the same thing. Besides, that damned Excalibur of Roman's needs to get a little pleasure out of life now and again."

So Elmer Scaggs, leaving the work at the hog company to his assistant, Tracy Benson, for the day, and instructing him to be careful and not blow anybody's foot off with the black powder, began a fury of activity at the stockyards, constructing what he called a "honeymoon stall." It was a bottleneck enclosure, narrow at the end where they would tie the mare's head and wider at the other where the railings would parallel her flanks with plenty of room left over for the sire to move around, yet not enough to let him prance and buck too much without coming up solidly against the restraining planks, which had been reinforced to resist his amorous kicking and shying.

"You gotta watch a big stud like that," Elmer explained. "He's liable to get a little frisky, and we don't want that little mare tore up too much."

"Well, she looks pretty good, all right," Mr. Hankins conceded. "Nice color, nice muscle, and a fine head. I'd say she's about six years old, and it looks to me like she's dropped at least one foal."

"All to the good," Elmer said. "Virgin mares needs a lot

of help sometimes, reachin' your hand into that ole puss to get the foal out. But, hell, she'll do fine. She'll be due for heat before long, likely as not, and if we can get a take from the sire, she'll drop that foal in early spring next year, it takin' about eleven months for such things with horses."

"Yes, Elmer, I know that," Mr. Hankins said irritably, because he didn't like hired help telling him things he already knew.

They kept Excalibur and the Morgan mare in adjoining pens so they didn't need to check too closely when she came into estrus. The stallion told them with his whistling and walleyed charging around and his stallionhood extended below his belly. Elmer had returned to his hog yard duties when Mr. Hankins sent one of the other hands for him and he rode to the stockyards on a Hasford Meat and Lard Company mule, whipping the brute along as though he might be a quarter horse.

Elmer took one look at Excalibur and said, "I think he knows what he's supposed to do!"

So they got the mare tied down in the stall and covered her back with blankets to avoid unnecessary damage to her hide from the sire's foreleg hooves, and greased her in the appropriate place with unsalted butter.

"You gotta give him all the help you can," Elmer said. "They ain't too gentle to their lady love sometimes."

Excalibur almost tore down the whole honeymoon stall before they even got him inside and into position. It took Elmer Scaggs and Mr. Hankins and two more stockyard hired men to hold him and get everything in place, and one of the employees complained that if he'd been looking for dangerous work he'd have hired on with the army to go west and shoot at Cheyennes.

Once they had everything positioned, both horses making a great deal of noise, it was over so quickly it surprised everyone, perhaps most of all Excalibur. He stepped down quietly, his snorting and whistling and squealing stilled, and the mare seemed happy that it was finished.

They led the subdued Excalibur to a far pen, well away

from the honeymoon stall. Then they rubbed down the mare and grained her and stabled her in one of the sheds behind the stockyard office where Mr. Hankins kept his buggy team and where Excalibur was kept as well, when the weather was cold.

"We don't want that big son of a bitch too close to her now," Elmer explained, still instructing Mr. Hankins on things he already knew. "She'll stay this way a while and before long, he'll want back at her. Best thing is to get him off somewhere on the other side of the stockyards and hope he forgets about what a good time he had. I'll tell you, Mr. Hankins, if this thing takes, it sure as hell won't be because that stud didn't do his job."

"All right," Mr. Hankins said. "You'd best get back to your job at the meat company."

"Yeah. I wasn't aimin' to lay around here waitin' to see whether we got us a pregnant horse or not. But by God, Mr. Hankins, I think tonight I might take a little visit into town and see a lady I know."

And all the rest of the day, after Elmer Scaggs had gone, Mr. Hankins marveled at the power of suggestion.

Custer parties were famous. And the one held on March 16, 1867, in the sandstone house just north of the stagecoach road between Manhattan and Junction City, which ran directly through Fort Riley, didn't disappoint anyone who attended.

There were the usual regimental commissioned ranks and civilian retainers who were always hanging about Custer and Libbie, including the flamboyant Tom Custer and Lieutenant James Sturgis, with his full lips and innocent eyes, and W. W. Cook, the Seventh Cavalry adjutant who had a beard parted on either side of a clean-shaven chin so that it flowed down across his chest in two outlandish vees, and Captain Myles Keogh, who was a veteran of the Papal Guard in Rome and a decorated hero of the Civil War.

There were two merchants from Junction City with whom Custer was apparently doing some kind of business, and August Bainbridge of the Kansas Railroad, bringing with him from Topeka a lady of considerable reputation as a mandolin player, who wore a deep purple dress with enough lace at collar and neck to make half a dozen sofa doilies, and of course Jared Dane, dressed in a black woolen suit with a knee-length coat and cut broad enough at the waist to conceal the fact that he was armed, which was rather absurd because everyone knew that Jared Dane always went armed, especially when he was accompanying his Boss in such uncivilized places as a frontier army post.

And Tallheimer Smith, a Leavenworth attorney who had been practicing law in Kansas since before the war because he had seen an opportunity there in all the new land acquisitions and arriving settlers, as only a lawyer could see such things. He had established a place for himself in history now by instructing in law at the University of Kansas at Lawrence, a university that consisted of a single two-story sandstone building on a rise above the town, with a cupola at the top, centered, looking very much like the gun turret on a naval ironclad of the recent hostilities.

And there were any number of enlisted dog robbers, who were not members of the party but who made the delightful hospitality possible, wearing dress blues minus the high, beehive helmets with plumes on top, much as French cavalry wore, this being before the French were mauled in the Franco-Prussian war, after which the American army discarded many of the Gallic accoutrements and took up those of the Germans.

And there was Roman Hasford.

Roman was astounded at the change in George Armstrong Custer from that confrontation at the reserve horse corral, when the Golden Cavalier had been icewater and vinegar, haughty and outside the human mold, as Roman saw it. As Roman entered Custer's home, he was struck first by the appearance of his hostess, her hair piled high over an animated face and bearing herself with the self-assurance of a general officer. Custer himself was smiling and cordial, handsome in a hawkish sort of way, extending his hand to all, especially the women, bowing and urbane, completely charming.

"Ah, my young friend," Custer said as he gripped Roman's hand at the door, showing fine teeth and no stammer at all. "My wife and I are honored to have you in our quarters. I do apologize for the spate of rain during the parade this afternoon, but I see you've adequately dried off and can now join in our festivities without discomfort."

There was cold mutton with mint jelly, Boston baked beans, sliced pickled tongue, a cold punch made from sweet apple cider, and an Irish potato salad that Mrs. Custer said she had learned to make in Texas.

The parlor was not spacious, but seemed so because the furniture, running to polished walnut and horsehair-stuffed chairs, had been moved back against the walls, baring a sanded oak floor. The whole place smelled of linseed oil, burning sycamore in the fireplace at one end of the room, and cinnamon. But there was no hint of liquor odor because there was neither wine nor whiskey.

Everyone stood around eating and talking, holding army-issue white china plates in their hands while three dogs as large as young deer wandered about the room sniffing everyone's feet and legs. Roman figured them as wolfhounds of some sort, but he wasn't sure because he'd never seen such dogs before.

Ugly as hell, he thought.

Elizabeth Custer was all about the room, seeing to her guests in the classic manner of great hostesses. Roman was fascinated by her, because she was a handsome woman who carried herself as he imagined Queen Victoria did. Her dress was nothing out of the ordinary, yet her bearing was such that she seemed to give each thread and pearl and button some special, hard-to-define quality.

Why, hell, Roman thought, that dress she's got on might bring a dollar and a half in some mercantile store, but on her it's worth at least ten dollars.

She paused in her rounds once, standing before Roman and smiling. She said she was happy he'd saved the mare that General Custer had told her about.

"Well," Roman said, "I thought she'd make a fine dame, being mostly Morgan like she is."

"And where is she now?" Elizabeth asked.

"Oh, back in the yards at Leavenworth. I expect by now she's already done with the first part of dropping a foal next spring."

He was a little embarrassed at the implications of what he'd said, but Elizabeth Custer continued to smile. Roman would write of her in his diary, "I reckon being in the cavalry all these years has made her understand how important a good horse can be. She is a pretty lady inside and out, and it's too bad she's married to that crazy man. But maybe she sees some horse in him."

The lady from Topeka who had come with Mr. Bainbridge played a few selections on the mandolin, and Roman thought the haunting sounds were more appropriate to hill country covered with hardwood timber than to this place on the plains, where one could stand on the Fort Riley main parade and see the rimrock to the north, and few trees.

For a moment, Roman could hear the foxhounds running in the deep valleys of the White River and smell the honey locust in bloom along the slope of ground before the Hasford farm and see the blue vistas of far hills on those cloudy, damp, yet rainless mornings in the Ozarks, when the only birds willing to advertise their presence were the flocks of crows in the hickory trees behind his father's barn, harshly making it known to all owls in the county that they were ill-tempered and ready for a fight. But he shook it off and concentrated on the delicate movement of the lady's fingers on the strings and frets.

The playing was well received and there was loud applause after her renditions of various European themes never heard before by most of her audience. And when she finished playing, the enlisted men passed among the guests with platters of little coconut pastries.

After the recital there were charades, played mostly by the army officers and their wives, with all the rest watching. It began to rain outside halfway through Tom Custer's attempt to portray the phrase "a rolling stone gathers no moss." The enlisted men passed around cups of hot chocolate while everyone stood about waiting as three enlisted soldiers with violin, banjo, and alto horn took their places in chairs beside the fireplace.

When the dance music began, Custer left the parlor and went into an adjoining room, closing the door behind him. As the dancing progressed, from time to time Elizabeth Custer went into that room, and when she returned she exclaimed to the ladies in ebullient tones that her Beau was the best dancer of all. No one else could judge, because after the charades George Armstrong Custer never came back into the parlor, where his guests sipped their hot chocolate and nibbled the oatmeal cookies left in various containers about the room.

One of the enlisted men was moving among the guests, offering roasted chestnuts in an amber glass compote. Roman recognized him as one of the men who had brought the Morgan mare out of the reserve herd for his inspection.

"Sir," the soldier said, holding out the nut-filled compote with both hands, "I like the way you do things."

That alone was enough to make the evening a success, as far as Roman was concerned. At least to that point.

It was only late into the festivities, approaching eight o'clock, when Tallheimer Smith came to Roman and introduced himself. Smith bulged largely at the front, affected a gold watch chain, and had a goatee of silver-white hair that was like an exclamation point below a tight little mouth with red lips.

"I am the attorney of Mr. Elisha Hankins," he said, "whom I believe is your employer. I am involved now in doing the legal work associated with your venture in the swine business."

"Oh?" said Roman.

"Yes. And this is my daughter, Olivia." The young lady curtseyed and Roman made an awkward bow. "I must tell you that I have seldom seen a young man with the foresight you have displayed in this business of the hogs. Perhaps you'd like to dance with my daughter."

So he danced with Olivia Smith and found that she stepped on his feet less than Victoria Cardin ever had.

"Mr. Hasford," she said, her hand on his shoulder, "which church do you attend in Leavenworth?"

"Well, I haven't quite made up my mind yet."

"If I may be so bold, would you come with Daddy and me some Sunday to services? We're Methodists."

"My family are all Methodists, too. I knew you weren't a Baptist. You dance too good."

She laughed then, and suddenly he found her less horsey and in fact attractive.

"We have a lot of social things."

"Well, maybe after we've got this army campaign finished for the summer."

Later still, Roman went to Jared Dane, who was standing behind the soldier ensemble with a cigar in his mouth and a cup of chocolate in his left hand. He always keeps the right hand free, Roman thought.

"Good evening, Roman Hasford," said Jared Dane, his eyes as dead as they usually were, hardly reflecting any of the light from the many lamps about the room. He watched the people, Roman noted, as though he were casually observing snakes in a rock pit, without any sense of being a part of the same breed.

They spoke of casual things like the weather and next year's elections, and Jared Dane said he would bet a lot on Grant's being elected President. It didn't matter to Roman one way or the other.

But then at last Jared Dane stared at Roman with some spark of life in his eyes.

"Whom do you know in Leavenworth," he asked, "who is connected with the Kansas state militia?"

"State militia?" Roman thought of Crider Peel, but had no desire to acknowledge any such acquaintance, and so avoided it. "Not much of anybody."

"Do you know Major William Claken?"

"Well, I know he's commander of the militia unit in Leavenworth."

"I'm very interested in those people," said Jared Dane, placing his cup carefully on a polished sideboard. "Being close to Fort Leavenworth as they are, they must be in tune, so to speak, with the military situation in Kansas."

"I suppose that's so," Roman said.

"Yes. It's so. And there are men among them who have knowledge of various moneys coming out of Topeka for militia purposes." Dane's eyes had taken on a deep light, intense and sharp-edged. "You know all about our good Governor Crawford. When he perceives an Indian scare, he calls up militia units and pays for it from the state treasury, and afterward sends a bill to the national Congress. And most generally he gets his reimbursement from the Federal taxpayer."

"I suppose that's so," Roman said, completely in the dark as to where this was leading.

"Yes. It's so. At various times and at various places, militia money is in repose." Jared Dane laughed, a short, abrupt, harsh sound, yet so quiet that it was obviously meant for Roman and no one else in the crowded room. "These funds are in the safe boxes of the Boss, waiting to be spent. Everybody trusts the express company safe boxes. But on more than one occasion, somebody knew that money was there and took it. All of which makes the Boss and his safe boxes appear less safe. This disturbs me a great deal."

"I can understand that," Roman said, beginning to get the implications of this talk. "I've read about robberies in the newspapers."

"Of course. Everybody has. Now I don't care a tinker's damn about that militia money. What I care about is that people might come to think they can't trust the express company to safeguard their funds."

"I can see that. Maybe some people would think their cash was safer in a hole in the ground."

"Exactly! And what I want you to tell me is this. How, in each of those robbery cases, did someone know the militia money was there in those express offices?"

"Somebody's been telling the robbers."

"Exactly! Somebody who knows the money's there. And

you can bet your hog farm that the one telling is having his share."

"You know about the hogs?"

Jared Dane leaned back against the wall, the twist of a smile at the corners of his mouth, but only at the corners.

"My God, Roman Hasford, don't you know by now that nothing in this state happens that the Boss doesn't know about?"

"Well," said Roman, shrugging, "I suppose so."

Now Dane was watching the dancers again, all the light gone from his eyes once more, as though he'd opened a curtain for a moment and then closed it.

"Of course, there's something else," he said. He lifted his dead cigar to his lips and clamped it between his teeth. "So far, there's been two of our people killed, and that disturbs me, too.

"So if you get some hint about who's marking the 'X' on our safe boxes, let me know. We're not talking about robbery alone. We're talking about murder, and I intend to find out who needs hanging.

"Well, I see the Boss is about ready to leave. I'd best go tell Mrs. Custer what a hell's-fire time I've had. Stay out of the rain, Roman Hasford."

Roman didn't have much time to think about what Jared Dane had said. Not then, anyway. The guests were all leaving and Mrs. Custer was bidding them a safe journey at the open door. The Golden Cavalier was still behind the closed door of the adjoining room.

Roman found himself in the line of guests leaving the Custer quarters immediately behind Tallheimer Smith and his daughter. Later he decided that this had been by Smith's design. After he had taken Libbie Custer's hand and expressed his appreciation for having been asked to her party, he walked onto the wide veranda, where the attorney was waiting for him.

"Mr. Hasford," Smith said, turning to Roman at the top of the stairs and stroking his white goat whiskers, which sprouted above his triple chins like horseradish, "I waited until this time to say it because it seemed more appropriate now than it would have been earlier. I have come directly from Leavenworth to this place. Mr. Hankins has asked that I instruct you to return at once."

"Return? If he wanted me back, why didn't he send a telegraph message?"

"Each penny saved goes on the right side of the ledger," said Tallheimer Smith, adjusting his tall silk hat on a head of flowing hair that fell to cover his ears. Roman thought it looked absurd here in the Wild West. "He said to tell you that he will come out to do the fieldwork and he wants you to manage the stockyards while he's away."

"Hell," Roman snorted, then touched the flopping brim of his slouch hat and made a little bow to Olivia, who was standing just behind her father, looking very horse-faced now that she was not smiling. "Pardon me, ma'am."

Tallheimer Smith continued to stroke his goatee and the three chins as well, frowning and staring down at the rain-splattered porch floor.

"You see, Mr. Hankins received a communication from General Custer to the effect that he, General Custer, could not trust you to do business with his regiment in the matter of remounts. Well, then, my message is delivered, and so good night to you, sir."

Roman stood on the Custer veranda, looking out into the rain. Officers and their ladies were hurrying along, capes pulled over their heads, going to post quarters near the Custer house. Civilians were climbing awkwardly into covered buggies that would return them to Junction City. Hitched to the rail fence along the Manhattan-Junction City road was his reserve herd horse, head down, its saddle glistening wet in the glow from a kerosene light at the gate.

"Why, that son of a bitch," he said softly. He pulled the collar of his coat up around his neck and stepped out into the rain, knowing that his chance of getting out to see any Cheyenne this summer had been foreclosed by George Armstrong Custer.

12

It was so bad I'd as soon not even talk about it," Emil Durand said in August, after he'd returned from the Hancock campaign, and was having a cool lemonade with Roman Hasford and Mr. Elisha Hankins in the stockyard office. The lemonade came in a small crock jar delivered each day of the hot season from Spankin's kitchen, along with a tray of ginger snaps or sugar cookies.

"No, sir, I'd as soon talk about all them fine hogs you got down by the creek, Roman."

Durand was holding his false teeth in one hand, shaking them like dice as he sipped lemonade and sucked on the cookies of the day because, as he explained in great detail, he liked cookies better when he just gummed them so they melted in his mouth like snow.

"No, sir, I'd as soon not talk about that campaign," he repeated, and then went on to talk about it.

Roman and Mr. Hankins were hanging on Durand's words because he was the first person they had had an opportunity to hear who actually rode against the Cheyennes during the past summer. Through it all, Min stood immobile against the wall near the door, yet there was a startling light in her eyes as she seemed to stare constantly at Roman's face.

"My wife never got into the hang of cookies and other civilized things," Durand explained.

"So, we started at Fort Larned, down on the Arkansas. The general rode his whole army down there because they was this big village close by on the Salt Fork, Cheyenne and Sioux. He went out to talk to some of their headmen and they had a few chats, but the headmen was unsettled about it because the general wanted to talk at night and the savages never talk serious things at night.

"Anyway. Right in amongst this chattin', the general taken his whole army right up to the edge of this village and it scared the dogshit out of them people and everybody run off, just leavin' all their truck behind in the lodges. Spooky thing, all them lodges standin' and nobody around. Just the wind blowin' and the general cussin'.

"So, when the general seen them empty lodges, he says to the Injun agents that it looked to him like a war had commenced. Well, it had, all right. Because the general and his soldiers had caused it, ridin' up on them folks with all their women and children. I allow they remembered Sand Creek, you see?

"We found a few old people left in the lodges. And this young girl. One of the general's surgeons said she'd been raped and then everybody started accusin' everybody else that they'd done it. The agents said the sojurs done it and the army said the savages done it. Anyway, she died right away. She wasn't no white girl, I know that. But I only saw her oncet, just a minute I seen her. I reckoned her about fourteen years old.

"So the general set Custer off after them as had run off. Then we heerd there was all this burnin' and killin' along the Smoky Hill and so the general said we'd burn that Salt Fork village and we done it and all the truck inside the lodges like they need to live. Stuff they'd made over the years, and cured hides and pemmican and suchlike. So then we heerd there was even more smokin' and shootin' along the Smoky Hill, and all them army people was too Gawd damned dumb to understand why.

"Anyway, the general, he talked to a few more chiefs like Pawnee Killer and Roman Nose. I thought you all'd be happy to hear he talked to a man called Roman Nose. Because of his name, like yours."

Emil Durand waved his lemonade cup in Roman's direction.

"Anyway, we talked to some more chiefs. This big Kiowa named Satanta. A mean, nasty man, but sugar in his mouth when he wants to be sweet. The general give him an officer's coat with shoulder boards and all. And a little afterward, Satanta showed how happy it made him by stealing all the army's horses outa the corral at Fort Dodge. They tell me Satanta likes to blow this old bugle he's got, but I never heerd it done.

"Then the general and his infantry and wagon guns come back home, but he leaves Custer out to chase down the savages. The general sent me along with Custer, which suited me about like green persimmons, and him and his boys got into a few skirmishes but nothin' that was too serious. We went up to Fort McPherson on the Platte, then made a long loop into Colorado Territory, almost to the South Platte, and then come back down to Fort Wallace. Mostly hard ridin'. Time we got to Wallace, the horses was about dead and the men not much better off.

"Right in the middle of all this, some of the boys started desertin' and it made Custer furious mad. He sent a detail after some of 'em and they killed one and wounded two others, which wasn't likely to make the rest of the troops love Custer too much.

"But sojurs they got out here are mostly dumb. I don't care how bad a man hates his outfit, anybody'd desert and go wanderin' off when he's out in western Kansas right in the middle of a Cheyenne war is dumb. Hell, look what happened to Kidder."

In late June, Lieutenant Lyman Kidder, with ten troopers and a Sioux scout, had departed Fort Sedgewick in Colorado Territory with dispatches for the Seventh Cavalry, which was operating then along the Republican River. Kidder never got there. What was left of his body and those of the ten troopers and the Sioux scout was found some time later.

"Did you see the pitchers they had in that *Harper's Weekly?*" Durand said, still rolling his false teeth in one hand. "There's all them Kidder boys on the ground and each one's got at least two dozen arrows in him. Them pitchers was drawed by a man named Howland, who was with Hancock when the campaign started. A feisty greenhorn who had on some brand-new St. Louis buckskins and was carryin' a Colt pistol like he knowed what the hell's goin' on out here.

"You know how long it takes to make a single arrow? I've set in Crow lodges in the wintertime and watched the old men do it. Gotta find the right kinda wood, hone it down with sandstone, and sometimes season it with heat and shape it with your hands, then glue on the vane and splice the arrowhead into the business end and tie it with sinew and then make all the tribal designs on it or the medicine won't work. Hell, it takes five or six hours just to do one arrow, and that's after you've got the right wood."

He drained his lemonade cup and slammed it down on Mr. Hankins's desk for emphasis.

"But this Howland drawer showed all them arrows just left to rot in them bodies. They ain't a buck on the plains who'd ride off and leave arrows like that. You don't go down to the mercantile store and buy the damned things.

"Anyway, when me and Custer got to Fort Wallace he up and leaves his regiment there, which suited most of them fine, and him and a few sojurs and me took the best horses Wallace could give us and come on to Fort Harker and then he takes the train back to Fort Riley to see his wife."

"For which General Hancock court-martialed him," said Mr. Hankins with some satisfaction. "And he was convicted and sentenced to a year's suspension of service without pay."

"Which likely satisfies a lot of sojurs in the Seventh Cavalry," said Durand.

"Yes, but which don't satisfy Phil Sheridan a damned bit," Mr. Hankins said.

"That's right. Phil Sheridan, who's on his way to take

General Hancock's place at Fort Leavenworth, so it's rumored. And I'd bet a mangy otter pelt that Custer won't stay gone no year or nothin' like it.

"So now I've heerd they decided to stop shootin' and start talkin'," Durand said.

"There was a resolution passed in Congress," said Mr. Hankins. "So this fall there's going to be a big Peace Commission sent out here, and I don't know what that means, but, by God, we'll sell a lot of horses and wagons to 'em, Roman."

"I hope they got somebody who can draw better than that Howland fella," Durand said. He slipped his teeth back into his mouth with one quick, easy motion and turned and looked at his Crow wife, still standing with her luminous eyes fixed on Roman's face. "By Gawd. That heathen savage of mine can't stop lookin' at you, Roman. She's told me you're the prettiest white man she's ever saw. Except me, of course."

So after all of Roman Hasford's anticipation and expectation of excitement with Hancock's campaign, there was nothing much to remember from it except that a Crow squaw thought he was pretty. He knew it was an even greater disappointment for General Hancock. Roman couldn't help feeling compassion for the general, though he knew Hancock hardly at all. He seemed a nice man even though he was a Yankee whose soldiers had likely tried to kill Martin Hasford at one time or another on the battlefields of Virginia. It made Roman feel a little guilty, admiring a man who had been his father's mortal enemy.

He wrote in his diary, "I don't know why I am always being ashamed over thoughts about Papa. I wonder if he is ever ashamed when he thinks about me. I wonder if the way he acted after he came home from the war was maybe partly because of something I did."

Everyone agreed the Cheyenne campaign had been a dreadful fizzle. And now a Peace Commission was taking shape to make its trek into hostile country, on the northern plains and in Kansas as well, the preparations being documented in great detail by the newspapers, some of which Roman had formed the habit of reading each night before bedtime, sitting under his dried-finger necklace and lamp and trying not to listen to Mr. Moffet's protests about the Anglicans exporting their ideas from Victoria's realm into America, or some such topic.

"The Church of England is as devious as the church of the Pope." So said Mr. Moffet. Roman could never see that it made much damn difference. He often wondered what Mr. Moffet's reaction might be if he suddenly exclaimed that he had become a Hindu. He wasn't sure what a Hindu was, but he knew it had nothing to do with Methodism, which Mr. Moffet extolled constantly, to the irritation of Roman and all the other boarders at Mrs. Condon Murphy's.

"Mrs. Murphy," Roman said to the mistress of the house, "Mr. Moffet is a kind and gentle man and full of virtue, but he is driving me crazy. May I have a room to myself? I'd pay the extra cost."

"As soon as one becomes available, dear boy," she said, patting his shoulder. "Now come in the kitchen with me. I've just gotten a keg of bock beer." That was in the spring.

Since then, Roman had not mentioned it again, but from time to time Mrs. Murphy caught his eye over her breakfast biscuits and smiled and nodded, and he knew she had not forgotten.

That summer it was hot and dry and the dust marked all the streets of Leavenworth with a powdery cloud that smelled like chalk. Victoria Cardin was still off in the East, in New York or wherever it was, and Roman did his work at the hog pens, where there were a lot of brood sows heavy with pigs in their bellies, as Elmer Scaggs put it, and he bargained for mules and wagons because Mr. Hankins, with his usual wisdom in such things, had decided that when the Peace Commission came to Fort Leavenworth, and it would surely come, opportunity waited for those with foresight.

"They'll have a lot of truck to carry along and a lot of gifts for the tribes," he explained to Roman. "Now the army's responsible for escorting them around, and General Sherman has already said that every commander is supposed to support them. But hell, son, the army don't keep enough mules and wagons to take care of the problem."

The Morgan mare was with foal, no doubt about that, a bright omen in what had been a dismal time. But they had to wrap her forelegs in burlap every day and keep her as quiet as they could so she would have a chance of coming to maturity with Excalibur's offspring before she got so bad they had to destroy her.

"There's gotta be something we can do for that mare," said Roman.

"Not much that anybody's figured out yet," Mr. Hankins said. "Once a horse gets that far gone with what she's got, it's just a matter of time. At least bad fetlocks hadn't ought to affect her rear end, so we'll just have to wait and hope that foal comes before she gets so she can't stand on her own front feet."

Orvile Tucker, the Negro smith who did all of Mr. Hankins's hoof work, told Roman it hurt the mare like hell to keep her forefeet shod, so Roman instructed him to forget the metal shoes and wrap her feet each day along with the fetlocks. But she'd been shod all her life, and without the metal pinning she moved very gingerly around the little pen they had for her next to the blacksmith shop.

Orvile Tucker was Roman's mainstay in the business of the mare, once Elmer Scaggs and Mr. Hankins had taken care of her love life. He seemed to understand better than anyone else what it meant, not only to Roman but to the horse. As he said one afternoon when he was a little drunk from elderberry wine and growing overly sentimental, because that's what elderberry wine does to a man sometimes, the mare had a lot of light in her eyes and he knew it meant a will to make it through to the time of dropping in the spring.

"By the Lord, Mr. Hasford," he said, his eyes so red one might expect blood to start running down his cheeks, "that Morgan mare's got more gumption than any horse I ever seen."

Orvile Tucker and Roman spent a lot of time together that

summer, with Roman standing beside the hot forge and sometimes pumping the bellows. Or else, after the day's work of fitting shoes to all the mules Roman was bringing into the yards, they squatted under the shade of the smithy and watched the Morgan mare in her little pen nearby.

So reticent had the Negro man been that when he first knew him Roman thought him mute. But slowly, Orvile Tucker had begun to talk, and now it was a constant stream flowing from his wide mouth. He had learned the smithing trade, he said, in western Tennessee when he was a slave, but two years before the war he had run away, leaving a wife and three children and a master who had been kind enough at least to allow him to learn something other than grubbing in a white man's fields. He'd made his way north and east, helped all along by various people who would become known as stationmasters on the Underground Railroad.

"So I come to Kansas to make my fortune puttin' shoes on the animals," he told Roman in his soft, liquid voice, which almost had a color to it, a color like his skin of pure milk chocolate, shining with his sweat. "I come to Kansas to see the whole world, like you done, Mr. Hasford."

"You left your children?" Roman asked.

And Orvile Tucker, watching the mare and smiling, shook his head. There were beads of sweat in his bushy hair, like clear pearls on black coral.

"Oh, Mr. Hasford, I think about that. But freedom was what I had to have." He wiped a large, well-veined hand across his full lips. "Sometimes freedom ain't so good, either. But it's better than what I had."

"If you'd stayed just a few more years, you'd all been free."

"Oh, Mr. Hasford, I thought about that, too. But even one more day was too much."

"Did your master whip you?"

"Only now and then." Tucker laughed softly. "But that wasn't what it was. It was somethin' else I can't even tell you or myself. It was freedom. It was like a handful of dirt you can hold in your hand and know it all belongs to you."

Roman also learned that this blacksmith shop had been financed by Mr. Elisha Hankins solely on the word of a brawny but ragged Negro who had come by the stockyard one day and claimed to be the best smith in western Tennessee before he'd run away.

"Well, hell," Mr. Hankins explained, "he had the arms for it. You know, there's something about a well-muscled colored man that reminds me of a tiger cat I saw once back east, before the war. This was a black tiger cat, all ripples and light."

It had been a long time since Roman had gone to Sunday worship. He reckoned his listening to Mr. Moffet each night was as good as hearing three or four sermons a week. But now he began to attend the Methodist church with Tallheimer Smith and his daughter. He and the goateed attorney walked on either side of the blushing Olivia down to one of the front pews in the little white frame building with its belfry, at the end of Miami Street.

The preacher, a Reverend Hezekiah Sample, was less of a hell fire-and-brimstoner than Roman had expected him to be, and it felt rather good to be sitting there with the summer sun coming through the south windows and the smell of lilac water all about him, singing the hymns, putting his dime in the passing plate, trying to keep from dozing in the final minutes before the benediction. Even though he knew that church was not the place for pride, he was satisfied with the way he looked in his new seersucker suit and silk necktie and low-topped shoes that laced instead of buttoning.

Of course, the experience recalled for him the times at home when a circuit parson came to the valley of Little Sugar Creek, and Martin Hasford would take his family to the services in Leetown. They always went in the spring wagon drawn by the little bay mare, which Calpurnia and Allan Pay had later ridden off to Missouri after they were married. Martin Hasford had been away at the war then, and Roman wondered if perhaps his father would not have allowed the horse to leave the farm had he been there.

Sometimes after the Sunday services he went to the Smith home for dinner, and usually the Reverend Hezekiah Sample was there as well, popping the fried chicken into his mouth and making noises about the Pope, just as Mr. Moffet did at the boardinghouse. But what Roman failed to gain in spiritual inspiration he made up for with Olivia's cooking, which was just as good as he ever had at the Hankinses' and a lot better than Sunday meals at Mrs. Condon Murphy's, which had a reputation for lack of imagination.

On Independence Day the church sponsored a picnic on one of the sandbars along the Missouri River south of town, and Roman bought Olivia's box lunch at the auction, which everyone seemed to expect him to do, and they sat together in the dark shade of the black willows and ate the dried-peach pie and talked about the Indian War and life after death and meadowlarks.

He attended a punch party that summer, held in the unfinished parsonage next to the church building. Everyone stood about drinking apple cider and munching pound cake and then there was square dancing—as opposed to round dancing. Roman reckoned that the church couldn't afford to put its name to round dancing, as the Custers could, what with bodies coming dangerously close together sometimes during the course of the movements.

Roman wasn't sure when it occurred to him that maybe Olivia and her father and everybody else in the Methodist congregation expected that after a proper time he and Olivia would become engaged to be married, since she was the respected maiden daughter of a respected father who was a widower and made a lot of money, and Roman was a rising businessman with good manners. It scared the hell out of him, so he stopped making a regular thing of the Sunday visits to the church and to the Smiths'.

He wrote in his diary, "She's a very nice lady, but some word might be said that could be misrepresented somehow and then she and her papa could put meanings to things that aren't there and I'd be hooked. I am not ready to be hooked by Olivia Smith."

So the summer went down toward autumn, with Roman falling into a pattern of behavior: Mrs. Condon Murphy's

breakfast to stockyards to hog pens and smokehouse to supper at Mr. Hankins's to bedroom at the boardinghouse, there
to sit for a while before the open window, where some breeze
and smell of water might be coming from the river to help cool
him as he listened to Mr. Moffet's sermons, all the while
thinking in these gentle hours of early darkness only of Victoria Cardin and when she might return.

It was the summer that Crider Peel's life began to close in on
him. And he knew that some changes had to be made, not because of any pangs of conscience about anything he'd done,
but because of fear that he was about to be caught up and held
accountable.

Fear had always been a part of Crider Peel's life, as much
as breathing or drinking water. For as long as he could remember, he had been apprehensive in the company of any
person larger than himself, either physically or intellectually.
In the classic manner of bullies he therefore let out his frus-
trations against those whom he knew he could brutalize,
which didn't include very many people other than his own
daughter.

But in the summer of 1867 the fear began to overcome all
other thinking. He could see a hangman's noose in his hazy,
liquor-soaked dreaming; even worse, he thought of it all day
as he went about his duties at the icehouse and the tannery.
His customary response to such pressures had been the bottle and wild orgies of violence against Catrina, but those no
longer worked.

And so he decided that something had to be done to eliminate the apprehension and the danger.

Crider Peel knew that Sequal and Tanner were in Leavenworth. He saw them almost every night in the Owl Head
Saloon at the corner of Delaware and First streets. They were
there from the Indian Territory, waiting for his signal that a
fat strong box was in some Kansas railroad express office. It
was a routine that Crider Peel had played out before, and he
knew all its movements, but this thing that had begun as a

marvelously beneficial adjunct to his meager pay at the ice-house and tannery had become the peril of his life.

In recent days, Sequal and Tanner had not favored him with friendly glances as he passed them each night standing at the Owl Head bar, and he knew it was because the information they waited for was not forthcoming. Such looks from men like these did little to calm him.

He knew their capacity for violence. They were what would have been called "border ruffians" during the Bleeding Kansas days. In fact, at that time, they had been exactly that, hiring to anyone with the proper amount of money, no matter the side or the cause. Now they operated out of the Indian Territory immediately south of the Kansas line, a part of that large body of men who took refuge in the Five Civilized Tribe Nations because there was little white law there. Staying in Leavenworth or any other organized town gave them the itch, and Crider Peel knew this. But he also knew, now that he'd made his decision, that they could be the instrument of his relief.

Sequal and Tanner were the only names Crider Peel knew for these men. But he knew their dimensions. Sequal was a large, ruddy-complected man with slack lips and a vacant stare, and some said he depended absolutely on his companion, Tanner, who was as small as Crider Peel but who had a hardness about his mouth and eyes that was enough to make decent citizens give way to him on the sidewalks.

These two disdained the town's comforts, and while they were in Leavenworth they slept each night along the river, rolled in a single blanket, even though the town was large enough to absorb them without suspicion. But now the year was turning toward cold weather, which would make sleeping along the river on some sandbar uncomfortable, and they were becoming increasingly impatient with Crider Peel's failure to bring them the information they wanted.

On the night that he reached his decision, Crider Peel walked into the Owl Head Saloon as always, and passing the two bushwhackers at the bar, he gave his signal, a touch of his fingers to the brim of his hat. Later, when he left the saloon and walked to the back of the tannery and waited on the loading dock there, the two men from the Indian Territory were close behind.

There was a lemon-yellow full moon, and it illuminated Crider Peel's face and glinted in his dark eyes. The other two wore wide-brim hats and their faces were in deep shadow, so Crider Peel was unable to see their expressions, which made him frightfully timorous. The two men loomed before him like the cigar-store Indian in front of the Seventh Street tobacconist, stolid, immobile, and hostile, Tanner standing immediately in front of the larger Sequal. There was about them the smell of snuff and old sweat and, to Crider Peel, a hint of acid, indefinable but repugnant.

"All right, Peel," said Tanner.

His voice was like a harsh whisper because he had been wounded in the throat in some gone year when a man with a knife took exception to his display of cards in a euchre game in Sedalia, Missouri, and tried to remove his head from his body.

"It's took you a long time, friend."

"I can't help it," Crider Peel said, then turned and walked the length of the dock and peered off into the darkness to ensure that no one was there. He came back to Sequal and Tanner, who remained in the moonlight without movement. "This is something else."

"What else?"

"There's a man who works for the railroad. He's been in and out of town, nosin' into things. Sometimes he's got a couple of Pinkerton detectives with him. They smell something, boys, and it could send us all to the rope."

"What is it they smell?"

"I don't know. They've talked to ole Major Claken and out at the fort, I don't know who-all they've talked to."

"Major Claken?"

"Sure, you know. The militia commander here."

"Maybe they're lookin' to enlist."

Sequal's large shoulders shook with silent laughter.

"This is a serious thing," Crider Peel said. "They're askin' all these questions."

"Just mind you don't give 'em no answers."

"Hell, they ain't talked to me."

"If they do, don't give 'em no answers," Tanner wheezed, then coughed and cleared his damaged throat and spat off toward the edge of the dock, making a silvery thread of liquid through the moonlight.

"But somebody could say something," said Crider Peel, and he reached to Tanner's coat but then drew his hand back quickly.

"You stay mum, Peel."

"You know I wouldn't tell nothin'," Crider Peel whispered. "But this is a bad man."

With his hands shaking, he took a cigar from a vest pocket, and the flare of his match turned the dark shapes of the two faces under the slouch hats to brilliant orange for an instant before the flame was gone. Crider Peel puffed rapidly at the stogie, inhaling great mouthfuls of smoke. His forehead and cheeks glistened with sweat.

"He's smart, too, and . . ."

The two dark figures waited silently for Crider Peel to continue, but he only puffed the cigar, his fingers twitching as he seemed to caress it, his teeth shining as he clamped it, almost biting off the end.

"Peel, if this man got you in a room with a barrel stave, I reckon you'd have a lot to say, wouldn't you?"

"No, no," Crider Peel whimpered, his voice rasping as though he might be trying to imitate Tanner. "No, I wouldn't do that. But this man has got to be . . ."

He couldn't say it, and the other two waited, watching him mouth the cigar, watching the dense clouds of smoke lift like an ice balloon, blue-white in the moonlight.

"He's gotta be killed," said Tanner casually, as he would say *I'm thirsty*.

"Yes," Crider Peel said, and they could hardly hear him.

"Then why don't you kill him?"

"Me? My God, I ain't even got a weapon," Crider Peel said, trying to keep the desperation out of his voice.

"Yeah, all you can do is soak up whiskey and weasel for us so we can do the work and then you take a share."

"But don't you understand? I'll pay you to do it."

Sequal and Tanner were silent for a long time, but they gave no indication that it was a proposition that was in any way unusual.

"It's for all of us," said Peel.

"Yeah, except it's you seems so Gawd damned anxious to get it done. Well, how much?"

"How much?"

"Yeah, how much? You said you'd pay. How much?"

"Fifty dollars. I'd give you fifty dollars."

Sequal grunted and Tanner turned his head toward the larger man and laughed, a harsh little sound in his cut throat.

"Sweet Jesus, Peel, you think me and my friend's gonna do Jared Dane for just fifty dollars?"

"You knew who I was talkin' about?"

"Who the hell'd you figure we'd think it was? Governor Crawford? Shit! Jared Dane for fifty dollars! We'd have to stalk that son of a bitch like a panther."

"It's for all of us," said Peel. "But all right. How much, then?"

Tanner stood silently, breathing hard, and behind him Sequal shifted from one foot to the other. Crider Peel heard a dog barking somewhere close by in the town, and along the river there was a steamboat whistle, all of it from another world, as though breaking into this capsule of colorless light that held the three of them on the tannery dock.

"We'll do it for a hundred."

"All right. All right," Crider Peel said, almost laughing with relief.

"Where's the money?"

"I'll have to get it. But I'll get it. You stay in town, maybe a day or two. Then I'll have it. And after you do it, there's another thing."

"I thought there might be another thing," said Tanner.

"After you do it, you ride down to the Territory and you tell your headman that I'm finished with all this. I ain't gonna say anything about what's gone before, but I can't do no more for him. I got a little girl to raise."

Tanner turned away, and Crider Peel could see his teeth glowing in a sardonic smile.

"Yeah, you yellow-backed son of a bitch, I figured that'd be the other thing. But you get the money, and when you do, Jared Dane's a dead man."

Crider Peel was soaked with sweat from his head to the crotch of his underwear, and he heaved air into his lungs as he watched the two dark figures move noiselessly along the loading dock and off into the night.

"God," he whispered aloud. "A hundred dollars!"

Crider Peel didn't have a hundred dollars. He didn't even have fifty. The last time he'd seen such money was after the affair at Bonner Springs, and all of that had long since disappeared into the cash drawers at the Owl Head and other such establishments. But he already knew where he might get it because there was Catrina, and he knew now how he could use her.

When Crider Peel went to the only man he knew who might advance him a hundred dollars, Roman Hasford was at the stockyards, grading out mules just brought into the pens by one of Mr. Hankins's Missouri agents. Elmer Scaggs was there, up from the meat company to report on the brood sows, and Orville Tucker was with Elmer and they were discussing the merits of pickled pig's feet and sweetbreads, the former being a thing Orville Tucker could recall as a delicacy when he was a slave and the latter being a thing Elmer Scaggs called "white butter," fit only to be fed to the surviving hogs.

"Well, sometimes we'd get sweetbreads because in the white fambly where I was at, they never eat no sweetbreads," Orville Tucker was saying.

"Damned smart white family," said Elmer. "Now, when I eat hog, I want some substance to put my teeth into. Like pork chops or ham."

"Sweetbreads mighty tasty in white gravy."

"That's the trouble with you niggers," said Elmer. "You cover somethin' up with white gravy and it's good."

"Mr. Scaggs," said Orvile Tucker, laughing his soft, liquid laugh, "you got an indelicate tongue."

And after Crider Peel advanced his proposition, Roman Hasford said, "Why, hell, what would you do with a hundred dollars?"

And Crider Peel, bowing and scraping as though Roman were at least a Federal senator, explained that with cold weather coming on, his little daughter needed some clothes and shoes, warm and satisfying, and he was immediately rewarded with a look on Roman Hasford's face that told him he had struck home.

"It's been a bad summer, Mr. Hasford," Crider Peel said. "Now I'm a little short and I need to buy some pretty things for that pretty little girl."

"My God, you could buy her half of Leavenworth with a hundred dollars."

"There's grub as well. And I'll pay back every penny, over time, because that's the only way I can, just a working man like I am."

Crider Peel knew that Roman Hasford knew that none of that hundred dollars would ever be seen again, but it was a charity Roman Hasford could not resist. So reasoned Crider Peel, and he was right.

"You'd drink it all away," said Roman.

"No, I'll do the best with it that I can."

And as Roman Hasford looked into his eyes, with Elmer Scaggs and Orvile Tucker just behind him, both huge and, to Crider Peel, menacing and malignant, it was a time to sweat almost as heavily as on the moonlit night when he'd stood before those two assassins from the Indian Territory.

"I'll have to go to the express office and get the money," Roman said, and Crider Peel, his black eyes glinting suddenly because he knew that now his problems were resolved, reached out and took Roman's hand in both of his and shook it violently, babbling his appreciation.

But on the walk back into town, Crider Peel began to

think of Roman Hasford making a visit to his mule-pen home to see for himself if any clothes or grub had been bought with his generosity. And it frightened Crider Peel, because he could see in his mind the hands and arms of Elmer Scaggs and Orvile Tucker, who were Roman Hasford's friends. They were likely willing to break faces and backs at his demand.

And so, because of this fear, he decided he would stop drinking, at least for a while, and use his earned money for a pair of shoes and a pinafore or two and maybe a petticoat and stockings and a coat for the child.

He was afraid of Roman Hasford because he sensed some antagonism there, and this young man who had come to Leavenworth as a gangling youth was no longer so gangling, taking on weight each day, it seemed, about the arms and shoulders. And of course there was his friend Elmer Scaggs and even that colored man, Orvile Tucker. Nor was it lost on Crider Peel that the first time he had seen Roman Hasford the young man was in the company of Tyne Fawley, and unless he was blind drunk, the very thought of Tyne Fawley terrified Crider Peel to a greater extent than all the others put together.

He was surrounded by evil shapes and forces, each waiting to devour him for the slightest excuse, and all of them beyond his control—that is, until this most recent brilliant idea, namely the hiring of professional assassins to dispatch Jared Dane, which had a double dimension. It would halt Dane's inquiries and it would please Tyne Fawley to understand that Crider Peel had a lot of guts. And initiative. And his resolve to use whiskey money to buy a few things for Catrina would mollify Roman Hasford, who was not an uncivilized man like all the others.

That same night Roman wrote in his diary, "Well, I can only hope the money goes to the good cause he outlined. What's money for, if not for such benevolent purposes?"

13

The Peace Commission came, and it helped Roman Hasford through late September and all of October, because there was so much to do that he didn't have the time or energy to think very long about Victoria Cardin before he fell into a deep sleep each night, the dronings of Mr. Moffet still in his ear. And it also gave him an excellent excuse to ignore the little notes that came frequently from Olivia Smith on blue and pink stationery, inviting him to attend a pie supper or choir practice or the coming Sunday's worship. Each of these with the hint of wonderful food, as though Roman were starving, which he resented a little.

Why, hell, he thought, if I want beefsteak I can buy it any time I want, same as her papa can!

He was buried in work, getting the wagons and mules and supplies and arranging for them to be shipped to end-of-track at Ellsworth. And besides all that, he was helping to purchase items on the accounts current of Mr. John Sanborn, who was the Peace Commission commissary officer. Among those items were things unavailable in Leavenworth, such as canned lobster and French wine. These Mr. Sanborn shipped by rail from St. Louis. They were intended for the civilian and military members of the commission.

Other things Roman could find: Irish potatoes, cured hams, bacon, and hardtack purchased through the commissary department of the army, dessicated vegetables from the same source because nobody else would eat them, and canned sardines. All of this truck was for the Indians and teamsters and the press corps, of which there were eight men, and for the members of the commission on a daily basis, when they tired of the lobster and French wine.

And a lot of dried beans and plug tobacco, and nine one-gallon kegs of applejack, which were listed in the accounts current as brandy. Commission members were expected to bring their own spirits. Indians and teamsters were expected not to drink anything so strong, which Roman and everyone else associated with the enterprise recognized as absurd. On special occasions, certain chiefs might be given a sip. Teamsters, never.

It seemed to Roman that some of the newspaper correspondents who were responsible for reporting what was happening were in a constant state of drunkenness, or something close to it. But at least one of them was considered capable of holding a pencil because he was appointed as the Peace Commission's shorthand stenographic secretary. When Emil Durand heard about it, he launched into a blasphemous and obscene tirade directed toward anyone who could write in general and against newspapermen in particular, for the man chosen to keep notes for the peacemakers was none other than the same John Howland of *Harper's Weekly* who had drawn those pictures of Kidder's men looking like porcupines with Cheyenne arrows.

As it turned out, the nine gallons of applejack were insufficient. Before the party returned to civilization after the talks, the kegs had run dry. And the commission had been gone for a little less than three weeks. Roman thought maybe that was the reason some of the correspondents wrote such nasty things about John Sanborn, claiming among other libels that he was interested only in making money off the American taxpayer.

Roman Hasford liked Mr. Sanborn, even though his enthusiasm was enough to drive most men to distraction. He dashed about, coattails flying, red-faced, his voice gushing out in bursts of sometimes unintelligible language. But he never swore, and even though he seemed disorganized about his duties, all the mules and wagons and supplies began to accumulate, which Roman never admitted was part of his own doing. Mr. Sanborn wore a little hat not quite large enough for his head. It had a high crown and almost no brim at all, and as he charged along Leavenworth's sidewalks he looked like an animated ear of corn, missing only the silk tassel on top.

Other things were happening that Roman tried to ignore so he could put all his thinking to the Peace Commission work. Why, hell, he thought, these people are paying me a salary, and most of what I do makes a profit for the stockyards besides.

During these busy times Mr. Hankins reminded Roman of how he had looked on that first day, when the yardmaster had been trying to control those wild ponies Tyne Fawley brought in from the Indian Territory. He ran about the pens, shouting orders to the hired help, and the little white dog was always barking at his heels, thinking everything was a wild game.

Each day Elmer Scaggs came from the hog farm and followed Roman about, slapping his hat against his legs and yelling about the productivity of Hampshire hogs.

"By Gawd, boss," Elmer would shout, "them sows has started droppin' piglets like buckshot."

"Well, what the hell did you expect? It's been four months since you turned the boars loose on them, so that's what's supposed to happen," Roman would say, without pausing in his checking of Mr. Sanborn's lists, supervising his wagon crews greasing axles, seeing to new mules coming into the pen near the blacksmith shop, where Orvile Tucker sweated and glistened and beat the red-hot iron on the anvil.

"Hell, boss," Elmer would say, undismayed by Roman's lack of proper excitement, "them sows are droppin' half a dozen pigs apiece and more. We're gonna be arse-deep in hogs by winter."

"Just see that none of 'em freeze."

"Freeze? Hogs, freeze? Hell's own fire, boss, you know they ain't no sensible hog ever gonna freeze so long as they're safe in our pens. And they're eatin' like the kings of all hogs, them slops from the fort and town and that grain. Why, we'll have more bacon next year than they got in the whole rest of the state of Kansas.

"And that Tracy Benson, he's the best hog man I ever saw. By Gawd, boss, you ever notice? Ol' Tracy even looks a little like a hog."

Then, seeing that Roman was paying no attention, Elmer Scaggs would leap on his mule and ride in a flurry of dust back to his pens and his smokehouse with the satisfaction of knowing that Roman Hasford was leaving the whole enterprise to him.

They collected the Peace Commission supply train at Ellsworth, the army escort having already arrived at nearby Fort Harker. Roman Hasford rode the Kansas Railroad many times that autumn, back and forth between Leavenworth and end-of-track, and each time he passed through Abilene he marveled at how the town had grown. The year before, when he'd been there buying horses, it was mostly tents and mudholes and hang-tail dogs, with only the beginning of Texas herds coming into the pens along the main-line track. Now, after its first summer of full-scale drives from south of the Red River, Abilene was a roaring, slab-sided, whiskey-soaked hellion with more saloons than Leavenworth could boast.

The newspapers carried all the stories of mayhem and fatal shootings when the former Confederate drovers got cross-legged with Abilene peace officers of Yankee vintage, or tangled with ordinary citizens who were foolish enough to wander through the streets after dark, making known their dear sentiments about Ole Abe within hearing of riders from the Brazos out slaking a two-month thirst. Roman decided it was a good place to stay clear of, even though it had become a sensational tourist attraction for greenhorns seeking vicarious excitement and for newspapermen gouging stories out of the Kansas dust for gore-hungry editors, now that the Indian War had cooled down in anticipation of a peace council.

Why, hell, thought Roman, I wouldn't get off the train in Abilene unless I had a loaded shotgun in one hand and Jared Dane in the other.

And Ellsworth defied description, being mostly a tent city, with less than five hundred souls living there, and most of them each night collecting in the canvas-covered bars, where planks were laid across empty beer barrels to serve as counters for dispensing the spirits. But cattle pens were already being built along the railroad, and Roman suspected that by the following year Ellsworth would take its honored place among the hell-raising trail towns that dotted the railroad like beads along a string.

Fort Harker was neat and clean, compared to the adjoining civilian community, but there were still some long faces among the garrison because of the summer cholera epidemic that had taken off at least a dozen people, and it was reputedly even worse at the forts farther west. But somehow the spirit of something new about to happen with the Peace Commission made almost everybody forget the puking sickness as they prepared to receive the worthy men who would go among the savages to talk peace along the Medicine Lodge Creek, south of the big bend of the Arkansas.

The meeting on the Medicine Lodge was supposed to commence during the first full moon of October, and well before that time, one hundred seventy-five wagons and more than twelve hundred mules and horses had been brought together at Harker, the animals picketed and hobbled on the open prairie under the supervision of men whom Roman had hired mostly in Leavenworth and Lawrence. The military escort for the commission was already there: two companies of cavalry and two of infantry, the latter of which would ride to southern Kansas in army ambulance wagons, and a battery of Gatling guns.

Finally the Peace Commission arrived by rail and was escorted to the fort, and there a military band played martial airs while the ladies of the garrison served lemonade and smiled bravely and said there was no longer any threat from the cholera, which was commendable because, as good army wives, they knew that disease was deadlier than Cheyenne arrows and harder to defend against. Between sips of lemonade, many members of the commission took a tot of rye whiskey here and there, not provided by the ladies but by their husbands or by sutlers or licensed traders to the Indians or by men like Emil Durand, who understood the requirements of great decision-making.

It was a decision-making group, that Peace Commission. There was a United States senator, the governor of Kansas, the Superintendent of Indian Affairs, and a whole covey of military officers, the most prominent of which was General William Harney, an old Indian fighter and the ranking army officer now that Cump Sherman had been recalled to Washington City. Some said Sherman had been replaced because he was too rough on tender Indian sensibilities. There were the newspaper correspondents and the commission secretaries and the scouts and the escort commander, Major Joel Elliot of the Seventh Cavalry, and interpreters and Indian agents and hangers-on. There were enough people, Emil Durand would later observe, to operate a whole Gawd damned country, provided it was a small country where nobody was mad at anyone else.

Emil Durand was scouting for the army escort, but Roman didn't have an opportunity to talk with him. The Peace Commission broke down into three parts: peacemakers, escort troopers, and teamsters, and Roman was always with the mules. In fact, he didn't see much of anyone except for the hard-handed, grimy-faced mule drivers. It was a little disappointing, not being able to hear some of the high-powered talk from people like Governor Crawford and Senator Henderson and General Alfred Terry. The group of newspaper correspondents appeared at a distance to be a vocal and fun-loving bunch, and Roman thought maybe he could learn something just sitting near them and listening as they tapped into Mr. Sanborn's kegs of applejack. But he had a job to do, and he didn't figure any part of it was hobnobbing with the dignitaries, so he stayed throughout with the rough lot who would handle the teams pulling the wagons. At least he had the satisfaction of having them all call him "mister."

The peace party moved across the Smoky Hill River on Tuesday, October 8, and camped for the first time on the open prairie, and Roman was with them. He'd shipped Excalibur out to Ellsworth for just this purpose, because he wanted to be sure his mules and teamsters were well adjusted to their duties before he left them to Mr. Sanborn alone.

"It's unnecessary, Mr. Hasford," Sanborn had said.

"I sold you some service," said Roman, "and I don't want any of it to fall flat. I'll just ride along for a while."

"I appreciate your consideration," Sanborn had said, and it made Roman feel important to the whole peace effort.

It took four days for the party to reach Larned, a desolate little fort on the big bend of the Arkansas, the column stretching out each day for over three miles, with the army escort outriders on either flank. Each night they could see the glow of grass fires to the west, set by Cheyennes, so everybody said, and creating a nervous tension around the camps each night while the black orderlies fried the bacon and opened the cans of sardines. Of course, in Roman's teamster camp there were no black orderlies, but hired cooks who fed the men as cattle-drive riders were fed—half-cooked dried beans and beef jerky and hardtack and scalding black coffee. It all smelled better than it tasted.

At Fort Larned the Indian agents had arranged for a few chiefs to be present to greet the commission, and Roman asked Mr. Sanborn if he might come in to the post to see them, even though there were no Cheyennes among the tribesmen, but only an Arapaho or two, and some Kiowas.

"You can stay beside me throughout," said Sanborn.

"Well, I'd better get on back pretty soon. My boss is expecting me."

Everyone gathered in the sutler's store, and the agents

gave the chiefs some whiskey. It became a very convivial meeting after a time, and Satanta, who was wearing the army officer's coat given him by General Hancock and carrying an old army bugle on a long leather thong, moved about among the white men, shouting various insults in the little English he knew. He was wearing ocher and yellow paint on his face, and each time he embraced one of the commissioners he left a smear of color along his cheek.

When it was time for Roman to get his hug from the big Kiowa, he was astonished at the overpowering odor of smoke and horses and cooked meat that seemed to cling to Satanta. He stood motionless as the great muscular arms enfolded him, and a little happy at that moment that he'd had two large tots of the sutler's whiskey, because it helped the situation.

"White man's corn hurts my teeth like hell!" shouted Satanta, and everyone laughed and slapped the chief on the back, raising clouds of dust from the Hancock coat.

Roman slipped out of the sutler's store after that. There was an army courier detail that departed for Fort Harker each day, and he decided to ride with it now, satisfied that his obligations were at an end and that Mr. Sanborn could manage without him. He wanted to go on, but he knew he was already beyond the bounds of what Mr. Hankins had told him to do.

On the ride to Harker, which took two days, he had the opportunity to see the land, and it was a pleasant sight, the earth seeming to move off flat in all directions, with few trees and a carpet of lush grass. He and the two army couriers saw three small buffalo herds at a distance, and they looked more in their element than those Roman had seen while a guest of Mr. August Bainbridge on the hunt train.

The two courier soldiers were happy to ride along without much conversation, which suited Roman. One of them was a youth about Roman's age, and he spoke almost no English. The other was a corporal who claimed to have been at the Battle of Shiloh as an infantryman, which he said was about the worst way to see a war. He was a reader, and on the only night they spent together on the plains, he pulled a book from his saddlebags as soon as he'd instructed the other soldier on making a fire and bringing water and feeding the horses.

Well, Roman thought, I wonder what that is he's reading, but I reckon I won't ask. He's such a tightmouthed son of a bitch!

It felt good to be free of his part of the Peace Commission business and riding Excalibur across open spaces. It gave him a sense of freedom he hadn't felt for a long time. The days were gloriously bright and cool and the green of the prairie had returned after a rain the week before, making everything smell like spring, a last breath of warm weather before the earth turned brown and the cold winds came. The winds now were still moderate but constant, and they felt refreshing against Roman's cheeks.

But the nights turned chill and a fire felt wonderful and the smell of bacon spitted on a stick over the flames made the salivary glands do little dances and afterward the blanket was snug and above all the stars sparkled like sharp-edged diamonds in a black sky devoid of clouds.

So instead of taking the train back to Leavenworth as he had originally planned, Roman stopped in Ellsworth long enough to buy a sack of grain for Excalibur and a sack of hardtack and bacon and coffee for himself and the necessary pot and skillet to cook it all in and rode out, telegraphing Mr. Hankins that he was on the way home but would be a little later than expected.

It was two hundred miles from Ellsworth to Leavenworth, and the horse made it in a week. Roman rode along the line of the Kansas Railroad, and twice they stayed in towns, Excalibur in a livery and well grained, and Roman in a hotel room, bedbugs and all. He stopped overnight in Topeka in hopes of seeing Jared Dane, but was told by the depot stationmaster that Mr. Bainbridge was now in St. Louis and Jared Dane beside him.

So Roman and Excalibur went on, easily, the man thinking about many things that had happened and nobody knowing what the horse was thinking, but both enjoying the land. As they went east there were more and more trees, more and more farms and ranches, more and more streambeds with water in them. Sitting loosely in the saddle, the horse moving smoothly beneath him, Roman's mind traced back and the images of faces came, those of Victoria Cardin and Olivia Smith and Catrina Peel and Min, the little Crow wife of Emil Durand. And of Calpurnia and his mother. All women, he thought. And Katie Rose Rouse as well.

He wondered briefly where Min was now, her husband being with the commission on the Medicine Lodge, where so many Kiowa Sun Dances had been held. Likely at Fort Harker, he thought, making herself useful to the soldiers.

He didn't pursue that thought any further.

On October 20, a Sunday, he rode into Leavenworth and past the Methodist church, where they were singing a hymn he didn't recognize, and he thought he could hear the high soprano of Olivia Smith. He laughed to think what the members of that congregation would say if he strode into the house of worship, dusty and showing a fawn-colored growth of beard and his boots scuffed and the Navy Colt at his waistband like a walnut plow handle.

He could visualize Hezekiah Sample's lantern jaw dropping as he stood there at his pulpit scrubbed and pink and the black stubble showing on his cheeks and his hair plastered down with bay rum and his Adam's apple likely already bobbing in anticipation of fried chicken at the table of Tallheimer Smith.

But Roman didn't stop. He rode past the church, the sound of the singing growing faint in his ears as he went into the streets of Leavenworth on the way to Mrs. Condon Murphy's boardinghouse, where he would order up hot water for a bath and a shave. And he would shave his upper lip along with chin and jowls because after thinking about it for a long time he had decided that a mustache was not what he wanted.

He felt a little guilty because he had intentionally ridden a wide circle around the hog pens and smokehouse in order to avoid Elmer Scaggs coming out and throwing his hat in the air and swearing and jumping around like a kid with cotton candy and wanting to show him all the new piglets.

Well, after all, he reckoned, there's a certain loss of dignity in being the new hog king of Leavenworth, Kansas.

Winter came cold and blustering and the Treaty of Medicine Lodge was history. Reservations had been assigned to the Cheyennes, Arapahos, Kiowas, Kiowa-Apaches, and Comanches, all in the western Indian Territory. That land had been designated exclusively for the Five Civilized Tribes during the Removals of President Andrew Jackson, but now it had been taken away, perhaps as punishment because some men of the Civilized Tribes had fought for the South during the Civil War.

And besides, the white man didn't have anyplace else to put the wild tribes, because no politician in Kansas, sensitive to the interests and aspirations of constituent businessman or railroader or settler, would consider a savage reservation on the surface of *his* state.

There was a great deal of jubilation and euphoria expressed in certain newspapers about the Central Plains being safe for the expansion of civilization. But here and there, some of the men who had been at the treaty councils gave the opinion that the chiefs hadn't really understood what they had put an *X* to.

Emil Durand said, "They wasn't a whole lot of fightin' chiefs at that treaty meeting. Roman Nose, I never seen him. And the chiefs that was—by Gawd, come spring and warm weather, them young bucks is gonna roll outa the blankets they been in all winter with the women and ride out lookin' for horses to steal and hair to take, no matter what the chiefs say. Anybody who thinks the Cheyenne ain't gonna hunt their buffalo 'long the Smoky Hill and so rub up agin a lot of white folks just because of some ink scratches on a piece of paper is Gawd damned crazy. It's like your hogs and their slops, Roman. If it's there, they're gonna go after it because that's their nature."

"So how do you have peace?" Roman asked.

"You don't, by Gawd, as long as there's any buffalo where

the white man's at. But they'll be peace one day. In the big rock mountains, they ain't much beaver no more. And in your lifetime and mine, they ain't gonna be no more buffalo, neither. And when they ain't, then the savages will learn to eat beans and corn and they'll be peace. Maybe."

Mr. Elisha Hankins was finely tuned to the whole situation because now more and more emigrants were going westward on railroad cars instead of in ox-drawn wagons, so his best customer was the army. If real peace settled on the plains, those troop units would begin to dwindle away, and with them Mr. Hankins's business.

"Son," he said to Roman, "I can almost feel the smoke in those Cheyenne lodges where they're all just sitting around in their winter camps, waiting to see if we live up to that treaty. And I have to say I haven't got much faith in our doing it."

Said hopefully, Roman thought.

Well, hell, Roman thought again. There was that one report. It was an ominous warning from one of the old Comanche chiefs who had been at the Medicine Lodge councils. He'd said that they'd wait until spring, and if the white man didn't keep his promises, all the brave young warriors would ride out again to join their wild brothers.

"You can bet your Gawd damned hat the Cheyennes are thinkin' the same way," said Emil Durand.

In its usual fashion, Congress was very slow in appropriating any money for Indian annuities, and there was bickering in the Indian Bureau about how to distribute promised goods. The army was nervous about all those guns and ammunition that had been specified for the tribes in the treaty, and there was a notion among many average citizens that a reservation system meant any Indian caught off the reserve was fair game for good shooting. And then it developed that there were a lot of white men who couldn't agree on exactly what the treaty terms meant in the way of hunting rights for the wild tribes. All winter, the buffalo hunters stayed in their lodges south of the Arkansas and waited and watched to see what would happen.

"This is a damned mess," Roman said one night.

"Yes," Mr. Moffet replied as he sat in bed in his winter nightcap. "The only answer is to bring the savage heathen to the Lord with good Methodist ministers of the chosen church leading the way."

"Maybe we could get the Pope to help," said Roman, feeling petulant and tired after a hard day at the stockyards in the blistering cold wind.

Mr. Moffet glared at him for a moment only, and then turned his back and slid down in the bed and yanked the quilted covers over his head.

"I'm disappointed in you, Roman." The voice came muffled from beneath Mrs. Condon Murphy's quilted comforter.

And Roman, sitting at the desk under the window and looking at the dried-finger necklace and trying to think of something to write in his diary, thought that he was maybe a little disappointed in himself.

Some Eastern newspapers continued to wax jubilant and euphoric because it was a winter of peace. They failed to remember that most winters on the plains were peaceful because the buffalo hunters didn't particularly enjoy leaving warm tipis to flounder about in the snow. But the people on the frontier, who knew a little more about the volatile nature of things, treaties or no treaties, waited for the spring with loaded weapons.

"You'll see, Roman," said Emil Durand. "I'll show you some Cheyennes with black paint on their faces yet, by Gawd!"

And Roman wrote his mother:

> I didn't see much of it except at the start, with all the mules and wagons Mr. Hankins and I collected, but I feel a part of the treaty, no matter how small, although I can't tell you how any of it will turn out.
>
> I'm very busy now with my various enterprises. It appears that I may not get home for Christmas again

this year. So much has happened here. I often go to the services at the local Methodist church. There is a certain sanctuary from all the violence, which we saw enough of during the war.

But maybe soon I will be there. If another real Indian war doesn't break out. I hope I can be there because sometimes it comes to me how good it is at home with you and Papa at Christmastime.

I have written often to Calpurnia and I have a number of letters from her about how handsome her young son Eben Pay is becoming, though he is not old enough yet to have any teeth.

My best regards to Papa.

So things went on as they were ordained. Elmer Scaggs, as he himself had predicted, was arse-deep in growing pigs at the Hasford Meat and Lard Company. Orvile Tucker was watching the bulging Morgan mare. Crider Peel had stopped drinking long enough to buy a few dresses and a pair of shoes for his little girl. Katie Rose Rouse entertained her gentlemen friends as the winds whispered about her eaves, all the while thinking of planting corn on her property around the hog pens. Jared Dane was back in Topeka for the winter, along with Mr. August Bainbridge, who was planning his summer assault on the line to Denver. More and more, Roman Hasford was running the stockyards.

And Victoria Cardin did not come home.

14

There was a migration of mourning doves into eastern Kansas in February, which was somewhat unusual because they mostly wintered only as far south and west as Iowa. But no matter why they were there, Jared Dane had gone out late in the afternoon, walking along the railroad tracks from the Topeka freightyards to the edge of town, carrying the latest of Mr. August Bainbridge's collection of firearms, a new Belgian double-barreled twenty-gauge shotgun that loaded from the muzzle with linen cartridges, and within twenty minutes he had a dozen birds, enough for a nice pie.

Fletcher, the black cook who had been with the Boss since slave days in Maryland, was especially good at bird pies, and this one was no exception. He built it in the well-equipped kitchen of the Bainbridge private railroad car, which was resting in the Topeka yards while Mr. Bainbridge went about his business of making money and cultivating politicians from a suite at the Albon Inn. The car was left temporarily to Jared Dane and Fletcher.

It was an elaborate car, plush and paneled and well lighted, and even the two compartments at the end of the coach where Dane and the cook slept boasted better accoutrements than most hotels to be found west of St. Louis. For two years the three of them had spent more time on that car than they had at all the Bainbridge estates scattered about the country.

Jared Dane and Fletcher, feeling themselves equals when alone, had eaten together as they always did when the Boss was away, sitting at the dining table where only the Boss and his guests usually sat, smoking the cigars afterward that only the Boss and his guests usually smoked. The pie had been wonderful, thick with yellow butter sauce and spiced delicately with black pepper, thyme, and a dash of marjoram, and the whole business covered with golden pastry that was at the same time both fluffy and crisp.

"You are a master of your art, Mr. Fletcher," Jared Dane had said.

"It ain't nothin' to brag about, Mr. Jared," Fletcher had replied, showing his gold front tooth that Mr. Bainbridge had hired the best dentist in Cincinnati to install as a freedom gift after the passage of the Thirteenth Amendment.

"Whatever, I am stuffed to the very gills."

And chuckling, showing the tooth that gleamed in the lamplight, Fletcher had risen to clear away the table.

Now Jared Dane was on the rear platform of the car, enjoying the last of his cigar and feeling the sharp night air, looking at the stars and listening to the coughing sounds of a switch engine somewhere farther along in the yard. Down the tracks from the car there was a light outlining the window of the yardmaster's shack, where green and red lanterns hung on the outside wall—some sort of signal, he supposed—and close alongside the Bainbridge coach was the dark outline of a row of empty boxcars on an adjoining track.

He flipped the cigar off into the darkness, where it made a shower of red sparks and then was gone. From somewhere in the town he could hear the faint notes of a piano, which clashed discordantly with the switch engine's bell, the echoes of each coming like waves on water. In the windless night he could smell onions being fried nearby, and satiated as he was with dove pie, the odor wasn't particularly pleasant to him.

He started down from the platform to take his evening walk before bedtime and then paused, holding the railings, somehow feeling the absence of his pistol. He didn't know why, nor was there any sense of danger, yet he had learned a long time ago that it was always safest to heed the unknown stirrings in his mind, and so he turned back into the car, took the ivory-handled Colt that had been the gift of Baxter Springs, and slipped it into his waistband. He started to take an overcoat, but decided that his stay outdoors would not be long enough to require any more than his waistcoat.

Back on the platform, he waited long enough for his eyes to become accustomed to the darkness and then stepped down into the chunk cinders that carpeted the lane between the tracks of the siding. He walked slowly, taking deep breaths through his nose and liking the stinging sensation in his chest. Over the line of boxcars was a faint silver glow, and he knew the moon would soon be up.

He was about fifty paces from the Bainbridge car when he thought he heard a new sound above the crunching of his own shoes in the cinders. He stopped and lifted his hand to the butt of the pistol and moved his head back and forth, trying to make out details in the black shapes and shadows along the yard, standing motionless now and breathing hardly at all and smelling the onions frying and hearing the clank of the switch-engine bell and seeing vaguely, out of a corner of his eye, the orange rectangle of the yardmaster's shack window. Far to the east there was the distant whistle of a passenger train coming, and behind him a cat squalled in agony or ecstasy, but all of his senses were tuned only to the small sound near the boxcars.

"Dane?" The voice was very close and very loud, coming from the line of dark shadows that were the boxcars, and he turned toward it, the pistol now firmly in his grip. "Dane? I want you."

As the yellowish flash came, and the explosion flat and echoing against the cars along the siding, he was already moving to his right, crablike, the revolver coming up in his hand. He felt the impact of metal against his left arm and side. There was no pain, just a solid strike as though he had been hit with a hammer, and then he was down in the cinders, rolling back against the rail. He saw the massive form, blacker than the night around it, moving toward him and he fired once, lying on his side, and heard the loud grunt and saw the form fold like a book closing, and then he saw the other one, coming along the tracks with the light of the yardmaster's shack window behind him, and he wondered how anyone in such a business could be so stupid as to have light behind him, and fired again.

"You shit," he heard the second one gasp, and then, before he could thumb back the hammer for a second shot, he saw the man turn and run away, back toward the yardmaster's shack and then off into the black line of cars, and Jared Dane thought he could hear a whispered cursing and the clatter of a weapon dropped and he knew that this second one had been hit hard, not as hard as the first, but hard enough.

There was a hot, soaking liquid running along his side, and his arm there had no feeling at all. The slow throbbing began and increased with each breath into a stab of pain all along his side and down into his leg. He thought it was a long time before anyone came, but actually it was only a matter of seconds until Fletcher was coming, shouting.

"Mr. Jared! Mr. Jared!"

Then they were there from all directions, the railroad men carrying their lanterns, everyone talking at once in the high, staccato tones born of shock. They bent down and turned Jared Dane onto his back and saw the bloodied left arm and side where the buckshot had hit.

"Jesus, it was a full-choke gun," somebody said.

"Here's a dead man," somebody else shouted, waving his light near the line of boxcars. "If he ain't dead, he'll be in a minute."

"Mr. Jared," said Fletcher, his face close to Dane's. "Can you hear me, Mr. Jared?"

"Mr. Fletcher," Dane said, the pain coming hard now and his teeth grinding together, "I think I'm about to waste that fine bird pie of yours."

He rolled his head to one side and vomited and the doves did not taste as good as they had before and when he was fin-

ished Fletcher tore a sleeve from his own shirt and wiped
Jared Dane's face, all the while holding his other hand tight
to the left arm above the wound, pinching the blood vessels
to stop the spurting flow of red.

"You men help me get Mr. Jared to a doctor," the black
man shouted. "If you don't, my boss gonna fire ever' white
ass in sight around here."

By the time a peace officer arrived at the scene, there were
at least two dozen railroaders, most of them with lanterns.
The peace officer ran up and down the track with a pistol in
his hand until he realized how foolish he looked, and then he
slipped the weapon back inside his coat. Under the light of
the lanterns, they inspected the blood-spattered rail where
Jared Dane had lain, and farther along the tracks toward the
yardmaster's shack they found more blood and followed its
trail as though they were tracking a deer, but after leading
them around the end of the empty boxcars on the siding, it
stopped. They stood over the large form of Jared Dane's first
assailant, lying on his own shotgun, and when they turned
him over, the lips were slack and one eye was half open, the
other closed.

"Anybody know who this is?" the peace officer asked.

Nobody did, so they went through his pockets and found
fifty dollars in yellow-back currency, as well as a jackknife, a
small ball of twine string, two pennies, and four horseshoe
nails, but no identification.

"He's dead as hell, ain't he?" asked one of the railroaders.

"We'll carry him down to Sims's Photographic Gallery,"
said the peace officer, "and tie him to that barn door Mr. Sims
keeps in back, and tomorrow Mr. Sims can take a picture of
him."

Everybody knew that this peace officer and all the others
in Topeka had an arrangement with Mr. Sims, the photographic artist. Any fatal casualties of shootings in town were
brought there by the law, who then shared a percentage of the
profits made from selling the postal-card-sized pictures to

tourists and greenhorns and other morbidly curious citizens who might be passing through on Mr. August Bainbridge's trains. This one would bring a lot, even from local residents, because he was the victim of Mr. Bainbridge's own man, Jared Dane.

And so it was all done in accordance with practices long established in such places, and the man Sequal was planted in the potter's-field section of the smallest and meanest graveyard in Topeka with no name on his marker. In fact he had no marker except a hand-lettered oak plank that proclaimed, HERE LIES A MAN WHO TRIED TO KILL JARED DANE, and whoever put it there knew it would be stolen for firewood before the spring winds came to warm the prairie.

Unknown to any of the good people of Topeka and the Kansas Railroad, the second man, Tanner, made it all the way back to the Indian Territory to tell his chief what had happened, and then died in agony from an infection of the groin wound Jared Dane had inflicted on him. Afterward, a considerable legend grew up around Going Snake, Cherokee Nation, to the effect that Tyne Fawley, watching his subordinate in great pain and lingering, put an end to the man's misery himself, shooting Tanner through the head with a .44-caliber Dragoon-model Colt pistol.

The incident in the Topeka railroad yard did not go unnoticed in the Kansas press. Two days after the affair, the *Leavenworth Conservative* printed a story on the second page, which was the page for important news, the first being taken over completely by advertising, as was also the custom in British newspapers. Informed of it, then reading it himself, Crider Peel took to his bed and was absent from his duties at the tannery for four days. Then he slipped from his den like a wounded fox just long enough to walk to First Street and buy three bottles of the cheapest rye and after that go back to his mule-shed home, where he got drunk for the first time in weeks, muttering to himself and striking out at Catrina when she came close enough, bringing him the food she had prepared.

"God damn, ain't you old enough yet to know how to cook beans?" he'd shout.

And when he rose from his blankets long enough to go outside to the privy, he was so drunk that she was able to avoid him with her agility, her quick black eyes watching him for any sign that he might be advancing on her with his fist raised.

Then he would lie crying, and the child would come to his bunk and wipe his face with a dry towel and he'd lament his sinful ways and his lost life, but then, on some hateful impulse, he would lash out at her. But during that time when he was home, making a good start on his next bout of daily drunkenness, she suffered few serious blows. She was sure of his moods and as quick as a cat on her feet.

"Tough it through," Crider Peel would mutter. "Tough it through."

For the first time in his life, perhaps, he *had* to tough it through. He couldn't run because he had no place to run and no means to do it, not even a horse or mule. He could only wait and see. But even in his stupor, he knew the most important reason he could not run was the child.

"Man can't make no headway on the road, draggin' along a tyke," he'd mutter.

And he would not leave her because in his strange, mangled thinking he realized that he loved her more than anything else he had ever had.

"Well, son," Mr. Elisha Hankins said to Roman over a tureen of Spankin's beef stew, "your friend sure got himself into a mess in that Topeka railroad yard. But at least the newspaper says he'll live. Had to take off his left arm, though."

"A pity, such a fine-looking man," said Spankin.

"That's a debate," Mr. Hankins said. "He always looked mighty cold to me, like maybe he was as much dead as alive."

"Don't talk that way about one of Roman's friends," she said. "A man's not just what he looks like."

"Well, you're the one brought it up, how fine he looks."

Roman sat with his head over his stew bowl, spooning

chunks of beef and potatoes into his mouth. The other two waited for him to speak, but he was silent, spooning the stew.

"They got a nice hospital down in Topeka," said Mr. Hankins. "A couple of fine doctors, they say, all that experience during the war. One thing about that war, it sure taught a lot of them doctors how to cut off arms and legs."

"Mr. Hankins!" said Spankin.

Roman straightened in his chair and wiped his mouth with the linen napkin that Spankin always provided at her table. The Hankinses watched him, leaning forward a little, but they already suspected what he'd say.

"I'll be away a few days," Roman said. "It's the slow time at the yards anyway."

"That's right, slow until the Indian War breaks out again," Mr. Hankins said. "You take whatever time you want, son. I guess you'll be goin' down to Topeka to see him."

"Yes. I'll ride down on the train. I'd appreciate it if you'd keep your eye on that Morgan mare. She's not far from due."

"Hell, son, Orvile Tucker practically takes that horse to bed with him every night, but I'll do what you ask."

"Take a warm coat, Roman," said Spankin.

Later, Roman wrote in his diary:

> *Hospitals are terrible places. The smells are enough to keep a man sick. And all those people in white coats running around and looking mad at the world, and the patients in rows of beds, and glass cases with shelves and shiny metal things lying on them that are painful just to look at.*
>
> *At least they had Jared Dane in his own place, a little room at one end of the long building, but barely big enough for his bed and a small table with brown and green bottles on it. Anyway, he had some privacy. I suspect that Mr. August Bainbridge was mostly responsible for that private room. Mr. B. owns a lot of things in Kansas and for all I know he owns that hospital as well, although I doubt it because it doesn't impress me as a kind of thing to make much money.*

I suppose Jared Dane was glad to see me. He looked bad. Like Mr. Hankins said, as much dead as alive with no light on his face and no shine in his eyes. And when I come to think on it, he didn't look much different than he always had when I saw him before the terrible wound. When I came close to him I began to understand that most of the evil smell in hospitals comes from the patients, what with all that medicine they pour down them and rub on them. It is no wonder that people don't want to go there whether they need to or not.

I didn't stay long at any one time. Mr. B. was kind enough to invite me to stay in his private railroad car during the week I was in Topeka and I got to see the places where Jared Dane had bled on the tracks and where the man he killed had died in the cinders. This colored man who works for Mr. B. showed all of it to me and told me about the racket of the shooting and how everybody came running. He is a nice colored man and reminds me very much of a slave I knew at Elkhorn Tavern whose name was Lark and who was the best beekeeper in Benton County.

Mr. B. didn't stay in the railroad car while I was there, having urgent business in town, I suppose. But twice he came and had supper with me and we talked. He is an educated man and I thought of Papa telling Calpurnia and me the stories of Greece and Rome and King Arthur's court because those were the kind of things Mr. B. liked to talk about.

When he started on the French Revolution I think maybe I offered some good comments that he enjoyed, thanks mostly to a book I read in the evenings when I visited Calpurnia in St. Louis. I can't remember who wrote it. Some Frenchman, I suppose. Papa wouldn't be too happy with me reading books by a Frenchman because he was never much for the French and always seemed proud that one of his grandfathers had fought against them a long time ago in Europe.

There were a lot of books in Mr. B.'s car and I spent considerable time in reading between visits to the hospital. There was one called Oliver Twist *by an Englishman named Dickens and because I couldn't finish it in the time I was there, Mr. B. inscribed his name in it and gave me the book and it lies* now beside my hand as I write in this diary. It's what they call a novel, a story of imagination such as I have never read before, and it's sad but I hope by the time I reach the end things will work out all right for the hero.

I felt a little guilty about staying away from my business in Leavenworth for so long but I somehow had a duty to be near Jared Dane for a while at least. And within a few days he began to look much better, although I can't take any credit for it.

There was a time during the battle around my mama's farm that I saw a lot of men die. And yet it held no meaning for me. Now, seeing one I know, even though slightly, on the brink of death is a horrible experience. I suppose it would be even worse if he were kinfolk. If I must face that one day I can only hope that my life's experiences have better prepared me for it. And no matter how such a thing should come, it seems to be better to come outside of a hospital whether it's for me or for someone I love.

Mr. B. had a couple of Pinkerton detectives hanging about Jared Dane's room all the while I was there. I suppose they were two of the men he told me about in Fort Riley who are helping him solve the express robberies and murders. They are a strange lot with their small black derbies and spats on their shoes and clothes that appear too tight for their little bodies. As often as I went to the hospital I don't reckon those two men spoke half a dozen words to me. In fact, they looked at me as though they thought I might be there to strangle Jared Dane in his bed.

It was hard to look at the place under the covers where Jared Dane's arm was supposed to be. It was embarrassing because I didn't know what to say to compensate for his loss. But Jared Dane might have understood what I was feeling and he acted as though all he had was a little croup, and after my first two or three visits he started scolding me for shooting so badly in our first contest together at the Fort Leavenworth turkey confrontation of pistols. And speaking of pistols, I saw from the first that the ivory-handled pistol had been retrieved from the railyard and now lay on the small table with all the

*brown and green bottles and within reach of the only hand he
had left. It occurred to me that even in his reduced state it
would be very dangerous for anyone to come through his door
unless he wanted them to.*

*It wasn't a new feeling, this seeing a man I knew without
something he originally had. I remember the night Mama sent
me to the loft while they cut off Allan Pay's hand after the battle of Elkhorn Tavern, doing it in our kitchen and everything
cleared away before I came down the next morning, and after
that I was somehow ashamed to look directly at Allan Pay as
he sat in the front porch rocker with one sleeve empty at the
end. It's much worse with Jared Dane because with Allan Pay
only the hand is gone but with Jared Dane it is all of the arm
to the shoulder, making it appear that one whole side of him
has melted away.*

*I wonder why it is that men who come close to me stand
such a chance of losing parts of themselves. I've seen many veterans on the streets of Leavenworth without arms or legs,
wounded during the war, but it seems I get more than my share
among friends and relatives. At least Papa came back whole.
Well, anyway, if he lost something it's not visible to the eye.*

*But it's crazy to feel bad about it when they don't. I can't
speak for all wounded men, but of the two I've known they
make it out a great lark which is confusing yet somehow magnificent. I reckon the only consolation for me is that I didn't
fire that minié ball that took Allan's hand nor was I trying
to shotgun Jared Dane in the Topeka railyard. But if I did
such a thing to a complete stranger the burden would be ex-
treme.*

*Jared Dane said to me, "Don't look glum, Roman Has-
ford. It could have been my head."*

*But there is a sickness in it all. I don't know what it is.
Maybe like seeing someone die in pieces which surely is worse
than having them die all at once. But maybe not. Dying all
at once is final as hell.*

*Now I have to find out what those papers are, the ones Mr.
B. gave me. He said it was a little gift because I was Jared
Dane's friend and had come to visit him. It seemed a little silly*

to me, a gift for doing something any decent man would do
without thought of reward. But Mr. B. insisted, and when Mr.
B. insists it's hard to argue.

Tallheimer Smith's office was on the second floor of the
Kansas Bank and Trust Company, and when Roman went
there he remembered that his own brother-in-law was above
a bank in St. Louis and wondered if there was something
about second floors of banks that held a particular fascination
for attorneys.

It was a tiny space, not much larger than Jared Dane's
room in the Topeka hospital, and when Roman seated himself across the desk from Tallheimer Smith, he had the sensation that the lawyer's back was brushing the window that
opened onto the street below and that his own was tight
against the opposite wall. Along either side were shelves
stuffed with legal-looking books, floor to ceiling, and Roman
wondered how anybody in a lifetime could possibly read all
the words in so many volumes.

The place smelled of dust and cigar smoke. From Chestnut Street beneath the window came the sounds of wagons
and horses and of men conversing in the warming sun that had
come in an early burst of good weather before spring actually
arrived.

Tallheimer Smith slipped the papers from the fat envelope Roman had given him, and placing a pair of steel-rimmed
spectacles on the end of his nose, he began to read, stroking
his goatee all the while with his short fingers that reminded
Roman of the cartridges Jared Dane had used in his rifle the
day of the Bainbridge buffalo hunt. As Smith read, Roman
grew more and more uncomfortable with the heat. There was
a stove in one corner behind Tallheimer Smith's desk, with
a coal scuttle and a small shovel beside it. There was the
feeling that flies should be buzzing about the place, speck-
ing the already dirty windowpane, but it was too early in the
year for flies.

"These certificates are signed by Mr. August Bainbridge,"
said Tallheimer Smith.

"Yes."

"Then they are authentic. There are some that are counterfeit, sold on the streets to unsuspecting victims. Did you have them from his hand?"

"Yes, he gave them to me in Topeka last week."

"It states that they were issued in appropriate consideration, but no price is listed. What did you pay for them?"

"I didn't pay anything for them. They were a gift."

Tallheimer Smith glanced quickly over the tops of his spectacles and his eyebrows lifted in what Roman assumed was an expression of surprise. But it was quickly gone.

"I see," said Tallheimer Smith. "They are worth a great deal of money."

"Exactly what are they?"

"They are stock certificates in the Kansas Railway and Telegraph Construction Company of Cincinnati, Ohio. This is a company incorporated under special act of the Ohio legislature."

"I read that, but I'd like to know what it means."

"These certificates assign to you shares in capital stock in the company, called the KRTC. Kansas Railway and Telegraph Construction Company."

"So what does it really mean?"

Tallheimer Smith folded the stock certificates and replaced them in the envelope and passed the envelope back to Roman and then leaned back in his chair and swiveled around to look through his dirty window, gazing across the roofs of Leavenworth's buildings. He laced his fingers across his ample belly and sighed.

At last he said, "Have you ever heard of the Crédit Mobilier?"

"No."

"It's a company that was founded in connection with the construction of the Union Pacific Railroad across Nebraska and beyond. The KRTC is the same kind of company. Crédit Mobilier is more famous, but the two work the same way. Of course, nobody is supposed to know exactly how they work.

But their purpose is to build railroads and, in the case of KRTC, telegraph lines as well."

Tallheimer Smith swiveled back toward Roman and placed his elbows on the desk, his hands locked beneath the goatee so that it thrust out like the end of a lancer's blade. He looked at Roman for a long time, sighed again, and took off the steel-rimmed spectacles and threw them onto the desk among all the stacks of papers and ledgers. And smiled.

"It works this way. The Kansas Railroad obtains various moneys from the Congress and from the sale of its stock to the public. Controlling stock is held by members of the board of directors, of course, but you can buy stock in the company without being an official in the organization.

"Now, the Kansas Railroad Company is not in the business of building railroads. It is in the business of running them. So the KRTC was formed to do the building.

"So the KRTC contracts with the Kansas Railroad Company to lay its tracks and string its telegraph. The stockholders receive dividends from the profits of that construction. And believe me, they are considerable."

Tallheimer Smith stopped talking and bent forward, leaning on his elbows and rubbing his palms together and waiting for Roman to respond, but Roman sat mute, waiting for the rest, and by this time he knew there was a lot more.

"Now," Tallheimer Smith resumed, "when the KRTC submits a proposal for a certain length of track, there is no chance for competitors. Because there are no competitors. And just as important, Mr. August Bainbridge is not only the prime owner of KRTC but also of the Kansas Railroad Company."

"So he's selling to himself," said Roman.

"Exactly. Now. Let's say the KRTC submits a bid on ten miles of track and they say they need twenty thousand dollars to do it, although everybody knows they could likely do it for less than half that. The Kansas Railroad accepts the bid and the money is paid and the work is done and it costs ten thousand dollars. The rest of that money is paid out as dividends to the stockholders. There is, you see, an inflated margin of profit built right into the bid for the work.

"So. Some of the money the Kansas Railroad Company pays out for this work comes originally from private investors. But largely it comes from the Congress in the way of direct cash payments, government bonds, or title to great tracts of land along the proposed right-of-way, which can easily be turned into money by sale to towns and immigrants.

"You see, there have been many gratuitous issues of stock from Mr. Bainbridge and his friends who are on the boards of directors of both the rail company and the construction company to various important members of Congress. These men, therefore, are most happy to vote appropriations in Mr. Bainbridge's interest because they know that some of that money will end up back in their own private pockets by way of construction company dividends.

"Do you understand all this?"

"I'm afraid so."

"Well, everybody involved makes a nice profit, eventually even those private investors who are paying twice or more than twice what they should to build this thing, because when the railroad is finished and starts making profits, they will share them."

"It's like buying a ten-dollar mule for twenty dollars."

"Exactly, but you see, in this case, that ten-dollar mule is going to appreciate in value as the years go by. And the railroad is getting built. The government is not in the railroad-building business. Private enterprise must do it, and without this system, it would be years before we had tracks connecting the East and West Coasts, or even going from St. Louis to Denver.

"Yes, these stock certificates are a very special gift indeed."

Roman sat for a long time, frowning and turning the bulging envelope in his hand. He felt as though he had just been made privy to the worst-kept secret on the border.

"Then it works this way," he finally said. "Everybody gets

what he wants, and a few who were smart enough to figure out how are making a hell of a lot of money."

"I think you've understood my explanation perfectly. And now you are among that happy few." Tallheimer Smith smiled and leaned far back in his swivel chair. "And if you have some discomfort with the arrangement, remember this. Without these enterprising men like Mr. Bainbridge, no matter how greedy you may think them, there would be no Western railroads built at all in our time and in our place here at the edge of things."

On the street, walking back toward the stockyards, Roman was troubled. And suddenly it hit him that something like this railroad business was going on with Mr. Hankins. He recalled the first sale of horses he'd recorded in the ledger, when some of the money the army had paid was not entered, on Mr. Hankins's instructions. What had happened to it? In whose pocket did it end up? He couldn't bring himself to believe that Mr. Hankins would be involved in something dishonest.

But, hell, he thought, it's Mr. Hankins's business and Mr. Hankins's ledger. If he doesn't want to show something in his books, whose damned business is it anyway?

He made a detour past the express office and deposited the stock certificates with the rest of his growing account. He couldn't help but feel himself to be a man of some substance. After all, during the past year he'd bought a new suit of clothes and boots besides, and the old slouch hat he'd worn from Arkansas had long ago gone into the trash bin and been replaced by a new one, fawn-colored and with a stiff brim.

But it had been a disquieting day. Perhaps most of all because as he had left the law office, Tallheimer Smith had invited him for supper. It would be the first time he'd seen Olivia in weeks, so for the rest of the afternoon among the smells of horse manure and hay, he braced himself for the coming scent of lilac water.

While Olivia prepared the supper, Tallheimer Smith engaged Roman in some rather boring conversation about the rising value of property along the railroad right-of-way toward Ellsworth, Roman all the while fidgeting uncomfortably on a new horsehair couch that had only that day arrived by freight from St. Louis. When it came, the meal was satisfying enough, although not the best he had ever taken at the Smiths' board, being composed mostly of baked sweet potatoes and somewhat overdone roast duck, the latter given in fee payment to Tallheimer Smith by one of his clients who, like many others who lived along the edges of prosperity, paid some of their indebtedness with occasional wild game and birds taken on the river bottoms or the prairie uplands west of the city.

Olivia seemed to lose all her shy and ladylike manner when not entertaining the Reverend Hezekiah Sample, and throughout the meal she talked constantly about how to cook marsh fowl, and after that she went into a detailed explanation of the migratory habits of pintails and mallards. Roman, his mouth full throughout, wondered where she had acquired all this wildlife knowledge. He found little to command his attention from start to finish, except for the pickled peaches and one comment Tallheimer Smith made.

"You know, Olivia, Mr. Hasford has become the owner of a few valuable shares of capital stock in the Kansas Rail and Telegraph Company."

It seemed a thing Tallheimer Smith had to say, but at the moment Roman couldn't understand why. It made him feel like a prize bull being examined for brand.

Then there were the cigars, as Roman's behind was once more abused by the horsehair couch, and from the kitchen where she was clearing up the dishes they could hear Olivia singing in her high soprano—a little too loudly, Roman thought, for her own benefit alone. Tallheimer Smith stroked his goatee and smiled, cocking his head the better to hear the notes issuing from his daughter's throat.

"Lovely voice," he said. "What a fine woman she is, Mr. Hasford, such a homebody. She loves to cook and keep her house as clean as a whistle and she sews like a professional seamstress. Why, I seldom have to buy her a single stitch of clothing."

Roman thought it sounded like the overblown praise of a mule-seller when one of his highbreds was on the block, and was a little startled at himself because lately he had seldom thought of Olivia except in terms of livestock of one kind or another. He would have liked it much better to be able to recall her as she had been when they sat together under the willows along the river, talking about things that had absolutely no significance and where there were no overtones of conspiracy. But Tallheimer Smith's conversation did little to dispel the image of two dedicated hunters about to corral a wild mustang, and when that metaphor leaped to his mind of its own accord, Roman winced because of the animal part again, and he felt a cold sweat breaking out across his brow.

"When I see her ready for church," Tallheimer Smith was saying, "I'm proud that I can be seen with her in public. Well mannered and from excellent stock, it goes without saying, my own family known in the vicinity of Paducah, Kentucky, since the days of the Polk administration and her mother, rest her dear soul, from a Rhode Island family that traces its lineage back to the Pilgrim Fathers. Yes, good stock. It has all given her a frugal nature, too. She never goes spending money unnecessarily. And such wonderful taste. She selected that superb couch you're sitting on now."

"Yes," said Roman. "It's a nice couch."

When she had completed her chores, Olivia came into the parlor and made straight for the couch, as Roman somehow knew she would, and placed herself close beside him and began to describe a yellow canary she had kept in a cage as a child and all the tribulations of keeping it away from the family cats until finally the thing died—of natural causes, Roman supposed—and she had buried it in the flower garden behind her Grandmother Smith's gazebo in Paducah, Kentucky. Through the whole grisly tale the sweat dripped from the hair above Roman's collar, making sticky little paths of moisture down the back of his neck. And all the while, too, he was smelling the overpowering odor of dish soap and having to look at Olivia's parboiled hands.

God Almighty, Roman thought.

Throughout all of the canary discourse, Tallheimer Smith was showing signs of drowsiness, and once the bird was buried, he rose and excused himself with a parting word to Olivia not to keep Mr. Hasford too long, and then he was gone up the stairs.

God Almighty, Roman thought again.

He saw the danger in this situation, alone in the Smith parlor with Olivia completely unchaperoned and a father who had made it quite clear that he was nudging Roman in his daughter's direction. She had edged along the couch, and now, with her father's footsteps hardly stilled along the stairway, she was tight against Roman's side. Although she was still mouthing words about the gazebo in Paducah, her eyes had gone wide and moist and she fixed her gaze on Roman's face. She reached up and touched her fingertips against the hair above his ear, and he felt her leg moving against his.

Suddenly the talk about gazebos and canaries and pintails and all the rest was finished, and while she continued to stare into his eyes with a sad, lip-trembling expression, Roman could hear her breath coming fast, with little jerking sounds, as though she might have some obstruction in her lungs.

"You must be so lonely, living in that boardinghouse," Olivia said, and the roving fingertips moved along his wet cheek.

"Well, no, I'm pretty busy."

"Father says it's such a wonderful country here, to start life. To start the things that will mean so much in older age. With your own home. I think about it all the time. Don't you?"

"Well, I reckon it's as good a place as any for that kind of thing."

"Oh, Roman," she gasped, and threw herself against him, her arms lacing behind his neck in a stranglehold and her face coming toward his, and before he could avoid it, her lips were pressed against his so hard that he felt her teeth bruising the inside of his mouth.

Later he tried to put in his diary, but couldn't, the things that were now rushing to his mind. Tallheimer Smith as father-in-law, Olivia singing her high soprano as she washed dishes, the gazebo in Paducah, the migration of pintail ducks, the horsehair couch. And he pushed himself away from her violently and at least managed to disengage his face from hers, but she was clutching at him and her body was lying against his, seeming to throb and pulsate like the bellows on Orvile Tucker's blacksmith forge.

"Oh, Roman, yes," she whispered.

"God Almighty," he said.

And as unexpectedly as she had advanced, she retreated, throwing herself away from him and flat onto her back along the couch, eyes closed, lips parted, arms extended stiffly to either side as though she were expecting to be crucified.

"Yes, Roman, yes," she wailed. "I'm swooning."

"God Almighty!"

Roman was up and across the room in two long strides, and as he yanked his hat from the clothes tree beside the door, he could still hear her on the couch, calling him and threatening to faint. He pulled open the door and she was up then, the little heels of her shoes clicking across the floor. And she had begun to shout.

"Come back here! Roman, come back here!"

He ran across the porch and went down the steps in one leap and was up into Excalibur's saddle without touching a stirrup, pulling back on the reins, and she was on the porch screaming.

"You come back here, Roman Hasford, before I tell my father what a rude man you are, you scoundrel!"

"God Almighty! Go, horse!"

Excalibur grunted with surprise as Roman's heels slammed into his flanks and was in a dead run after two strides along the street, and behind him Roman could still hear Olivia shouting.

Pounding through the dark streets of Leavenworth, he thought, I never reckoned a good Methodist girl would carry on like that to get a husband.

He felt fear, fear of a father's wrath. And bewilderment and disappointment that something he had always thought to be only a friendship could turn into such passion. Despite all that, it was funny, too. Funny as hell, because even if she'd stripped off all her clothes right there in her father's parlor, he would have felt no desire at all. At least he didn't think he would have. Of course, no girl had ever stripped off her clothing in front of him, but he had the uneasy feeling that Olivia had been close to that.

God, he thought, if Mama ever imagined I was thinking about girls taking off all their clothes in front of me, she'd come all the way from Arkansas with a willow branch and beat hell out of my butt!

Excalibur was into the mood of things and would have run all the way to the fort, but Roman reined him in at the newspaper office and tethered him in the street and went up the outside staircase to the rooms of Katie Rose Rouse. On this night he would impose on her friendship and he knew he'd be accepted, because she would understand that even though there was no desire centered around the home of Tallheimer Smith, a young man was still a young man. With each step up the stairs, Roman felt more and more disturbed and pained by the thought of Olivia Smith.

Well, hell, he thought as he gently knocked on the door of his partner in the pig business, I feel sorry for that girl, but a man can't go around getting married to just everybody he feels sorry for.

And later, in the dark morning, he lay awake on Katie Rose's bed and thought about Victoria Cardin. It wasn't the place or the time to think about Victoria, but he couldn't force his mind away from her.

And when he was dressed and departing into the light of the coming sun, Katie Rose stood behind him in her doorway and said, "Roman, I hope to God you're a better hog raiser than you are a lover."

"Shit!" Roman said, and all the frustration of the past few hours was in the word.

Roman Hasford waited two weeks for the anger of Tallheimer Smith to descend upon him, but it never did. Finally it came to him that despite her threats and shouting, Olivia had said nothing to her father about what had happened on the horse-hair couch, either real or fancied, and Roman felt sorrier for her than he had before.

But no matter how much he might have thought that what had happened was partly his responsibility, he bruted it away, as his papa used to say before the war about situations one could do nothing about. He made his resolution. He thought, I've gotta stay clear of that damned Smith bunch.

Then Olivia and Tallheimer and their horsehair couch slipped easily from his thinking, because finally Victoria Cardin came home.

15

The invitation came by way of an enlisted man riding a dray horse that would have made a cavalryman blush, but once he saw the writing on the envelope, Roman Hasford stopped thinking about the horse. He recognized the hand of Captain Edwin Cardin, and inside was a cryptic note asking him to dine on the post the following Saturday night. At the bottom was a postscript notation that the captain's daughter had returned from the East and the dinner was in her honor, but until Saturday she would be resting and receiving no visitors.

Hell, he thought, here I've got three days to try and keep busy with Victoria not two miles away and her papa telling me to stay away.

It never occurred to him that the postscript might have been Victoria's idea.

He did the best he could with what was at hand to soak up time. Part of it was spent pampering the Morgan mare.

"She's about ready," said Orvile Tucker. "Any day now. She can't hardly walk at all, an' that girl has got a load of grit."

"You watch her night and day," Roman said. "I'll pay you extra."

"Ain't no need for extra, Mr. Hasford. I feel like that foal is mine as much as Excalibur's."

"I'm depending on you."

"You can do that."

Roman went shopping along Miami and Chestnut streets, looking for a gift. He had a terrible time trying to locate anything suitable, because he reckoned Victoria Cardin had everything any woman needed. He finally settled on a small bottle of perfume no larger than a silver dollar and weighing less than half of that. But it had an impressive label. It was called Lavender Dream, and the shopkeeper assured Roman it was made with the finest ambergris that any sperm whale could produce.

"It's a hell of a lot of money," Roman said.

"Just think of it on the lady's neck, a tiny drop."

So Roman threw two coins on the counter with instructions to wrap the perfume in white tissue and all tied with a nice blue ribbon.

Another diversion that came up was the move at the boardinghouse. Mrs. Condon Murphy announced to him at breakfast on Friday morning that her only single room had become available because the usual tenant there had gotten himself married and moved to Missouri to run his father-in-law's sorghum mill in the vicinity of Osceola.

It took Roman less than an hour to move all his trappings, and Mr. Moffet helped, repeating on each of his passages down the hall with an armload of Roman's clothes that he hoped his next bedmate would be as good about not snoring as Roman had been, which led to a long explanation that before Roman there had been this Mormon Bible salesman who constantly gave Mr. Moffet hell for the fruit-jar beer and, besides that, snored loud enough to draw return honks from riverboats tied up at the Leavenworth docks. Worse still, the Mormon had taken exception to Mr. Moffet's philosophy of communion in the Methodist church.

After the chore was done, Mr. Moffet solemnly offered his hand, and Roman thought him a little teary-eyed.

"Come back and visit whenever you feel inclined, Roman, and we can have a sip of beer," Mr. Moffet said, looking up into Roman's face with the kind of pained expression that suggested a hound dog caught in a barbed-wire fence.

Roman thought, You'd think I was gone off to Abyssinia or Japan or some such place, and me not twenty paces away down the hall from him.

The new room was small, with a window opening toward the west, and Roman knew he would miss his view of the river when he was writing in his diary. But this room had a fine walnut desk with three drawers, and there was a new coal-burning space heater in one corner and everything smelled fresh as clothing left all day in the sun in summer. Mrs. Murphy brought him a special bedcover that had so many colors she called it her Joseph's-coat quilt. She claimed it had never been used by any other boarder.

"Three other men wanted this room," she said proudly. "But I wanted you to have it. Now that you're all fixed, let's go down to the kitchen. It's the bock-beer season again."

Roman always enjoyed Mrs. Murphy's kitchen. It was spacious and clean and reminded him of his mama's kitchen, except there was no bed at one end. It always smelled better than the food that issued from it tasted. On that Friday there were thick slices of red onion and cold fried chicken livers and a sip of Irish whiskey along with the bock beer.

For the first time, Roman began to understand what it meant to be a man of means. Little things came your way that otherwise eluded you. People gave you special consideration. There was almost a bowing and scraping, if only in the eyes, and the greater the means, the more pronounced the bowing and scraping.

What's wrong with being a garbage collector and a pig grower in this town, he thought, and having a good job besides?

But he knew it was more than the hogs and the garbage. The word had seeped across Leavenworth like molasses across a hunk of cornbread that he owned capital stock in the Kansas Railway and Telegraph Construction Company, something normally thought of in connection with men who wore diamond stickpins or politicians in Topeka or Washington City who knew governors or Presidents and had the power to make laws that affected people they had never seen.

He wondered if maybe he ought to buy one of those diamond stickpins so that Victoria Cardin might more fully understand his status.

It's a thing that doesn't take much getting used to, he thought as he sat in Mrs. Condon Murphy's kitchen, nibbling red onions and drinking bock beer. Being poor is what takes a lot of getting used to.

Yet even as he thought it, he knew he had never been really poor, even in the times during the war when he and his mama had lived from hand to mouth because the partisans came and took their grub. But he also knew that throughout his life he had never known anyone in Arkansas who could consistently rub two silver coins together. And that included Papa.

Maybe there are better things to rub against each other, he thought, but right now I can't call one to mind.

And so, with this and that, he managed to live through the hours before he could brush his best suit and the new fawn-colored hat, polish his shoes, trim the long-hanging blond hair around his ears with a pair of scissors he borrowed from Mrs. Murphy, shave carefully with his bone-handled straight razor, inspect himself in front of the oval mirror attached to the back of his door, put the blue-ribboned package in a coat pocket, and walk to the stockyards, where Orvile Tucker would have Excalibur saddled and shined for the ride to the quarters of Captain Edwin Cardin.

And he thought, with almost every step, God Almighty, I feel pretty good.

Roman carried visions in his head all the way along the ride to Fort Leavenworth, thinking how it would be. He would sit beside Victoria Cardin at her father's table just as he had before, and she would touch his arm just as she had before. He would entertain her guests with his stories about partisans in the hills, just as he had before. And when it was over, he and

Victoria would stand in the darkness on her front porch and kiss. Just as they had before.

It was a wonderful night, warm and clear and the wind low. There were mockingbirds singing in the timber along the river, announcing the arrival of good weather over the land. There was the smell of new life that always came in this time of year, with the profusion of early prairie wildflowers creating color and aroma that were there at no other time. But on his ride to the Cardins', Roman noticed none of this, though he was usually so attuned to such natural things.

He worked out in his mind the best possible time to present his gift, wallowing it about from one side of his thinking to the other and back again. At once, perhaps, when she ran to meet him at the door. Or maybe at the table, where all could see. Or after all of it was finished and they were alone together, or maybe, still better, just before that, when he and Victoria and her father were in front of the fireplace, with the captain holding his brandy snifter and smiling his approval.

But at last, just before he tied Excalibur to the hitch rail in front of officers' row, he determined that the sooner it was done, the better, so she would understand his serious intentions at once, and respond in kind.

As he walked along the gravel pathway to the steps, he could hear organ music from inside, but there was no singing, only a great babble of voices and laughter, as though perhaps everyone had had a good deal of time at the punch bowl. Roman couldn't help wondering if maybe his invitation had stated a later time than all the others, and a little twitch of apprehension began in the pit of his stomach.

Melissa answered his knock immediately, as though she might have been standing behind the door waiting; her expression was anything but encouraging, and her words were no more so.

"I didn't even know if you'd come, Mr. Roman," she said, opening the door. "Bein' the only civilian invited. I hope you like my victuals, 'cause you ain't gonna like much more about it. Lemme take that new hat."

The twitch in his belly moved up halfway to his throat, like the heartburn from too many half-cooked pinto beans.

The parlor was crowded with people Roman had never seen before, the men in dress blue uniforms and the ladies in what appeared to be their best finery. In the center of the room were Captain Cardin and Lieutenant Thaddeus Archer, and between them stood Victoria. She was so lovely it almost made Roman catch his breath, and he marveled that during her absence he had been capable of losing the details of her features in his mind.

He was there for only a moment before she saw him. She gave him a smile, making Roman gulp, then turned and touched Lieutenant Archer on one arm, saying something to him, and came across the room, avoiding officers and their ladies with deft movements of her little feet under a flowing yellow silk taffeta gown. She wore a double string of pearls tight about her neck, just above the flared collar of the dress.

"Roman," she said, still smiling, the tiny rows of pearls behind her lips gleaming like the choker at her throat. She held out her hand, palm down.

He had no idea what possessed him, but he took her hand and bent and kissed it. It embarrassed him and he felt his face growing hot, and quickly he slipped the small package from his coat pocket and gave it to her.

"Welcome home," he said, so softly that he wasn't sure she heard him above the noise of conversation in the room, so he said it again, this time a little too loudly. "Welcome home."

Nearby heads turned, and unsympathetic eyes inspected him. But he didn't mind because she was still smiling when she spoke, moving close so he could hear her words.

"How very considerate of you, Roman. Come, let me introduce you to our guests."

He thought it sounded wonderful, her saying "our," even though he knew she meant hers and her father's. Then there was the dizzying round of the room; people he had never seen before measured him, with polite smiles, quick handshakes, and bobbing heads. Lieutenant This and Captain That and Major Something-or-other and Mrs. Lieutenant This and

Mrs. Captain That and Mrs. Major Something-or-other. He hardly heard the names, they went by so fast, and could no more remember them once they had been announced than he could recite the Greek alphabet.

Then he had Lieutenant Archer's hand in his and found it firm and dry; he knew his own was wet, and the lump in his chest became almost painful. Finally it was the host himself, and the captain said he was glad to see Roman because he wasn't sure the invitation had ever been delivered, the reliability of common soldiers being so poor nowadays, and Roman couldn't help thinking that if there was some doubt about the envelope arriving at its destination, Cardin should have brought it himself or else mounted his courier on a better horse.

He had no opportunity to sample the punch being served from a large etched-glass bowl at the parlor sideboard, because Melissa announced dinner and everyone trooped slowly into the dining room, remarking on the divine nature of Philadelphia Fish House. Roman could only assume they were talking about the yellowish liquid he'd had no taste of; from the level of their voices he thought it must be as lively and powerful as First Street rye.

There were three enlisted attendants in dress uniform standing along the walls. There was a place card on the table above each folded linen napkin, and although he had never experienced such a thing before, he knew at once that they were meant to assign everyone to a specific stall, like horses in a stable. His stall was midway along one side of the board, and as he pulled back his chair he saw that Victoria was in her usual place at one end of the table, on her left a major with Medical Corps piping on his uniform and on her right Lieutenant Thaddeus Archer.

There were the pungent odors of spices and garlic and cooked roast beef. The blur of conversation around the table was army talk, and even though the windows were open there was an oppressive heat, as though a spring twister storm were in the offing, even though Roman knew the sky was clear to the west. As he sat there, he tried to remember what had happened to his little gift package, but couldn't. Sometime during the course of all those introductions it had effectively disappeared.

As soon as the guests were seated, the soldier orderlies began to march back and forth from the kitchen to the dining room, bringing out platters and bowls of steaming food. The beef was served by the captain, standing at the head of the table and slicing, placing a slab on each plate that was passed around the board. While all of this was happening, the lady on Roman's left turned to him and said that she understood he knew the infamous ruffian who worked for the railroad, Jared Dane.

"Well, yes, ma'am, I know him, all right. He's a fine gentleman."

That was the last of the conversation between Roman and his dining partners on either side, their backs turned to him throughout the meal as they chatted with officers on their far flanks. And across the table the diners bent toward one another, laughing and sipping their wine between bites, talking about Custer's court-martial and about Elizabeth's amber hair and about the divine quarters at Fort Hamilton in Brooklyn and about a certain troop first sergeant who had imbibed so heavily the day before Easter that in chapel the following morning he had passed out cold during the rising anthem.

And there was talk of the Cheyenne restlessness since the snow had gone from the prairies, and of how they had already harassed a few settlers and stolen a few horses because they weren't satisfied with how the provisions of the Treaty of Medicine Lodge were being fulfilled.

Only now and again did Roman find anyone acknowledging his presence, and then with fleeting glances, as though they were noticing, with nothing more than a passing interest, the intrusion of a moth about the candle flames.

The eating took an interminably long time. Each soldier who came to stand behind Roman's chair with a wine bottle raised noted that he always had an empty glass, and filled it. But for him the wine did little to dissolve the growing knot that had now risen to the area of his throat.

At last it was finished, and Captain Cardin said that all the men would forgo their after-dinner cigars while everyone gathered once more before the fireplace in the parlor for an announcement. There the soldier orderlies passed around dainty stemmed glasses and everyone was served a small portion of port, the guests standing in a semicircle about the room, with the captain, his daughter, and Lieutenant Archer in the center. When all had been served, Captain Cardin raised his glass.

"Ladies and gentlemen," he said, "I now propose a toast to my daughter, Victoria, who wishes me to announce that she is engaged to be married to Lieutenant Thaddeus Archer, Quartermaster Corps, United States Army."

There were exclamations of delight and a few shouts of "Bravo!" and Victoria was smiling and her father was setting aside his port with some distaste and one of the soldier orderlies was handing him a snifter of brandy and Lieutenant Archer was standing like a fencepost clad in blue and Roman suddenly realized that with only a little more pressure from his fingers the wineglass would shatter in his hand.

The guests began to pass before the couple, shaking hands, the ladies kissing Victoria on the cheek as the tiny teeth shone behind her wide smile. Roman joined the line, trancelike, having deposited his untouched port on a parlor end table. He shook Captain Cardin's hand, and the words coming from the captain's lips were a bumble-bee-buzz of confusion, reaching Roman's conscious ear in little hums of noise, senseless and unaccountably syrupy. Then came Victoria, whose hand was cold and whose expression was the same as it had been when he'd given her the wrapped bottle of perfume, but her gaze darted away from him at once, going to the next well-wisher, who was shoving Roman along. And there was Archer, staring straight into his eyes with a glow of triumph in his face.

He was in a corner then, under the same photograph of Civil War cavalrymen that Lieutenant Archer had stood under on Roman's last visit to this place, and he watched dully, a smile fixed on his face like something pasted there, as soldier musicians arrived and the officers began moving furniture back from the center of the room so there could be dancing. And the twitch in his gut was like the one he'd had after the battle at Elkhorn Tavern, when they came to him and told him his friend, the old Jew at the Sugar Creek mill, had been hanged with baling wire by the partisans.

Before the music started, Roman moved to where Captain Cardin was standing, holding his snifter in one hand and a cigar in the other.

"I appreciate your hospitality, Captain," Roman said. "But now I have to be going."

"So soon on a Saturday night?" the captain said, his eyes a little glassy. "Very well. I'll see you again soon, or at least one of my officers will, because we need to buy some more horses now that the Cheyenne are showing signs of kicking up again."

Roman didn't shake the captain's hand because they were both filled, so he turned abruptly away and walked to the outer hall and took his hat from the rack there. Melissa was at the door, her dark eyes on him and a grim set to her lips, which looked purple in the evening lamplight.

"You shoulda knowed she wasn't gonna marry no civilian," she said, and swung the door open.

As he rode back to town, there was no pleasure in feeling Excalibur's strength between his legs. There seemed no source of strength or joy anywhere. There was only a black, dismal void that reached coldly into each secret place of his inner self, and everything in the exterior world was suddenly useless and meaningless and cruel. The mockingbirds made no impression on him, nor did the sweet smell of the river or the bright stars that sprinkled the darkening night sky.

He went through the routine of stabling, rubbing down, and graining his horse automatically, without the pleasure that such things usually gave him, and walked to the boardinghouse scuffing his shined shoes in the dust and thinking about Mama and what a fool he'd been and happy that he'd never mentioned Victoria Cardin in any of his letters home.

God, he thought—the first coherent thing that had come to his mind since Captain Cardin stood before the fireplace making his toast—I wish I was home.

He felt no bitterness toward Victoria, or even toward Lieutenant Archer. It surprised him a little. Once, if such a thing had happened, he'd have lost his temper, gone into a rage, sworn and stomped and threatened mayhem. But somehow it had left him desperately calm, desperately lonely. If he felt bitterness toward anyone, it was directed inwardly, toward himself.

Mrs. Condon Murphy was still clearing up her supper table when he walked into the boardinghouse. Her eyes lighted when she saw him, and she smiled and waved.

"Aw, Mr. Hasford. I thought you'd be gone into the wee hours this night."

And Roman had the feeling that everyone in creation knew where he'd been and what his aspirations were along officers' row at Fort Leavenworth, and he rudely remained silent as he crossed the parlor and mounted the steps two at a time, thinking that a man of means can afford to be rude when he damn well pleases.

Going along the hall to his room, he saw a light under Mr. Moffet's door.

"Come in," Mr. Moffet called to his knock, and even as he moved into the familiar room where the little beer salesman was sitting in bed, nightcap in place and a fruit jar in his hand, Roman had no idea why he had turned in here.

"Roman, Roman," Mr. Moffet said, obviously delighted. "Have some beer."

Taking a full jar from the nightstand, Roman went to his old chair before the small desk, moved it over against one wall, and sat down, tilting the chair back and unscrewing the cap from the jar.

"Tell me about John Wesley," he said.

"Aw," said Mr. Moffet. "A great and gentle man."

Roman heard none of the dissertation that followed. It was background music, like the singing of cicadas in a locust grove during early evening summer conversation on the front porch of the farm in Benton County, Arkansas. He allowed the impressions of this day and of his life to drift across his thinking without direction as Mr. Moffet droned on. The chatter of voices at the Cardins', strange and incomprehensible; the sounds of the river alongside the boat when he and Victoria came upriver from St. Louis; the day Calpurnia was married in their mama's living room, all in white, in a dress made there in that same room; the cold day he had seen the ghostlike formation of horsemen coming along Wire Road clothed in the vapor of breathing; the feel of the Navy Colt in his hand when he had stood beside Jared Dane at the Fort Leavenworth turkey shoot; the sad determination of Olivia Smith's face in the instant before she threw herself against him on the horsehair couch; the feeling of Victoria's lips on his over a snow-covered cannon above the Missouri River; the quaint little face of Catrina Peel as she stood silently beside him for an instant, her tiny hand touching his sleeve on that far-gone night when he had first come to this border land, and after that being afraid ever to appear before him again.

At one point he thought, Why, hell, women have some kind of a hex on me. They are either too much or not enough. So the fault must lie somewhere with me. My face too long for one, not long enough for another. My hair too straight for one and not straight enough for another. My conversation too ignorant for one and too smart for another. Well, at least there's always my dear Katie Rose.

In the middle of Mr. Moffet's discourse on the great founder of Methodism, there were loud noises downstairs that broke Roman out of his reverie. Then the thump of heavy shoes up the stairs and along the hallway and someone calling his name. He slammed the front legs of the tilted chair down onto the floor and jumped to the door, hoping that news had come of Lieutenant Thaddeus Archer suddenly dead of some foreign disease.

It was Orvile Tucker, hat in hand, standing in the dim hallway with his bloodshot eyes wide and his great mouth gaped open to show an astonishing array of white teeth.

"Mr. Hasford," Orvile Tucker shouted, almost slavering. "She done come down!"

"What?" For Roman it was like trying to come up from deep water to catch a breath.

"The Morgan mare, Mr. Hasford. She done come down. A fine, blood-red colt, gonna be big as his pappy an' have the soul of that brave ole girl."

"What?"

"The Morgan mare, Mr. Hasford. She done foaled. A little man horse fine as you ever seen!"

Roman stared at the great chocolate face before him, the teeth shining, the eyes red, the sweat running off his cheeks, the hat in his hand, the hair like coal cotton packed over the round head, and it struck him like a blow that to this black man he, Roman, was not a man of means but only a lover of good horses.

"A colt?"

"Mr. Hasford, the bes' Gawd damn lookin' colt I ever seen."

"God Almighty!"

Roman threw his arms around Orvile Tucker and he felt Orvile Tucker's laughter and felt Orvile Tucker's great muscular arms around his waist and felt Orvile Tucker's wet face against his own and he began to cry. It was uncontrollable, but he didn't care. They stood holding one another there in the hall of Mrs. Condon Murphy's boardinghouse, the black man laughing, the white man crying, the sweat from one cheek mixing with the tears from the other, each trembling with the thought. The Morgan mare had come down!

When he pushed away, Roman made no effort to brush away his tears. It didn't matter. He held Orvile Tucker's shoulders and shook him, but it was like trying to shake a hickory stump, and Orvile Tucker laughed a great new burst of laughter.

"She done it, Mr. Hasford, that Morgan mare done it!"

"Come in here, come in here and have some beer," Roman said, pulling Orvile Tucker into Mr. Moffet's room, where Mr. Moffet sat in his bed wide-eyed, his nightcap askew.

Roman took a fresh mason jar from the night table, unscrewed the lid, and handed it to Orvile Tucker.

"Thank you, Mr. Hasford," said Orvile Tucker, and lifting the jar to his lips he drank it all, the whole quart, without lowering it from his lips.

Mr. Moffet had only a limited number of fruit jars on his nightstand, but beneath his bed was a cardboard box filled with two dozen more. So the three of them sat drinking deep into the night, Orvile Tucker telling them of horses he had known and Roman constantly asking if the new colt was healthy and Orvile Tucker assuring him that it was all right and one of the yard men was even now sitting there watching to ensure that nothing bad happened, on penalty of his very balls.

But later Orvile Tucker grew serious.

"Mr. Hasford, we'll have to wet-nurse that colt a little later, 'cause it's the Morgan's time. She hurtin' bad an' we gone hafta destroy her."

"I know," Roman said. "You'll have to do that, Orvile, because I couldn't find the stomach. I'll have to get away. I want to get away anyway."

"Where you goin', Mr. Hasford?"

"I don't know. But I need to take Excalibur and ride out along the tracks and see all the towns and get drunk and go on beyond where the railroad runs and watch the Cheyenne kicking up their dust, I reckon."

"When you goin'?"

"Maybe tomorrow."

Beyond civilization, Roman thought.

Thinking about Orvile killing the Morgan mare, Roman began to cry again, wiping his nose between gulps of Mr. Moffet's beer. There were no sobs or trembling lips, just the water running down his face.

"God Almighty," Roman said.

Mr. Moffet tried to resume his history of John Wesley but finally gave it up because he saw that neither Roman nor Orvile Tucker was paying any attention. So he rose from his bed and bent awkwardly to slide another cardboard box from beneath the bed, his knobby little knees and hairless ankles showing below his nightshirt.

After Orvile Tucker was finally gone, back to the stockyards to check on the new bay colt, Mr. Moffet, feeling the effects of his own produce, sat owlishly in his bed, and with his nightcap lost somewhere under the covers, he bade Roman good night and observed that he had never until this very night shared his fine beer with a nigger. And then slid down and was asleep.

Standing over the bed, Roman looked down at the small figure, like a twig under cotton cloth. He laughed, took another drink from the mason jar in his hand, and said, "Well, you little son of a bitch, he likely never had a drink of beer with such as you, either."

He started toward his room but stopped, returned to Mr. Moffet's, and took two more full jars of beer and only then made his rather staggering way along the hall. He sat heavily on the edge of his bed in the dark, and drank a little more and cried a little more, though whether from joy or grief he was never sure.

Finally Roman lighted his lamp and attempted to write a few words in the diary, but his mind would not bring anything to his hand that made sense, and all he produced were a few unintelligible scratchings on the paper. He blew out the light but still sat for a time in the darkness before undressing and crawling beneath Mrs. Condon Murphy's Joseph's-coat quilt. And as he sat in the dark, hearing the mockingbirds now through the open window, he wondered if words that were written but never read were still words.

PART THREE

When men come together to kill or maim one another, there is a certain fascination if for no other reason than to see what real fear is. It's been said that there are men who have no fear or else enjoy the control of it, and I suppose these are the ones who relish war.

—from Roman's diary

Tyne Fawley began his ride from the green hills of the eastern Indian Territory in early summer. He rode slowly, sleeping each night under a single piece of tarpaulin, the reins of his haltered horse tied to his wrist. He made himself go slowly, even though every instinct urged him to ride as fast as he could. But he knew that a man in a hurry attracted attention, and he wanted nothing he did to bring him under suspicion.

Some of his friends had already been hanged and others shot, like the two who went to Topeka for a small job of work; one had ended up dead in the cinders of a railyard and the other had made his way back to the Territory, only to suffer so horribly from his wound that he had to be put out of his misery like a dog gut-squashed under a log wagon's wheels. It had become a dangerous time. Various forces of the law seemed to buzz around his ears. And so he was off to the western plains for a short time, to lose himself in what he expected would be the next round of wild-tribe hostilities. He knew it was easy for a man to lose himself inside a war, because he had had some experience at it.

As he rode, he inspected the land before and behind him and to either flank, wary as a wolf. With the horse moving easily beneath him he sat in the saddle loosely, every muscle relaxed and so all the more ready to tense for action. He rode always with his mouth slightly open, for he had never learned to breathe through his nose, and besides, he suspected that his hearing was sharper when his mouth was open. The parted lips exposed the row of large, crooked teeth the color of pinewood cut two days before and left in the sun to dry. And the long-fingered hands with the pronounced knuckles lifting up the skin in knots were never far from the weapons he carried on his person and in the rifle scabbard under the fender of his saddle.

To pass the endless days he chewed tobacco, of which he had an inordinate supply, and hummed soundlessly behind his crooked teeth, tunes that came to him from his days in the wooded mountains when he was a child and his mother and all his brothers and his one sister would gather on the front gallery of their home above the Buffalo River and sing to the accompaniment of his father's Jew's-harp, and sometimes dance together and then watch the light of a going sun touch the far hilltop timber with a lace of red and gold and orange and yellow before the blues and purples of evening came on and the summer cicadas and crickets began to send their little messages. Sometimes, too, they could hear the sounds of hounds running foxes across distant ridges with that haunting, melodious song at the same time beautiful and terrifying, having in it the power and timbre of all living things that had ever hunted one another.

Of course, these were not the words he would have used to describe such things, but he felt all of it in his soul just as he did the humming behind crooked teeth, silent because it was only in his mind, like the images of his childhood.

There was plenty of time on this journey to think about what a son of a bitch he was, never having gone back to see his mother and father, never having written, never having shown the least interest in what had happened to his two brothers who went off in the first year of the war to fight for whichever side they found first, never having tried to find out how many times over he was an uncle because he knew his sister was married and spewing out young'uns one a year, as long as she could manage it. He'd cut himself off completely on the very day he rode away to the north and Missouri, losing himself to everything that had ever happened before, as he was trying now to lose himself to those damned Pinkertons and deputy United States marshals and jake-leg sheriffs here and there along the borders of the Indian Nations. And so he thought about those things a great deal, but they didn't bother him a lot.

He traveled light, with only two saddlebags and a yellow slicker and the tarpaulin tied behind the saddle pommel. In the saddlebags he carried a packet of beef jerky and some extra stockings and powder and lead and percussion caps, a small hatchet, a folder of needles and thread, another of fishhooks and line, matches in a metal box that was supposed to be waterproof, and a bag of dried corn. The corn was for himself, not the horse, because the horse was an Indian pony and expected to live off grass. At night he tried to find water, which wasn't always easy, and he liked rolling into sleep among trees, but before long that wasn't easy, either.

By the time he reached the Arkansas River below where it flowed south from Kansas into the Indian Territory, trees became scattered and small. Even more so when he moved into the Cherokee Outlet and then turned the horse due north and across into Kansas somewhere southwest of Fort Larned. He had a picture of the land in his mind, a rough map, so that he always knew approximately where he was at any time, even though he avoided all habitation because he reckoned that the fewer people he saw, the fewer would see him.

He had to wait one full day in a small thicket of stunted willows along the Salt Fork of the Arkansas while a herd of Texas cattle passed, going toward Ellsworth most likely or anywhere along the railroad where there were buyers from Kansas City.

Those same cattle he followed for two days, trailing their droppings, but far enough behind to be out of sight of the drovers. Then on the third night he walked on foot into the herd, avoiding the singing perimeter riders, took a young steer, and led it out. With the dawn, knowing nothing was missed and the herd moving far off to the north, he slaughtered the steer, peeled off only a part of the forequarter hide, sliced off a good bit of meat, and roasted some of it over a low fire for his supper.

The rest of the forequarter roast he'd cut off he carried in a slab hanging over the rump of the pony, running blood until finally the meat dried and the fibers parted like melting snow and it all began to give off a noxious odor. But at least for three days he had fresh beef.

Now he was in the high plains, where the sky and earth at the far horizon blended into one and where the clouds seemed to stand motionless and the flat land lay like a dish filled with shallow water that reflected each ray of the sun's passage overhead. An endless flatness more heaven than earth, except that the horse beneath him kicked up prairie birds and the ground was dotted with buffalo droppings. A land where he could almost see the earth's curve, or at least feel it, the ground dropping off at all points around him to infinity.

By then he was pushing the horse harder. He saw no Indians but he saw the signs of their ponies many times. Whether these were hunters or war parties he had no way of knowing. He took no chances, and each night dug a foot-deep hole to start his fire in and before rolling into the tarp he let it die and only then moved off some distance in the darkness and slept with two revolvers beside his head.

Finally he came to Hays City, a new, sprawling town where everyone was expecting the railroad soon, already wild and uninhibited and mostly lawless like her sister towns to the east, and already building cattle pens in anticipation of the Texas beef traffic. He saw plenty of Indians here, but they were old or drunk or both and he paid them no mind.

He spent a few gold pieces on a bath, a few more on a good meal—at least as good as he could find in one of the tent cafés—and a few more on a woman. The women, like everyone else waiting for the tracks, had already arrived in force and had begun to ply their trade in a large tent like those found at prairie revival meetings. This particular tent had a wooden false front with fake windows and an enticing signboard that proclaimed "entertainment."

He went on about the business of getting himself lost until the curiosity of Pinkerton detectives and railroad troubleshooters and deputy United States marshals out of Fort Smith and Topeka cooled a little back in the green hills of the Cherokee Nation and in eastern Kansas. He knew he'd go back there, as soon as it was safe, if for no other reason than to take care of a little business having to do with a certain party becoming nervous about past accomplishments. But for now, that would have to wait.

He had allowed his beard to grow and now he looked like a great many other wanderers of the western frontier. There was a tangle of hair hiding his neck, and a crooked mustache that hung on either side of his mouth like the clutching fingers and thumb of a hand.

When he saddled his horse in the livery corral on his last day in Hays City, the man in attendance remarked on what a nice pony it was.

"His name's Going Snake," said Tyne Fawley.

"Well now, that's a strange name."

"Well now," Tyne Fawley said, "this here is a strange horse."

16

In that year Philip Sheridan came, and no sooner had he taken command of the Department of the Missouri than he was out into the field. This tough little Irish fighter had so distinguished himself on the battlegrounds of the Civil War that he stood in the nation's esteem next only to Grant and Sherman, at least to those living north of Mason and Dixon's line. They were of like mind, those three soldiers, believing in total war, something familiar to many former Confederates from the Shenandoah Valley to Atlanta, who had seen the smoke-blackened chimneys where farm houses once stood. It was a way of warfare about to become equally familiar to the wild tribes of the high plains.

He came to Fort Hays, sixty miles west of Ellsworth in the true high plains, forsaking at least temporarily the plush headquarters accommodations at Fort Leavenworth, to get things started, as the sergeants said. And no reason why not, he being first and foremost a soldier and after thirty-six years of life still a bachelor with no wife or kiddies to tie him down. The sergeants did not speculate as to whether this meant that Sheridan wanted no woman or that no woman wanted him.

Now he sat behind a small folding desk in his tiny command-post room in the guardhouse at Fort Hays, one of only two buildings on the post not constructed of rough-cut lumber. He wore a long coat, open and showing a double row of brass buttons across a growing little belly. Behind him was one miserable window with no glass, and on one side of that the red standard of a general officer and on the other a map of the Department of the Missouri, and a broad blue line marking the course of the westering railroad along the Smoky Hill route. The line stopped just short of Fort Hays where he sat, but was poised to be extended west toward Denver with each passing day, like a snake stretching out across a flat, sun-faded dooryard.

He was completely at ease in the heat of midafternoon, no trace of perspiration on the high brow above his slightly Mongolian-looking eyes. His black mustache was well clipped and the hair across his round head was cropped so short that one hardly noticed he was almost totally gray.

From behind him came the sounds of a frontier post, floating through the window like high-noon shadows, harsh and distinct. A noncommissioned officer was barking commands to a group of men doing their turn at dismounted drill. From somewhere there sounded the brittle clang of a hammer on an anvil, and the dim beat of horses' hooves trotting in close formation. And very near, a troop sergeant was bellowing at one of his enlisted men.

"You Gawd damned hammerheaded kraut-eating heathen, pick that weapon up out of the dirt and you drop it again and you'll Gawd damn well sleep with the son of a bitch!"

But even with the heat, the acrid smell of dust and horse droppings, and the noisy distractions from outside, Sheridan directed his entire attention to the young man seated across the desk from him, the fierce black eyes darting from one detail to the next. This was a fair young man whom Sheridan studied, long of leg and with sloping shoulders and straight hair that was light brown and kept falling across his brow and into the pale blue eyes that gazed unwaveringly into the general's own. On his lap was a fawn-colored hat, wide-brimmed, and from beneath a light duck jacket protruded the butt of a Navy Colt revolver. His trousers, of the same material as the jacket, were tucked into low-heeled boots of soft leather.

"I've been traveling from Leavenworth, mostly along the railroad right-of-way, taking some leisure from my work," Roman Hasford was saying. "Camping on the prairie or else spending a night here and there in the towns beside the tracks."

"I see. It could be a dangerous time to camp on the prairie," Sheridan said. "I advise against it. But perhaps no more dangerous than a night spent in one of these trail towns, from what I've been told."

A smile flickered across one corner of the general's mouth like the quick flight of a hummingbird, gone almost before it had appeared.

"Yes, sir," Roman said, returning what he assumed was Sheridan's smile. "But I've been in good company since Abilene. A man who was coming here to Fort Hays."

"What man?" Sheridan asked.

"A Mr. Emil Durand."

Sheridan's eyebrows lifted for an instant and a crease appeared in his bright forehead, but it was gone as quickly as his smile had been.

"Ah. Yes. A man who has scouted for us—" He broke off and leaned forward, his fingers clutching the edge of the desk before him as though he were about to leap up. "Hasford! Of course. When I assumed command of the Department, my quartermaster staff informed me that you were Mr. Elisha Hankins's principal agent in dealings with the army. But although my adjutant tells me that you know me, I do not recognize you."

"No, sir, I don't reckon you've ever seen me," Roman said. "But you came to my mother's house in the valley of Little Sugar Creek in northwest Arkansas after the battle of Pea Ridge. Your men later left some food for us, and I want to take this opportunity to thank you because without those beans and that flour, we might have starved."

Sheridan frowned, fingering the buttons on his tunic.

"Northwest Arkansas?"

"Yes, sir. After the battle of Pea Ridge. We called it Elkhorn Tavern."

"Yes. At the time I was commissary and quartermaster officer for the Army of Southwest Missouri."

"Yes, sir, my brother-in-law told me that. His name is Allan Eben Pay, of St. Louis."

"Oh, yes," said Sheridan, and the faint smile returned and remained. "A young officer, I believe, who had lost a hand."

"Yes, sir. He married my sister."

"Now I recall. I was still a captain then. Only two months later I received my commission as a colonel in the volunteer Michigan cavalry. Which was good. The Army of Southwest Missouri did not set well with me, nor me with it."

"And so from there on to all the rest," said Roman.

"Yes," said Sheridan. And now his eyes were not so intently inquisitive and his face seemed to soften.

"I remember your mother. A strong and remarkable woman."

"She still is," said Roman.

"And I seem to recollect that your father was away in the Rebel army. I hope he returned safely and whole."

"Yes, sir, he did. He served with General Lee in Virginia. He was a member of the Third Arkansas Infantry."

"Ah. Texas Brigade. A fearful group," and Sheridan laughed an explosive little laugh, like the burst of a round of cannister.

"When I heard you were here," said Roman, "I thought it only proper to visit with you and tell you we appreciated those beans."

Sheridan laughed again, a rather startling sound, as though it happened infrequently and he was not accustomed to controlling it.

"Not according to regulations, giving rations to civilians," he said. "But I thank you for coming. Now what sights do you expect to see here in western Kansas?"

"Cheyennes. I have always wanted to see some Cheyennes. I'd heard about them before I left home. I sort of like that name. Cheyenne."

"Yes, I can understand it."

Sheridan leaned far back in his chair, holding his hands with fingers laced across his belly. He studied Roman for a long time without speaking. Somewhere a bugler blew Stables, and the sounds of hoofbeats came nearer.

"Perhaps I can help you," Sheridan finally said. "Can you shoot and ride?"

"As good as the next man. Better than most," said Roman.

"I suspected as much. Until you came to the city of Leavenworth, I assume you lived in the outdoors most of your life."

"Yes, sir. All of my life, until then."

"Very well. There's a special scout unit forming right here at Fort Hays. You might be interested in that. It's not an enlistment, you understand. We have no authority to recruit soldiers. We are signing everyone on as civilian quartermaster employees."

"Well, I'm sorry, sir, but quartermaster work is the kind of thing I've been doing ever since I came to Kansas, and I haven't seen any Cheyennes yet."

"My young friend," said Sheridan, laughing once more. "If you join this group, which is commanded by a major named George Forsyth, who is one of my aides, I can assure that you will see a great many Cheyennes!"

It had been two weeks in which Victoria Cardin was far from Roman's mind. In the first days after he'd left Leavenworth she was always there, the vision of her face haunting him and the sound of her laughter echoing hollowly in his mind. He'd spent a lot of time in Topeka, visiting Jared Dane, who was up and about now, the left sleeve of his coat pinned up neatly. And he'd dined once with Mr. August Bainbridge at a place called the Crosstie Club, where he'd felt out of place among all the white shirts with stiff collars. And he hadn't been too comfortable with the lamb chops, either. He'd attended a traveling circus and gone twice to the Topeka Opera House to watch presentations of the Stratford Performing Arts Company, which he had never heard of, although the playbill indicated they were world-renowned and had presented themselves before Queen Victoria in London and Francis Joseph in Vienna. He'd watched a parade featuring the Topeka Silver Cornet Band and afterward a political address by one Horatio Seymour, a Democrat who was running for President against U. S. Grant. From the look and sound of him, Roman didn't reckon Seymour had much chance, particularly in view of the fact that citizenship and the franchise had not yet been restored to most people who had been Confederates.

But in all of it, Victoria was there, as though she were standing just behind him whispering in his ear. That changed when he happened on Emil Durand and Min in Abilene. Roman found them squatting beside a railside cattle pen, and after that moment Victoria's face faded from his thinking because there was no room left in his mind for anything except hell-raising and sightseeing in the company of this old man whom he enjoyed just as he had the old Jew at the Sugar Creek mill before the partisans hanged him.

I reckon I like to soak up the wisdom of old age, Roman thought.

They watched the drovers bringing in the herds, and the huffing engines aligning cars to load cattle, and they roved the streets at night, noisy and boisterous and wild, not only in Abilene but in Ellsworth as well, the two towns being duplicates of each other. They gulped rye whiskey from four-ounce glasses seldom clean, visited a few ladies of the evening, danced, played billiards or dominoes, watched fistfights, listened to heated arguments about which side had won this battle or that in the late war.

And always Min hunkered patiently outside each building or shack or tent while the men passed the rowdy time inside, and then helped them stagger out along the railroad tracks beyond the stockpens, where Emil Durand made his little camps, opposed as he was to sleeping within the confines of Sodom-and-Gomorrah towns, as he put it, even though Roman offered to pay for beds in some flophouse.

And always Emil Durand explained in fanciful detail that

the Cheyennes were out again, making war on their old enemies the Pawnees, so they claimed. But war parties, once launched, were never reluctant to stop a stagecoach, shoot at a gandy dancer, steal a horse, or set fire to some isolated homestead—at least to those few that were not built of prairie sod.

"So when Cheyennes start doin' such things," said the old mountain man, "there's bound to be a mite of firearms put in use on both sides and that means a mite of sudden death on both sides and that means one thing leads to another, by Gawd!"

During the course of these dialogues it was made clear to Roman that Durand was headed for Fort Hays, where he could do some scouting for the army, and maybe even some for the new Tenth Cavalry, two troops of which would be there soon.

"I ain't ever worked with any of them nigger sojurs before," he said. "So I figured to take me a whack at it."

Roman took a bit of drunken offense at Durand's language and grasped the opportunity to point out his superior breeding, as drunk men often do.

"My mama always said it was impolite to call them that," he said. "She said to call 'em colored folks."

"Well, I had a different mama," said Durand. "She could have been a big, fat Shoshone squaw who could skin out a full-growed bull elk before a man could get his fire started."

In the rye haze, Roman couldn't recall whether that Shoshone squaw squared with what Durand had told him earlier about his antecedents, but before he could pursue it, a fight broke out farther along the plank bar where they were standing, and one Texas drover very nearly bit off the nose of another.

"Damn good squabble," observed Durand.

On the journey between towns, Emil Durand rode beside Roman, pointing out signs—pony tracks here, a buffalo trail there, the path of a rushing jackrabbit across a sandy swale along the a tributary of the Smoky Hill. Min rode behind, leading a pack mule, her gaze constantly on Roman's back.

At least it seemed so to him, for each time he turned to look at her she was watching him.

At night they dug a small fire hole and brewed coffee and fried bacon, and after they ate, Min would bring a tattered banjo from the mule's pack, and then the mountain man would show Roman how to hold his fingers on the frets until the fire died into total darkness, the cries of the coyotes seeming to draw nearer as the purple shadows became black.

"I knew an old Jew man once who sang a song about baboons with red arses," Roman said one night. "Do you know it?"

"No, but by Gawd I can sing you one about ladies with pink arses," said Durand, and he proceeded to do so, twanging the banjo in accompaniment, but Roman couldn't understand any of it because Durand sang it in French.

At first Roman was a little apprehensive about sleeping on the open plains this far west, what with all of the old mountain man's stories about the Cheyenne being out again. But Durand was so confident that the feeling soon passed. Besides, Roman had bought a gallon of rum from a wine merchant in Abilene specifically to provide the refreshment necessary for such a long and dusty horseback ride, so by nightfall he didn't really give a damn whether the Cheyenne appeared or not.

Roman was glad he'd had the foresight to bring along a double fistful of gold coins, for Emil Durand appeared to be penniless. He didn't mind spending them, because Durand did no bowing and scraping or suggesting or anything else that a lot of men might have done. He took what was offered, and Roman offered it all, because he was glad to have such company.

"A gallon of rum," said Durand. "By Gawd, that ort to keep our throats slick till we get to Hays and plenty left over to offer friends a sip after we get there. If we find any friends."

And so they came to this outpost of the army in western Kansas, and Roman, finding Sheridan there, paid his respects and with a what-the-hell attitude joined Forsyth's scouts, as did Durand.

That same day Min disappeared, Roman had no idea where, but Durand suggested that maybe while he and Roman and the rest of Forsyth's band were out hunting Cheyennes, she might make a few dimes and quarters scrubbing clothes for soldiers of the Fort Hays garrison.

Major George Forsyth signed on his last twenty quartermaster civilians at Fort Hays, bringing his little scout unit to fifty. They were actually anything but quartermaster civilians. Most of them couldn't read or write, but they could shoot and ride. They were tough, plains-hardened, Indian-wise men for the most part, exactly what Forsyth wanted in accordance with Sheridan's instructions; collect some good men and go hunting for hostiles and scald them.

They would ride fast and light, stringing no baggage train behind, carrying what they needed on their horses, a little coffee and dried beef and a lot of ammunition for the Spencer repeating carbines that each was issued from Civil War cavalry ordnance stores.

Major Forsyth was the right man for the job, a stocky, squarejawed soldier who, like his commander, believed in straightforward, decisive action. A brown mustache accented the firm set of his full-lipped mouth, but somehow there was a soft look about him, which had to do with his slightly waved hair, parted on the left and swept back like a dandy's over each ear. Appearances to the contrary, there was nothing soft about him.

Second-in-command was Lieutenant Frederick Beecher, and he was equally suited to the task. He was a somewhat frail-looking soldier, especially when he stood near Forsyth, but there was a determined cast to his rather cadaverous features, which may have been a legacy of the wounds he'd received during the war that had left him with a decided limp. But limp or no, he had already seen much service on the frontier.

It was Lieutenant Beecher's duty to hire the men of the command after either Sheridan or Forsyth had taken his own look at each applicant and indicated his approval.

On the day that Roman Hasford inscribed his name on the rolls and Durand made his mark—the last two men to sign on—the others of the group were billeted in two of the fort's barracks, staying out of the sun and sleeping or making weapons ready or squatting on earthen floors and spinning yarns to one another about old Indian fights. As Roman and Durand left the mule shed where they had been issued their Spencers and one blanket each, they saw no signs of any of their comrades, but only the usual regularly uniformed soldiers of the post going about garrison duties or drill.

"It ain't exactly what I had in mind," said Durand. "I wanted to spend a spell with them nigger sojurs, but this is likely better. No lollin' around at some army post, gettin' drunk and whorin'. Right out after the red savages, so I hear. That Lieutenant Beecher's a good man. I served with him before. Forsyth, I ain't ever been with him nowhere. By the bye, where-at's our rum?"

"With the horse gear in the stables," said Roman, feeling an urge to gag at the very mention of it.

"Well, that's the last we'll see of the rum," Durand said. "Horse sojurs can smell evil spirits in a keg as good as they can sniff out a wanton woman."

They moved into the dusky dimness of one of the assigned barracks and saw the shadowy figures of other men, some on the bunk beds abutted to the walls, others on the floor. The place smelled of gun oil and dust and sweat, all of it having a hard, metallic substance to it that stung the nose.

"Find a place," Durand said.

From a dark corner came a voice with a nasal, brittle twang that sounded vaguely familiar to Roman. He moved in that direction, blinking, trying to make out the face of the man slouched on a bunk there. At first all he could see was a fan of whiskers and a long mustache and pale eyes gleaming beneath the wide brim of a hat.

"Never expected to see you out here in the wilderness, sprout."

Roman stared, his eyes slowly becoming accustomed to

the shadows after the harsh sunlight outside. Then he laughed and dropped his gear and held out his hand.

"Tyne Fawley! For hell's sake, where'd you get all that hay on your face?"

"Lost my razor," Fawley said, rising and showing his rows of pine-chip teeth. "You been raisin' a lot of tarnation in Leavenworth since I seen you last?"

"Not much to speak of."

"I expect you're joshin' me. Last time I recollect you and me teamin' up, we got drunk enough for ten men. You ever see my ole gal Katie Rose?"

"Now and again," Roman said, and he was glad for the lack of light in this place, because he could feel his face flushing. And he determined there and then that he would make no mention of the fact that he and Katie Rose Rouse were business partners. And that made him feel a little guilty because it was like being ashamed of the association, which he wasn't.

"I reckon from the looks of that Spencer you just dropped impolite on the floor that you and me and these other bushwhackers is gonna go out and kill a few Cheyennes."

"I reckon so," said Roman, and a little chill of gooseflesh ran up his back at the words Tyne Fawley spoke and at the tone in his voice. Not because there was menace in it, but because Fawley said it as casually as he would have remarked on shooting crows.

On the first morning of his service with Forsyth's scouts, Roman was awakened by a great, booming voice before dawn had made any impression on the night's darkness. Rising from his blanket pallet he saw the figure of a man in the doorway of the barracks, a lighted lantern in one hand and a Spencer carbine in the other. The orange light flickered across the man's face, and Roman stared in horrified fascination and supposed he must be dreaming, because he had never seen such a face before.

The man himself was tall, taller than the door was high,

and slender to the point of frailty, clad in a long coat and fringed leggings and moccasins like canoes with beadwork across the instep. On his head was a low-crowned hat with the widest brim Roman had ever seen, so wide that around the edges it drooped like a great wet sycamore leaf. From beneath the hat hung straight, greasy-looking hair, shoulder-length, that framed a face as fleshless as a skull.

His eyes were deepset under brows that appeared to be chiseled from feldspar, and he had a long nose with tiny nostrils; his wide, lipless mouth was intersected by a deep scar at one corner. The scar was the color of yellow rat cheese and ran up the side of the face, disappearing into the hair in front of the right ear.

And the voice was like close thunder, round and resonant and making painful vibrations in the ear.

"Hark now, you scoundrels and fornicators," the man bellowed. "Pray to the Lord God of Hosts for strength against his enemies on this ninth day of September, 1868, *Anno Domini*. Cast out the vulgar dreams of sleep and wanton desire and get off your arses and come get the sowbelly and beans God Almighty has provided."

And then he was gone, ducking through the door.

Roman heard Emil Durand groan from his own pallet nearby, then go into a coughing fit; then there was the explosive sound of a nose blown between finger and thumb.

"What the hell was *that?*" Roman asked.

Emil Durand spent another moment hawking like a choked dog.

"That's Jacob," he said. "He's a good wilderness man, like me. Only not as old. He starts each day like that, with a God spiel. He's been down south the last few years, sellin' Injun scalps to the Mexicans. Good man to have around in a fight, Roman, and a man of God besides."

Roman started to laugh but sensed a note of seriousness in Durand's voice, and so kept quiet. After the mountain man rose, with accompanying grunts and groans, and stumbled along the rows of scouts coming from their sleep to go outside and relieve himself against the barracks wall, Tyne Fawley chuckled from Roman's other side.

"Sprout, we've done got ourselves in with a batch of crazy men. But don't ever laugh at that crazy son of a bitch parson. He might take the notion of sellin' *your* scalp to somebody."

How the hell did Tyne Fawley know I was about to laugh? Roman wondered. Unless maybe he's had the same urge when that wild-looking man talks.

When he went out to join Emil Durand standing close to the barracks wall, the old man taking a long time to finish, Roman felt the bite of a hard wind from the west, sending before it little particles of sand that felt like birdshot against the skin. He thought of what might lie ahead somewhere out there on the still dark, desolate plain, and wondered if he was destined to put down his grave there where no one would know how his bones rested, not Mama or Cal or Katie Rose. Or Catrina Peel.

Facing the dark barracks wall, he wondered why he should think of Catrina Peel.

"Stand aside, sprout, and let a real stud horse water this army house," said Tyne Fawley, moving close beside him. And Roman felt safe, being in the company of such good men.

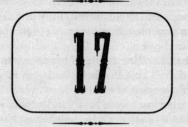

17

They rode out of Fort Hays and on to Fort Wallace, more than a hundred miles to the west. The horses were dust-covered almost before they were well started, and the men's lips were dry and cracked, each man going to his canteen only occasionally, because they all understood the lack of water in this parched land. Emil Durand said the September sun was in a growling mood. Each night they camped without fire, chewing the salty dried beef that made thirst a thing to trouble sleep. Forsyth posted almost a third of them to sentry duty throughout each night, while the brittle stars turned overhead.

Roman Hasford saw little of the well-drilled Fort Leavenworth discipline in these encampments or on the march, either, Forsyth fitting his method of handling the group to the natures of those involved. Yet there were always men to respond to any order, men to move each day to the far flanks to protect them from surprise, men to stay awake during long hours of darkness. And no command was necessary for all of them to keep their weapons ready and their eyes open.

They saw a few buffalo at a distance and twice rode through brown grasslands where there were larks that rose up at the approach of the horses, fluttering and looking like white and yellow slashes of silver and gold in the sun. There were a few hawks overhead, but not nearly as many as Roman could recall seeing in the greener country east of Topeka. At night there was an unending chorus of coyote songs from all around.

For the first time Roman began to appreciate the strange fascination of the Great Plains flatlands, where during daylight the earth seemed to stretch out forever in every direction but at night closed in tight so that the edge of the world seemed within walking distance, only the arch of stars overhead to indicate the vast emptiness. There was a compelling but harsh beauty about it, completely foreign to his childhood hills and deep valleys with their cold-water streams and dense stands everywhere of oak and hickory and walnut.

Once they paused at a sod house where a man and his work-hardened wife and three sons came out to greet them, each of the boys carrying a rifle. These people offered water from their well, and Roman wondered at the hard labor that had put that well down. The water was warm and had a brackish taste, like copper and salt. Everyone took only a few sips, because they all knew what water meant to this man and his family, how precious it was. But because the man seemed so eager to help, they took a few sips and then rode on, the rearguard among them waving goodbye to the five figures standing beside their sod corral where two old horses stood, heads down. As the wind pressed their clothes against their scrawny legs, the three boys waved back forlornly, as though they were saying farewell to the last human beings they would ever see.

"Damned hard place to take root," said Tyne Fawley, his teeth working on the cud of tobacco that was always there now, bulging his lean, whiskered cheeks.

"Waitin' fer the railroad, or salvation in some other form," Durand said. "Say, Fawley, you reckon you could spare a little bite of that eatin' tabacky?"

Fort Wallace was as desolate as Fort Hays had been, a cluster of slab-sides on the open plain with only two sandstone structures to give it any dignity, and a flagpole that looked to be the tallest thing between here and all the rest of eternity, and on it the standard garrison bunting showing the red, white, and blue, whipping out in the wind and frayed at the end.

"You'd think the Yankee army might buy itself a new flag now and again," said Tyne Fawley.

"They ain't often got enough money for ammunition, much less things like flags and payin' their sojurs the sixteen dollars a month promised by the recruiters," Emil Durand said.

A troop of the Tenth Cavalry was at Wallace, but nobody had time to give these new black soldiers more than a quick glance, because they'd no sooner arrived than a telegraph message came over the army wire from Sheridan, who reported that a small settlement to the north of the Smoky Hill had been attacked and a string of wagons caught and burned and two Mexican drivers killed. So Forsyth's men ate quickly and slept briefly, and prepared to ride out hard at the next dawning.

At least they had one heavy meal of boiled beans and sowbelly, and a solid feed of grain for the horses. For many of them, horses and men alike, it would be the last garrison food they would ever eat.

It was difficult to keep track of time on that march. It was blistering sun and cold nights. And watching the endless plains pass under their horses' hooves. Only a few days out of Fort Wallace they picked up the sign of a great many unshod ponies and travois etchings in the dust. Roman didn't know much about such things, but it appeared to him as though they were in pursuit of a lot of Indians.

"Do they know we're here?" he asked.

"They know," said Durand.

"They don't act like they're too concerned. I don't see much evidence they're in any great hurry."

"They ain't," said the mountain man. "They reckon such a piddlin' small bunch as us can't do 'em much harm. Which is what Forsyth wants. Them movin' slow, us fast. So we'll catch up soon."

"The more I measure that trail they're making, the less such a prospect appeals to me."

Tyne Fawley, riding on Roman's other flank, laughed and sent a huge spurt of amber juice into the chopped dirt of the Indian trail.

"They ain't nothin' to get in a lather about, sprout, us with all these repeatin' carbines and most of these bushwhackers with us mean as ole Billy in hell."

"Yes, well, they may have a few ole Billies themselves."

"We'll soon find out what they got," said Durand. "That horseshit they dropped along here ain't more'n a day old."

They were mostly a quiet, purposeful group, little conversation passing among them. Emil Durand was the epitome of all the rest, his old eyes sharp and watchful under the narrow brim of his beaver hat, looking to the distance and glancing down now and again to study the marks in the earth where the ponies had passed. The usual sounds were the scuffing of the horses' hooves and sometimes a small protest from one or the other of the two mules that constituted their entire baggage train. The mules carried extra ammunition, even though each man was weighted down with his own, one hundred forty rounds for the Spencers and another thirty for the revolvers.

Roman was becoming concerned about Excalibur. Each man in the troop carried grain in his saddlebags, but the big stud was accustomed to more than the frugal handful that Roman gave him each night. At least he could take some comfort in knowing that Forsyth and Beecher and the surgeon were riding big army mounts like Excalibur that also needed grain, yet he could detect no concern in their faces.

Only once during their ride from Fort Hays to Fort Wallace and on out to find the Indian trail had the troop commander said anything directly to Roman. On the dusty march between the forts, he'd reined his horse back to ride beside Roman and ask if he was as good with a carbine as with a pistol.

"Your friend Durand here told me you outshot Jared Dane at that turkey contest in Leavenworth."

"Pistol's my worst weapon," said Roman, bloating up a little with pride at the attention. "Long gun's my best. I used to hunt squirrels with a rifle."

"That's good," Forsyth said with the hint of a smile showing beneath his mustache. "Because the things we're after are considerably easier to hit than squirrels."

"Yes, sir," Durand said. "And a damn sight harder to kill."

First there were the shots, and Roman came awake in the half-light of dawn, reaching for Excalibur's reins. This group slept by their mounts, so there was never a necessity for running down a picket line.

After the shots, he heard Jacob's great booming voice.

"Rise and smite the heathen this seventeenth day of September, 1868, *Anno Domini*, and saddle them horses quick, you bleary-eyed sons of bitches!"

All around him were the shadowy figures of men throwing saddles on their horses, pulling down cinches, going up onto mounts with carbines in hand, fully clothed from their sleep, cursing and grunting and spitting. Excalibur caught the excitement, and Roman had a hard time getting the saddle on him until Tyne Fawley rode up on the stud's far flank and held him while Roman threw on the gear and tightened the straps, yanking hard on the leather and smelling the stallion's excitement and cursing him for the first time.

"You hammerheaded bastard, hold still! Hold still, God damn it!"

He was aware of the high crown of Emil Durand's beaver hat going past above his head, the beard flowing beneath, and Durand shouting something Roman couldn't make out. All he heard was the hard pounding of iron-shod horses wheeling and coming to a gallop and still the shots, closer, and the voice of Jacob.

"Roll, Jordan, roll, Jordan!"

Then up into the saddle and the other riders whirling

around him and going to the commanding voice of Beecher, who was waving a hand with a pistol in it, shouting, unheard, but everyone coming into line behind him and his prancing gelding. The night before, they'd ridden into the floodplain of a little stream called the Arikaree, a river that Roman had never heard of, close on the tracks of the many Indian ponies. Now, in the half-light, they were out of sleep, with weapons in their hands.

"They're tryin' to run off some of the horses!" a high voice shouted, and then more shots.

"Roll, Jordan!"

"Pull along the Gawd damned mules!"

"Open fire on those red sonsabitches!"

"They're runnin' now, pour it on."

"Roll, Jordan!"

Roman saw Forsyth turning his mount among them and pointing toward the Arikaree, and they all jerked their rearing horses in behind him as he made a dash for a small island in the mostly bonedry riverbed, where a few stunted willows and a single ragged cottonwood made their mark against the sand.

"There they be, Roman!" Emil Durand shouted, and Roman saw them then, misty riders in cloudbanks of dust, raising a shrill keening that brought out gooseflesh along Roman's back, and the sound unaccountably called back a flashing memory of home and an old man named Ruter who played the saw, holding it clamped between his knees and working a fiddle bow across it until the chill whispers came, a hard vibration of metal, quavering and distant and somehow defiant, everything about it beyond comprehension, as were the voices of the naked horsemen now.

"Stay together!" Beecher shouted. "Stay together for the island!"

There was a renewed burst of firing, and then Excalibur was driving under him and there were little whippets of sound around his face and he knew these were bullets, the firing now suddenly close on one flank, and he heard a horse squeal when it was hit and he heard the men around him cursing and he heard the slashing sounds of quirts across horses' rumps, and there was the thick taste and smell of dust and the confused mass of charging horsemen, but less confused than they appeared, going as a solid body toward the island, and now all around the snap of ricocheting slugs that had struck the ground and whined up among the riders like a fingernail dragged across rusty iron.

Excalibur was surging, going with the others, and Roman let him go, making no effort to guide him but only clutching the saddlehorn in one hand, the Spencer in the other, as the big stud powered his way into the midst of the other running horses. Roman felt a jolt and thought it was a rider behind crowding into him, but then almost at once felt a froth of blood across his lips, hot and salty, flying back from Excalibur's face, and knew the stud had been hit hard with one of those bullets.

There was another little jerk through Excalibur's frame as they came across the sandy stream bottom and onto the island, a little spasm of muscle, and Roman knew his horse was hit again and he tried to ready himself for quick disentanglement when Excalibur went down, so he wouldn't be caught with a leg under the half-ton of horse.

But Excalibur kept running to the point on the island where Roman pulled him in and then he settled, going down with a loud grunt and a moan, sliding to earth gently, as though to make sure he didn't catch the rider under his fall.

"God damn it!" Roman cried, tears starting in his eyes. "They've killed my mule!"

And in the wild melee of sound and smell and surging action, he was not even aware that his mind had jumped to that morning in the yard of Elkhorn Tavern when he was a boy and had been caught in a Rebel charge and his mule had died.

Excalibur's legs were going up, jerking, and his eyes rolled back to Roman and there was a bubbling gush of red at his muzzle and nostrils and Roman shot him once, behind the right ear, the Spencer kicking in the one hand that held it. Roman was crying full out now and cursing and his nose running, his fury making him shake as he dove down behind his dying horse to scoop out a little shelter in the sand.

"God damned Cheyennes," he gasped, and then Tyne Fawley was with him, pulling the saddlebags off the back of Excalibur's saddle, heaving to bring them loose.

"Gotta get that ammunition free of him, sprout," Fawley yelled above the din of general firing now. " 'Cause you're sure'n hell gonna need it."

"Barricade with horses," Beecher was shouting, dismounted now and running among the men, waving a pistol in one hand, his hat gone and his gaunt face red with excitement. "Stay behind the horses!"

All of them were down now, turning their horses' flanks toward the enemy, toward the embankments on either side of the streambed, where Roman could see the ponies and the riders and the blossom of quick white smoke when they fired their weapons. Struck horses were screaming and there was the sudden howl of a wounded man, a sound not nearly so terrifying to Roman's ears as the agony of the horses. Some of the scouts were shooting their own mounts, bringing them down to form a barrier against the shots coming from the far banks, and then firing themselves, the barrels of their carbines laid across the still quivering bodies of their horses.

Then the keening mass charged down the streambed, waving rifles and lances and hatchets, and everyone on the island opened on them and Roman worked the lever of the Spencer until he realized he'd shot the magazine dry. He snapped open the wooden ammunition carrier to reload, noticing with some amazement that his hands were no longer shaking, that his eyes, even with the sweat pouring into them, were clear and his vision sharp.

The charge broke off to either side of the island and they breathed heavily, gulping in the dirty air, but the respite was short and the ponies came again, and they aimed for the horses, bringing some down in a catapulting whirl of dust so thick that it became hard to see what was happening only a few yards from the tip of the island. The naked warriors veered off to either side again and Roman gritted his teeth against the taste of black powder. The barrel of the Spencer was so hot it blistered his hand when he touched it.

Roman couldn't believe how far the sun had moved across the eastern sky. It had all happened so quickly, the abrupt rousing from sleep, the run to the island, the two charges. As though all time had been compressed into a few flaming moments. As he waited for the next charge he felt the sun's hot presence almost squarely overhead. He was amazed that he felt no hunger at all, only thirst, and that was somehow magnified by the swarms of biting gnats that feasted on his eyelids and lips.

"Here they come again!" someone shouted.

Then Forsyth yelled, "Volley fire. Full magazines, men, and volley fire. And this time, don't shoot until I say."

And they came, more than before, filling the streambed, and in front rode a huge warrior waving a rifle and wearing a feather headdress of a kind that few except the Cheyenne wore.

"Roman Nose," Jacob was shouting. "Roman Nose. The son of a bitch fornicator, heathen Satan abomination, kill him, kill him! Lord Gawd Almighty, kill him!"

Roman was at the point of the island and he saw the big Cheyenne coming fast, waving his arms and riding a large chestnut painted in yellows and reds.

The lever on the Spencer jammed for a second and Roman clawed at it, cursing, and frantically rolled to one side, the carbine working now and a round going into the chamber as the big Cheyenne's pony went directly over him, soaring, blotting out the sun for an instant. Roman lifted the Spencer in one hand and fired at the Cheyenne's broad back and the chestnut pony broke away to one side and off the island and through the thick dust of the dry streambed and there were other warriors around Roman Nose then, and all Roman could understand of it were the shouts.

"We got him, we got Roman Nose."

And that charge was finished, split like the others, and a lot of their ponies down and warriors riding past their fallen companions and lifting them up from the dust and carrying them out of range. And Roman Nose, too, was carried off, slipped from the back of his pony by many hands, the pony running free and ass-shot at the far bank and then rolling back screaming and thrashing and a few of the scouts shouting with joy, Jacob among them.

"Roman Nose, you son of evil, blight on the children of God, damn you, damn you, bleed."

Roman lay panting and wondering if it had been his snap shot that did it. It was close, too close to miss, but he felt no jubilation, only a vast relief that now the Cheyenne and Sioux were drawing back. Not far, but at least not coming on again. *The things we're after are considerably easier to hit than squirrels,* Forsyth had said.

God Almighty, Roman thought, I've been shooting at men here. I wonder if maybe Papa felt a little sick about it, too, when he was in the war.

Jacob was prancing among the stunted willows, shouting, his mouth wide open beside the livid scar.

"Bleed, you heathen, bleed."

God Almighty, thought Roman, I'd a lot rather shoot *that* son of a bitch than one of those pony riders.

Now came the calm and the thirst and the gnats. And Forsyth was down with three wounds, one to the thigh, the slug deeply embedded. Beecher was dead. The surgeon was dead. And already half of the men in the command were either dead or wounded.

Trying to find some reality to hang on to, Roman rolled over behind Excalibur's huge form and looked at Tyne Fawley, only a few feet away, behind his own dead horse. Tyne Fawley was grinning and chewing his cud and showing teeth through the tangled beard that was now colored with the brown juice of his chewing.

"Well, sprout, you sure'n hell seen some Cheyennes now, ain't you?"

"I never reckoned to see 'em just like this," Roman said, and his voice broke a little.

Tyne Fawley stopped grinning and spat off to one side and then crawled over, dragging his hot Spencer alongside, and put one hand on Roman's shoulder and shook him. And then the grin came again and he shook Roman's shoulder once more and Roman felt the hardwood texture of his fingers.

"Don't worry, sprout," he said. "It ain't nothin' you can change. We all of us do what we hafta do when we're set down in a place."

"I never reckoned it'd be like this," Roman said, lying back with his head against Excalibur's dead flank. "I saw some of it once, but watching it and doing it is two different things."

"Don't worry about it," said Tyne Fawley, shaking Roman's shoulder again. "Have a little chew. It'll ease your mind."

And Roman did.

The Cheyennes didn't come again that day. The sun moved slowly across the sky and the men dug pits in the sand of the island so the water would seep in and they could replenish empty canteens. With the surgeon dead, they tended one another's wounds and Jacob showed some aptitude for such things and Emil Durand, his own face scarred and bloody from a Cheyenne bullet, said it was because the Holy Roller son of a bitch had all that experience from skinning hair off people's heads down in the Southwest.

But the man with the horrible scar on his face and the hair that hung like dyed Spanish moss saved a few of them, pronouncing, after each application of his skill, a fiery benediction over the bloody bandages.

He refused to treat Forsyth's thigh wound. After considerable probing with dirty fingers, with Forsyth gritting his teeth, Jacob announced that the ball was so close to the big artery that cutting out the lead could only bring death by excessive bleeding.

So, in great pain, Forsyth cut the bullet out himself, using a straight razor.

"Gawd damn," said Emil Durand. "That man's got some real sand in him, ain't he?"

Then the stars came with the evening and Roman could see Venus and thought about the times when he and his father would sit on the porch and talk about the heavens and that lovely white planet hanging far down on the horizon and seeming to touch Pea Ridge with its light, and the smell of late locust blossoms in their noses and the sound of the springhouse hollow mockingbird in their ears, a long time before the Yankees came and a long time before Roman's father marched off to the war.

After that, when the purple along the eastern horizon gave way to black, there came the singing of chants and incantations, or whatever they were, floating to them in a serenade from the banks of the Arikaree, sharply discordant to the white men's ears but like waves of water, as though somehow in the night the river had run full again to cleanse everything away, all the dust and blood and dying.

18

That night they lifted up only one song in defiant response to the Sioux and Cheyennes' singing from beyond the Arikaree's banks, and that was only the single ragged voice of a man wounded in the cheek and the shoulder, and the song he sang was in defiance not only of the red man but of other, former enemies as well. He mouthed the words to the tune of "Joe Bowers," a song much heard among the Texas drovers in saloons from Abilene to Hays City, but the quality of his singing was not as good, because his voice was not oiled with drygulch whiskey as the Texans' always were, and besides, the bullet that struck his cheek had knocked out half a dozen of his few remaining teeth.

Oh, I'm a good old Rebel! Now that's just what I am . . .

With nightfall the pitiful noises on the island had gone. The horses were all dead and the wounded men tended to, though roughly, their pain at least dulled by generous draughts of laudanum dispensed from the dead surgeon's bag. Some said that Jacob, who administered this tincture of opium, had taken a few sips himself, although he was unscathed by ball or arrow. And so the cries of wounded men were stilled.

They lay behind their dead horses beside damp rifle pits they had scooped out of the island's sands, chewing dried beef. A few of them were already skinning back the hide from a horse's rump to slice off a mouthful or two of fresh raw meat, raw because Forsyth had ordered no fires. And with good cause, for even now there was an occasional shot from the far banks, the bullet winging off harmlessly into the night with no light of fire to make an aiming point.

"Just to let us know they ain't forgot about us," said Emil Durand.

And on this night they heard no coyotes, although since leaving Fort Wallace, and Fort Hays before that, they had not known a moment of darkness when the calls were not frequent and close.

Forsyth called a council of war after evening came. He sat propped against a dead horse under the cottonwood tree, the bandage on his thigh showing ghostly white in the darkness, and his two senior scouts bent over him.

"If they leave tonight," said Forsyth, "they might get a relief column to us within a week or so."

"If the red bastards don't cotch 'em on the way," one scout said.

"We'll send another pair tomorrow night."

"If we're still here," said the second scout.

"I'll take the first swing at it," the first scout said.

"No. I want you two here. I need you here. Somebody else. But neither one of you."

"All right. There's Emil. He's old but he's still got some hard bark on him."

"And who else?" asked Forsyth.

"That young Hasford. He's got some guts, maybe. Besides, he's strong as a pullin' mule, and levelheaded besides."

"The squirrel shooter," Forsyth said, and rubbed his wounded leg. "Well, he's a woodsman, coming from where he does. I suspect he can read his path by the stars."

"Damn few woods here, Major, but a mite of stars," said the first scout.

"Yes," Forsyth said, letting his head fall back against the

dead horse's flank and gazing up through the thin branches of the cottonwood and holding his wounded thigh in both hands, gently.

"Damn! It hurts like hell, but I can't get myself bamboozled with any of that painkiller. All right. Young Hasford. I like the set of his jaw. Stubborn, I'll bet. Young and tough."

"All right," said the first scout. "If it ain't me and Big John here, then them two. They got as good a chance as any, I reckon."

"Get 'em over here, quick. Moon's due in a few minutes."

As the scouts slithered off through the darkness, Forsyth rubbed his wounded leg, smiling as he heard the words of the song coming from beneath the hanging limbs of a nearby willow.

> . . . *For this fair land of freedom I do not care a damn.*
> *I'm glad I fit against it, I only wisht we'd won.*
> *An' I don't want no pardon for anything I've done.*

Roman Hasford heard the singing, too, and it was a welcome counterpoint to the deep, throbbing chants coming along the wind from the night beyond. He had tried since darkness fell to see Sioux and Cheyenne fires out in the flat Arikaree floodplain, but there was only starlit blackness, the foreign voices seeming to come from the bodiless, impersonal plains.

They're singing in the dark, he thought, or else they've kindled their fires too far back for us to see.

It disturbed him a little. If he could have seen a glimmer of fire he might have been able to put some kind of human quality on it, but as things stood, there was only the night and the vibrating sound, interchangeable and meaningless except for its menace; a threat he could associate only with lying in bed in the dark as a very young child and wondering what kind of terrible thing might be ready to crawl from the rafters and devour him.

And they know that, he thought. They know it's meaner to play on my mind than on my flesh.

It was like being at the bottom of a deep well with the brilliant stars above, watching him like animal eyes. And the animal voices murmuring their challenge. And so the old soldier's song, coming in a quavering voice from the willow close to where Forsyth lay, was welcome. Because it assured him that no matter what else, there was no unmentionable thing oozing down from the rafters to consume him. Only men, who were vulnerable to bullets.

As he chewed his jerked beef, looking at the night sky, listening to the old Rebel's song, the picture came into his mind of an engraving he'd seen a long time ago, when he first came to Kansas. It had been in *Harper's Weekly* and had portrayed a scene set near the Capitol Building in Washington City, the dome unfinished, truncated, and a scaffold in the foreground where the Federal Union had hanged a man named Wirz, the commandant of the Andersonville prison, because his treatment of Yankee prisoners of war had been inhuman.

God Almighty, Roman thought, what makes a man's mind jump all that way to someplace he's never been, from Colorado Territory to a far town and an execution?

And thinking of his own position here on this small island, surrounded by hostiles, the word *execution* made his skin crawl.

Roman lay with his hat off and his head against Excalibur's cold flank, done with crying now about the big stud's demise in battle. His teeth worked methodically on a hunk of cold dried beef that seemed to grow larger in his mouth as the chewing progressed. He heard Tyne Fawley nearby, breathing heavily, and knew the yellow-eyed man was sleeping. And pulling his mind away from his situation, Roman thought of things. Just things. How gooseberries tasted so sour and yet so sweet in one of his mother's cobblers; how his father's face had taken on new lines after he'd seen the war with General Lee, and how maybe now his own face would be somehow changed too, somehow different; how little Catrina Peel's black eyes, the few times he'd seen them, had exposed a depth that was frightening; and how mysterious it was to watch a hand and five fingers holding a pen or pencil and making symbols on a sheet of foolscap that others who knew the code could comprehend.

> *. . . I can't take up my musket and fight 'em now no more.*
> *But I ain't agonna love 'em and that's fer certain shore!*

Maybe Papa had crazy things like this go through his mind after a battle, Roman thought.

And lying there in the darkness he felt a worm of disquiet squirming in his brain because he'd given his father such short-tempered consideration when he came home from the war, had even come close to hating him because of the change in his manner. Now, listening to the old Rebel's song, he felt closer to Martin Hasford than he had since he was a boy and his father took him into the woods in dawn's light and showed him where wild turkeys had roosted in low cedars, or where a vixen and her kits had played in the leaf mold of the oaks and hickories along some Ozark ridge. And that made the disquiet even worse because here he was beyond all chance of telling his father as much. And he knew that even if they were face to face, the old hill-family reticence when it came to showing emotion would stand like a wall between them.

One of the senior scouts touched Roman's shoulder and he jumped.

"Major wants to see you."

As they slipped through the darkness to where Forsyth lay, Roman could hear two others behind them, and he knew one of them was Emil Durand. When they came to the cottonwood tree and the dead horse there, they grouped tightly around the commander and Roman could smell the sweat of the others, old and going cold now, and he could smell blood and some sour odor that he supposed was either vomit or else the harsh water that had seeped up into the many rifle pits.

Forsyth didn't waste any time getting to it, because moonrise would come before long.

"Do you two men think you can slip out of this mess?" he asked.

"We can sure'n hell give 'er a try, Major," said Durand instantly.

"Hasford?"

"Yes, sir, I think so."

"All right. There's considerable urgency here, so listen carefully, because I won't say it a second time."

"We're listenin', Major," said Durand.

"We need somebody to know what's happened to us here. We need help as fast as we can get it. So you two will get away from here, right now, and go to Fort Wallace. There likely aren't any troops closer than that. Due south for most of the way, but once you're clear of the hostiles, veer a little to the east or you might end up in Texas two weeks from now. You'll have to travel at night, at first anyway. But you've got to move as fast as you can, and not get lost and not get caught by the hostiles."

"Yes, sir," Roman said, but Durand only grunted.

"Take one full canteen each, a pocketful of dried beef, and revolvers. If they catch you, no amount of weapons two men might have will make any difference, and Spencers and their ammunition are heavy. Besides, we'll likely be able to use those Spencers here.

"I suspect you'll find hostile activity all the way to the Smoky Hill. So you've got to be on the lookout."

They were all silent a moment, Forsyth holding his wounded thigh. Roman could hear Durand breathing heavily.

"Major," Roman asked, "how far is it to Fort Wallace?"

"Not far," Forsyth said. "About a hundred miles."

The voice of the old Rebel, singing his song, came distant and haunting to Roman's ears.

> *. . . And I don't want no pardon fer what I was and am,*
> *And I won't be reconstructed 'cause I don't give a damn!*

They left the island on the upstream side and went about a mile along the center of the riverbed, sometimes walking through spongy sand, sometimes on bare rock, and Roman tried to move as quietly as did Emil Durand, who seemed to float above the ground, the tips of his moccasins feeling out each contour like the fingers of a sensitive hand.

"Don't look at anything direct," Durand had whispered as they departed the besieged scouts. "Look a little off to the side. You can see better in the dark that way."

"I know that," said Roman.

"An' if we sight anything along these banks, just go down easy. Like you was molasses meltin' into the ground. Then we can decide what to do when we're belly-down."

Twice while they were moving along the streamline, they sank down as war parties of mounted warriors rode along the banks. The second time, the Indians were very close, and as he lay panting, Roman clutched the Navy Colt in his hand and listened to the talking of the passing hostiles. He was struck by how confident they seemed, as though out on a summer lark, in no hurry, their lances and rifles shining in the coming moonlight.

When they moved, it was like creeping along a dark tunnel except for the stars overhead. They could hear the Sioux and Cheyenne singing in the darkness on either side, as though the whole exuberant mass of warriors were moving beside them along the banks, teasing them, daring them to try to break away.

Sometimes there was shouting and laughter, and once Roman was sure he heard the trilling voices of women, and often they heard the pounding of pony hooves, as though races were being held. Once they were so close to the Indian camps that Roman thought he could smell the odor of cooking meat, spitted over a fire, but he saw no fire glow anywhere, only the night beginning to lighten as the moon rose. He heard the call of a night bird, sharp and mournful, but Roman couldn't recognize it and that was enough to make him wonder.

What the hell am I doing out here on this pool-table land where I don't even know the birds, much less the damned naked people?

Finally, with the banks of the river closing in on them from both sides, they moved to the southern escarpment and pressed themselves against the wall of hard-baked sand and took a sip of water.

"God Almighty, that tastes awful," Roman said.

"All right," Durand whispered. "What we do now . . ."

He stopped and his hand went to Roman's shoulder and he made a little hissing noise and Roman could see a hand coming up and a large revolver in it, and hear the click of the hammer as Durand pulled it back.

Then Roman saw, coming up the draw of the dry riverbed, a dark form, coming the way they had come, and he lifted his Navy Colt and felt a huge lump growing in his chest and heard a soft grunt as a foot struck a protruding rock in the streambed and saw the dark outline of a low-crowned, wide-brimmed hat.

"Wait," Roman whispered. "It's Fawley!"

Tyne Fawley crawled up to them, his teeth shining among the mustache whiskers that the moon turned to silver cornsilk.

"That you, boys?" he whispered.

"You dumb son of a bitch," Durand said, lowering his pistol. "You about got your damn fool head shot off."

"Couldn't let you two pilgrims get lost in the dark," Tyne Fawley whispered. "Took me some leave of that bunch back there. Now. I'll tag along to Fort Wallace."

"You crazy son of a bitch," said Durand. "Likely Forsyth'll hang you to a plum tree when he catches up to you. Iffen the Cheyenne don't get your arse first."

"Hush, old man, and take a chew of this," said Tyne Fawley, and passed Emil Durand his plug of tobacco.

By then Durand's shoulders were shaking with silent laughter.

"Jesus Gawd, I'm in with a walleyed insane posse of men," he said, worrying off a good cud of tobacco with his teeth. "I wisht to Gawd we all had us a good drink of whiskey!"

Roman took a chew as well, and then Tyne Fawley reached out and squeezed his arm and Roman could see the shine of Fawley's eyes and the glint of his teeth inside the tangle of hair. And though he knew they were smack-dab in the midst of a lot of hostiles, he felt better than he had all day, since first seeing those riders in the dust at dawn, trying to run off their horses.

"So let's trot on outa here, what say, sprout?"

And they crept up over the sandy bank and out onto the flat, high plain where the coming moon had begun to give a pale distinction to the land.

The first night they made less than ten miles, crawling some of the time, Emil Durand leading. They could hear the hostiles all around them as the moon arched overhead, but the presence of white men was so unexpected by the warriors that they were something less than alert. Each time a party of horsemen passed close by, Roman lay face down in the dried short grass and hoped none of the ponies would step on him.

As the first hint of dawn came to the east, they were still in the midst of Sioux and Cheyenne. There were little encampments scattered across the prairie, stretching out like a great Sun Dance gathering or some such thing, and the tribes seemed to have taken up semipermanent residence around the Arikaree, with tipis up and pony herds in little clusters and guarded by the young boys. About two miles south of the river they had begun to see fires, the women apparently so confident of their security that many of the blazes were not set in holes to conceal them, as was the usual custom.

Before full light, Durand found a small dry-wash tributary of the Arikaree and they slithered into a bend of it and slept through the sun time under a hedge of overhanging dry grass along the southern rim, so they would be in shadow during the day, each of them taking a shift as sentry. Roman spent his time on watch peering over the edge of the embankment, his hat off and his face hidden in the weeds, and saw many horsemen, but none of them came close enough for him to hear their voices.

The second night they traveled almost twenty miles, according to Durand's reckoning, and only had to go down twice with the near approach of riders. They walked well into the daylight and finally took cover along a rock outcrop that ran across the plain for almost a mile like a low wall that some ancient man or god had put in place at a whim.

"We're out of the main bunch now," said Durand. "But there'll be some more of the sonsabitches, you can wager. Just driftin' around on the edge of what's happenin' at the Arikaree."

"Outriders," Tyne Fawley said.

"Some, maybe. But mostly just the curious, hangin' on to the edge of big doin's they ain't quite ready to throw in with yet. But any we see out here'll be mean as a wounded wolf, 'specially they see there's only the three of us."

The next night Durand found a small sump hole, a place in the plains where the ground water oozed up through the underlying rock, an artesian seep of water that came all the way from the snows in the Rockies and was there even in the dry seasons. They refilled their canteens, the water brackish but welcome, despite the bad taste. Roman's canteen was already empty.

"Sprout," Tyne Fawley said, "you gotta take it a little on the easy side with that water."

"The damned beef is salty and makes me thirsty."

"Get yourself a little stone," said Durand. "Suck on it like rock candy. That'll help. But don't swaller it."

Roman laughed, remembering how his mother had always been concerned with his bowel movements. It had been a long time now since he'd dropped his pants.

"It's bad on the constipation, I reckon," he said.

Durand snorted. "Doin' a shit each mornin' is the least of what we got to worry about now. I reckon we still got about sixty miles to go. After we get to Fort Wallace, you can fill ever' latrine they dug there. And meantime, you gotta fart when they's savage Injuns about, do it quiet in your own pants."

Roman bristled, but the old mountain man turned away and Roman took it all as good advice and kept his mouth shut. But he thought, God Almighty! He's not dealing with some greenhorn!

Each night they did better than the last. And on the fourth day they walked well into the sun until they came to an old buffalo wallow, a wide, round dish of dust sinking below the level of the plain. At one edge of the wallow was the carcass of a long-dead buffalo, the meat rotted away or taken by the buzzards and coyotes, but the hide stretched like a mossy tent over the ribs.

"Damn fine hidin' place," Durand said. "An' I can sure'n hell use me some sleep."

They packed themselves into the carcass under the hide, where it didn't smell very good and where there were still big-bellied September flies and a swarm of gnats and a few green-backed beetles with shells hard as a fingernail and bigger than cartridges for a Spencer repeating rifle.

"You oughta feel right at home, sprout," said Tyne Faw-ley, chuckling. "It's pert' near as good as that boardin'house you've been stayin' in Leavenworth."

"Except there's no crock of cool beer," Roman said.

"Don't talk about no beer," Durand said, making himself comfortable between the other two. "I'm so Gawd damned thirsty I could drink horse piss iffen it was cold enough."

"I always reckoned that's what you mostly drunk anyway, mean as you be," said Fawley, but Durand only grunted and closed his eyes.

The drone of flies had almost lulled Roman to sleep when he gave a start at Tyne Fawley's sudden hiss.

"We got us some company, boys!"

Coming across the flat yellow plain in the morning sun were half a dozen naked men riding ponies daubed with paint, the tails clubbed and feathers hanging from the manes. Roman could see lances and at least two rifles, and he eased the Navy Colt from his belt because this war party was headed directly toward the buffalo wallow.

"Easy now," whispered Durand, his eyes wide and shin-ing now. "They ain't too many, and we got five, six shots each of us."

"I got twelve," said Fawley, and he held a cocked revolver in each hand.

The war party was close enough now for them to see the features of each face, the cheeks high-boned and glistening with black paint.

"Let 'em get close," Durand said. "Shoot 'em all right off, because if we leave any they'll ride back for friends who can't be a far piece, and then we're bear grease in the cookpot. Them's Cheyennes."

As they hunkered in the old buffalo carcass, the Cheyenne came closer, then stopped less than a pistol shot away, talking loudly and making little signs with their hands. They began to dismount and started grooming their ponies, pulling dried grass from the plains floor and rubbing down flanks and rumps and then taking fresh paint from loincloth belt pouches to refurbish the red and blue and black designs on the horses' hides.

Roman was holding the Navy Colt, feeling the sweat on his palms, and there was a little tug at his left leg. Just a little tug and then a stinging, searing pain in the calf just above the boot top.

"God Almighty," he whispered, and Emil Durand turned to him with his hand up before his mouth and then they saw it, sliding fat-bodied and turnip-headed from beneath the buffalo carcass. It was a prairie rattlesnake about three feet long, the scales greenish yellow with black markings all along the back.

"It got me," Roman gasped. "The son of a bitch got me."

"What the hell?" Tyne Fawley said, turning from his watching post at the ass end of the carcass, and he saw the snake going away and cursed.

"Be quiet, for Gawd's sake," said Durand.

Then the snake turned and started back toward the sheltering shade of the buffalo hide and Tyne Fawley bent toward it and shot a stream of amber from between his wide-spaced teeth. The tobacco juice hit the snake square in the face and it recoiled, rattled dryly, and slowly turned away, weaving a pattern through the dust of the wallow, moving away from them like a fat sausage.

"God Almighty, it stings," Roman whispered.

"Take care of the bite," Fawley said to Emil Durand. Taking a large, bone-handled jackknife from his trousers pocket, he opened it with his teeth and handed it to the mountain man. "I'll take care of the Cheyenne."

Working in the cramped quarters of the old carcass, Durand picked up the dropped Navy Colt, let down the hammer, and positioned the knife.

"This ain't gonna be too Gawd damned pleasant," he said. "So tighten up your gut, Roman, and don't make no noise."

Roman pressed his head back against the ribs of the dead buffalo, feeling the heat of the sun against the hide over his face. The sweat was running along his neck, and when Emil Durand cut the trouser away from his leg and slit the boot top and made the incisions over the two tiny puncture holes in his calf, he hardly felt it at all, but knowing it was happening, he ground his teeth together and refused to look at the bloody work the mountain man was doing on his leg. And didn't really know what was being done.

"Gimme that cud," Emil Durand said, and taking Fawley's soggy wad of tobacco, he pressed it against the wound and Roman could hear the rip of cloth as Durand took part of the trouser leg and cut it again and made a bandage. He wrapped it tight around the snakebite, the tobacco making an odd lump. To Roman the leg began to feel more like an oak stump than a leg.

"The red niggers are leavin'," Tyne Fawley said.

"Which way?" asked Durand.

"Off north," said Fawley. "Mountin' up now, jabberin' like crows. By Gawd, old man, I kinda wanted them sonsabitches to come close enough to kill."

"You're crazy as hell," Durand said.

"God Almighty, it feels like a hot iron," Roman said.

"Don't worry about it," Tyne Fawley said, still watching the departing warriors. "You ain't no man until you been bred and until you been snakebit."

"Horseshit," said Durand. "This here is a bad time for snakebite. We're in a hurry, and if this boy walks now, he'll die sure as hell."

"Wait a minute," Roman said, but the other two continued to talk as though he weren't there. Fawley watched as the Cheyenne rode off, disappearing finally into the yellow plains. Then he sighed and let down the hammers of his revolvers and replaced the pistols in his waistband holsters, and Emil Durand took up a canteen and sloshed a mouthful of water into Roman.

"Don't forget what we're out here for," said Durand. "We gotta get to Fort Wallace, or else them men back yonder is dog meat."

"I don't give a damn about those men back there," Fawley said. "They took their chance. But you go on if you feel like it."

"This boy can't walk. You don't walk around the prairies with a snakebite. You keep your arse still and quiet."

"I ain't talkin' about this boy walkin'," Fawley said. "I'm talkin' about *you* walkin'. You go ahead and light out when the sun's down and me and him'll come on."

"Come on, hell!"

"You heard me, old man."

"This boy can't come on now."

"I'll carry him."

"Wait a minute," Roman said. By now the pain in his leg had run up the whole left side of his body like hot syrup spilled from the bubbling pan.

"Hush, Roman, you ain't got nothin' to do with this," said Durand.

"That's right, just hush," Fawley said. "Lay back and sleep, and give him some more water, old man."

"I was fixin' to."

Roman Hasford had only a hazy, unclear notion of when Emil Durand set off on his own, walking with the sun casting little halos of brilliant light around the top of his beaver hat. And never looking back as his slouching, long-gaited walk took him farther and farther away. He seemed to grow smaller and smaller until he was finally gone in the last lingering copper shine of evening.

They'd moved out of the buffalo carcass by then, and before the shadows began their creep across the wallow, Roman's leg was swollen so badly that Tyne Fawley had to slit the boot all the way to the instep. The fever had come on strong, and Fawley wiped Roman's face with a piece of cloth torn from the trouser leg, only just barely dampened. Emil Durand had left his canteen, but even so they had no abundance of water.

Before they moved, Fawley lightened his load, disassembling one of his revolvers with a jackknife that he used as a screwdriver. After taking out the cylinder, he threw it as far as he could in one direction, then threw the impotent pistol as far as he could in the other.

"No need leavin' a gun that works for some painted heathen to pick up," he said, knowing even as he said it that Roman was incapable of understanding his words.

Then he thought, What the hell, and went through the same operation with his second revolver. He dumped all of his ammunition into the dust of the wallow, and Roman's as well, keeping only the Navy Colt with five chambers charged, and slipping it—their only defense now—into his waistband.

He consolidated the water, and there was barely enough to fill one canteen. He threw away his bowie knife and its heavy sheath and decided what the hell again, and cut off both of Roman's boots with the jackknife and threw the boots into the surrounding grass and reckoned maybe he'd saved two pounds. But he slipped the closed jackknife back into his trousers because he always felt a little more comfortable with a blade at hand.

He thought about taking off his own boots, but decided against it. He knew his soles were no longer as tough as they had been when he was a child, running the Ozark hardwood forests in his bare feet.

Finally, with the light fading, he took up Roman Hasford's limp form piggyback and started south.

There was mostly just the pain in the leg and the smell of Tyne Fawley's sweat and the blackness around them. Before midnight, the hallucinations began. He thought it was Calpurnia carrying him past the chicken coop and on down into the springhouse hollow that summer when he was five years old and had gotten a splinter in his foot from the rough planks of the back porch and Cal had said she'd carry him to the springhouse but he'd damn well have to walk back on his own, because she'd be carrying the crock of buttermilk.

Sometimes glaring silver balls came up through the night to blind him and he tried to hide his face behind the tangle of Tyne Fawley's hair, and then he could feel the sweat and taste its saltiness. And he knew it wasn't his sweat but Tyne Fawley's, because his own skin was as parched and dry as old bull hide left in the sun. And sometimes the balls, coming at him like gigantic bullets, were black, blacker than the night, with a shine behind them, terrifying with their size and speed and with the sounds that accompanied them, which were really the songs of coyotes nearby.

And sometimes his left leg below the knee, where Tyne Fawley's arm hooked under it, felt like a railroad tie, heavy and split and dead, all the sap of the wood bubbled out with interior heat and dripping off his stocking-clad toes. And sometimes he saw in his fevered mind the shapes and forms of things past, now wavering on the horizon like mirages of water that constantly retreated before him over a sun-bleached field.

There was no orderly progression in his images, because after he thought it was Cal carrying him, he could see himself on the kitchen table where his mother and the old Jew from the Sugar Creek mill had dug out the splinter, Cal and his father holding him, and the smell of coal oil as his mother drenched the foot in it before she used the knife, and the old Jew holding his foot and singing a song about baboons with red tails.

And the voice of his mother was clearer to him than Tyne Fawley's heavy breathing. She was holding the stone-sharpened knife and saying that this wasn't anything compared to the time the barber in Bentonville had to cut out old man Ruter's appendix with no painkiller except a few swallows of white whiskey.

"Don't hurt me, Mama," Roman gasped as he had that night on the kitchen table.

"I ain't gonna hurt you, sprout," said Tyne Fawley, striding through the darkness.

The next day they went on after sunrise, Tyne Fawley saying to hell with the Cheyennes, and if they appeared they'd do so at their own risk. They stopped often, and Fawley forced a few bites of dried beef that he'd already chewed into a mush himself into Roman's mouth. And he gave Roman a few sips of water, but only a few because the water was almost gone.

Of it all, the only thing that Roman could make sense of was Tyne Fawley's hairy face bent close to his own like a bushy slab of planed lumber, and the sound of Tyne Fawley's hard voice.

"It ain't far now, sprout. It ain't far."

And then the babbling delirium came and he was thrashing like a fish just out of water, the hook still in his mouth, and Tyne Fawley struggled to hold him in place, piggyback, as they went on, step by step, across the miles.

And then nothing.

19

First were the September flies. They came to him from what seemed a great distance, but soon their faint buzzing was a roar in his ears and he could feel their sticky feet across his nose and open lips.

Then the strong odor of carbolic and talcum and alcohol liniment, and even before he came to full consciousness it re-called to his mind the smells of the little room in the Topeka hospital and Jared Dane lying in bed with a white sheet to his chin and a smile so faint it could hardly be called a smile at all, and the sagging, vacant place under the sheet where his left arm should have been.

Then the sensation of wetness clinging to him as though he were underwater in a cold pool, yet his body hot, and as he rose to full awareness he knew he was lying on his back, naked except for some kind of knee-length gown that was soaked with sweat, and the sheet covering him from neck to toes wet as well. And remembering Jared Dane and what had happened in the buffalo wallow, he had a moment of panic, wondering if he still had both his legs, but then he was sure he did, because of the pain just below the knee where the snake had struck.

The ceiling of the room came into focus slowly and he

knew his eyes had been open for a long time, but sight came with halting, blurred hesitation. There were heavy rafters below a low-peaked roof, all of it whitewashed and the whitewash peeling and showing spots of bare wood like brown rot on bleached bones. He waited a long time before he tried to move his head, and when he finally did, he saw the rows of white-covered empty beds between his own and a far wall, where a door stood open to the yellow glare of sunlight. There were windows in the wall facing him, two of them, and the sunbeams slanting into the room through them were shafts of golden gauze in the fine dust that hung suspended.

After a long while he looked the other way. Sitting beside his bed, brushing at the flies with an eagle-feather fan, was Min, her black eyes fixed piercingly on his face, and seeming, in their deep intensity, to generate all the heat that made the perspiration pour from his body. As he looked at her, trying to decide who she was, Min placed the eagle-feather fan on her lap, lifted his head with one hand behind his neck, and took a blue-enameled cup from a bedside table and placed it to his lips.

His first coherent thought was, Why, hell, this is some kind of soup and no hotter than the air in this place and about as salty.

And only after he had swallowed it all, even though his throat felt tight and swollen, did Min lower his head to the straw-stuffed pillow and he, with one last look at the skeletal rafters overhead, closed his eyes and fell into a deep, sweaty sleep.

He woke once during the night, and the ward was dark because since nobody else was there, Min had taken it on herself to blow out the single coal-oil lamp bracketed alongside the door. He was lucid but weak, and she had to help him outside to the adjoining privy, which he suspected in this place was called a latrine, and he thought, as he sat on one of the three holes he had groped for in the dark, that his mother would be happy that he'd finally had a bowel movement, though small and insignificant. At the same time he knew, too, that she wouldn't appreciate at all that he'd been helped in the endeavor by a godless Crow squaw, who had indeed helped even to the extent of holding up his hospital gown while he sat there.

Oh, Mama, you're not here, he thought, recalling the times when he was less than five years old and constipated, and it had been her beside him on the pot, holding his bare belly in her wonderfully soft yet strong hands and urging, "Do it, do it, just push it out."

As Min helped him back into the building, he thought, God Almighty, there's all kinds of terribly personal things a man thinks of after he's been snakebit.

Back in his bed, the Crow woman fed him another cup of cold soup, and this time he sat up to take it, though he didn't really want it, but felt she would force it down his throat one way or the other. The room was misty silver in the moonlight coming through the two windows, and he could see the shine of her eyes like coals lighted with some flameless fire. He thought of the men on that dry island in the Arikaree and wondered briefly if the moon, the same moon, was shining there and on the Cheyenne and Sioux around them.

He slept again, never once wondering where he was or how it had come about that Min was there, but this time going into deep slumber, wet with new, hot sweat. Near dawn he woke, the silver moonlight at the windows gone and in its place the gray, colorless herald of coming day. He was shivering with chills, and then, as he lay on his side, he felt the Crow woman slip under the sheet and move tight against his back like half of a glove onto a cold hand, and with her warm body pressed to his, he slept again and dreamed of a sunny day beside Wire Road in Arkansas, and his father coming toward him through the new, knee-length corn and the sun hot against his father's face.

When he woke again he was dry and knew his gown and the covering sheet had been changed, and perhaps even the flannel mattress cover on which he lay. It was midmorning, and Min was still there on the three-legged stool beside the bed, watching his face. But now standing over him was a tall, bony-faced man with a thatch of hair that seemed to grow only across the crown of his skull. He had huge ears and was wearing a long, cream-colored duster, the sleeves of which came only an inch or so below the elbows, revealing knobby wrists and hands as disproportionately large as the ears, and the backs of which were covered with a fine black hair so long it looked ready for the curling iron.

"Welcome back to the living, young man," the duster-clad man shouted, his voice a grating rasp on Roman's ears. "I'm Doctor Hubert Slamons, contract surgeon and general roustabout for this godforsaken hole, and you're damned lucky to be alive, no thanks to me and mine, and the only patient I've ever had that's attracted his own private nurse."

Roman tried to speak but was only able to expel a harsh grunt of air from his swollen throat. Min gave him a drink of water from another of the ever-present blue-enameled cups, and he gagged and coughed and felt his neck muscles convulsing, then slowly opening. He took a deep breath after the Crow woman moved the cup away from his mouth.

"We've poured plenty of that down you the last two days," said Dr. Hubert Slamons as he drew another stool up to the bed and sat down and took Roman's right wrist in his huge fingers to test the pulse. "The snakebite fever burned out all the moisture by the time that wild-looking man carried you in here."

"What is this place?" Roman asked, his words coming like a frog's croak.

"Fort Wallace infirmary," Slamons said. "The best medical facility in western Kansas by virtue of the fact that it's the only one."

Min gave Roman more water and then wiped his brow with a damp cloth, her eyes never leaving his face and seeming completely unaware of the frock-clad white doctor who sat across the bed from her.

"Where is he?" Roman whispered.

"Her husband?" the doctor said, glancing at the Crow woman. "He came in here three days ago, feet bloody, and he led out the troops of the Tenth Cavalry to relieve Forsyth. Up north, or wherever it was you scouts got crosswise with the hostiles. Said you and this other fellow was on the way but he didn't know if you'd make it. But said he'd make a beeline with the troops for Forsyth or else all those men would be dog meat. That's what he said, and then rode out leading the troops."

"Not him. Tyne Fawley."

And saying it, he felt a little knot of resentment toward Emil Durand for leaving them out there on the dry plains, but then, almost before that thought was finished, he was ashamed of his selfishness, knowing the old mountain man had done the right thing, and that if he hadn't, those men on the Arikaree might indeed be dog meat—and in fact might be anyway.

"Oh, that wild man who brought you. It was the day after the troopers rode out, the day before yesterday. You were as hot as a baked sweet potato and babbling on about a splinter in your foot, out of your mind with the fever. Fever does that sometimes. You're lucky it didn't convulse you. Snakebite'll do that to a man, too. Then yesterday your fever broke and you started sweating like a squeezed sponge, and so he left. He rode out of here with some empty supply wagons going back to Fort Hays."

Roman thought about it for a while and finally asked where his clothes were. Slamons bent and pulled a bundle from beneath the bed.

"You want to see what's here?"

Roman nodded and the doctor unrolled the bundle. There were the underwear, the waist shirt, the trousers and jacket, and the Navy Colt. But no fawn-colored hat. Roman couldn't remember when he'd lost it. There was a small belt bag, too, and Dr. Slamons bounced it in his hands.

"You want to count this?"

Roman nodded again and Slamons poured into the palm of one hand two double eagles, an eagle, and seven silver dollars.

"I make it fifty-seven dollars. Does that sound right?"

Roman didn't say anything, but stared at the scale of whitewash on the rafters above. The doctor looked at the Crow woman as he replaced the coins in the leather pouch, rolled everything together again, and shoved it under the bed. He seemed to feel impelled to absolve his own orderlies as opposed to outsiders, most especially outsiders who were Indians.

"This woman was doing some washing for the soldiers out south of the fort," the doctor said.

"I know who she is," said Roman.

"She came in here when that wild man brought you in. I don't know how she knew anything about it, your being here and all, but there she was. I understand they're always watching. She wouldn't be moved, so, to avoid a fuss, I left her be. Your own private nurse, so it is. She's served some purpose, I suppose, shorthanded as I am. And I'm glad your inventory's up to snuff."

"If your soldiers wouldn't steal my goods, why do you think she might?" Roman asked with what little heat he could command in his weakened condition. And looking at the woman, he thought he saw a new gleam in her eyes.

"Oh, I didn't mean that," the doctor replied, a little too quickly and vehemently. "She made it known you were a friend. But now I think it's time she left my infirmary. I've been good about this and stretched a point. But now she's in a place she's not supposed to be."

"Where's she supposed to be?" Roman asked, but even as he spoke, Min was rising from her stool and moving away, out into the aisle between the empty beds, and going toward the door, her back straight and her feet making little searching steps, toed inward. And as she went out into the sun, Roman knew she wouldn't be back.

"Doctor?" he asked. "What is it you've done to help me here?"

"Why, there wasn't much we could do. When you got here, snakebit, it was die or live, no matter what we might do. Except pour the water down you."

"Which the Crow woman did," Roman said, and his voice was coming stronger now.

"Why, yes. I suppose so."

"Then why don't you go piss in a barrel!"

Dr. Hubert Slamons sat upright on his stool, eyes bulging, mouth open, and Roman could almost see the large ears quivering. Then he stood up rigidly, and the hands below the too-short sleeves were stiff and the huge hands fisted.

"Why, you ungrateful wretch," Slamons gasped. "I should dump you out onto the prairie."

"You do that," Roman whispered. "But remember this. I was one of Forsyth's men, and if he gets back and you've acted like an ass more than you already have, he'll likely strip you down with a bullwhip."

"Why, this is . . ." The doctor stopped and gaped. His large hands clasped and unclasped at his sides. "You must still be delirious."

He wheeled and stalked out, the tails of his long coat whipping out behind him, and Roman thought it was a better medicine than he'd ever had, nipping this punctilious bastard in his own infirmary. No sooner was the doctor gone than he thought of Min, and wished she'd come back, but knew she wouldn't, and maybe it didn't matter. Maybe it was better that she wouldn't, because despite his show of indignation at Slamons's implications, he knew there was a double eagle missing from that money pouch. He remembered what Emil Durand had said about the Crows stealing a few things here and there, just for the fun of it. Not that he cared. Except for the accusation.

After the doctor had left, he felt alone in the empty ward. He lay for a long time allowing the flies to inspect his lips and eyelids, and was somehow disturbed that in all the times he'd been near her, he had never heard the Crow woman utter a single sound. He knew his memory of her would be only the bottomless black eyes, sparkling and yet subdued, deep and beyond understanding. And thinking of that, he saw in his mind the eyes of Catrina Peel, and the flies at his eyes made a tear run down along one cheek.

"God Almighty," he said aloud, and lifted one hand and clenched the fist and felt the strength coming back into his arm.

The Crow woman hadn't taken the twenty-dollar gold piece. Tyne Fawley had, on the last rest they'd made before going into Fort Wallace, and in fact with the fort actually in view and Roman out of his head with the fever. It was not a malicious act, nor even one of greed. It was a matter of necessity, because Tyne Fawley knew that before long he'd need a little money if he was to get away from this place and avoid the possibility of unpleasant events, if and when Forsyth got back from the Arikaree and started asking questions about his departure from *that* place. Maybe, if Forsyth never got back—which was a distinct possibility—the whole thing would go unnoticed, but even if there turned out to be no fuss over a small matter like desertion in the face of the enemy, Tyne Fawley had already made up his mind. Short as his tenure had been, he'd had a bellyful of getting himself lost in the Indian War, no matter how many tin stars were sniffing into his various enterprises in the green country to the east.

Something had been chewing on him. Just before he'd left Hays City to join the expedition, he'd heard news of a man arrested in Wichita for complicity in one of those express-office robberies, and odds were about a thousand to one that he'd be hanged as soon as some circuit judge could impanel a jury. And although Tyne Fawley couldn't understand one of his bushwhackers wandering around outside the sanctuary of the Indian Nations, even dumb as some of them were, the fact came home to him that it all looked suspiciously as if somebody within the group had turned informer.

With such a thing possibly going on, it might be difficult to lose oneself even in an Indian war, most especially since, when he'd signed on with Forsyth, he'd penned his right name—two of the few words he knew how to write with any confidence in the spelling. He'd never had the inclination or talent, when he'd been a pupil in the one-room hill schoolhouse, of absorbing much that was said. His father, realizing this, and not taken much himself with education anyway, had put this third son of his back in the rocky fields to work like a grown man, even while his two elder brothers continued to make chalk symbols on slates under the direction of a fiery little Baptist who doubled as minister to the community, performing his miracles of spellbinding in the only honest-to-God, stud-and-shiplap church that could be found within forty miles in any direction.

So, maybe in a spasm of superiority, having seen so many X's inscribed on Forsyth's roll, he had written "Tyne Fawley." And regretted it ever since. He remembered now, for the first time in many years, the words of Mother Fawley: "Pride goes before a fall." And for the first time ever, he understood what it meant.

He thought for a while about going to Colorado Territory, or maybe California or the Oregon country. But he knew the Nations was the only place for him, where he could hole up in some timbered valley and still be close enough to inspect the possibility of moonlight endeavors in adjoining states like Arkansas or Missouri or Kansas. And concentrate on taking a few horses and forget those Bainbridge express strongboxes, even though hanging for stealing a horse was likely as painful as doing the same thing for armed robbery and murder.

So when he saw that Roman Hasford was going to live, he made off for Fort Hays on the supply wagons, explaining to the quartermaster lieutenant in charge that Forsyth had instructed him to do so in order to recruit more men, and when the lieutenant swallowed the story, it confirmed what Tyne Fawley had always thought, that army quartermaster officers were stupid.

Once he was at Fort Hays, it was a short walk to Hays City, where he used Roman Hasford's double eagle to buy a few items required. First, a Smith & Wesson revolver, five-shot and .32-caliber. It wasn't as large a bore as Tyne Fawley preferred, but it was a good used gun and it took rimfire brass cartridges, which made loading a lot faster. Then a side of bacon and a can of coffee beans and a pot to cook them in, and a waxed box of ammunition for the pistol and a knife with a fourteen-inch blade and a razor. The last because he'd also had a bellyful of itching beard and was going to dispense with everything on his face but the mustache, which he'd boasted since he was sixteen years old, and by now he was accustomed to the itching there.

Most of all, he needed a horse. When he'd opened Roman

Hasford's money pouch, he'd seen immediately that there wasn't enough for a horse, even if he took it all, what with horse prices being so inflated because of the imminent arrival of the railroad in the area. If there'd been enough, he would have taken it all. But there hadn't been, so the horse would have to be obtained by other means.

He spent the last of Roman's money in one of the tent bordellos in Hays City, and afterward selected a tough-looking little buckskin mare tied in front of the place and hoped the real owner would be long at his carnal pleasure. He tied his duffel onto the saddle and rode south in the darkness.

He rode mostly at night, as though the Cheyennes were still after him, and hoped as he went that he didn't blunder into any Kiowa or Comanche war parties, once he was south of the Arkansas. He rode scab rock where he could find it in the dark, to hide tracks, but pursuit didn't bother him much. He rode with the North Star just over his left shoulder until he knew he was well into the Cherokee Outlet, and turned the buckskin mare to the east. Some nights he didn't bother to make a fire at all, but ate the bacon raw and chewed the coffee beans.

It was an uncomfortable ride, because strapped to this little mare was a Texas-style saddle with horn and pommel much larger than any he had ever become accustomed to, and he alternately cursed the Mexican leather worker who'd crafted the saddle, and brooded about informers, drawing up a list in his mind of who among his people might be the tattler.

George Forsyth came back to Fort Wallace with what was left of his scout unit; more than half had been killed or wounded. In honor of his second-in-command, the engagement on the Arikaree would be called the Battle of Beecher's Island. When Emil Durand had led the black troopers of the Tenth Cavalry into the dusty floodplain where Forsyth was besieged, everyone was whooping and shooting in all directions and making such a fuss that the Cheyenne and Sioux withdrew, mistaking bravado for ferocity. Forsyth and his men had been on the island for ten days, the last seven of which there had been little ammunition and nothing to eat but the putrefying dead horses.

"I've had to eat rotten meat many a time," said Emil Durand. "And it ain't all that bad if you can overcome the smell."

It was proclaimed by the western army and the press as a great victory, with at least two hundred of the savage heathen slain.

"More like a dozen, I'd wager," said Emil Durand. "You can't ever tell because they always carry off their dead and wounded, and them chiefs ain't gonna come into Leavenworth with a tally sheet of their bucks that was hit. But by Gawd, the boys of Forsyth did take off a bunch of Injun ponies. Even the Cheyenne can't carry off their dead horses."

For reasons known only to himself, Sheridan disbanded his little group of "quartermaster scouts" and Forsyth, after renewing himself with water and tough roast beef, returned to the headquarters of the Department of the Missouri, on the bluffs above the river at Leavenworth. And Emil Durand found his Crow woman among the washtubs of Fort Wallace and spent two days and one night under buffalo hides with her before signing on to scout for the black men of the Tenth Cavalry, whom he called the best Gawd damned nigger fighters he'd ever seen, failing to add that they had been the first ones.

And Roman Hasford was issued a new pair of army brogans to replace the boots Tyne Fawley had cut off him. He confessed his complete ignorance of Tyne Fawley's whereabouts, drew the seventeen dollars' pay he had coming, and headed for Fort Hays on the same kind of supply wagon Tyne Fawley had taken a week earlier. Beyond that, he took various kinds of army transport to end-of-track and then took the train to Leavenworth.

He was still weak and dehydrated, and made constant trips to the end of the coach, where the keg water cooler stood sweating in its niche. His leg was still painful and discolored and swollen above the army shoes. But there were distractions. He watched through the car windows as the high Kansas plains slid past and slowly turned to long-grass prairie.

He thought about Excalibur and regretted that he had taken the big stud out in his quest for Cheyennes.

God damn the Cheyenne, he thought. They killed the best horse I've ever seen.

He somehow felt betrayed by it all. Here he'd come from Arkansas to see the tall plains warriors he'd heard so much about from people like the old Jew at the Sugar Creek mill, and all he had for his troubles was a dead horse and a leg that hurt like hell.

Well, you can't blame the Cheyenne for the snake, he thought, and then thought again, The hell you can't! Because they're the ones who had me pinned under that stinking buffalo hide in the first place. And they sure'n hell killed Excalibur!

But he took some solace in the knowledge that maybe he'd had a hand in killing Roman Nose. On the other hand, it didn't set too well with him, killing his own namesake. There's got to be some special sin in that, he thought. It was a kind of sacrilege, like shooting yourself in the foot on purpose.

But God Almighty, he thought, none of those people riding down on us were blind baby birds!

He had to work hard to recall where the "baby birds" metaphor came from; it had welled up in his mind from almost forgotten times before he'd ever heard of Cheyennes or Kansas or Phil Sheridan or a war chief called Roman Nose. Then he remembered the time on Wire Road when those boys had stoned the birds in their nest, and he thought it must have been a strong image to last so long and to recur at least twice in recent years, like an unpleasant little dream that kept flitting in and out of his sleep.

"Well, you wanted to see 'em," said Emil Durand. "And now you have." Or was it Tyne Fawley who'd said that?

It had been a confused time, as bad as when the Yankees came to the valley of Little Sugar Creek and that old billygoat Earl Van Dorn had fought them to a standstill until he ran out of ammunition. Roman could understand that a little better now, after having been on Beecher's Island and remembering how he'd started to count the number of rounds left for the Spencer after the third charge. Like most civilians, he'd never had any notion of what logistics was about.

In fact, he'd learned a lot about soldiers in those days with Forsyth. And he realized that being involved was a lot different from just watching, as he had at the battle of Pea Ridge.

And when he thought of Tyne Fawley he remembered the snakebite and what had happened afterward, at least the first part of it clear in his mind, and sometimes as he sat alone in the railroad car, looking at the monotonous passage of landscape outside the window, he could still smell the sweat of Tyne Fawley and could almost feel the man's damp hair against his cheek as they moved through the night toward Fort Wallace.

The snake! When I write home about getting snakebit, he thought, Papa's not going to have much respect for me, what with all the times he told me how to go about avoiding Ozark rattlers and copperheads.

Well, he thought, maybe I won't even write about that part.

He stopped over in Topeka to give his regards to Jared Dane, but found that Jared Dane was off in places unknown, detecting along with some of his Pinkertons, still looking for the men who had robbed the express offices. And he found, too, that he himself was some kind of big hero because he'd been with Forsyth's men.

Mr. August Bainbridge took him as guest of honor to a dinner of wild turkey and English lamb at the Albon Inn, where there were a lot of men wearing silk cravats and striped trousers and clawhammer coats. All this after Roman had protested his lack of suitable clothes.

"My boy," said Mr. August Bainbridge, "as a stockholder in the Kansas Railway and Telegraph Construction Company, you are a man who can afford apparel. As a matter of fact, we've just paid a considerable amount in dividends to your account in Leavenworth."

And they proceeded together to visit three of the best clothiers in Kansas, so that on the evening of the banquet Roman found himself fitted out in the best of Eastern gentlemen's accoutrements, including a rose-and-white flowered vest, a wing-tipped collar with gold stud and black string tie, and a ruby ring on the little finger of his left hand.

There were some newspapermen at the Albon that night, and after the dinner, when everyone was standing about in the lobby bar, sipping brandy, they inquired about the Battle of Beecher's Island in some detail. Roman, feeling ill at ease and completely soaked with nervous perspiration, told them in halting phrases about the dust and sweat and confusion and the courage of the men who had been beside him.

"It seems to me that all you're saying," said a small, goateed man with hollow, fiery eyes, "is that you ran from them and then looked for a place to dig holes!"

And Roman, well into the brandy, his leg hurting and the winged collar choking him like a hangman's noose, retorted with considerable heat.

"That's right. Has anybody ever shot at you, you little son of a bitch!" And wasn't at all sorry that he'd said it.

Whereupon Mr. August Bainbridge took his arm and led him into the hotel vestibule, where a grinning Fletcher was waiting to take Roman to the private car in the Topeka railyards to spend the night.

"Well put, my boy, well put," Mr. Bainbridge said, chuckling. "That was the pipsqueak Milton Reynolds who publishes the newspaper in Lawrence."

"Milton Reynolds?" asked Roman. "My God, he was at the Treaty of Medicine Lodge. He's a well-known man. I only saw him once. I didn't recognize him."

"Small worry, my boy," said Bainbridge. "You go with Fletcher and have a restful night. I suspect he'll give you another sniff of my best brandy in the car. And good for you on putting the little Indian-lover in his place. Don't concern yourself with such pygmies."

But Roman did, rolling his ungentlemanly behavior around in his mind from one side to the other like a ball of twine chased by a kitten. But at least Mr. Bainbridge was right, and Fletcher gave him three drinks of good brandy in the car, and a fine cigar besides. And told stories about Jared Dane.

20

Winter came on strong, as it usually does in Kansas, but the Cheyenne continued their raids along the Smoky Hill right into snow time, their war parties slipping down into the western Indian Territory after each foray and leaving Phil Sheridan in a towering rage. Usually a quiet season, that year's cold weather saw an increase in army stock purchasing, which made Elisha Hankins very happy and kept Roman Hasford busy enough that only now and then in the evenings at Mrs. Condon Murphy's boardinghouse did he have time to think about Victoria Cardin Archer.

"I long to see her," he wrote in his diary, "but the prospect of encountering her on the streets of Leavenworth is unsettling because I have no inclination to be amicable, yet on the other hand could hardly restrain myself at sight of her lovely face."

But he saw Lieutenant Thaddeus Archer, who was buying the horses for what everyone who knew Sheridan's temperament suspected were remounts for a winter campaign. It was early November when Archer appeared at the yards, at a time when Elisha Hankins was off in Missouri contracting for livestock, and so the lieutenant and his retinue of enlisted men were shown the available horses in the holding pens by

Roman Hasford, who gritted his teeth at first sight of Victoria's husband, but then, throughout the rest of the negotiations, had to suppress his laughter at the young quartermaster's appearance.

Archer was wearing a calf-length greatcoat that seemed to swallow all of him except his face—a huge, cumbersome robe of heavy wool. And on his head was what Roman assumed to be a Russian-style army winter-issue hat, with flaps that tied over the woolly crown when not hanging down to protect one's ears from frostbite.

Roman followed Archer and his soldiers about among the pens, the enlisted men leading out the mounts Archer indicated and tying them all in a row on picket ropes before the yard office, and then going into that office where the little space heater was huffing and red hot at the bottom, with a full load of soft coal inside and the enamel coffeepot on top hissing aromatic steam.

There had been little conversation between them, and there was not much now as they seated themselves opposite one another across the top of Mr. Elisha Hankins's small, battered desk. Roman did his figuring with a pencil and a tablet of blue-lined paper, and came up with the price, a fair one and true market value: fifty horses at one hundred twenty-five dollars each, for a total of six thousand two hundred fifty dollars. When he'd checked his figures, he tore off the page and slid it across the desk for Lieutenant Archer's inspection.

Without a word, Archer drew from inside the greatcoat, which Roman thought was large enough to conceal an entire library, a small book of blank drafts appropriately inscribed with the name of the biggest bank in Kansas, the Bainbridge Mercantile Exchange. He used one of the quill pens kept in a small well inserted in the desk, and dipped the point into a pot of ink there, all of which was intended for that specific purpose. As Archer wrote the draft, Roman could hear the quill scratching against the paper. Having finished, Archer tore the draft from the book and passed it across the desk, replaced the book within the folds of the gigantic coat, and rose, retaining, as he had throughout the afternoon, a cold, haughty expression that Roman supposed the lieutenant reserved for dealings with servants, the lower enlisted ranks, and stray dogs.

"I would suggest, sir," Archer said, "that you obtain a great many more cavalry-qualified horses, and as soon as possible. We'll have the requirement for more within a short time, and I'll be back for the usual accommodation within the week."

He turned toward the door and Roman looked at the draft. It was made out for seven thousand dollars.

"Just a minute," Roman said. "You've misunderstood what I said. You've paid me more than the horses are worth."

One hand on the door, Lieutenant Archer smiled, an icy smirk.

"You may hold the draft until Mr. Hankins returns and give it to him," he said. "Apparently he declines to explain his operations to the stockyard lackey."

Archer had started to turn away when Roman spoke, and all the heat and rage and suppressed antagonism he felt was in the harsh tone of his voice.

"When Mr. Hankins is not here, I run this stockyard. And I won't accept your draft!"

"Oh?" said Archer. "Then destroy it and I'll write another when your employer is here."

"You do that," Roman said. "But meanwhile, you tell those dog robbers out there to run the horses back into the pens, because unless I've got money in hand, they don't leave here."

Glaring into Archer's eyes, Roman tore the draft in half and threw it on the floor. The lieutenant's face began to go as red as the cast-iron stove.

"There is an accommodation here," he said, seeming to have some difficulty in getting the words free of his tongue. "And I need delivery on those horses now. They have to be shipped to Fort Riley, and there is an urgency in this you wouldn't understand."

"You can have your delivery any time you pay me the quoted price."

"There's an accommodation, sir!" Archer shouted.

"I don't know anything about an accommodation. All I know is the fair price of horses."

Archer started to speak, his mouth open, and for a moment Roman could see the glint of a gold tooth, and then the lips clamped shut under the well-clipped mustache and Archer stalked to the desk. Without resuming his seat, he produced the checkbook from his coat, bent over the desk, and furiously scribbled out another draft in the amount Roman had specified. Then he went back to the door, his left arm crooked as though he were holding the hilt of a saber that wasn't there. He threw open the door, letting in a blast of cold air, and turned, obviously furious, the hatred clear in his eyes.

"I don't expect to find you here, once Mr. Hankins has heard of this," Archer said. It came out as a hiss, and Roman thought the words were as malevolent as that rattler's fangs had been in the buffalo wallow. Except that the snake had done what God intended it to do. "What's more, until that time, I will purchase army stock from some other source."

He wheeled about and marched out, leaving the door open, and Roman was up, knocking over his chair, charging to the door and out into the wind and shouting at Archer's retreating back.

"You do what you damn well please. And tell Victoria I send kind regards!"

Archer stopped dead still for a moment, and then turned, his greatcoat seeming to change direction a second after his body did. He ran back toward the yard office, raising his right arm as he came, and Roman, suddenly elated, stepped free of the doorway and as Archer came within reach, struck just above the mustache with a balled fist.

Archer staggered back, pain and astonishment on his face, and Roman stared at what he'd done, watching the gush of blood down across the upper lip, dripping in shiny droplets from the tips of the carefully trimmed mustache. The lieutenant made a movement inside his gigantic coat as though about to advance once more, and Roman raised both hands to strike again.

But instead of advancing, Archer stepped back and his arm dropped. Behind him along the horse line, his troops were staring, openmouthed. When he tried to speak, the blood running into his mouth sprayed out, and it took several efforts before any words came.

"You keep the name of my wife off your lips," he gasped.

"Ask her about the boat trip we made together up the Missouri," Roman said, his fists still up, and as soon as he'd said it he wondered why. God Almighty, he thought, what's the matter with me? I've hurt this slimy son of a bitch enough already without such foolishness.

"God damn you, sir," Archer sputtered, and wheeled once more, back toward his men. He strode to his horse, his left arm crooked, and mounted and rode away without giving his troops any command. Bewildered, his men slowly gathered up the just-purchased horses and their own and rode out onto Seventh Street, following their lieutenant.

Roman was shaking. Only after the last of the soldiers had disappeared along the road to the fort did he lower his fists and turn to the door. It was then that he saw, at the corner of the office shack, Orvile Tucker. In the smith's massive black hand was a five-pound sledgehammer.

"That was a good lick, Mr. Roman," he said, his chocolate face impassive.

"God Almighty," Roman said. "I haven't hit anybody with my fist since I was eight years old!"

"Well, you ain't forgot how, Mr. Roman." And bouncing the hammer in his hand, Orvile Tucker laughed.

Roman spent the next days worrying about Archer's "accommodation." He kept remembering the first time he'd registered a sale of army stock, when Mr. Elisha Hankins had instructed him to enter in the ledger a sum less than what had been received. He suspected this was all part of the same animal, and it made him squirm to think that somehow Mr. Hankins was involved in crooked dealings with the procurement people at the fort. He felt as he thought he might if he were to discover that his father was a stagecoach robber.

And thinking of his father, he knew the elder Hasford would have found out right away about those improper ledger entries and would have refused to have anything to do with such a thing without proper explanation. It made Roman feel immature and inadequate, and he wished he had some of his father's strength of character.

He did a lot of thinking about Tyne Fawley, too. There was a little wedge of guilt in his soul for not having thanked the man for saving his life. But he knew it was foolish because Tyne Fawley had departed his company before Roman had been capable of saying anything.

So, as was his habit in times of consternation, he threw himself into his work, spending a lot of effort at the Hasford Meat and Lard Company, where Elmer Scaggs was curing hams and bacon, having already sold fresh pork as fast as he could slaughter what he called the first generation of Scaggs hogs.

"Not a stone's weight of fresh meat to the army," said Scaggs, with Tracy Benson standing behind him, grinning and nodding vigorously with each statement. "All to the town's butcher shops. But every Gawd damned hunk of meat in that smokehouse is contracted to the troop messes at the fort. I tell you, boss, this is gonna be one helluva business!"

"Let's call that smoked meat Scaggs Ham and Bacon," Roman said. "I like the sound of it. I'll get one of the printers in town to do us some oil-paper lettering to wrap it all in. The fresh pork, too. Scaggs Home-Smoked Pork Chops. That kind of thing."

"Why, Gawd damn, boss," Scaggs said, puffing up like a bantam rooster walking past the hen coop. "I reckon that's a good notion."

To celebrate the new name, the three of them, Roman and Elmer and Tracy Benson, went into town to visit the First Street saloons—there being two additional full-time employees now to watch the hog pens and to keep the hickory and sassafras smoldering in the curing house—and Tracy Benson got into only two minor scuffles and one serious fist-fight.

"I like that Tracy," Elmer said. "He reminds me a lot of how I used to be."

"I can understand that," Roman said. "It wasn't too long ago that you were rioting around town."

"Yeah, but hell, boss, that was before I had a ham named after me."

And once he'd seen his two employees off toward the hog ranch, riding their mules crookedly into a growing snowfall, Roman went by to pay his respects to his business partner, Katie Rose Rouse, passing one of her gentleman callers coming down the outside stairway as he was going up.

They had a few sips of clear liquor from the dainty stemmed glasses, and Katie Rose sprawled half-naked across the room from Roman, looking like a great white sausage, with only the glittering eyes and the full mouth enclosing half the rim of her glass showing any signs that there was life within.

"Roman, you and me can own a big part of this state before we're through."

Roman laughed. "Why not all of it?"

"Because the most of it is already owned by your friend August Bainbridge."

Roman laughed again, feeling better than he had for a long time. He finished his third drink and went down to the sorrel gelding he'd recently taken from Mr. Hankins's inventory of stock and now used as his own, and would continue to use until the little blood-red colt offspring of Excalibur and the Morgan mare was big enough to break to saddle. There was a shed behind Mrs. Condon Murphy's boardinghouse where he kept the horse stabled at night so he could ride to work each day.

"Hell, son," Mr. Hankins had said. "You haven't got any business walking back and forth."

"It's not far."

"Men of means don't walk around getting their shoes dirty in Kansas dust," Mr. Hankins had said. "And sure as hell, heroes of Beecher's Island don't."

In the shed, as he was rubbing down the sorrel with empty

burlap bags and dipping a small bucket of oats from the hopper, he thought about Lieutenant Archer's accommodation again and thought about Victoria Cardin married to that ass, and for the first time he began to question her judgment.

"Sometimes," he muttered softly, "you're addle-brained and blind as a bat when it comes to people you care about."

As he trooped heavy-footed up Mrs. Condon Murphy's back stairs, he thought that maybe tomorrow he'd best take a side of bacon and some airtight canned peaches down to Crider Peel's mule-shed home so he could assure himself that Catrina had something to eat. And maybe a red ribbon for the child's raven hair.

And he remembered a line from an old song the Jew at the Sugar Creek mill used to sing: *Black, black, black is the color of my true love's hair*.

And wondered why such a thing would come to mind, because Victoria Cardin Archer's hair wasn't nearly so black as Catrina Peel's.

On the way along the hall to his room, he saw a dim light under Mr. Moffet's door and heard a low voice singing some hymn he didn't recognize, and he knew the little beer salesman was sitting up in bed, his nightcap askew on his head, a few empty mason jars on the bedside table, fighting off the incursions of the Pope or the Mormons or the Anglicans in his own unique way.

Roman laughed silently and went to a good night's rest under Mrs. Condon Murphy's Joseph's coat quilt. And he dreamed, without terror, of a huge and beautiful half-naked man with feathers in his hair riding toward him, but always fading into yellow dust before he came close enough for Roman to recognize his features.

Lin Chow was a Tonkin Chinese who had come to Leavenworth by various passages from his native Southeast Asia to India to Madagascar to Suez to Marseille to New York and finally to Kansas, bringing with him a family that consisted of a fat wife who knew how to cook fish in the old way—which meant mostly raw—four sons with their wives, and seven grandchildren.

The people of Leavenworth took one look at this company as they disembarked from the river steamer and said that now, with a Chinaman in town, maybe there would be a good laundry.

Knowing what was expected of him, Lin Chow opened the laundry in an old riverfront warehouse. The laundry and the family quarters were at the front of the long building and the family seldom moved beyond sight of it, establishing a kind of Oriental enclave whose only contact with the white citizens was across a new pine counter when dirty shirts were brought in, or when clean ones were picked up in snow-white wrapping paper.

Lin Chow occasionally went beyond his little domain and into the town to buy pork or carrots, usually taking one of his grandchildren with him. And although the man dressed as anyone else on Leavenworth's streets would dress, the child was always resplendent in a bright red silk brocade smock that brought admiring glances from the ladies along the sidewalk.

Later they would say to their husbands, "I saw one of those charming little Chinamen today," even if it had been one of Lin Chow's granddaughters walking beside him and clutching his hand.

Everyone admired Lin Chow. He was clean and industrious, always had plenty of coins in his trousers, and his sons were never seen in the town's saloons, drinking hard spirits and raising hell. It was assumed that the laundry business of Lin Chow was a good one, which it was. Some even suspected that Lin Chow was a wealthy man. Which he was.

Of course, Lin Chow was not his real name, but he had used it since passing through the city of New York because it seemed the kind of name the white men expected him to have. Nor was it the laundry business that had made him rich. The source of his wealth was located in the rear section of the old warehouse, where there were wooden bunks along the walls, each covered with a straw tick and having beside it a three-legged stool and a brass charcoal burner no larger than an army-issue coffee cup.

It had taken a long time to establish this business, because it involved messages going back to the homeland of Lin Chow and the product returning by ship to San Francisco and then by another ship to the Pacific side of Panama and then by mule train across to the Caribbean and then by another ship to New Orleans and then by steam packet up the river. The product came originally from India, then was smuggled into China by people in the employ of the British, and there was purchased by Lin Chow's business associates.

Lin Chow's acute sense of profit and loss told him that this was a terrible way to do business. There were too many middlemen. And so, when the Mississippi River opened up for commerce after the war, Lin Chow was ready, having made discreet inquiries. By 1865 his product was coming from Vera Cruz, in Mexico, and although its quality was not as good as the Asian variety, it was good enough for Lin Chow's customers, who didn't know the difference anyway.

It came in small bundles wrapped in cheesecloth, a dozen bundles to each wooden crate marked "dried vegetables." When Lin Chow and his eldest son unpacked and unwrapped these bundles, what they found inside was a blackish, gummy brick, slightly harder than bread dough. These they aligned along a rack specifically built for the purpose at the back side of the warehouse, where the sun could dry out the moisture until the bricks were hard enough to shred with a razor, then crush with a stone into a powder that looked much like snuff. This material was then tamped into the bowl of a long-stemmed pipe, heated over one of the charcoal braziers, and smoked like tobacco by the many customers who came to enjoy the evaporation of cares and worries in the blue haze.

By the winter of that year, when Sheridan managed to get George Armstrong Custer released from his court-martial sentence and sent him out with the Seventh Cavalry on a snowy campaign, Crider Peel had become one of Lin Chow's regular customers. And Lin Chow, being no fool, understood that Crider Peel did not make nearly enough money to afford the luxury of his product. So Lin Chow, who thought about such things but was wise enough never to do anything about them, studied the situation and listened to gossip in the butcher shops and watched with his own eyes the comings and goings of Crider Peel and finally decided he knew where the money was coming from, a fact that he did not divulge even to his fat wife, even on those evenings when they were on their sleeping mats and whispering and Lin Chow was content because she had prepared him fish caught that very day in the Missouri River, and he had washed it down with the rice wine that his youngest son made.

The money for Crider Peel's frequent visits came from Mr. August Bainbridge. Not from him directly, of course, but through his enforcer, and having come from Southeast Asia, Lin Chow knew what enforcers did. And this particular enforcer was Jared Dane.

There were tiny flurries of snow driven by gusting wind against the panes of the single window in the room. It was a bare room, drab and a little cold, with only a minute cast-iron stove to heat it, burning low. There was a rolltop desk against one wall, three straight-backed, cane-bottom chairs, and a brass cuspidor almost as large as the stove. The place smelled of coal smoke and money. It was the rear office of the Bainbridge Leavenworth Express Company, but the manager was not there in his usual place before the desk. He had scurried out to stand with his two employees in the wire cage at the front as soon as Jared Dane walked in, leaving the place to Mr. Bainbridge's pistoleer, which is what all of Mr. Bainbridge's employees called Jared Dane when they knew he was beyond earshot.

Jared Dane sat at the desk, his booted feet up and crossed among the scattering of drafts and ledgers and bills of lading on the desktop. He was still wearing his overcoat, although he had been in the room long enough for the snow across his shoulders to have turned to water. He was always cold, it seemed, since those surgeons in Topeka had cut off his arm.

Finally he pulled the glove from his right hand, using his teeth, and tossed it onto the desktop.

"I suppose it won't be long now," he said, his voice flat and sounding as cold as the day outside.

Facing him were two Pinkerton detectives, derby hats screwed hard down over their ears, their tight three-piece suits straining across lithe muscles, their topcoats across their knees, as they sat forward in the other two chairs, their eyes and faces and mustaches so similar that Jared Dane thought they looked like mirror images, only one being real, the other a wintery reflection.

"You've spent a lot of money cultivating him," said the first detective.

"I'm not cultivating the bastard. I'm buying him opium. And the Boss has plenty of money to spend on such enterprises, so don't concern yourself."

"I'm not," said the detective. "As you say, Mr. Bainbridge has a lot of money. But I'm not so sure it's been well spent in this case."

"It takes time," said Jared Dane, flexing the fingers of his remaining hand, then sniffing them. They smelled like sheepskin, from the glove.

"Maybe we ought to introduce that militia commander to the pipe, like we did Peel," said the second Pinkerton. "I still think he knows more than he's saying."

"Major Claken?" Jared Dane snorted. "Hell. He's a temperance man, so he's not a good candidate for the Chinaman's hog fat. You underestimate such good, solid citizens. You do him great injustice. After all, he's the one who told us this Peel was one of the few people who knew when those militia funds were in our safeboxes."

"Major Claken hasn't got much judgment, having a man around him like Peel and trusting him with such knowledge."

"The militia uses what they can get, which is usually dog shit," Jared Dane said. "What you don't like about the good major is his smell. Boiled cabbage and wet snuff."

"Well, at least we've got one name from this Peel weasel,

but that was last summer and the man's hanged already and moldering in his pine box," said the first detective.

"We'll get the big one soon. I feel it. All we have to do is keep assuring Peel we won't have him prosecuted. Then he gets addicted to that pipe in the Chinaman's place. When that happens, he'll tell us anything just to keep up his little journeys to dreamland."

"Yeah, and then what?" asked the second Pinkerton. "I despise the thought of letting him go free in return for a little information."

"Oh, no," said Dane quietly, rubbing the fingers of his right hand tenderly across the empty left sleeve of his overcoat. "Oh, no. A promise to a dishonest man can be justified if it's dishonest as well. When he tells us what we want to know, then we'll hang him, too!"

The snow made roast pork somehow appropriate, a nice shoulder direct from Elmer Scaggs's slaughtering pen and cooked all afternoon with Irish potatoes and onions and a heavy dash of black pepper and thyme, all served awash in its own brown gravy in a room thick with the smell of fried dried-apricot pies to follow.

"By God, it's good to be home for this kind of provender," Mr. Elisha Hankins said, wiping his hands across the blue-and-white-checked oilcloth he'd bought in Missouri for Spankin's table.

Roman had small appetite, knowing what he had to do later. But the Hankinses seemed oblivious to his preoccupation, forking everything into their smiling mouths and talking around the chunks of potato and pork about the terrible weather and how this was a downright wicked time to send soldiers out against the hostiles.

"Now the wild tribes, they know how to do it," said Mr. Hankins. "When the ice comes, stay in the lodge with a fat squaw."

"Mr. Hankins, don't be ugly," said Spankin, but she was laughing, too.

After the meat and vegetables had disappeared and then the fried pies, golden and crisp with butter, and Spankin had risen to clear the table and bring the coffeepot from the stove, and there were cigars and little mint candies, also from Missouri, Roman cautiously went into the affair with Lieutenant Thaddeus Archer.

Something like a chill came over the kitchen, although it was impossible for Roman to define. Spankin's face went as blank as one of her dish towels, and Mr. Elisha Hankins lowered his gaze and began to rub his forehead with the tips of his fingers.

"Did I do something terribly wrong?" Roman asked.

"No, no, no," said Mr. Hankins, and he looked up and Roman thought there was moisture in his eyes. "I should have told you a long time ago."

He leaned back in his chair and began to tap the edge of the table with his blunt fingers, staring at them as though he'd never seen them before.

"I should have told you a long time ago, son," he said, and sighed. In fact, throughout what followed, he sighed after almost every sentence that he spoke. "When I bought this stockyard, there were a lot of competitors around here. It was dog-eat-the-God-damned-dog.

"Back then, I was in the straits. I put everything I had into the business. If it didn't work out, me and Spankin would have been begging on the streets, I guess. So I hedged every bet I could. I took every edge anyone would give me. And there were those willing to help me at it. I didn't want to steal anything, I just wanted to make a living.

"There were some buyers from the fort then who made no bones about it. During the war. A rabble. Then when Archer came, he picked up on it. To deal with me, they wanted assurance of some remuneration for themselves. So I sold them stock above market. And the difference I paid back to the buyers. Not the army, you understand, but the procurement officers."

"God Almighty, that's the accommodation Archer was talking about," said Roman.

"I'm afraid so," Mr. Hankins said, sighing again, tapping the table now like a drum roll. "It was my price for doing business. Rebates. That's why I didn't want to be known as your partner in the pig business. I was afraid somebody would want the same circumstance."

"And this was with army men?"

"I'm afraid so. Not all. Just the jake-legs who came in here to buy. God damn, Roman, it started during the war, when a lot of unscrupulous men saw a way to line their pockets."

"You mean," asked Roman, "that the United States Army turned a blind eye to this?"

"Hell, no!" Mr. Hankins said. "It was just some of their people. They court-martialed a peck of them during the war. Not here, but other places. I hear that Sheridan himself was hell on such people. But they're hard to catch unless somebody like me goes hangdog in there to some general and starts to tattle, and who's going to do that when his whole business may depend on keeping things as they are?"

"And Captain Cardin?"

For the first time during this discourse, Mr. Hankins took his thumping fingers from the table and looked at Roman directly. He smiled and shook his head.

"I won't pretend I don't know why you're asking that. But I don't think the captain was ever involved. I think he don't know anything about it. I think he don't care a damn about this job he's got, and lets underlings like this Archer do his business. Oh, he came in a couple of times right after he got out here, but I never saw his name on a draft."

"Then it's Archer."

"So far as I can tell, it's been only him since he got here. Picked up on a good thing. A good thing for him. So that's all of it. Have another cup of coffee."

Roman shook his head. "I've had all I can stand."

As Roman rose, Mr. Hankins gazed up at him and Roman thought he looked like a whipped dog.

"I'm not really sorry for anything I've done. I haven't made a penny over the whole thing, just kept my business. Are you coming in tomorrow?"

Roman laughed, he didn't know why, except maybe that what Mr. Hankins had said reminded him of the song the old Rebel was singing on Beecher's Island when Forsyth called him and Emil Durand and asked them to go for help.

He pressed one hand to Mr. Hankins's shoulder and then moved around the table and put his arms around Spankin, who was standing at her stove with the most horrified expression Roman had ever seen on her face. Then he went to the wall peg where his overcoat was hanging.

"I'll be in, the usual time," he said.

Riding home to Mrs. Condon Murphy's boardinghouse, the snow driven hard against his back by the north wind, Roman Hasford thought, Why, hell, it doesn't make any difference.

And it amused him that now he could pass off something so lightly that three years ago would have sickened him—a man abetting crime, a man close to him, even though at no profit to himself. And maybe part of it was that he had been on the frontier long enough not to give a damn anymore how a man sifted through the possibilities of survival and finally came up with the nugget that made things work. So long as he didn't kill somebody. So long as he didn't take a pistol and demand the money, as that man Jesse James over in Missouri seemed to be doing more and more.

And maybe part of it was because the criminal now was Lieutenant Thaddeus Archer.

And knowing what he did now, maybe part of the amusement was because he could go to his friend Little Phil Sheridan, who had given his mother dry beans when starvation had threatened during the war, and who had said such wonderful things to the newspaper people about the men of Beecher's Island, and bring to justice the husband of Victoria Cardin, with spite and malice! It made him laugh again, the snow coating the back of his neck, because now he knew things a lot of people didn't know, and with that knowledge he could destroy an adversary. But never would! Maybe that was the best part of all—a sense of power he'd never known, yet would never use.

When he stopped behind Mrs. Condon Murphy's boarding-house, the wind suddenly calmed and he could smell hot bread at one of the Leavenworth bakeries. On impulse, he reined back into the street and rode there and walked in, snow-covered, and when he asked for two loaves of bread fresh from the ovens, a flour-sprinkled boy with a white cotton hat said, Yes, Mr. Hasford, right away, Mr. Hasford, and I'll put in two buckwheat buns besides, and thank you for the fighting at Beecher's Island!

God Almighty, Roman thought.

He bought four loaves instead of two and had a bonus of two more buckwheat buns from the flour-covered lad, and on the ride to Crider Peel's mule barn he held the bread under his coat to keep it from the moisture of snow, and felt the heat from it against his belly.

He made his usual call and knocked, and when he had the normal response, which was none at all, he pushed the door open and went inside. He saw no evidence of Crider Peel, in fact just the reverse, because everything seemed freshly cleaned and put in place and there was a pot of turnips boiling on the stove. The hanging burlap curtain that separated the two rooms of the place was still moving gently, as though someone had just passed through.

"Catrina," he called. "I've brought you some bread."

There was no response, nor had he expected any, and he took the loaves from beneath his coat and placed them on the table beside the burning lamp. Then quickly he looked about the room and saw that the woodbox was full and the water bucket as well, and on the shelf behind the stove lay an open burlap bag with what he estimated was about a peck of sweet potatoes.

So she's not cold and not starving, he thought, but no thanks to her father, I suspect.

Going to the door, he felt some new presence in the room and, turning, saw Catrina Peel holding back the burlap curtain and watching him.

"Thank you," she said, and backed into the rear room, and the burlap curtain swung down before her and Roman started to speak again, but knew the last appearance had been made.

"There's fresh bread on the table, Catrina," he called, and then he was out into the driving snow and riding back to Mrs. Condon Murphy's boardinghouse and thinking all the way, God Almighty, she spoke to me!

"She's still so tiny," he wrote in his diary that night, the Joseph's-coat quilt around his legs and ankles, "but has grown so large in some mysterious way. And still has the marks of her father's hands on her face."

Even so, it was a good feeling, and he knew that from this point on he would take more food to that place. Maybe some meat, he thought, maybe some of that bacon I was thinking about before. She seems capable of cooking as well as a grown woman.

And then he thought, The state of Kansas has this orphanage south of town on the road to Lansing. Maybe she should be there.

He wondered how such a thing might be arranged, since she was not a real orphan. Then he saw in his mind that grim limestone building, forbidding even in the light of summer sun, and recalled the stories he'd heard about the children there being treated like slave laborers and fed on thin potato soup, and the disobedient going under the leather strap. And thought, Maybe she's as well off where she is.

The sound of her tiny voice was with him when he fell asleep, a voice matching her tiny body, yet resonant and rich, like a silver bell heard through the muffling snow. But strangely it was not the voice of a child.

21

The lamp, suspended from one of the rough beam rafters, hung by its brass chain only two feet from the floor. It had a dark red globe, almost purple, and the glass was thick and frosted and deeply etched, so the light from the whale oil wick inside was diffuse and seemed to seek out every corner with a soft, sensual glow, not obvious or bright, but with a presence as solid as the blue-gray haze of smoke in the room. Crider Peel thought it the most wonderful lamp he'd ever seen, and he knew that soon it would be transformed and would be no lamp at all, but instead a living, pulsating sun, benevolent and kind and with a smile that touched his soul.

It was his own world within a bigger, incomprehensible one. He was screened off here with woven straw mats hanging on either side of his low bunk, and even though he knew this little cubicle was only a part of the warehouse, with his own sun beginning to gleam and the blue-gray haze beginning to thicken, he was all alone. And beyond his little universe, he knew—at least before the narcotic numbed his brain—that only a few paces away was the snow and the street and a small responsibility in his mule-shed home, a responsibility he'd never asked for and that tore his heart each time he thought of it.

Crider Peel moved the pipestem languidly to his mouth, in no hurry because it would be there as long as he wanted it, and his eyes were heavy-lidded, more heavy-lidded with each passing breath, as he gazed mesmerized at the red orb of the lamp. It had a quality of smell, that lamp, just like the smoke. Musty-sweet. As thick as olive oil. All of it one, smoke and light, everything calm here and without the compulsion to frenzied activity to stay alive, lashing out in fright at every passing shadow. All the apprehension gone, nothing to scar and bruise him, no tomorrow, no nothing except the faint glow. Not like whiskey, which made him wild, made him an animal, creating little many-legged creatures that crawled up the walls of his mind. Now there was just the half-sleep, where nothing had a sharp cutting edge, not even the prospect of raising a little girl, not even the horror of paying men to kill, not even the overwhelming burden of guilt for past associations that had led to armed robbery and murder.

Sometimes, during his early visits to this place, he recalled the terror of that night when he was standing at the Owl Head Saloon bar and Jared Dane had materialized beside him, offering to buy him a drink. And then suggesting something better at the Chinaman's. He had assumed that Dane smoked, too, but later, as Dane gave him money and made him promises and tried to coax information from him, Crider Peel came to Lin Chow's alone, with Jared Dane's money in his pocket and knowing full well then that the railroad executioner didn't take the pipe.

It hadn't been hard to shift sides, considering its compensations. But he'd never forget that first night, when he'd been afraid to accept Dane's companionship and afraid not to, expecting, as they walked along First Street to the old warehouse, that at any moment Dane would shoot him like a rabid dog. Then there was Lin Chow's panacea, and all the fear melted away in its misty pleasure.

Each time he came here, he thought for a few moments about the things that had gone before, and the irony did not escape him. The very man whose arm he had taken, through contractual arrangements with wicked men, was now his benefactor. Of course, in his lucid moments he knew that had Jared Dane known of his arrangement there would have been something less pleasant for him than the money and Lin Chow's.

But he finally realized that Dane was unaware of who was responsible for the affair in the Topeka railyard, and now Crider Peel had switched sides and no longer sought Jared Dane's life. Even so, thinking it through each day, and then each night at Lin Chow's, before the smoke dissipated any thinking at all, he was still reluctant to say the name that he knew would be a death warrant for the one man who *did* know he was responsible for Topeka. Tyne Fawley.

But he knew that eventually he must, because, playing the two of them off against one another, he understood that his loyalty had to be with the man who gave him the money for Lin Chow's, the man who assured him that no grand jury would call him, that no court would try him, that no hangman would adjust about his neck the rope loop with thirteen coils.

Sometimes, thinking this, he wondered if he should trust Jared Dane. He'd heard stories about Jared Dane, and none of them pleasing. But whom else could he trust? he asked himself. Not Tyne Fawley, who was as dangerous as a shedding snake—especially now, after the fiasco in Topeka, when two of his best men had gone up the flue.

And so he drew on the pipe each night because after a short while, in the gentle glow of the red lamp, enveloped in the fog of blue-gray smoke, such worries went away and everyone was his friend and everywhere was peace and everything was as sweet as wild honey.

Wild honey! Almost every time he went into the semi-sleep of Lin Chow's opium, he recalled that day in the wooded hills above Wheeling, which then had still been a part of Virginia, when he and his younger brother had found the bee tree. Crider afraid of the bees, but his brother going up the old oak snag to steal the comb, and stung horribly, but still skinning back down the tree laughing, and the two of them eating until the sweetness clogged their throats and then his brother screaming and Crider Peel leading him home. And there the brother died, his neck and chest swollen internally from the beestings, and nobody could do anything about it because nobody had ever seen anything like it before.

But always Crider Peel loved honey, even though after his brother died he always ate it with the vision of a choking boy. The red lamp and the blue-gray haze chased that vision from his mind and he could think of honey, taste it in his mouth as he sucked the pipe. And chased away the vision, too, of the last time he had struck his daughter with his fist, and of all the times before.

It was a lovely pipe, he thought, ivory and delicately carved and with a small bowl. Crider Peel always lay on his side with the stem in his mouth, the bowl over the charcoal brazier. And each time, even more than the last, he knew that his troubles had now vanished, drifting upward to the rafters of Lin Chow's warehouse to disappear in the friendly darkness.

It was a good winter for Roman. He still thought of Victoria Cardin Archer now and again, but the deep pain that had accompanied such thinking when he'd gone to the western plains had diminished and now finally he could recall his times with her as a necessary kind of heartbreak that went with growing up, like the bittersweet black chocolate that looked so fine and tasted so good when he bought a pound of it from the confectioner's, but which, after a dozen or so chunks, could be laid aside without many second thoughts. Even though a hint of the taste lingered.

Maybe Forsyth's mission against the Cheyennes had burned the puppy love out of him. That's what he called it now. Puppy love. Just as his mother had called it back in the Ozarks when he'd gone to school in Leetown and had gotten calf-eyed and tangle-footed every time he thought about another ten-year-old, Maybelle Hopshire, whose daddy made corn liquor in a valley still hidden somewhere in the wild country of War Eagle Creek and spent a lot of his time in the jailhouse after he'd sampled his own wares excessively and took it upon himself to chastise one of his wife's brothers with a bullwhip. No matter which of the six brothers he chose for such treatment, it was bound to cause him pain, because not one of them weighed less than three hundred pounds, little of which was fat, and the eldest of them was sheriff of Benton County.

It gave Roman a chuckle now to think about Maybelle Hopshire and the total disaster of his courtship, which had ended one spring day when he'd asked to walk home with her and maybe whittle her a willow whistle, and she'd kicked him in the stomach. For a week he'd been in the depths of despair, and then school was out for the summer and his burning love for Maybelle vanished from his heart forever.

So he began to equate Maybelle with Victoria, and it was a good feeling because instead of getting kicked in the stomach he'd had the pleasure of giving Victoria's husband a bloody nose, right before a group of soldiers who he knew would spread the tale through every troop mess at Fort Leavenworth.

"It is my savage nature, I suppose," he wrote in his diary. "After the first shock, it seems I have taken a certain pleasure in having assaulted the good Lieutenant T. Archer."

But he never wrote anything in his diary about having been either partially or totally responsible for the death of Roman Nose. He tried not to think of that at all.

It was a joy to work in the snow with Excalibur's bay colt—putting a halter on him, letting him feel the weight of a saddle blanket, leading him on a long rope in circles around one of the stock enclosures, teaching him to come at the whistle, which promised a cube of sugar or a winter-wrinkled carrot. Orvile Tucker had found a farmer south of the town who had a root cellar stuffed with last summer's carrots, and when he brought them into the stockyards, Roman used half of them for the colt, the other half as a gift to Spankin Hankins's kitchen, where they always ended in a rich stew.

They named the colt Excalibur Junior, but were soon calling him just Junior.

"That Junior," Orvile Tucker said. "He's gonna be almost as big as his pappy and with those Morgan lines and color of his mammy."

"Just see he gets plenty of oats," said Roman.

"Mr. Roman, I feeds that colt like he was my own chile."

And on the day that Orvile Tucker fashioned the first set of iron shoes for the colt, they had a little celebration. Mr. Hankins bought two gallon jugs of cherry wine, and Elmer Scaggs and Tracy Benson came from the hog ranch to join in, and afterward, when Mr. Hankins invited them to supper at his house, Spankin was furious because they were all a bit drunk.

Lieutenant Thaddeus Archer's threat not to return was fulfilled, but other quartermaster officers came and bought horses to be sent to Fort Riley and then to a place called Camp Supply, in the Indian Territory. What everyone suspected would happen did. Sheridan turned Custer and the Seventh Cavalry loose on a Cheyenne winter village, and it was destroyed along with its chief and his wife and some women and children. To most people, the only sour note was that Major Joel Elliot and some of his men were killed as well, and there were ugly rumors going the rounds of the saloons and hinted at in some of the newspapers that Custer had ridden off and left Elliot and his men when hostiles from nearby camps appeared.

"God Almighty," Roman said to Elmer Scaggs. "Elliot was with the Medicine Lodge Treaty bunch. I saw him a few times and he seemed well respected by his troops. When is all this killing going to end?"

"Well, if they leave Sheridan and Custer alone, it can't last much longer," said Elmer Scaggs. "They won't be none of them savages left to kill. Say, boss, it sure is nice now to collect that garbage at the fort. You can smell our bacon cookin' in all the troop messes each morning. And at Christmastime we could've sold four times as many hams as we had. By Gawd, next year we'll *have* four times as many."

All of this business enterprise was a little scary. Roman's account at the express office was growing, what with his dividends from the railway construction stocks and the proceeds from the garbage collection effort and the sale of meat and lard from the hog ranch. He had already paid Katie Rose and Mr. Hankins for his initial investment deficit, and now everything was showing a profit. And of course he was still drawing his salary at the yards, where Mr. Hankins had made him the foreman with an appropriate raise in pay. His express book showed, by New Year's, that he was worth more than eight thousand dollars in cash money. He suspected that his father had never made that much during his entire lifetime, and it embarrassed him a little. In his letters home, he only alluded to the fact that he was doing well. He never mentioned figures. Somehow it all seemed a bit sinful.

During January, Roman made one concession to his wickedness. He went to church. He didn't go with Tallheimer Smith and Olivia, as he always had before, but sat in one of the rear pews, from which he could escape after the services before they saw him. They were in their usual place down front, within range of the blasts of hot air that issued from the Reverend Hezekiah Sample's mouth. After his sermon, Hezekiah blistered somebody, but to Roman's vast relief he didn't name names.

He wrote in his diary:

Hezekiah quoted from Matthew. I have the verse before me in Mrs. Murphy's Bible, which I borrowed for the occasion of research. "Tell it unto the church." And then from Corinthians. "It is reported there is fornication among you. Put away from yourselves that wicked person." Well, I hope he doesn't take out an advertisement in the Leavenworth Conservative. *He did the next best thing, I suppose, by announcing such a thing from his pulpit, even though he didn't identify any of the sinners. It seems a strange way to practice what Papa always said was a benevolent religion. You might expect they'd have the courtesy to make charges behind closed doors if they're trying to bring lost souls to salvation.*

He hoped the reverend wasn't talking about Olivia Smith, remembering the incident on the horsehair couch in her living room. But he didn't put that down in his diary.

That church service continued to disturb him—not only the calling out of sinners, but the fact that he himself had never made his peace with any God. He'd spent many evenings on the front porch of the Benton County farm, he and Cal listening to their father quote Scripture, and both had done a large part of their early learning in reading from the Book from which those Scriptures came. But as he grew older, reading the Bible himself from end to end and watching people in various churches and camp meetings, some of whom frothed at the mouth and talked in tongues, his doubts edged up like unwelcome bile and his questions increased.

Even though he didn't clearly perceive it until he was in Kansas, it had been a heavy burden to him that he could not completely conform to his father's faith, a faith that recognized a Divine Being who ordered all things. It made him feel as if he'd been deceiving the elder Hasford, had turned enemy to his own kind.

But maybe what Cal once called "Papa's holy light" had been dimmed by his exposure to all those terrible things during the war. That thought came like a revelation to Roman. Maybe this accounted for the change between the Martin Hasford who went away in 1861 and the Martin Hasford who came home in 1865. Maybe, Roman thought, his father was struggling with himself after everything he'd seen, trying to integrate the world as it was with the world as he had always imagined it.

And that thought was comforting. It made Roman feel a little closer to his father, though they were separated by a lot of time and many miles. He felt closer to him now than he had since the two of them were in the woods together, the elder Hasford showing the younger how nature worked.

It was during this time that he was on the streets of Leavenworth one snowy afternoon, browsing through the hardware stores in search of a shotgun. Elmer Scaggs had mentioned dove hunting when the season was right in the spring, and Roman had decided that for all the good work Elmer had done at the hog ranch he might deserve a little gift.

Perhaps a good shotgun, one of the new ones that loaded center-fire brass cartridges from the breech.

At the corner of Sixth and Miami streets, walking with his head bent into the harsh wind and snow, Roman almost collided with a little man on the sidewalk who was wearing a long Union Army overcoat, stained and torn, and a woolen stocking cap pulled down over his ears. The man was selling white paper pamphlets, and Roman bought one and gave the man a silver dollar and shoved the pamphlet into a coat pocket and forgot about it, wondering, as he moved away, how long it might have been since that man had enjoyed a full, hot meal.

For some time the tract rested in the overcoat pocket. Then one night in his room at Mrs. Condon Murphy's boardinghouse, having finished the last pages of a new book called *Innocents Abroad* by a Missouri man named Samuel Langhorne Clemens, and in no wise ready for sleep yet, Roman remembered the pamphlet and retrieved it from the hanging coat.

The pamphlet was entitled "Defense for the Rational Adorers of God." It had been translated from German, and there were numerous comments appended by a Leland Converse, who had put the whole thing together in the city of Boston.

Roman began reading casually—"time-passing reading" he called it—but quickly there was nothing casual about it. He finished the tract and then reread it, making notes along the margins. There was a tremendous excitement about it, and he fingered back and forth in the little booklet until well past midnight. And he kept thinking, I'm not alone!

Before he slept, he took the diary from his desk drawer and dipped the quill into the pot of ink, afraid that if he didn't make his notes now, they would slip away during the night. As he wrote, his fingers were almost blue with the cold but he didn't have time to throw more coal into the stove.

> *It's about an all-powerful God that created the world and everything in it in some mysterious way that we can't yet comprehend. And then He went away from it so it could fend for*

itself. It was the religion of John Adams and Thomas Jefferson, according to Mr. Converse, and of Benjamin Franklin, too, who said, "The Ten Commandments and the Sermon on the Mount contain my religion." No church dogma, Mr. Converse writes, and no faith through revelation but through the force of reason!

And afterward, under the Joseph's-coat quilt and unable to sleep because of the cold and the enormity of this thing, he thought, Why, hell, it fits the way I've been thinking for a long time. Not faith through revelation.

Revelation was supposed to mean the process of God talking to people in one way or the other, revealing himself. He'd read about people like that in his father's Bible, and he'd even known a few back in the hills, the ones who frothed at the mouth and talked in tongues. It had always made him a little uncomfortable to think of mortal man claiming to have a conversation with the Great Maker. He was glad his own father had never come close to making such a claim.

I should stop cussing so much, he thought before sleep came. And even with his feet cold under the Joseph's-coat quilt, he felt wonderful.

Before he went to the stockyards on the morning after he'd discovered that he was a Deist, Roman Hasford rode downtown and guided the sorrel up and down the streets, looking for the little man in the Union greatcoat. He wanted to buy him a good meal and talk to him about the tract and maybe find a few more things that had been published on the subject. It was bitter cold and few people were on the streets, and those few were hurrying along with mufflers around their faces. There was hardly a wagon in sight, and no horses were tethered to the hitch rails along the fronts of most buildings.

After riding all the streets, his toes feeling like chunks of ice inside his boots, Roman reined in at the city marshal's office on Chestnut Street. Inside were most of the men who made up the corps of peace officers in the town, staying in out of the cold, feet propped on a large cast-iron stove, two of them playing checkers on a board held between them on their knees.

"Shut that Gawd damned door," one of them shouted, and then looked up and grinned. "Sorry, Mr. Hasford. Didn't pay no mind to who it was. Cold's got my head stifled."

From behind his desk, the city's chief marshal, Eldon Harvesty, made a signal of salutation with one hand and shifted a massive cud of chewing tobacco from one cheek to the other. It struck Roman that this whole place smelled of tobacco juice.

"Mr. Hasford!" said Marshal Harvesty. "What can we help you with?"

Roman described the man from whom he'd purchased the Deist tract, and asked if anyone had seen him. Marshal Harvesty blinked a number of times in rapid succession as he shifted his cud once more, the process making his outlandishly huge brindled mustache twitch at the pointed ends.

"Him? You know him?"

"No. But I wanted to talk with him."

"Is they anything we can help you with, Mr. Hasford? That man, he drifted in here a few weeks ago, just a drifter and panhandler from southern Illinois, so he claimed. We figured he wasn't doin' much harm, so we let him sell his little books."

"I'd like to find him."

"Well," said Marshal Harvesty, rubbing his face with his hands and darting his eyes around the room, where everyone was suddenly still and watching. "You could see him over at Turkimer's undertaking parlor. We found him this morning in an alley off First Street, down by the river. He was froze to death."

And riding back through town to the stockyard, Roman kept thinking, There's no benevolent God. We fend for ourselves and some do a damned poor job of it. And most of those get little help from the rest of us!

22

The chief peace officer of Leavenworth, Kansas, sat in the pantry just off Mrs. Condon Murphy's kitchen at a small table normally used for keeping accounts and making menus, such as they were. He felt surrounded by shelves and bins, although there were only a few of these along one wall, where sacks and tins and jars held the victuals in quantities necessary for Mrs. Murphy's line of work. It had no windows, and seemed to him like a jail cell. The only opening was the door that led into the kitchen where the widow was preparing her tenants' breakfast, thereby broadcasting the odor of fresh bread and bacon into all corners, even into the corner where Eldon Harvesty sat. His fat hands were folded before him on the tiny table and his bald head gleamed under the light of a lamp bracketed to the wall beside a year-old calendar with a scene of what some unknown artist thought an Indian maiden would look like, dipping her bare feet into a limpid pool of water where lilies grew.

Harvesty was dressed for warm spring weather because that's what it was. He wore no coat, just a vest over a white linen shirt and a pair of cotton trousers too small for his expanded belly. He was beginning to sweat a little, especially across his bald pate, and some of the thick moisture made its way along his temples and cheeks and finally into the extravagant mustache that was waxed heavily but already wilting, even though it was barely sunup of a new day.

When Roman Hasford came, he filled the doorway, and Eldon Harvesty marveled at how this young man had grown in the few years he'd been in Leavenworth. The marshal had marked his arrival closely, as he did the coming of all strangers, especially those from the South, and noted that Hasford had grown in wealth and influence as well as in muscle and bone. Taking his derby hat off an almost nonexistent lap and placing it on the table before him, Eldon Harvesty rose and nodded.

"Good morning, Mr. Hasford," he said.

"I'm told you want to see me," said Roman. "Is there some kind of trouble?"

"I'm sorry to have wakened you," the marshal said. "But I thought it best."

"It was time to get up anyway."

"Please sit down with me for a minute, Mr. Hasford, I've got a few things to say to you."

There was no place to sit except for the swivel chair the marshal was occupying, but on cue, as though she'd had an ear to the door, Mrs. Murphy appeared with a stool, and Roman moved into the room with it. Mrs. Murphy asked if Harvesty wanted a cup of coffee, *too*, indicating by her tone that her guest Mr. Hasford was eligible for one, but bringing two cups might be a slight imposition.

"That'd be real nice, Mrs. Murphy," said Harvesty.

Eldon Harvesty was embarrassed. As Mrs. Murphy carried in two steaming mugs, he made every effort to look at potatoes and sassafras roots and coffee bins rather than at the pillow-tousled hair and sleep-puffed eyes of Roman Hasford.

"Mr. Hasford, I'm a family man," he began at last, his eyes still taking an inventory of Mrs. Murphy's supplies. "I've got four young'uns, all girls. I hate to think of those little ones and others like them gone off to spend their lives in the state's orphan asylum."

Roman Hasford sipped his coffee, coming more awake

and alert with each of the marshal's words, but he said nothing. Harvesty, being in the line of business that he was, understood that he'd left no opening for response, and that was what he intended because this was a very sensitive issue and he wanted to approach it with care and without interruption of his thinking.

"Some of the church people have such places, too, but they aren't much better than the one the state's got. Most generally the state gets these poor little waifs and they put 'em in that place in Lansing and God knows the abuse they suffer. I could tell you stories about some of the older ones taken out of there, too. Kids thirteen, fourteen years old, adopted to be carted off to St. Louis or some other place for carnal purposes."

Roman Hasford was wide awake now, holding his coffee mug before his face, and Harvesty could see him watching with a sharp intensity, as though measuring each word. Harvesty had known it would be like this because although he had never had much direct contact with Roman Hasford, he'd heard stories and he knew the kinds of friends Hasford seemed to collect. Like General Phil Sheridan and Mr. August Bainbridge. Even though he was perhaps twice as old as this young man and an established politician in eastern Kansas, he did not consider himself to be Roman Hasford's equal in the hierarchy of Leavenworth society.

"Now, I am aware of your interest in the daughter of Crider Peel," Harvesty said. "And I know you have no evil intent in that regard, like some of those people who take young girls off to St. Louis."

"How do you know of any such interest?" Roman Hasford asked, and his voice was quiet, but his tone had a grainy substance, Harvesty thought, like metal filings.

"You've made no secret of it," said the marshal, then took a loud sip at the mug and elaborately wiped the dewdrops of brown liquid from his mustache. "Nor did Crider Peel, when we had him in our jail for drunkenness. He bragged about it, a fine gentleman like you with many business interests. Besides, it's my duty as a peace officer to know what's happening in my town."

Roman Hasford placed his mug carefully on the table, as though he were handling the most delicate crystal, and drew a deep breath.

"Have I broken some law?"

"No, no, no," Harvesty said, waving one hand and shaking his head. "Nothing of the kind."

"Well, why do you have to tell me this so early in the morning, and to what purpose?"

Harvesty could hear the irritation in the words, and he placed his large hands on the table before him, assumed his best vote-winning expression, and for the first time looked directly into Roman Hasford's eyes.

"Just a short time ago, Mr. Lin Chow, the Chinaman, came to me and led me to his establishment down by the river. You know Mr. Lin Chow?"

"No. But I know about him. Mrs. Murphy takes all my dirty clothes to him."

"And did you know that he sells opium in the rear quarters of his establishment?"

Harvesty had some small satisfaction in seeing the look of startled surprise that crossed Roman Hasford's face, but it was quickly gone, a reaction the marshal had seen many times, a concentrated effort to hide any emotion from a peace officer, even if the peace officer was doing nothing more than wondering about the weather.

"It's true. Mr. Lin Chow has been in that business since before the war. It doesn't seem to do anybody much harm, so we've overlooked it. Besides, when we need donations for the city's improvement, like putting gravel on the streets or hiring a scavenger to empty our privies or improving the docks so all the boats don't pass us by and go on upriver to St. Joe, Mr. Lin Chow gives more than his share. He always gives more than the Odd Fellows or the Masons or any of the churches. He always gives pert' near as much as Miss Katie Rose Rouse."

Marshal Harvesty lifted his coffee mug to his lips once

more, allowing all of what he'd said to sink in, and knowing full well that Roman Hasford knew he knew of the business association at the hog ranch. He smacked his lips, wiped his mustache, and placed the mug back on the table.

"Now, Mr. Lin Chow understands good citizenship. And so he came to me this morning, even though he knows I'm going to have to close him down for a little while because of what happened."

"And what happened?"

"At Mr. Lin Chow's, in one of those little beds he keeps for his customers, was Crider Peel. It was a bloody mess. Somebody had cut him several times with a knife. Mr. Lin Chow claims that anyone could have come in and done it. I asked him how come Crider Peel hadn't made any racket, getting stabbed so many times, and Mr. Lin Chow said that in his condition he maybe didn't even know he was being stabbed at all.

"You see, Mr. Hasford, there's a river door to that place, in back, so Mr. Lin Chow's customers can go in and nobody in the street up front will see them. There's this rope along the ceiling, like a train car emergency cord, and when somebody comes in that back door he just finds himself a bed and pulls the cord and it rings a little bell up front and then Mr. Lin Chow takes back what is necessary to do this smoking. So Mr. Lin Chow claims it could have been anyone. And I believe him. After all, Crider Peel wasn't famous for making friends. But he don't have to worry about it now, because he's dead as a doornail."

Roman Hasford didn't simply rise from his chair, he leaped, and Harvesty could see his pale cheeks and his clamped jaw. He watched as the young man went to the door, hesitated, turned, then turned again to look into the kitchen, where Mrs. Murphy was pouring cream gravy into a china tureen and shoveling hot biscuits from a flat cast-iron skillet. Abruptly he turned back to his stool and sat down, leaning on his elbows and pushing his face close to the marshal's.

"Why are you telling me this?" he asked.

"Mr. Hasford," said Harvesty, spreading his hands as

though he were laying out pages of a large book. "I wanted to give you the opportunity to do something about that little girl. As soon as I make this known to the city fathers, away she goes to that asylum in Lansing. A delegation of the good men will march down to that mule shed and take her."

"Maybe they should have taken her a long time ago."

"Maybe so. Crider Peel likely wasn't a very good daddy, but at least he *was* a daddy, and she's not even got that now. I think you are concerned with the child's welfare. As I am, Mr. Hasford. But I have no means. And I know you wouldn't sell her off to some evil man in St. Louis or some-place like that."

The marshal could almost see Roman Hasford's mind working behind the pale blue eyes, not dismayed now but coldly calculating.

"Where's the body?"

"Still in the opium den. But very soon now, I'll have to send someone down there from Turkimer's funeral parlor. That's when the cat's out of the bag, as they say. I thought you might have something better than the state orphan asylum."

"God Almighty, man, I can't take her. I live in a board-inghouse and I'm not old enough to be her father."

"I understand that, Mr. Hasford. I'm not suggesting you take her in adoption. I only thought you might help get her into some decent place. Like maybe the Hankinses'. Of course, the authorities might raise a stink about the child going to the Hankins home, what with that trouble he had in Illinois."

"What trouble?"

"He helped a bunch of them Mormons a long time ago. Got tar-and-feather clothes for his trouble, because a lot of people there didn't take to Mormons. A lot of them here don't either. So maybe you might think of a better place."

Roman Hasford rose again, more calmly now, and paced back and forth in the pantry. With his long legs, two steps in each direction were all he could manage in the small space.

"How much time can you give me?" he finally asked, look-ing down at Marshal Harvesty's wet pate.

"Well," said the marshal, "not long. I've got my duty. An hour, maybe."

"An hour?" Roman Hasford said. "I can't do anything in an hour."

"I've got my duty."

"I'll give you a thousand dollars to give me five."

At the mention of such a sum, the marshal jumped as though he'd been bitten.

"Oh, well," he said, wiping his mustache furiously. "I had no intention of your doing such a thing. I only thought to give you some chance of doing what we both know is right."

"A thousand dollars."

"Well, maybe two hours."

"Four."

Marshal Harvesty's hands moved down across his belly, caressing the lines of the bulging linen shirt. He avoided Roman Hasford's eyes.

"Well. Do you have such an amount here with you?"

"Of course not! But you'll have it."

"But when, Mr. Hasford?"

"In four hours. The express office will be open in time for that."

"You'll bring it to me?"

"No. I don't expect to see you again today, and I don't want you nosing around, seeing what I'm doing."

"Then where?"

"You can pick up the money at Katie Rose Rouse's place. In four hours. She'll have it."

And the marshal thought that maybe Roman Hasford had imagined such a possibility before this morning.

"Well."

"A thousand dollars. In gold."

Harvesty shrugged, trying to put it on a casual basis.

"All right. Four hours. That's all I can give you."

Roman Hasford spun toward the door, but paused there and turned back, pointing a finger at the marshal's face as though he were aiming a pistol.

"You'll have your money. But if you do me wrong on this,

Marshal, if I don't get that time you say you'll allow, and if you try to find out what I'm up to, you'll be doing yourself a great disservice."

And then the young man was gone and Harvesty heaved a great sigh of relief and wiped his bald head with both hands and then lifted the mug to his lips and drank, even though the coffee was long since cold. Then he thought of the things he could do with a thousand dollars in gold, and laughed.

But he didn't laugh long. He thought of Roman Hasford's final words and reckoned they might mean a great many things, but he was a wise man in such situations, and was concerned with only one of those. He thought, By God, I'll give the young man five hours just to be sure that son of a bitch Jared Dane don't come around after my ass when all this is over.

As a man accustomed to such dealings, he was most concerned with the well-known association between Roman Hasford and Jared Dane, which could become very dangerous indeed.

And Harvesty was perhaps better acquainted with what Jared Dane had been doing to Crider Peel than anyone else in Leavenworth. But he had intentionally avoided the subject. The marshal didn't even like to *think* of Jared Dane.

Yes, he thought. It's only right. I'll give Mr. Hasford five hours.

It took less time than Roman had reckoned. His mind was in turmoil over this whole business, but he had to admit it didn't surprise him much, and maybe without even knowing it he'd made some plans for this day. Knifed to death in an opium den! That was a wonderful thing for a girl to grow up with, and Roman began to realize that his own relationship with his father wasn't so bad after all.

As for the murderer, Roman didn't speculate. With a man like Crider Peel, there were too many possibilities, and Roman didn't know all of them. So he tried to keep from speculating, concentrating all his thinking on what he had to do.

As he threw the saddle on the sorrel in the shed behind Mrs. Murphy's, and rode to the stockyard, leisurely because he didn't want to attract attention to himself on this day, he listed in his head the necessary stops to be made, just like running figures down one of his ledgers at the hog ranch.

First, to Mr. Hankins's to pick up another horse and gear, though he didn't even know if Catrina Peel could ride. She'll damn well have to learn in a hurry, he thought.

He'd tell Mr. Hankins that he needed to be gone about three weeks, maybe more, on personal business. That was all he'd say, because the fewer people who knew what he was doing, the better.

Next, to the express office to draw out the money for Harvesty and some more for himself. And if the express office wasn't open yet, the manager would be in back, getting ready for the day, and he'd open for Roman Hasford because he knew as well as Harvesty did that the Boss would raise hell later if he didn't.

Then to Wilmot's General Mercantile, for coffee beans and bacon and cornmeal and a pot for the coffee and a skillet for the bacon and bread. It would be sparse fare, but he'd lived on sparse fare before and he knew the girl had as well. He'd buy two blankets because spring nights could be cold in the direction where he was headed, and a large bag of corn for the horses, and one of those new Winchester repeating rifles and two boxes of brass cartridges, just in case. In case of what, he wasn't sure because he'd never kidnapped anyone before, but he hoped that because she was nobody special and just a little girl, insignificant in the greater scheme of things, the authorities wouldn't make a fuss, much less bother to pursue him.

Then to Katie Rose; no explanations necessary there, just leave the money and tell her to mark well the time that Harvesty came for it.

Next, to the hog ranch, to tell Elmer Scaggs he'd be on his own for a while, which would tickle Elmer Scaggs to death because Roman was aware that the big man enjoyed any new responsibility that might be pushed his way. And Roman knew Elmer Scaggs could handle it.

And finally, to the mule-shed home of Crider Peel.

When Roman Hasford knocked and quickly pushed back the door, he could smell ham cooking. Standing on a wooden crate before the stove was Catrina Peel, turning to him, wide-eyed, holding a spatula in one hand. It struck Roman that the stove looked massive and forbidding behind such a small figure.

"Catrina," he said softly, expecting her to bolt toward the burlap-curtained door that marked off her territory, but she didn't. She stood on the crate, the ham spitting in the pan behind her and the spatula in her hand, and her eyes looked the deepest brown that Roman had ever seen.

"Catrina, you've got to come with me now. To a good place where nobody will ever hurt you again."

She looked at him for a long time, then turned on her crate and with the spatula pushed the pan of ham from the hot end of the stove. With her back to him, she spoke so softly that Roman could hardly hear her.

"Is my daddy not coming anymore?"

God Almighty, Roman thought, this is the hard part.

"No, Catrina, your daddy isn't coming anymore. So we'll go away now to a good place and you'll be with kind people and learn how to read."

Learn how to read? Why the hell did I say that? he thought. But then he had no time to think further because Catrina dropped the spatula and leaped off the crate and darted to the burlap door and disappeared behind it, as quickly and furtively as a mouse, and he could hear her crying. And then her voice, high-pitched, yet somehow with that resonance he'd noted once before.

"My daddy's dead, isn't he?"

Where did she learn about dead? Roman thought. But, hell, living her whole life with somebody like Crider Peel, who knows what-all she understands, what-all she's seen?

He walked to the burlap door, which had been a kind of

symbol in his mind all this time, a kind of shield that held him off from this child, no matter how hard he'd tried to penetrate it. He still heard her crying beyond it and took a deep breath.

It was a bare room. There was a long bed like a woodbox with straw, and a cover of ragged blankets. There was a little pole rack across the back of the room, holding a few pitiful items of clothing, and a pressboard box containing what appeared to be cotton underwear and stockings and, beside it, two pairs of men's brogans without laces. And Catrina Peel was crying as she stuffed her clothes into a flour sack, her hands moving quickly, as though she sensed some urgency, and going about it all like an adult, yet at the same time making the sounds of a child crying, her tiny shoulders shaking.

"That's good, Catrina, and don't forget your doll."

"Daddy took it away when I was bad," she said, and Roman ground his teeth and turned back to the other room. He went to the stove and found a stale loaf of bread on a shelf, bread he'd brought less than a week ago. He tore it open and fingered up the hot ham and placed it inside the bread and remembered bringing the ham as well, only the day before yesterday. He wrapped the crude sandwich in a dish towel that wasn't completely clean, and by the time he turned from the stove, Catrina Peel was standing in her doorway, holding the cotton flour sack. She was no longer crying but her cheeks were tear-streaked.

My God, Roman thought, how old is this child anyway, knowing what we've got to do and asking me no question but willing to have me take her? And maybe it was from that moment, seeing Catrina Peel waiting for whatever he might do, that he stopped thinking of her as a child.

"Let's go," he said, moving toward the door and the early-morning sunlight outside. "I've got a nice little horse for you."

"Will he bite me?" she asked, running along behind.

"No. You just sit on her and hold the saddlehorn. I'll show you how. And we'll go to a good place."

* * *

The first day they made only about twenty miles, according to Roman's reckoning. They took the ferry at Woolcot, just a short distance south of Leavenworth, because Roman wanted to get out of Kansas as fast as he could. It meant having to cross the Missouri again at Sugar Creek, east of Kansas City, and they did that at dawn of the second day. After that they drove straight south, Roman pushing the horses as fast as they could handle the pace.

Catrina rode behind him on the dappled mare he'd selected from the stock pens, silent but watching him, her legs too short for her feet to reach the stirrups, holding on to the saddlehorn as Roman led her horse. He looked back often and smiled. She never smiled back. But there was no hostility or fear or uncertainty in her face. Roman felt a greater and greater weight of responsibility on him as they rode, because he knew she trusted him and depended on him for whatever might come.

It's almost as bad as thinking about protecting Mama from the partisans after the battle of Pea Ridge, he thought. Only Mama was tough enough to be the one protecting me.

On their first night out, after he'd cooked bacon and spoonbread in a willow-choked break just north of the Missouri and she'd eaten like a wolf, she smiled. And she spoke for the first time since they'd left that Leavenworth mule shed.

"It's good."

There was a small victory in that, and he gave her a blanket and tried to pull it up around her neck, but she pushed his hands away.

"I can do it," she said.

And a little later, Roman saw her squirm out of the blanket and go off into the darkness to do whatever she needed to do, and he thought, Well, she can pretty well take care of herself in most ways.

It was a pattern that would obtain for the next week, and Roman couldn't help thinking that this was a better way to travel than being on foot, as he had been coming north. It was almost as if he were alone, concentrating on avoiding towns or heavily used roads. It didn't hurt to play things safe, he reckoned. Sometimes he even forgot there was anyone behind him and then he'd be brought back to reality by the sound of the mare's iron-shod hooves, and he'd turn and look and Catrina would be there, watching him. She's as bad as that Crow squaw of Emil Durand's, always watching me, he thought, but there wasn't anything disquieting about this. In fact, he rather enjoyed it. Even so, he couldn't help feeling like a bank robber running from the law.

Then they forded the Cygnes River and began to move into the northern reaches of the Ozark Plateau, where the trees and the terrain were something he understood. There were gentle valleys here, and rolling hills, but everything grew more rugged as they rode south. By then he began to feel secure and thought maybe it was because the trees were so familiar to him, the oak and sycamore and hickory and walnut. He began to talk to her constantly as they went, never turning but pointing out this blooming dogwood or that leafing redbud, and the new spring flowers like the wild blue violets along the many tiny streams they crossed, or the white yarrow beside the roads, or the green shoots of pokeweed just sprouting. He explained to her that his mother cooked pokeweed sprouts in the spring and called them greens, but that the roots and stems and the clusters of blue-black berries that would come later were poisonous.

Spiderwort and bull thistle and milkweed: he reckoned he'd forgotten all those names since he first learned them from his parents a long time ago. But they came as easily to the tongue as did his names for all the birds: cardinals, the cocks beginning to search for mating territory or else already defending the nesting places of last year, and mockingbirds and the many varieties of woodpeckers. At night there were the songs of whippoorwills and the trembling cries of screech owls.

The farther south they rode, the more dense became the hardwood forests. Even though the leaves were new, they filtered out the sunlight. When they left the roads and went overland through the timber it was like a womb, those tall, thick-growing trees sheltering them with green, protecting them from everything. And it all smelled so familiar, an' earthy, new smell. It reminded him in flashes of his mother churning, of Calpurnia teasing him when he came in from a hunt with squirrels not all head-shot, of his father blazing locust trees with a hatchet, marking those to be cut later in the year to sell as fenceposts in Bentonville.

There was so much it almost overwhelmed him, and although he tried to explain to Catrina all the sensations of it, he knew there was so much he could never explain. Even to himself.

One night, after they'd built their little fire and cooked the bacon, Catrina looked at him and said, "Why do you keep sniffing, Mr. Hasford?"

"Oh, I reckon just to see if I smell rain," he said.

"How do you smell rain?"

"I don't know. But sometimes you can. And I didn't bring any slickers, so if it rains, we'll get wet. And don't call me Mr. Hasford. Down here in the hills, I'm just Roman."

She looked into the fire for a while, its light reflected in her eyes in dazzling flares of luminescence, and he thought, No, she's not like that Crow squaw of Emil Durand's. These are eyes such as I've never seen before.

"Will we just ride the horses on and on?" she asked.

"No. It won't be long now."

And wrapped in his blankets that night, listening to her steady breathing as she slept, he felt an intense satisfaction because on this day she had spoken more than he'd ever heard her speak before.

It didn't rain, even though it was the season for such things, and so they rode on, dry and warm at night, as all the while the country became more rugged and more familiar. And then, south of Cassville, they turned onto Wire Road, which within a few miles led directly through the old battlefield of Pea Ridge and past the farm of Martin and Ora Hasford, the place where Roman had lived most of his life, the place that was home.

* * *

Four days after Roman Hasford and Catrina Peel departed the environs of Leavenworth, Kansas, a minor news item appeared on the third page of the *Conservative*:

> Another murder has blemished the fair face of our city much in the manner of what happens in places farther west, where the rowdies and roustabouts of Texas bring their bovines for sale.
>
> Mr. Crider Peel, late employee of the Denison Tannery and Ice House, was found stabbed by a party or parties unknown in a First Street establishment.
>
> Mr. Peel had been a resident of the city for some years. He left a young daughter whom a Kind Providence decreed would be adequately cared for. Friends of Mr. Peel indicated that just two days before his misfortune he had said a Mr. and Mrs. Conmister, he being an uncle to the child, had come to Leavenworth and taken the child back to their home in Youngstown, Ohio, for the purpose of educating her. It is assumed that the child will now make her permanent home there.

No source was quoted for this information. But the source had been Marshal Eldon Harvesty. As was often the case among newspapers of that time and place, small importance was given to the origins of a story. In this case, Marshal Harvesty had suggested that his name not be used since he actually had no part in the incident. He and the editor being of the same political persuasion, this request seemed reasonable. As in all times and places, political favors were not unknown in Leavenworth. Marshal Harvesty was proud of his work.

In his little journalistic ruse, the marshal had protected Mr. Lin Chow, that wonderful benefactor, by keeping his name from public view and warding off any possible outcry by the do-gooders. And now it would be only a short time before the marshal could inform Mr. Lin Chow that he might resume his enterprise in the rear of the warehouse, which was such a valuable source of revenue for underpaid peace officers.

Even more important, the marshal had provided Mr. Roman Hasford with the protection he needed against the biddies and busybodies of various church groups who might start nosing about.

Of course, the marshal did not know anybody named Conmister. In fact, he was more than a little proud of having invented a new name he had never heard of, one he hoped nobody else had heard of, either.

Marshal Harvesty kept a fine finger on the pulse of his city. He was certain that once his story had wide circulation those biddies and busybodies, and more especially the city fathers, would put the thought of an orphan from their minds, since this orphan was the daughter of a notoriously wicked man who patronized barrooms and whores. There would be much sighing among the matrons of the churches, who would say, "Well, now the child will have a good home." And they'd heave another sigh of relief because they wouldn't have to worry about it. And he was right.

Eldon Harvesty saw all of it as a stroke of genius. It was the least he could do, he thought. And the most he could do for himself, to stay on the good side of Mr. Roman Hasford's friends. And so he rested easy in his bed each night and thought about the many ways he could spend a thousand dollars. Only occasionally would he start from sleep after dreaming that Jared Dane was knocking on his door.

PART FOUR

After I told him I was at the Battle of Beecher's Island, Papa and I never once spoke of it again, no more than we spoke of his experiences with General Lee. But there was in his eyes a new respect, I thought, as though maybe now he looked at me as one man looks at another when both have shared similar trials of body and soul.

—from Roman's diary

When Martin Hasford looked up from his work in the field alongside Wire Road, where he had finished his cutting of winter wheat and was making the earth ready for a summer stand of corn, and saw his son on the sorrel, he felt his heart suddenly pounding just as he had felt it pounding one morning in September of 1862 on the rise of ground above a little stream called the Antietam.

He had never expected to see his son again, taking it as a punishment for all his blasphemous language when he'd been a soldier, and for his doubts about a God who would preordain butchery on a battlefield. That doubt was still strong in his unspoken thoughts.

He shouted, but Roman had already seen him and reined to a stop before turning up through the locust-covered slope to the farmhouse. Martin Hasford dropped his grub hoe and ran to the fenceline bordering the road, wondering only vaguely who the girl on the led mare might be. All of his mind was taken with the tall young man who was grinning as he came down from the saddle.

Later, Martin Hasford would remember that moment, as he and his son looked into one another's eyes, Martin having to tilt his head back a little now, and amazed at the size of this young man whose face had hardly changed at all since he'd left home, except that now there was a stubble of blond beard on the cheeks. And then the quick, somehow embarrassed handclasp and his own eyes dimming. No word was spoken, and as Martin Hasford released his son's hand, they were suddenly embracing, still silent. It seemed to the older man that now he was finally coming home from the war—a crazy idea, he thought, because it was actually his son coming home.

And later, too, he had to chuckle when he recalled the first words spoken after all that time away from each other, after all the things he had rehearsed saying in case Roman ever did come back.

"Your mama's baking a gooseberry pie, the first of the season!"

As they walked side by side up the locust slope, Martin said, "I reckon you're still in Kansas."

"Yes. I've made a good business there."

And never a word about who the girl might be who rode the led horse and who had the biggest eyes Martin Hasford had ever seen. I guess he's married a very young girl, Martin Hasford thought, but nothing else because he was still buried in the excitement of his son's return. And besides, men marrying young girls in northwest Arkansas was nothing new.

"Your mama's going to have a fit," he said.

Ora Hasford came to the front porch at her husband's call, stocky and solid as a hickory rain barrel in her ankle-length calico dress and white half-apron. She stopped and stared and then squealed. She didn't scream or shout or speak any known word, but squealed and ran down the steps and threw herself at her son, and he laughed and picked her up in both arms and whirled her around as though she might have been as tiny and light as the girl on the mare.

Of course, Ora Hasford lost no time in wondering about the girl, as her husband knew she wouldn't. She asked straightforward and to the point. And her son told her that this girl was very special and had no place to live because she was an orphan, and Ora Hasford said she had a place to live now, just as Martin Hasford suspected she would, because everyone in this valley knew Ora Hasford could no more restrain her affection for babies and children and young people, even ugly ones, than she could stop the sun's rising each morning. And this one wasn't at all ugly.

It was like most reunions of people who cared deeply for one another and had been long separated, Martin supposed. Frantic and unhinged a little and confusing and everyone either embarrassed about speaking or else babbling on like an idiot. And the strange sound of Roman's voice made Martin realize that long absence plays tricks. The face might look the same because it had remained solidly in memory, but the sound of a voice could never be remembered as distinctly.

It was like that throughout the first day, Ora and Roman helping the girl down from the mare, Martin bringing a bucket of cool water to the porch because he could think of nothing else to do, Ora clucking and saying they'd get right to work making some decent clothes and then asking Catrina Peel if she was tired, and Catrina Peel saying she was, and Ora taking her up to the old loft room that had been Calpurnia's, which would now be hers, and Martin Hasford for the first time hearing the resonant voice. And in the loft, Ora insisting that Catrina take a little nap before supper while Martin and his son fiddle-footed and tried to think of something to say on the porch.

When Ora came down from the loft and joined them on the porch, the smell of baking coming by now out through the open windows, her face was set in grim lines and her eyes had a flinty spark that Martin Hasford recognized as seething anger. Then Roman told them all of what he knew about this child, and Ora, when he was finished, balled her fists and said she'd thought as much, from the deep scars on Catrina Peel's face.

"People who do such things ought to be dragged on a rope behind a good running horse," she said.

Then Roman told them what he'd been doing, even repeating a lot of things he'd already written in his letters home, and they listened to the catbirds mewing in the sumac scrub along the sides of Wire Road, and a crow making a fuss somewhere in the timber behind the barn.

"It sounds good," Roman said, and Martin Hasford was glad because it was somehow something he himself had saved just for his son.

The days and evenings all rushed together after that, and it reminded Martin Hasford of the times before the war, he and his son sweating together in the field across Wire Road, getting the crop planted, and Ora with Catrina Peel, making bread in the kitchen or feeding corn to the chickens or slopping the hogs or walking to the springhouse in the hollow for a crock of milk or a covered dish of butter. Just like before the war, Martin thought, my son beside me in the fields and my daughter at the house with Mama.

On the third evening, Martin Hasford could hold out no longer. He took down the old and battered blue-covered primers that Roman and Calpurnia had used when they went to school in Leetown, and began to sound out the alphabet for Catrina Peel, and the words, and the sentences. And so the reading lessons began. By that time Catrina had begun to speak frequently, especially to Ora, and smile to all. She didn't chatter, as Cal once had, but spoke only when she had something to say that was important, at least to her. And everything she said was important to Martin Hasford as well.

And after a few nights of the readers, Martin took down his big Bible and his copy of Mr. Gibbon's *Decline and Fall* and read aloud under lamplight, and was elated to see the expression on his grown son's face, as though he were recalling the many, many evenings in the gone years when he'd been a child and had heard that same voice saying those same words.

"She's smart as an owl," said Ora Hasford, although she didn't hold so much with reading and writing for a female as she did with Catrina's quick grasp of how to function in a large and well-equipped kitchen. And Martin Hasford remembered that his wife had said the same thing about Calpurnia.

It was all such a peaceful joy, seeing his son look at all the old, familiar things with a deep pool of remembrance in his eyes: the sprouting green garden beside the house, the heavy oaks that rose in formation up the slope behind the barn, the wide yellow fields across the road, and beyond that the lifted, timbered hills, blue and distant, and the ragged edge of Pea Ridge. And it was equally joyful to see his wife bubbling with an enthusiasm he hadn't seen since before the war, all because now there was another daughter to rear.

One day Roman saddled the mare and the sorrel and took Catrina on a tour of the area, and Martin Hasford felt included because his son had said he wanted her to see the things that he had seen, and said it in a way that made Martin Hasford think that it was part of them all. He showed her the mill on Little Sugar Creek where the old Jew once lived, which was now run by the former black slave named Lark; the foundations of the burned-out Elkhorn Tavern at the base of Big Mountain; the ridge behind the barn where the wild plum trees grew, which had been a special place for Calpurnia. And that evening Catrina talked more than she had ever talked before.

But a few days later, Catrina talked not at all because Roman was leaving, going back to his business in Kansas. The sun was shining and the larks across Wire Road were already looking for nests and making their sweet calls, and there was the scent of honeysuckle from the springhouse hollow. But it was a dismal day for them all. Yet Roman laughed and gave gifts. He left the little mare and all its gear for Catrina. He gave Martin Hasford a new Winchester repeating rifle and ammunition to go with it. And to his mother he gave five shining double eagles.

"It's from me and Allan Pay for the ones you gave him when he and Cal were married," Roman said.

And there was another thing, a dog-eared pamphlet that explained Deism. And after Roman was gone, riding back north along Wire Road, and the two females were in the kitchen with tears still gleaming on their faces, and after he'd sat on the porch reading the tract, Martin Hasford knew why Roman had given it to him.

My son, he thought, wanted me to know that he is not god-less. And more besides.

Martin had said nothing about such things. He hadn't asked Roman if he'd been going to church, maybe because Martin himself had found little solace in the few services he'd attended since his return from the war. Yet somehow his son had sensed the torment, sensed that Martin Hasford could not understand how the old God who willed all things could allow the horrors he'd seen during the campaigns in Virginia and Tennessee. Maybe it was because Roman had seen part of the battle of Pea Ridge. Or more likely because he'd been at Beecher's Island, and had actually taken part in deadly combat.

So Roman, having grown up with my God, understands, thought Martin. He was sure of it. And the greatest gift Roman Hasford could give to his father was an apology for that belief. No, not an apology, Martin thought. Instead, an answer to my agony, a remedy for my inner pain.

Well, it's going to take a little getting used to. But if Thomas Jefferson and Benjamin Franklin and my own son are right about it, I've got the free will to work it all through without worrying about everything being laid out for me in advance. It's nice to think that all the bad words I heard from my own mouth in battle and all the bullets I put into young Yankee soldiers were my own doing and not God's.

23

General U. S. Grant was inaugurated as President in March of that year, and by the time Roman Hasford returned to Leavenworth in the summer, some of the new administration's policies were being hotly debated, especially those concerning the wild tribes. "Old Sam" was discussed by the old soldiers and the young ones as well over steins of cold beer in the First Street saloons, and by the officers in their parlors as they held snifters of brandy, their women standing well back and silent because they understood that women were supposed to be seen and not heard when the subject of Grant came up.

What Old Sam had done irked a lot of people. He'd made a turnabout, they said. It had been assumed that when he became Commander-in-Chief he would do everything possible to have Indian affairs taken away from the Interior Department's Indian Bureau and given back to the army, the way Cump Sherman and Phil Sheridan said they ought to be.

Everybody knew, they said, that the Indian Bureau was staffed with incompetent and corrupt politically appointed scalawags who were doing nothing less than lining their own pockets and who knew absolutely nothing about the red man. They couldn't distinguish a painted Cheyenne Dog Soldier from a squash-eating Iowa, the soldiers said. Most of the newspapers made the same claim.

Once in office, however, Old Sam ignored all that and did nothing to give the Indians back to the army, but listened instead to the humanitarians who said troops provoked war, made mistakes in deciding who was hostile and who was not, and killed a lot of women and children. So the Peace Policy was begun, under which many of the agencies were staffed with church people, particularly Mormons, and the law was laid down: the army couldn't touch an Indian within any reservation boundary unless the resident agent asked them to. Old Cump Sherman was as mad as a wet snake, they said.

Of course, as some editors pointed out, Old Sam hadn't realigned his thinking on the spur of the moment. He realized that Congress, where almost everybody was getting damned tired of spending money on this or that little Indian war, was dead set against moving the Indian Bureau out of Interior. So Old Sam had to forget what he might have wanted most to do, because now he was a politician. He had been a fine soldier, but only time would tell what kind of a politician he was.

Roman Hasford got a firsthand viewpoint on some of this from Emil Durand, who had left the employ of Colonel Ben Grierson and his black Tenth Cavalry to come east. The first morning Roman appeared at the stockyard after going his rounds to greet Katie Rose Rouse, and Elmer Scaggs at the hog ranch, and the Hankinses at their breakfast table, he found the old mountain man leaning against an outside wall of the yard office, sitting on a rough wooden bench, his hat off, the hot breeze making his hair fly, gumming mouthfuls of coarse bread as he held his false teeth in one hand.

"Roman, I'm coming to the end of my road," he said without any preliminaries as they shook hands. "And I decided I wanted to do it among the whores and featherbeds of St. Louis."

Roman looked about and saw Durand's Indian pony, hung with gear, but no sign of the Crow woman.

"Where's Min?" he asked. "I have a mite of appreciation for her helping me get over that snakebite."

"She lit out," Emil Durand said. "Back to her own people, I allow. When I decided to leave the service of them Tenth Cavalry troopers, I went back to Fort Wallace to fetch her. By Gawd, they told me she'd departed by moonlight and taken two army horses with her. I hope she made it back to Montana Territory. But she may have ended up in some Cheyenne buck's lodge, doin' what she likes best. I suppose she showed you all the delights of heathen copulation in that Fort Wallace horspittle."

"No," Roman said, and laughed. "She was true to you, Emil."

"Like hell," the mountain man said, but he laughed as well, sodden breadcrumbs spilling from his mouth and into the gray beard. "But I never ast her to be."

"Why'd you leave the Tenth? Didn't you like those colored troopers?"

"Why, hell, Roman, them's some of the best sojurs I ever seen. And Ben Grierson's as good a man as you could find. No, it was politics."

He finished his bread and brushed the residue from his whiskers and clapped his false teeth back into his mouth with a loud clack before continuing, "They put the Tenth down in the Indian Territory along Medicine Bluff Creek. Smack in the middle of that Kiowa-Comanche reservation, where they can't do nothin' agin red hellions unless the agent ast 'em to. They got them sojurs buildin' a fort. They call it Camp Wichita now, but I hear they'll finally name it Fort Sill. So I left. Never was much on buildin' white mens' houses."

"But now you say you're going to a place that's got more white mens' houses than anything else. There aren't many skin lodges in St. Louis."

"Listen, Roman, buildin' 'em and layin' with a woman in one of 'em is two separate things."

"How will you live?" Roman asked, sitting down now beside Durand. He took his hat off to let the breeze comb through his damp hair, and suddenly the scent of horses was very strong on the wind and he realized how much he'd missed this place and that smell.

"Oh, hell, I'm gonna play my banjo and sing bawdy songs in the saloons and tell the pilgrims from the East all about the savages and their women. I got some stories about their women that them pilgrims will like. Then I'll build me a little still somewheres along the river, and just run out the days I've got left."

"How old are you, Emil?"

For a long time Durand chewed on his false teeth, making them click gently, and watched the horses in the nearest pen as they tail-switched flies on their rumps. When at last he spoke it was not in his usual manner—somewhat like a braying mule, Roman had always thought—but quietly.

"That's a good-lookin' bay mare over yonder." He seemed to shake himself. "How old am I? Damned if I know, Roman. But I was a young man when I seen this century start. Not long after that, there was this pretty little Mandan squaw who lived in one of them villages along the Missouri before the smallpox killed all of 'em."

Then his voice ceased suddenly, as though it had come up against an unscalable escarpment. He watched the horses, and his lips were stilled on his false teeth. Finally he spoke very quietly.

"I gotta be ridin' east."

And so Roman Hasford escorted his friend through town, and there in one of the general mercantile stores he bought him a new hat and a banjo inlaid along the neck with mother-of-pearl. And then on to the old ferry. Riding the streets, they made a strange contrast, Roman on his big sorrel and well suited out with trousers and vest and coat that matched, and polished boots and a felt hat, and the old man on a tired pinto in his ragged plains garb, most of the fringes on the buckskin rotted off and his feet in moccasins that showed a hint of toe at the ends.

Without dismounting, they shook hands and Durand looked a long time into Roman Hasford's eyes. His grip was dry and strong against Roman's fingers.

"I've got a sister in St. Louis," said Roman. "Go look up her husband and tell him you're a friend of mine. He's a lawyer, and anybody in town can tell you where his office is. His name's Allan Pay."

"I'll do it, Roman. I'll tell him about you and me bein' heroes at Beecher's Island. So goodbye."

Roman watched the old man riding down the wide gangway and onto the ferry skiff and there turning to wave, but only briefly, and then facing the wide Missouri. Roman thought, There goes a man who helped bury my Uncle Oscar in a world that is about gone. Along with most everybody who was in it.

And that night in his room at Mrs. Condon Murphy's boardinghouse, he wrote in his diary, "When I think of Emil Durand now, I can almost see the high rock mountains he talked so much about, with the snow on top as white as washed cotton and where there were no white men, only red, and where the streams ran clear and cold and the beavers made their dams. He's had a long life and it saddens me to know that it has run its course. And that I can never see the things he has seen."

And before he slept he reckoned that now he understood a little of the camaraderie that old soldiers feel for one another after they've seen war together. It made him appreciate more than ever the reveries he had seen his own father fall into, remembering, perhaps, old friends he'd seen die on one of those terrible battlefields in Virginia or Tennessee. There are so many ways that one has to say goodbye, and all of them are bittersweet.

Leavenworth was becoming a modern city. There was a new fire engine, horsedrawn, and the pumper for a three-hundred-gallon tank, powered by a steam engine. And there were a lot of hoses that could be dropped into wells or the river, provided, in the latter case, that the fire was close to the banks of the Missouri. The contraption was painted red, with yellow wheel spokes much like some of Mr. August Bainbridge's locomotives, and some said it spat out more live sparks than it doused, but only when the volunteer firemen could get the damned engine going. Most citizens couldn't see any appreciable decrease in the number of buildings that burned to the ground after the thing was installed in a shed next to the Odd Fellows Hall on Sixth Street. Everyone called the machine the Town Fathers' Folly.

The volunteer firemen approached Roman Hasford with an offer to be one of their fire marshals, and with the job offer came a metal hat that was painted white, with a red star on the front. It looked a good deal like a decorated chamber pot. Roman respectfully declined, but gave them a ten-dollar gold piece to help in the maintenance of the fancy equipment, knowing even as he did so that the delegation who had offered the white chamber pot would likely head straight for the nearest saloon and liquidate his contribution in a pleasant afternoon drunk. He hoped that nothing caught fire during the course of their celebration.

There was a new apothecary on Miami Street, and the druggist carried a line of books that he sold from bins at the rear of the store, behind all the shelves of liniments and pills and nostrums. He also had available a line of European picture postal cards showing ladies in various stages of undress. These he sold from beneath the counter at the front of the store, where he also kept razors, surgical bandages, and artificial limbs.

The books disappointed Roman. Mostly this literature was confined to dime novels like Beadle's Pocket Library editions, detailing hair-raising exploits of the now-defunct Pony Express, and tales of the infamous Missouri bandit Jesse James, that made him out to be a sort of Robin Hood. There was one issue devoted solely to the Battle of Beecher's Island. It was so wildly fictional that it made Roman laugh, and he realized that such things were probably composed by men who had never been west of Philadelphia.

"It's the stuff of history," said the little apothecary, blinking like an owl. "The stuff of history."

"It's the stuff of horseshit," said Roman. "No, I apologize to the horseshit. That is real stuff and it also smells better than this. Why don't you stock some books by Mr. Charles Dickens or Mr. Sam Clemens?"

The apothecary blinked.

"Who?"

There was also a new ice cream parlor, neat and clean along its street side, but in back, on a loading platform, city urchins were paid seven pennies a day to grind the cranks on the machines, which overlooked the empty bottles lying in the alley, cast out by the saloonkeeper in the next street. Roman had two thoughts: first, that maybe he should start a dairy herd to supply milk; and second, that he'd best have Elmer Scaggs mention that saloonkeeper to the city fathers so that a little pressure might be applied to get him on the rolls of the Hasford Garbage Collection Agency.

The newspapers had begun to concentrate their considerable populist venom on the various entrepreneurs of the state, particularly Mr. August Bainbridge. The heat was focused on his practice of slashing prices and paying rebates for freight and passengers on the many stagecoach routes he had established as feeder lines to the railroad. It was a highly successful campaign to squeeze out competitors.

The *Conservative*, in almost every one of its weekly editions, seared Mr. Bainbridge as completely lacking in honesty, morality, or common decency.

"Mr. August Bainbridge," the *Conservative* proclaimed, "is a public nuisance who should be abated by the Congress."

Roman read all of these charges each evening that the *Conservative* was published, sitting on the back porch of Mrs. Condon Murphy's boardinghouse, sipping lemonade and smoking one of Mr. Elisha Hankins's cigars. And he always had a chuckle about it because he knew that Mr. August Bainbridge didn't give a good damn what the newspapers or anybody else said about him, just as long as people rode his trains and coaches and deposited their money in his express offices.

Some of what happened that summer had the smell of disaster. For a number of days, just after noon, two officers of the judge advocate general visited the stockyard, where they cloistered themselves with Mr. Elisha Hankins in the hot little yard office. Afterward, Mr. Hankins would appear as the officers rode away, gasping for what little fresh air was blowing in from the river, looking haggard and worn, a deep misery in his eyes.

After four straight days, the officers came no more, but Mr. Hankins continued to look horsewhipped and Roman could contain himself no longer.

"Is there anything I can do?" he asked.

"No," said Mr. Hankins, avoiding his eyes. "They're not after me, son. They're after their own kind."

"The rebates on stock sales?"

"Yes. Don't say anything about this to Spankin." He turned and walked away, and Roman thought he looked as though he might be carrying an anvil on his shoulders.

Damn! Roman thought. Somebody should have shot that Thaddeus Archer a long time ago.

And for the first time in many weeks he thought about Victoria.

In early August, Mr. Elisha Hankins announced his intention of traveling to the western posts of the army to investigate the possibility of stock sales. But Roman knew it was just an excuse to get away from Leavenworth for a while. After all, those western posts got their remounts and beef out of Fort Leavenworth. But he said nothing.

There was a lot of furor up the river at Omaha, because the Union Pacific had connected with the Central Pacific at Promontory Point, Utah, giving the nation its first transcontinental railroad. There were flyers all over Leavenworth, tacked to the sides of buildings, pasted in store windows, blowing loose in the street, to the effect that anyone could board a car in Omaha and ride all the way to Sacramento for a flat one hundred dollars.

Of course, the Kansas Railroad people, whose tracks hadn't reached Denver yet, made light of it, saying that after all, there had been a transcontinental telegraph line since the first year of the war, more than eight years ago.

But there were some unpleasant rumblings about the Union Pacific, and the ugliness was bound to slosh over into Kansas. Because of that, a visitor came to Mrs. Condon Murphy's boardinghouse on a hot Sunday afternoon, asking after Roman Hasford. He was shown to the back porch.

"Well, I'm damned," Roman said, rising and offering his hand. And he could hardly keep from laughing, for this visitor wore a straw Panama hat with a brim hanging out beyond his ears at least a foot or more, and it seemed to emphasize the shallow, lifeless cast of eye and pallor of skin. "How are you, Jared Dane?"

After some casual conversation on Mrs. Condon Murphy's back porch, mostly concerning the progress of the railroad toward Denver, Roman Hasford and Jared Dane walked downtown to the Garrison Hotel to take their supper. It was a lazy afternoon, with little traffic on the streets. The sun was lowering but still bright, and the westward-facing buildings gave off a blinding glare, as though the light were reflecting from mirrors. At the intersection of Seventh and Delaware streets a gang of boys were playing kickball while a few Sunday strollers stood on the sidewalks and watched, encouraging the boys with shouts and applause.

As Roman and his friend approached, the game went on but the spectators fell silent, watching as Dane passed. Roman would write in his diary, "It seems he spreads a cold chill over people who know him only by reputation. Such a thing has never affected me. Still, there is a strange vacancy in his eyes sometimes, but I suspect that even then his mind is covering much ground."

In the Garrison Hotel dining room, all the hired help paid great attention to them. They were not unaware that these two men were associates of Mr. August Bainbridge, and rumor had it that Mr. August Bainbridge was the real owner of the hotel, even though the tax rolls indicated that two gentlemen from Lawrence were the proprietors.

The room was done in red velvet wallpaper, and the heavy drapes over the windows looking out on Chestnut Street were of the same rich color, the whole place decorated in the manner of some famous café in the city of New York, so Roman had heard, but he couldn't recall the name. It smelled of cinnamon and cloves and frying beefsteak.

Jared Dane had the baked ham with apple butter, but Roman opted for the fish, supposedly taken that same morning from the Missouri. He was sorry for it afterward, and thought, as he had often thought before, that apparently nobody north of Sedalia knew how to fry fish. He admitted to himself that this was a little unfair, because he had grown up on perch and smallmouth bass taken from cold hill streams and cooked by his mother to a crisp delicacy, although it was full of tiny bones.

It was fascinating to watch Jared Dane eating with only one hand, using first the knife, then the fork, one at a time, and having no difficulty with it. Roman tried to keep his eyes on his own food or the surrounding diners, but he had the sense that Jared Dane didn't care whether he was observed in what might have been an awkward and embarrassing operation. Everything was facilitated by his obviously strong right hand, even though it was a hand that looked fragile and doll-like.

Their conversation was casual—almost a forced casualness, Roman thought, because he knew Jared Dane had come for a purpose. He asked about the investigation of the express-office robberies and Dane said it was making headway, although recently the Boss had been infuriated when one of his stages had been stopped south of Topeka. Not much loss, Dane said, except for passengers' pocket money and the four coach horses. And, of course, the dignity and reputation of Mr. August Bainbridge.

Jared Dane said he understood that Roman had been at Beecher's Island and Roman replied that he had, knowing that most likely Dane knew a great deal about that operation, as he did about most things happening in Kansas and thereabouts. Roman added that he never expected to get himself involved in such a thing again.

"So now you've seen your Cheyennes," said Dane, and Roman couldn't remember whether he'd ever said anything to Dane about coming to Kansas partly to see some Indians.

"Yes," Roman said, expecting Dane to inquire further

about details. But Dane abruptly changed the subject to sage hens, of all things, saying he'd hunted them once in Dakota Territory but that he preferred the meat of upland quail, which he'd had in great abundance while a peace officer in Baxter Springs. So that was the end, before its beginning, of any discussion about Roman being a military hero on the Arikaree—which suited Roman.

They ended the meal with rice pudding and brandy and coffee, and the waiters brought cigars without being asked, a whole box of them, which was placed open on the table between them, along with a carton of the newest safety matches, which would strike only on the sandpaper strip along the side of the box. When struck, they burst into a bright yellow flame and smelled like sulfur.

A cigar looked out of place in Jared Dane's thin-lipped mouth. As they puffed, Roman studied Dane's face and was struck by the mannikinlike quality of this greatly feared man; his flesh was pallid and his eyes lifeless, and the thin, rust-colored hair across the skull was equally so. Roman did not recall him looking that way in the early days of their association, and he knew the loss of an arm had taken its toll.

He would write in his diary, "Or maybe I can see things more clearly now."

As they sat at their corner table, Roman became aware of Jared Dane's eyes constantly darting about to inspect the room, as though he was looking for something. And it came to Roman that when they'd entered, Dane had gone directly to this table and placed his chair to the wall so that no one could get at his back. It made little prickles of gooseflesh climb up Roman's back.

"The Boss has gone to Washington City," Dane said, puffing his cigar and watching the rest of the room indifferently, as if nothing interested him, which Roman knew was not true. "A little trip to offer condolences to some old associates because now the dance is about over."

"The dance?" asked Roman.

"The highly profitable dance of the Kansas Railway and Telegraph Construction Company."

"Is Mr. Bainbridge in trouble?"

"Oh, hell no," Dane said, and gave a short, harsh little laugh that did not change the expression on his face at all. "The dance is never over for the Boss. But it's over for some of his friends in the Congress. Certain parties are making a loud racket about congressmen who were given stock in the company in return for votes. The Crédit Mobilier started the whole thing, because those people have been too greedy. Now the smell of scandal and corruption is spilling over, and some of those gentlemen may be in trouble."

"Jail?"

"Maybe."

"Mr. Bainbridge?"

Jared Dane laughed again.

"Nobody has ever been sent to jail in this country for bribing a congressman. There are not enough jails to hold them all. But some of the Boss's friends who helped with large appropriations may or may not be brought to account. Surely they'll be in some trouble the next election, which to a politician is likely worse than the thought of jail."

All of this had suddenly made Roman apprehensive, because he didn't know what was coming next. The room became hotter than it really was, and he felt a small bead of sweat escape his hair and roll down the back of his neck.

"So the Boss asked me to come have a visit with you," said Jared Dane.

Even though he had expected as much, hearing Dane say he'd come on business and not as a friend was a bit bruising to Roman's pride.

"Oh." Despite his best efforts, his voice sounded impersonally hard. "And what did the Boss think was important enough to take you away from your work?"

"Don't get into a snit, Roman Hasford," Dane said, and this time his laugh seemed to have at least a modicum of warmth. "This railroad scandal business. The Boss allows that you need to get shed of your stock in the company."

"But he gave it to me."

"There's a time for giving and a time for taking away.

That may not be biblical, but it should be. The giving in this case was for friendship. The taking away is for politics. Mutually exclusive terms, of course."

"Well, hell, if he wants it back, he can have it. That's fine with me." But he squirmed a little because this whole thing had something else in it that Jared Dane seemed to be holding out.

"He'll buy it back."

"Buy it? God Almighty, Jared, he can *have* it. I don't want any money for it."

"No, the Boss insists. And what the Boss insists on, he gets."

Jared Dane's gaze fastened on Roman's eyes; there was some new spark of metallic light there, and although Roman was inclined to protest, he thought better of it. Play out the hand, he thought.

"The Boss reckons there shouldn't be any hint of corruption attached to a man he expects to put in the Kansas state legislature next election."

Roman's mouth came open but no sound issued forth. He stared at Jared Dane, thinking it was a joke, but even with the tiny smile that twitched at the corners of Jared Dane's lips, he knew it was not.

"God Almighty!"

"The Boss says first Topeka and later Washington City, in the Senate. He says you're a good man and there aren't many of those in either place. I suppose I have to agree with him."

It was the most devastating thing anyone had ever said to Roman Hasford, the most outrageous. And yet it was appealing. Everything that came within the next hour was a mere muddle of impressions on a mind awhirl with the implications. And the words flashed through his mind. Politics! State legislature! The United States Senate! And he knew, as surely as he could see Jared Dane's pale face before him, that Mr. August Bainbridge was a man who had the power to make these words a reality if anyone on earth did.

God Almighty, he kept thinking, I don't think Mama even knows what a United States senator is!

They went to the express office, and even though it was Sunday night, Roman, in a daze, didn't mark the unusual fact that the office manager was there, unlocking to Jared Dane's short knock at the front door. Inside, Roman's stock certificates were laid before him. He signed them over to the ownership of August Bainbridge, and Jared Dane gave him four thousand dollars Federal greenback currency, which was placed in the safe and credited to his account in the ledger books.

Outside, the air was cool, the sun already gone beyond the western high plains. They stood for a moment, Jared Dane finishing his Garrison Hotel cigar and flipping the butt into the dark street. Farther along the sidewalk toward the railroad depot Roman could see two figures in derby hats and knew they were Pinkertons. He wondered if they'd been somewhere in the background all along, bodyguards to Jared Dane.

They could hear a locomotive bell ringing and from the river a steamboat whistling as it came into the docks, and back in the direction of the residential area, a shrill-voiced woman was calling her child. With the heat waves from the gone sun subsiding, there was the smell of settled dust, and in the evening half-light everything had a deep purple cast to it.

Jared Dane reached over and squeezed Roman's arm and laughed his brittle little laugh.

"Off to Topeka now," he said. "And some of Fletcher's fine companionship. Better than those two cretins I'm working with. But the Boss admires Mr. Allan Pinkerton and thinks his men are infallible. He's misguided."

Roman was only momentarily amazed that Jared Dane knew he had seen those two derby hats.

"I remember Fletcher," he said. "Give him my kind regards."

"He remembers you, too. That's the thing about you, Roman Hasford. People remember you. You'll make a fine United States senator, although it'll have to wait a few years."

With a final squeeze of Roman's arm, Jared Dane turned and moved away toward the waiting detectives, an insignificant, slender figure in his thigh-length coat and outlandish Panama hat.

As he walked to Mrs. Condon Murphy's boardinghouse, Roman's elation made his feet seem to move on a cushion of air above the rough sidewalk. But as he went, he recalled all of Jared Dane's little speech. Mr. August Bainbridge would put him in high office. And so, he thought, I'll be the man of Mr. August Bainbridge. Bought or sold or traded.

Jared Dane had said the Senate would have to wait a few years.

Why, hell, Roman thought, that's a long way down the line before I'll be old enough to run. What age? Thirty-five? No, that's the President. But a ways off, nonetheless, and Mr. August Bainbridge owning me all the way, I suppose. Nobody ever owned me before. Not Papa or Mama or anybody else. Maybe it's good, I don't know. It's power. I'm just beginning to know what power is.

That thinking cooled everything. But as he mounted the steps to Mrs. Condon Murphy's front porch, he couldn't suppress the elation. That someone like the Kansas railroad mogul might think Roman Hasford would make a good United States senator, a hill boy who could never milk a cow as effectively or as quickly as his sister, now considered for an exalted place!

"Hello, Roman," said Mr. Moffet, sitting in one of Mrs. Murphy's porch rockers, well back in the darkness against the wall. "I'm glad to see you."

"Hello, Mr. Moffet," Roman said, and the sound of the little beer salesman's voice brought him back down to earth. He wondered if this strange man would vote for him, and knew he would.

"I've brought down a few jars of beer," Mr. Moffet said, almost apologetically. "It's very hot upstairs. I was just having a few sips and listening to the tree frogs. Perhaps you'd join me."

Roman laughed and swept off his hat and slapped it against his leg.

"Why, hell, Mr. Moffet, I think I will."

24

Some people called it Quick Killer because its victims were often dead before the symptoms had been recognized. It came usually at the same time that typhoid fever did, in the heat of summer, but not with the same frequency. Nobody was sure what caused it. There were a great many who thought it was the result of vapors breathed at night, vapors that floated on the air from dead and rotting things.

Before the Civil War, there had been an obscure Englishman who claimed it came from polluted water, but nobody paid much attention to him. And those on the Kansas frontier had never even heard the claim, with the possible exception of a few army surgeons. It was still some time before the microscope came into widespread use and therefore nobody was aware of the wildlife in their drinking water.

Of course, the obscure Englishman had been right, and if there was one thing frontier towns had in abundance, it was bad water. Sewage was dumped indiscriminately in alleys or into convenient streams generally used for drinking water, and wells were cheek-by-jowl with outdoor privies. The army posts were a little better off, because during the war, regimental surgeons had observed that a clean camp sustained fewer serious diseases than did a dirty one. Of course, army surgeons were entirely ignorant of why this was true in most cases. And even in the clean compounds, Quick Killer appeared on occasion.

First came diarrhea, followed by violent vomiting, dehydration, withered skin, faint pulse. Then came agonizing convulsions, stupor, and death, each successive horror following on the last so swiftly that beginning to end was sometimes only a matter of hours.

It frightened the hell out of everybody because it was a thing that moved so swiftly the victim didn't have much chance to marshal his defenses against it. These were a people who firmly believed they could whip anything, if only they were allowed to set their jaws and plant their feet. But Quick Killer attacked so swiftly that it was gone almost as soon as it came, taking many of its victims with it.

Cholera had probably started in the Ganges Valley of India a few centuries before the birth of Christ, and was mostly confined to Asia until well into the nineteenth century, when global commerce spread the disease in the bowels of British and Dutch and Portuguese sailors. By the time of America's Civil War, it was known in Europe. And by the time of Roman Hasford in Kansas, it was known there as well.

And in that summer of his odyssey into the high plains, ostensibly to test the livestock market but really to escape the furor at Fort Leavenworth over kickback payments to army procurement officers, Mr. Elisha Hankins became acquainted with it. He was staying at that time in what passed for a hotel in Hays City. After the initial onset, which he attributed to a bad beefsteak he'd eaten the night before, he lasted twenty-seven hours.

Roman Hasford offered to accompany her, but Spankin said she preferred to make the trip alone, without anyone to take the edge off her grief. She took a rail coach to Hays City and rode back to Lawrence in the baggage car, sitting beside the pine box that held everything remaining on earth of her husband, pronounced dead and then embalmed by the medical people at Fort Hays and attended by a young lieutenant to the railroad siding, where there were pens containing herds of rust-colored Texas cattle waiting for shipment east.

Because it was hot, the baggage men left the sliding doors of the car open and she could sit beside Elisha and look out on the passing landscape, yellow and flat and treeless but finally, as they approached Topeka, changing to rolling terrain, with scrub marking the streamlines. On the night of their passage she stayed beside the coffin, her head resting on an arm crooked over the top of the pine box and the baggage men watching and talking only when necessary, and then in gentle tones. They brought her water from their wall-bracketed keg, but she ate nothing except one corn muffin that the conductor offered during a stop at Ellsworth.

There was one passenger coach behind the baggage van, and behind that a string of stock cars stuffed with longhorns. She could hear them bawling as though they were crying out in protest against what was coming for them: the slaughterhouse hammer in Kansas City.

Roman Hasford knew the plan, and so he met her in Lawrence. She would not take the spur back to Leavenworth, but go directly on to Kansas City and east from there. At Lawrence, the private car of Mr. August Bainbridge was waiting and the coffin was loaded into the parlor section. Fletcher, after the railroad baggage men had placed the box in the midst of plush carpets and horsehair armchairs and mahogany tables, said he'd make a nice chicken pie for supper. Flashing like a high cloud in his white shirt and trousers, he turned and went back into the kitchen to allow Roman a few last words with Spankin.

They had only a few moments before the two cars from the Leavenworth spur were coupled and the whole train moved eastward. It was early evening and the sunlight was slanting through the windows on one side of the car, and because each window was edged with leaded stained glass, the car was suffused with color—reds and purples and yellows and blues. Like a cathedral, Roman thought.

They stood beside the coffin, Spankin with one hand on

Roman's arm, looking into his face with eyes as dry as they had been from the start of this business, and Roman realized his own mother was not the only rock-hard woman in this world. With her voice and expression, she might as well have been doing nothing more than inviting him to supper, yet just behind her lay the man with whom she had spent the last five decades of her life.

"Roman," she said, "go see Tallheimer Smith. He's got all the papers. Mr. Hankins told me that if anything happened like this, I was to tell you to go see Tallheimer Smith."

"I will," said Roman. "But I wish you'd let me go with you."

"No. It's our last journey together, and best made alone. Back to southern Illinois, where all my people are, and all of his that are left."

The coach jolted forward as the last of the cars in the rear were coupled, and she quickly took his hand in both of hers.

"Go now, Roman."

Fletcher was back, standing at the rear of the car, and he made a little bow.

"Take special care of this lady," Roman said.

"Oh, Mr. Roman, I will. The Boss done said so, and she gonna ride this car all the way home."

Roman went to the platform. Already the locomotive up ahead was huffing and popping out the slack between the couplings. As he went down the steps, he turned. Spankin was there, and she bent down and, taking his face between her two hands, kissed him on the mouth.

Then he was just standing there between the crossties, watching as the eastbound pulled away, growing smaller as it went, the green and red lanterns on the rear of Mr. August Bainbridge's train finally just a glimmer as the night came down quickly. He was thinking about the man who had given him his first chance in Kansas and who had become his second father. And in his company, the lady with a laugh brighter than all her years and a kitchen choked with the smell of blackberry cobbler and good cheer.

Well, by God, he thought, if she won't cry, then I won't, either.

And so Roman Hasford walked the two blocks to the Cato Hotel, which he knew was owned by Mr. August Bainbridge, and took a seat in the saloon and drank himself into near oblivion, mostly with French brandy. And the waiter refused to take any of his gold pieces. He was vaguely aware that nearby was a man in an Eastern derby hat, watching him. Finally he could hardly talk at all, and all the lamplight in the place melded into a single, solid golden glow, like molten iron.

And then someone was helping him out of his chair, the one with the derby hat, and just behind the derby hat was the pale face of Jared Dane.

"Let's get you to bed now, Roman Hasford."

He heard the words and he knew the voice. A hard, impersonal voice. He allowed himself to be helped from his chair by the Pinkerton, and that was all he remembered.

Tallheimer Smith's cramped office was much as Roman remembered it from the only other visit he'd ever made there. Except now the window behind the attorney's chair was wide open, allowing free access to the room by every bluebottle fly in eastern Kansas. The noise from the street below was so loud that they might as well have been sitting on the sidewalk.

It was apparent that Tallheimer Smith was in an evil mood. There were deep frown puckers above the new steel-rimmed spectacles he wore, the metal frames glinting like the sweat that hung in tiny beads on his forehead.

"I am in bad sorts this day, Roman," he said, and Roman had the uncomfortable feeling that he was about to be used to unburden somebody else's problems. "Olivia has been announced for marriage to the Reverend Hezekiah Sample— our minister, as I'm sure you recall. In which I am supposed to rejoice. But I find little to make me joyous. She'll live like a pauper, of course, and besides that, the good reverend has

taken a mission to the Navajos or some such heathen group
in the Territory of Arizona, a wilderness. Once the vows are
taken and they depart, I'll likely never see her again and will
expect daily a telegraph detailing her massacre and dismem-
berment."

The thought crossed Roman's mind that maybe Olivia
had prostrated herself before the preacher on that horsehair
couch in Tallheimer Smith's living room. And for her sake it
was likely all to the good, because the old Jew at the Sugar
Creek mill had always said that there were only two things in
nature more randy than a three-year-old billygoat, and those
were rabbis and Methodist preachers.

"Give them both my wish for happiness," Roman said.

Tallheimer Smith grunted and leafed through a number
of legal-sized papers before him, then threw them, along with
the new spectacles, onto the desktop, leaned back and
groaned, and laced his fingers across his belly.

"Young man, do you know anything about your late departed employer?"

"That he was my friend."

"Did you know he lost two sons at Shiloh?"

"God, no," Roman said. "Neither of them ever mentioned
such a thing."

"They did. Two sons. The youngest about your age. I tell
this to you so that you won't be surprised at what follows."

"I didn't know," Roman said, because there was nothing
else he could say. "They were both good people."

"Yes."

Tallheimer Smith replaced the spectacles and lifted the
sheaf of papers from the desktop and read them, although
Roman was sure Smith knew, without looking at every word,
what was contained in the document.

"Last will and testament, leaving one Roman Hasford the
one-third interest held by Mr. Elisha Hankins in the hog and
trash-collection business. The same Roman Hasford appointed as agent to sell the stockyard on Seventh Street, taking thirty percent of the gross for his commission. The same
figure on all intervening sales of cattle or horses or mules

until the yards are liquidated. And until then, the same Roman Hasford drawing salary commensurate with his duties as manager of the yards. Money generated by sales going to the widow, transferred by letter of credit to a bank in Vandalia, Illinois, or personally hand-carried in draft by one Tallheimer Smith. And the Hankins residence to be sold and the gain therefrom to one colored man, Orvile Tucker, former slave."

"God, that's wonderful," Roman said, and then thought what it meant. "But where will she live?"

"Yes, it was a grand gesture to a faithful employee." And Tallheimer Smith once more threw his spectacles onto the desk.

"But where will she live?"

Tallheimer Smith sighed. "She's not coming back here," he said. "She told me the day she left to claim Elisha's body. It would be too painful, she said. So it's good you went to Lawrence to see her there. Otherwise you would never have seen her again. I assume you have developed some affection for her."

And with all this last will and testament and money and agents and percentages, the only thing Roman could think of was lost suppers in the little blue-and-white-checked kitchen with the smell of ginger and coffee and fresh bread. And the thick flow of good fellowship.

Riding the sorrel back to the yards, he felt as though he were suddenly in a foreign country.

25

When Sam Grant went to the White House, the other two great heroes of the Union were bound to move up a notch or two as well. And they did. Cump Sherman was named Commanding General of the Army, a title that he knew meant almost nothing, because all the policy and operation of the army was vested in the office of Secretary of War. To add insult to injury, he was asked to move to Washington City, a place he held in utter and absolute contempt, even though he had a brother there who was a United States senator.

None of this was of much concern to the citizens of Kansas. But what it created at Fort Leavenworth was concern indeed. As Sherman moved upward, so did Little Phil Sheridan, and there were even reports in the newspapers about his dining on roast squab and morel mushrooms in the various beaneries of Chicago, his new headquarters. He now reigned as overlord of the Division of the Missouri, which included everything west of the Mississippi.

And in his place at Fort Leavenworth was General John Pope.

"Pope!" the old soldiers exclaimed. "Holy mule shit! The Rebs run that son of a bitch halfway into Maryland after he claimed he'd beat their arses at Second Manassas."

The civilians were no less vehement, although generally less colorful in their language.

But at least they had one consolation. Pope was charging ahead on Little Phil's program to eliminate corruption in the procurement department. This was not surprising, in view of the fact that Sheridan was Pope's immediate superior and everyone knew Sheridan could scald a subordinate with the same hot water he used on enemies.

"Old Pope," the soldiers said, "is gonna make his reputation on courts-martial to compensate for all those lads he left in the dust at Groveton."

And so this cleansing campaign began, and ultimately brought Roman Hasford and Victoria Cardin Archer face to face once more.

The river was a dark mirror in the night, with a dull shine that faded into the Missouri shore at the far side, the horizon there outlined, an uncertain fringe along the bottom of the night sky. Only the strongest stars were visible, because there was a high veil of thin cloud, the threat of coming autumn, that shut off the more timid ones. Somewhere in the night above where Roman Hasford sat on the sorrel, there was a flight of southward-migrating geese, and their honking gave a ghostly echo to all the river's quiet little noises.

There was a road here, the riverbank hard on one side and the cliff that rose to the Fort Leavenworth compound on the other. There was talk of building a railroad along this right-of-way, north to Atchison and on to Falls City in Nebraska, but so far there was no metal on the ground. The bluff rising to the fort was a forbidding mass, blacker somehow than all the rest of the surrounding night's blackness. A short distance to the north, there were willows and some sycamores along the water's edge, and from there a horned owl was hooting, a soft and velvet sound that seemed to come from everywhere yet nowhere.

Roman hoped he was in the right place. When the note had come that afternoon, carried by a Fort Leavenworth sol-

dier who came on foot and looked as though he would rather
have been almost anywhere else, Roman read it quickly and
stuffed it into a trousers pocket. And seeing the soldier staring at him with a slope to his shoulders that was both inso-
lent and obedient at the same time, waiting for some reply,
Roman had sent him packing without any answer or even the
thought of giving one, because the thing was dumbfounding.

Roman,
Can you please meet me in the road alongside the river
below the fort bluff tonight as soon as it gets dark?

Victoria

P.S. Very important. Come alone.

A locomotive whistle from south of town moaned dismally
in the night, a long way off. And Roman shivered even though
it was warm from the day's sun. Still, there was a certain bite
to the air, and he wondered if that meant there was another
harsh winter on the way.

He heard it a long time before he could see it, the shod
hooves of the single horse making a soft drumming along the
roadbed. When the sound finally materialized out of the
night, he could see it was a buggy with a canvas top, the front
bent down like the brim of a man's hat.

The buggy came abreast of him, the horse snorting as it
was reined in. Roman dismounted and expected to see a soldier driving the little trap, but there was only the one dark
figure under the canopy, and as he stepped close he could see
the faint gleam of a collar like little wings in the darkness.

"Come in with me, Roman," said Victoria Cardin Archer,
and as Roman mounted the buggy seat, the little vehicle
tilted as though it might overturn with his weight.

"Hello, Victoria," he said, not knowing what to expect
and not caring at the moment, his heart pounding.

"It's been so long since I've seen you," she said, her voice
almost a whisper. Her hand came through the dark and she
touched his arm, but then quickly her fingers were with-

drawn, like a night animal retreating suddenly after coming too far into the light. "Why haven't you come to visit us?"

"Well," Roman said, resisting the impulse to point out that since her marriage he'd never been invited, "I've been pretty busy."

"I know you have, with all those hogs and lard and that garbage." Roman thought he could feel her shudder. "I've been so busy, too, with the sewing circle and the Ladies Aid and all."

While she went on about the social whirl of Fort Leavenworth, Roman tried to make out the details of her features. But no matter how hard he tried, there was nothing there but a pale blur. It could have been anybody. And he hardly recognized the voice. And maybe because of that, because he couldn't see the pouting lips and the fluttering lashes, his heart was no longer thumping. It was like being lectured by a disembodied spirit, even though the spirit smelled of lilac water and talcum powder. He had the urge to reach out and touch her, just to see if she was real.

But he didn't. He was, in fact, extremely uncomfortable with this whole business, now that it had begun. No matter his excitement at the note with her name on it. He kept thinking of what his mother would say about his meeting like this in the dark of night with a married woman.

"We heard about you being at that awful battle of Beecher's Island," she was saying. "All those thousands of savages. We were all so proud of you."

"It didn't amount to very much."

"Modest, modest, modest. You've always been so modest," she said. "When I heard about it I told everyone that I knew you. I told everyone how we'd come together on the boat from St. Louis. And Daddy thought you were so nice on the boat, before we ever got here."

"I have a great deal of respect for your father."

"And Thaddeus just *knew* how much I enjoyed your company," she said, and laughed quietly. "He was always so jealous. Such a dear husband."

And Roman wondered if she knew that he'd bloodied her

husband's nose. Maybe not or maybe so. He suddenly real-ized that he couldn't say which, and that all along, from the time of that boat ride she'd mentioned through all the rest, he was the one of the two of them who had no notion what was happening.

"Remember that first winter?" she was asking. "We walked along the bluff and looked at the river?"

"Yes, I remember."

"You kissed me, remember?"

"More than once, Victoria," he said, trying now to bring some of the wonder back. It struggled for only a second and wouldn't come.

"It was such fun," she said.

God Almighty!

"I suppose so," he said, hearing his own words and know-ing that he would have described it in different terms. He wasn't sure in exactly what terms, but different terms. Fun! God Almighty.

"Daddy said you were a friend of General Sheridan's," she said. "I never knew that. You should have told me."

"Well, not a friend. I just happen to know him."

He was sure that at some time he'd told the story of Gen-eral Phil Sheridan bringing food to his mother's farm after the battle of Pea Ridge, told it to Victoria and her father and pos-sibly even some of his dinner guests. It caused a small twinge of resentment in his gut that maybe she had never listened very closely to anything he'd said. Maybe she'd never listened at all.

"Victoria," he said, "what's this all about?"

"I just wanted to see you again, to visit an old friend."

"In the middle of the night, down here by the river? I could have come to your quarters and talked with your father and with your husband and with you. All you needed to do was ask me."

"In the first place, it's not the middle of the night," she said, and her voice was testy. "I haven't even had dinner yet. And besides that, Father's ill. And Thaddeus went to Chicago to see a lawyer. A civilian lawyer."

When she said *lawyer*, it was as though a hammer had struck an anvil in Roman's head. And he knew now what this was about. Not the details, but enough to put a cap on it.

"A lawyer?"

"Of course. That awful friend of yours, General Sheridan, just hates Daddy and Thaddeus. And even though he's gone from Fort Leavenworth, he's going to do them all the harm he can."

"Wait, Victoria. What harm can he do?"

"What harm? He's trying to get them brought up for court-martial! That's what harm."

He felt no shock or even surprise when she said *court-martial*. Maybe there was even a little elation.

"Haven't you heard what's happening?" Victoria asked, and now her voice was so harsh and strident that the horse in the buggy stays snorted and jerked on the lines.

"I'm afraid I don't keep up too much with what's going on at the fort."

"Oh, Roman," she said. "It's General Sheridan and that terrible old man you work for. Well, you worked for him until he died of cholera. Daddy heard about it. No small loss, and now you're the only one down there at the stockyard. You're the only *one*!"

Roman was stunned at the sudden venom in her voice, and he sat silently, even though he was ashamed for doing so, knowing that his mother would hide him with a willow switch if she ever heard that he hadn't rushed to the defense of a good friend and a good man.

Why the hell am I sitting here thinking about what Mama would do? he wondered.

"So I thought you should say something to your friend General Sheridan, about Daddy and Thaddeus being innocent of what they're all claiming."

"I don't know what anybody's claiming, Victoria," Roman said. When he'd entered this buggy he'd been anxious to be near her, to touch her. Now he was sitting back in his own corner as though he were talking to a spider.

"General Sheridan's saying they took money they weren't

supposed to take. Oh, hell, Roman," she said, and Roman marveled at how easily that word rolled from her tongue. "I don't really know what he's saying. Nobody tells me anything. But Daddy and Thaddeus are going around hangdog, and both of them suspended from their duties. You've got to say something to General Sheridan."

"Well, I don't get to Chicago very much," Roman said, and heard the sarcasm in his own voice.

"All right, all right," Victoria said, her voice rising once more and the horse snorting and pulling on the reins she held in one hand.

"That's a spooky horse you've got," he said.

"All right," she said, and he could feel her struggling to keep control of her temper. "At least you don't have to testify. When they come and ask you to testify, you just tell them you won't."

"Testify? In a court-martial? I think they can *make* me testify. But I couldn't tell them anything directly. All I know is what Mr. Hankins told me."

"You see? You see, that old man spreading lies about my daddy and Thaddeus!"

Then she was silent and Roman sat in his corner, gone cold inside, and uncomfortable, and wishing he'd never come at all. He thought that if this were Jared Dane or the chief marshal of Leavenworth or just about anybody else, he'd be blistering them with rebuttals. But because it was Victoria, he sat mute and his shame grew as he saw in his mind the faces of disapproval. The face of his mother and of Spankin and of Catrina Peel.

Catrina Peel? Why do I think of Catrina Peel now, on this dark night, in this dark buggy, with this dark woman that I don't think I even know?

"You could make one of those trips you're always making. I mean, when they have a trial. Just not be here," Victoria said at last, her voice calm and measured, calculating. "Then you wouldn't have to say anything about it."

"Well, I don't know if I could do that."

Then she touched him again, just a light pressure of her

fingers on his knee, and he could feel the heat of her hand through his trousers.

"Roman, I could make you very happy," she said.

Roman could hardly keep from laughing. Here was an offer he would never have dreamed of, and one he might once have leaped at. Or maybe not, because such things between Victoria and himself could only have been possible after marriage vows. He was acutely aware that he came from generations of hill people who believed that knowing a woman, in the biblical sense, without benefit of vows, was a mortal sin and a sure guarantee of spiritual and sometimes physical retribution. And he knew that a few years along this wild border hadn't washed that out of him.

Roman said nothing, waiting with some perverse pleasure to see how long she'd leave her fingers on his leg. But it was only a moment and then she withdrew her hand.

He pulled himself up from the corner of the buggy seat and swung down, the little vehicle swaying as it had when he entered it. Then he turned back to the dark figure with the bow of gray light at the neck.

"I'm sorry, Victoria. I'm sorry you've come to this misfortune, but I'm afraid I can't help much."

He didn't actually see her arm move in the darkness, but rather sensed it and stepped back quickly and heard the sharp little hiss of the buggy whip as she slashed at him. Then the reins snapped across the horse's rump and the horse bolted forward, the buggy springs groaning and the steel-rimmed wheels grinding through the river sand. Roman stood in the road watching until there was nothing more to see of the dark shape of horse and buggy going away.

It was a strange sensation, standing there in the darkness beside the river, all of his body like a forearm that had gone to sleep, the circulation now returning with a tingle down to the fingertips. He felt sorry for Victoria. Yet there was no longer that old bittersweet recollection of her presence, which he had once longed for as though it were the only reality in the whole world, as though nothing else mattered except being with her. Now other voices, other faces, had come between them.

What she'd said about Mr. Elisha Hankins made him hate her a little.

But I reckon in some crazy way I'll always love her, he thought. I know better, but I can't help myself.

Roman Hasford had ridden only a hundred yards or so along the river when he saw the horseman, large and commanding in the center of the road. The thought jumped into his head that Victoria had hired someone to shoot him. But then the voice came and he drew a deep breath of relief.

"You all right, boss?" shouted Elmer Scaggs, and Roman was sure anyone on the Missouri shore could have heard him.

"What the hell are you doing out here?" Roman asked, drawing in the sorrel beside Elmer's mule. At that close range he could make out the shotgun held across Elmer's saddle pommel.

"Orvile Tucker told me you'd rode off this direction at dark," Elmer said. "I just wanted to see if you was all right."

"I'm all right."

"Who was that in the buggy?"

"You didn't recognize anybody?"

"Hell, no, it's black as this mule's soul out here. But the damned thing pert' near run over me."

"Well, just forget you ever saw any buggy."

"That's fine with me, boss. I ain't seen nothin'."

"Good. Be sure it stays that way."

"Sure, boss. Say, you had supper yet?"

"No." Roman realized he was suddenly very hungry.

"By Gawd, let's you and me go in town and lay on some grub. And a tot or two of rye whiskey."

"The whiskey sounds like a good idea."

"They's this place called Efferidge's. Best Gawd damned white beans I ever et, cooked with one of our own ham hocks. And cornbread cooked with cracklin's in it. Our cracklin's, too."

"Lead on, Elmer."

"By Gawd, it's my treat, boss."

Roman was never sure where they were when he asked Elmer Scaggs the question. It may have been Efferidge's, or it may have been one of seven saloons they visited afterward.

He would write in his diary, "When a man needs solace, I suppose he thinks that almost anybody handy is a great philosopher."

"Elmer," Roman said. "Have you ever had a woman ask to be with you?"

"In a fornication way?" asked Elmer, his watery eyes blinking rapidly.

"Yes. In that way."

"Yes, by Gawd, I have. Once, in Toledo, Ohio, before the war. I was workin' the boats on the lake."

"Did you accept her offer?"

"No, by Gawd, I didn't. I can tell you why, too."

"Don't do that. It'll only confuse me more than I am. But it's happened to me twice in this town, and I turned away from it both times. What the hell's wrong with me?"

"Boss, they ain't nothin' wrong with you. You're a young gentleman. And don't worry about lost opportunities. Why, hell, once you're in the legislature, they'll be lots of 'em winking at you."

"Legislature? What the hell do you know about that?"

"Why, it's all around town, boss. Before long, you'll be representin' the whole shebang of folks around here, goin' to Topeka in top hat and stripe britches and walkin' with a cane."

"God Almighty, I hope not," Roman said, and even in the rye haze he realized it was the first time he had really, actually, down-to-the-marrow admitted to himself that Mr. August Bainbridge's plan to send him into politics scared the hell out of him. It scared him even more than Victoria Cardin Archer's proposition, and after he mulled it over a while, having another rye in the process, he decided that the two overtures amounted to about the same thing. It seemed to call for a switch to beer, which he made, and not long afterward he was sick in an alley, throwing up among a litter of cans and scrap paper while Elmer Scaggs held his head.

"Better back here where nobody can see you, boss," said Elmer. "You'd lose some Baptist votes in the election if they seen you like this."

"God," Roman sputtered, spitting and blowing his nose between finger and thumb and then kicking at the rubbish underfoot. "Elmer, why the hell aren't these people buying our garbage disposal?"

"By Gawd, you're right, boss. I'll talk to some councilmen tomorrow."

And Roman went into a fit of giggling, holding on to the gigantic Scaggs as they made their way back to the street.

It was well past midnight when Katie Rose Rouse opened to the knock at her door and beheld Roman Hasford, who had lost his hat, and Elmer Scaggs carrying a double-barreled shotgun.

"I see you're both good and drunk," she said.

"Ma'am, I ain't ever been drunk in my life," bellowed Scaggs, and as they staggered into her apartment she took the gun from Elmer's unresisting hand.

"They ain't anything in here to shoot with that thing," she said.

Roman threw his arms around her and gave her a very moist kiss on the neck.

"God Almighty," he kept saying.

It was a short visit for Elmer Scaggs, and after only one drink of her clear liquor in a stemmed glass, he retrieved his shotgun and left, and Katie Rose had to close the door behind him.

Roman remained in a state of semiconsciousness on the couch amid a profusion of needlepoint pillows, and spoke only once after Elmer left.

"Katie Rose Rouse, I am learning more and more and

more," he said, then seemed to forget for a moment what it was he remembered. Then he went on haltingly. "That you are a real, genuine woman."

"It will comfort me in my old age," she said, shaking her head and smiling and sipping her clear liquor.

Roman stared at her a moment, up on one elbow, but his eyes didn't seem to focus very well and finally he collapsed back into the bed of pillows and sighed and went to sleep.

Katie Rose threw a light quilt over him and stood for a while, looking at his face. Then she smiled, shook her head again, and turned to her own rear bedroom. The next morning, when she rose to have her corn muffin and buttermilk, Roman was gone.

On the end table with the porcelain-based lamp was a note, and she read it with the same smile she always had for children and men, who to her were about the same.

"I apologize for my unseemly conduct."

26

That winter, alone in managing the horse and cow business that had been Mr. Elisha Hankins's, Roman Hasford had time to evaluate. He knew there were major decisions ahead, any one of which could change the rest of his life for better or worse.

The trouble was, he didn't know what might turn out to be better or worse. He couldn't help remembering that when he'd come to Kansas he wanted to see buffalo and Cheyennes. He had seen both, and neither experience had added much on the good side of the ledger. He wrote in his diary:

> *Maybe the things a man expects to be wonderful are usually a disappointment. Maybe the wonderful things are just a tabulation of little bits and pieces, like a bowl of hot popcorn in Mrs. Condon Murphy's kitchen when the December wind is blowing Christmas closer, or when Elmer Scaggs gets drunk and cries and tries to hug me because I've made him the Pig King of Leavenworth, or seeing the deep light in Catrina Peel's eyes after she's well fed and knows she isn't going to be hit with a grown man's fist.*

More and more, he found himself sitting alone in the little stockyard office shack, with the cast-iron stove glowing red at the bottom, thinking about the Osage orange trees that grew on the south slopes of Ozark hills, and about clear running water, like Little Sugar Creek with its occasional pools of deep water where bullfrogs invited a gig, and about going to collect the new mushrooms in the apple orchard near Elkhorn Tavern after a spring rain, with his mother, who afterward would fry them in butter only long enough to put a crisp brown film across the spongelike surfaces.

And always he thought about Catrina Peel growing now in the bacon-and-sassafras-scented kitchen in the house above Wire Road, sleeping in Calpurnia's old bed in the south loft, learning her grammar from Martin Hasford's *Decline and Fall of the Roman Empire*.

And he thought about peace of mind, as opposed to the Kansas state legislature.

"You gotta run, boss," Elmer Scaggs said at each opportunity. "I ain't ever knowed anybody in the legislature."

"For God's sake," Roman finally exploded. "Stop telling me what I've got to do."

He wrote in his diary, "I seem to be imbibing too much of late. Not that there hasn't been cause, if one needs any cause for such things. But it seems to me that more and more I crave the sensation of strong spirits. It isn't a good thing because although it has the power to make one forget troubles, there's a loss of control that is both frightening and embarrassing once the Old Amber, as Elmer Scaggs calls it, evaporates in the muscles."

After the turn of the new year the scandal broke concerning the rebates in army procurement. It was a small thing compared to what was being said in the newspapers about railroad-construction fraud, but it loomed large in Leavenworth, a city that depended on army money.

The *Conservative* reported all the juicy details and spread a lot of conjecture and libel. Captain Edwin Cardin had been reassigned in disgrace, so the *Conservative* claimed, sent to some obscure post in the Territory of New Mexico, where there was nothing but cactus and lizards. Lieutenant Thaddeus Archer had resigned his commission, the newspapers reported, and gone off with his lovely young wife to upstate New York to make his way in real estate.

"It is suspected here that the state of New York takes more kindly to thieves than do our own local gentry!" the paper said.

Reading that, Roman couldn't help feeling a profound pity for Victoria. He could only hope that these new telegraph news services had not sent such stories beyond the borders of Kansas, because she deserved better than having to read such stuff in her new home.

There was a lot more, some of it castigating Phil Sheridan and General Pope for not bringing somebody to a court-martial. There was a lack of evidence, so it was said.

"Such bounders deserve to spend a long vacation in the Federal penitentiary at Detroit, or in some other such dungeon, well away from the temptations of preying on honest citizens."

Roman was sorry he'd not gone out to the post to say good-bye to the captain before he departed, knowing from what Mr. Elisha Hankins had said that Edwin Cardin was more the victim of his own casualness than a criminal. Yet Cardin was lucky, Roman thought, because Phil Sheridan had decided not to end his career with a court-martial. He wondered if perhaps Little Phil had not given Thaddeus Archer a choice: Get out or we'll try your ass! And Roman was glad Archer had opted for the former.

There was considerable selfish relief in all of this. Had Victoria's husband been tried, Roman knew he surely would have been called to testify. He was glad such a confrontation with justice had not occurred, despite his repugnance for Thaddeus Archer.

I wish I'd hit him a second time when I had the chance, he thought.

He and Orvile Tucker worked Junior in the snow again, and Roman had a saddle on the bay colt before the end of January. Soon he was riding him about the pens. The offspring of Excalibur and the Morgan mare was a gentle horse, but now and again his daddy's strain showed through, especially when a mare in some adjoining compound came into estrus. Then his eyes would go glassy and he would charge about his pen with muscles rippling, whistling so violently and shrilly they could hear him all the way to Miami Street.

"Mr. Roman, he's one fine animal," said Orvile Tucker.

"I know it. I'm going to breed him to some good stock when you think he's ready, somewhere down the line. You start looking over any of these yard horses that might make a good dame. I'm going to buy the good ones myself and start a little herd from this colt."

"Well, come to think of it, there's that big buckskin mare. And the little calico that the drunk Delaware sold us last week," Orvile said.

"I like those, too. I think I'll have one of the hands move them into that pen next to your shop, so the army won't be eyeing them when they come to buy stock."

"Not much market with the army now for them kinda horses, Mr. Roman," Orvile said. "They's mostly lookin' for mules and drays. Wagon-pullers."

And every day Mr. Elisha Hankins's little white dog looked at Roman as though he were asking about the master. Orvile Tucker kept him in his little lean-to bedroom behind the smith shop, which is where he'd always stayed because Spankin wouldn't allow him near her picket-fence house. At least, Roman thought, he doesn't have to think about that little house all empty and cold.

Finally the dog disappeared, and it was no big loss to Roman because he'd never liked the little son of a bitch anyway. Then Marshal Eldon Harvesty came one day and said the dog had been cut in a fight and died from loss of blood, and suddenly Roman wondered why he hadn't spent more time petting the square little white head.

"I thought you'd want to know," Harvesty said.

"I appreciate your telling me," said Roman.

"It happened on Second Street, right in front of Lippert's hardware. It was Lippert's big mastiff done it. Must weigh at least eighty pound. It drew a helluva crowd. The little white dog put up a good fight, they say."

"I would have expected as much," Roman said, and after giving Harvesty a cup of coffee from the blue-enameled pot on the cast-iron stove, he turned his back on the marshal and walked away.

In late February the telegram came.

Be ready to come when I call. May need your help sometime in the first week of March. Try not to make other plans. Important.

Jared Dane

What the hell is this all about? Roman wondered. But he knew, even though he was mystified, that if Jared Dane called, he would go.

It was only a small town on the north bank of the Neosho River, well south of the heavily traveled route along the Kaw and the Smoky Hill. Yet it was an important hub in Mr. August Bainbridge's network of stagecoach lines, which led out toward the Indian Territory, and because of that, Jared Dane selected it for his little ruse. He was convinced that the felonies committed against the Boss and the peace and dignity of the state of Kansas had their origins to the south in the Cherokee and Osage country along the Verdigris River.

His operatives had been working a long time, putting together bits and pieces of information overheard while munching cheese and crackers at crossroads stores or sometimes around campfires deep in the Indian Territory as far away as Tahlequah. Dane's men behaved like horse thieves and looked the part, bewhiskered and smelling of cheap whiskey, sleeping on the ground during good weather, in cow sheds during bad. They were willing to be Jared Dane's spies for only a few silver dollars each fortnight or so, which Mr. Bainbridge could certainly afford, and their information was generally credible because they had no more loyalty for kindred spirits than does a black widow for her husband. Besides, they were generally on the darker side of the law themselves, and had access to places where a Pinkerton with a derby hat or an Eastern accent would be as welcome as an outbreak of smallpox.

In short, Jared Dane was using a technique developed by Allan Pinkerton himself during the late war, although he would never admit to taking any idea from the feisty little detective whom he had met three times in the company of the Boss, and with whom, at each meeting, he'd been less impressed. One thing Jared Dane knew: the men he used were not unlike those he hoped to apprehend.

In February he had employed his spy network to send out false information, a thing he refused to credit to Allan Pinkerton, although Pinkerton had done the same thing for Mr. Lincoln. Instead of listening, his people talked. Only in bits and pieces, of course, so as not to make anything too obvious.

And what they said was that in the first week of March a very large express company payroll, in gold and greenbacks, would repose in the little town along the Neosho and would remain there for two days prior to disbursement, arriving on Friday and not moving until Monday. On the Friday in question, arrangements were made for a coach to arrive, heavily guarded, from which a strongbox would be handed down, so heavy it would require two men to carry, although the only thing in it would be sandstone rocks. And then coach and guards would go on their appointed way, as though the Boss's company were confident that the local express office manager was capable of safeguarding the goods.

Along with the coach there would arrive, unobtrusively and by back streets, Jared Dane and six Pinkertons specifically selected for their ruthlessness and marksmanship.

It was a chance shot, but Jared Dane had been in this sort of business long enough to understand that hunches needed to be played and instincts honored. He had some notion of the exact man he was after, but he wasn't sure. He had had indications over the past two years that maybe Roman Hasford knew that man.

Hence the telegraph message to Leavenworth.

All the snow was gone, and so, in the dawn light of Sunday, March 6, 1870, the alley behind the express office was a dull gray passageway between the scabby backs of buildings as the coming light began to expose its ugly contours. The express office itself was a single-story structure, but those on either side were two stories each, with windows facing onto the alley. On one side, the next building was flush against the wall of the express office. On the other side there was a small walkway that led to the main street, where the express office fronted on a wide, verandalike covered sidewalk.

There was a door and window on the alley side of the green-painted express office, and directly across the narrow alleyway there was a coop with head-high wire and a roost shed, and on either side of that were slab-sided structures, one with a loading dock, the other with a lean-to shed large enough to stable about three horses.

On that morning there were two men inside the express office, both at the window opening onto the alley, and both armed with ten-gauge shotguns. In each of the second-story windows of the buildings adjoining there was another man armed with a large-bore repeating rifle. In the horse shed that stood like a breakwater at one end of the alley were three more men, one with a rifle and one with a long-barreled shotgun, and Jared Dane, with his Baxter Springs pistol in its holster and two more revolvers thrust uncomfortably into his waistband.

They had all been there since late Friday night, waiting. And that morning one of the men with Jared Dane exclaimed for perhaps the tenth time that this whole thing was a bag of foolishness. And on that morning Jared Dane told him to clamp shut his God damned mouth.

Watching through a crack in the rough-cut vertical planking of the shed, Jared Dane saw the chickens come out of their coop and begin to inspect the new day. They were all white hens except for one gigantic Rhode Island Red rooster that strutted about, looking this way and that, and then planted his feet and crowed. And at that exact moment, from the far end of the alley, a single wagon appeared and turned in slowly toward the rear door of the express office, a man on the wagon seat clucking the mule team along. Beside the lead mule rode a tall man on horseback. He was clean-shaven except for a thatch-colored mustache. Behind him, single file beside the wagon, were four other riders, each with a rifle in hand.

"Just like they did it before," whispered Dane. "With a wagon."

The wagon drew up at the express office door and the horsemen began to dismount, but only after the leader took a long look up and down the alley. The rooster crowed again, and one of the mules snorted and pawed the loose dirt of the alley. The driver tried to hold it in, still clucking to it. Two of the men went to the express office door, one holding a wrecking bar he'd pulled from his belt.

"They're all on the ground," Jared Dane whispered. "Let's go."

He shoved open the door of the horse shed and it made a loud creak and the man with the blond mustache stiffened and his head jerked around and Dane lifted the Baxter Springs pistol, sensing that the two men with him were now out and beside him, their weapons coming ready.

"Throw up your hands," Dane shouted, and the alley exploded in sound, a blast of shotguns from the rear window of the express office and the sharp reports of the rifles from the upstairs windows.

"Son of a bitch!" someone shouted, and the wagon driver was on his feet, whipping the mules, and one of them went down screaming, throwing its weight against the other, its long yellow teeth shining. The second blast came from the express office windows and the living mule shied violently, pulling the dead weight of the other mule and the wagon into the coop fence, the chickens flying and hopping and squawking and releasing feathers like white snow, and then the driver pitched down onto the singletree as more shots came. Against the door of the express office went the man with the wrecking bar, crumpled like old taffy, and dense clouds of black-powder smoke roiled like water, punctuated with the long, yellowish tongues of flame, the shots echoing back and forth between the walls of the alley and the lead saddle horses trying to scramble back over the last in line, which were down and kicking, and two of the men clawing over the bloody hair and splattered leather and loose stirrups.

Someone was screaming obscenities, and then that was cut off as the roar of guns went on and the smoke grew thicker and a brown dog ran howling from beneath the loading dock and went tail-down past the horse shed, where Jared Dane and his two companions were still shooting.

Then Dane shouted, "In front! In front!" And he and his two men ran along the side of the building and out onto the sidewalk as the man with the blond mustache appeared from the walkway and emerged onto the boards and Jared Dane felt more than heard the blast of a shotgun near his ear, and then the rifle fired once, twice, three times. The man with the blond mustache was thrown against the wall, one arm flung back between the bars of the express office window, smashing the glass, his other arm bloodied and useless, flailing against his side like a washcloth hung to dry on a windy day. He staggered out onto the sidewalk and the shotgun fired once more, and he pitched down into the gutter and rolled onto his back.

"Jesus!" said Jared Dane. "We got the bastard. I hope he's the right one."

There were a still a few hollow explosions from the alley, and the wild squawking of chickens and the screaming of a wounded horse. But only for a little while. Jared Dane and his two men moved along the sidewalk cautiously, Dane holding the hot Baxter Springs pistol ready in his hand, even though he knew it had been shot empty.

The man had lost his hat and there was a spray of straw-colored hair across his forehead. A thick blotch of red ran from just below his neck to his crotch. His eyes were open, yellowish. And his wide mouth was open, too. Jared Dane bent near him and the man spoke, a gasping, harsh sound against the babble of voices from the townspeople who were running out into the street now.

"You been after me a long time, ain't you, you son of a bitch?"

"What's your name?" Dane asked.

"Go to hell," the man in the gutter gasped. "You just take care of the sprout."

"Who's the sprout?"

"You and your railroad and all the rest can go to hell," the man said.

There was no change in the expression as the last rattling breath came, the eyes open, the lips parted over teeth the color of wood chips, and Jared Dane stood over him a long time and then finally bent to close his eyelids.

It was only then that Roman Hasford came to appreciate the pervasive power of Mr. August Bainbridge. When the second telegraph message came, calling him to some community he'd never heard of, he went to the Leavenworth station and there found a locomotive and a caboose waiting. He was the only passenger on the breakneck run to Lawrence and then to Topeka, all other traffic being pulled onto sidings to let him pass. In the Topeka railyard stood a coach with six horses, and he was off to the south, into the afternoon and evening and night, the team changed twice on the way, until he arrived at the front of the green express office only about twenty-four hours after the shooting.

When the lathered horses were pulled to a snorting halt, Jared Dane was waiting.

"I'm sorry to inconvenience you," he said, taking Roman's arm and leading him along the street. "But I need your help."

There were little groups of townspeople all along the way, watching them silently as they passed.

"All right. You've cost me the worst night I've spent in a long time, trying to get a little sleep in that bouncing coach."

"I wanted you to be here. I didn't want you to learn about this from somebody else. Come on."

There was an undertaking parlor. It had the only plate-glass window in town, with gilt letters in an arch that proclaimed its purpose. They paused a moment before it.

"God Almighty," Roman whispered.

Inside the window, propped up on what appeared to be wooden doors so that passersby could get a good look, were three men. They were stripped down to woolen underdrawers. Across their chests and stomachs were blue-black pencil marks, punctures. The eyes of the one in the center were still open.

"Caught trying to rob the express office," said Jared Dane, and took Roman's arm again. "Come inside with me."

It was dark there because the skies were cloudy outside and there was a drape behind the three corpses, cutting off what little light there was, but in one corner on an ornate table was a coal-oil lamp that sent out a murky orange glow. There was a long table, or rather a number of nailed-together planks sitting on sawhorses, and on this lay a figure covered with a white sheet. A small fat man appeared, smiling and wiping his bald head with a brown handkerchief.

"At your service once more, Mr. Dane," he said.

"Take off the sheet."

The little man drew back the sheet, then, after a brief glance at Jared Dane, pulled it away from the body on the planks. There were a number of wounds in the torso and one just under the left eye, indenting the cheek in a grotesque pucker. Roman was finding it difficult to breathe.

"Do you know this man?" asked Dane.

Roman heaved air into his lungs and felt cold chills along his back.

"Yes. His name's Tyne Fawley. He saved my life after Beecher's Island."

"I suspected he was the one," Jared Dane said, his voice so low that Roman could hardly hear it. "But I needed to know. I've suspected him by name for a long time, but I needed to know. I didn't know what he looked like."

"Did you kill him?" Roman's voice was trembling and harsh.

"There were seven of us. There were six of them. Two got away."

Roman turned, and the fat little man was standing there

before him, smiling and bowing and wiping his face with the brown handkerchief.

"Cover him up again," said Jared Dane, and while the undertaker did it, wheezing and sweating, Roman took a wallet from his pocket, and from that a number of greenbacks. When the undertaker was finished covering Tyne Fawley, Roman thrust the bills into one of his fat hands, wadded into a ball.

"Bury him the best you can," he said. "And if you put him out there in your front window, I'll break your arms."

"Yes, sir, yes, sir." He glanced at Jared Dane, who nodded.

"Get him a nice suit of clothes. He's likely never had one before," Roman said.

"Yes, sir, yes, sir."

Choking, Roman turned away and went out to the sidewalk, and Jared Dane stepped close to the fat little undertaker and took one of his coat lapels in his fist.

"Do as the gentleman says or I'll be back to visit you myself."

On the street in front of the funeral parlor, Roman Hasford was waiting, looking at the townspeople, who were still standing about watching, as though they expected something else to happen.

"Accommodations here are sparse," said Jared Dane, "but we can have a meal and ride back together on the coach that brought you."

"No," Roman said. "If I may, I'd like to go back now, and alone. I'm not sure I can talk to you."

"You be the judge, Roman Hasford," said Jared Dane, and his voice was as cold as Roman had ever heard it. Roman avoided looking at him. "I appreciate your coming. The Boss will be glad to pay you whatever you reckon your time was worth."

"Oh? Well, tell the Boss he can kiss my ass."

Roman rode back alone on the coach to Topeka, and from there took a regular passenger train to Lawrence and then to Leavenworth. And he remembered all the way how Tyne

Fawley had carried him at least forty miles through hostile country to Fort Wallace.

Back in his room at Mrs. Condon Murphy's boarding-house, he wrote in his diary, "My God, I knew he was no saint. Mr. Hankins told me so. But if he was the worst of all men to others, he was at least always good to me."

Then he laid his head on the small desk and cried, until Mr. Moffet rapped gently on his door and announced through the oak panel that he had a fresh new batch of beer, all nicely cool in mason jars, and wondered if maybe Roman would enjoy having a few sips.

"I suppose so," Roman called, and after splashing cold water on his face from the bowl on the dry sink and wiping his eyes with the fresh towel Mrs. Murphy always placed in his room each morning, he walked down the hall to Mr. Moffet's room, thinking, What the hell, Tyne Fawley would have wanted me to take a few swigs for him!

27

Lin Chow always held something back to ensure that there were tricks left to play as the game went on. He imagined a little red lacquer box at the base of his brain, and in the little box were many things he kept only to himself and released one by one as he needed them. The box was so full that he knew there would be many items left at the end of his life, and this was good because he could go to his ancestors with knowledge nobody else had, and would make a gift of it to them. Which was the kind of thing Lin Chow assumed ancestors enjoyed.

It was a technique he had developed as a child in China, where he found it an advantage while growing up with four older brothers. He'd had no sisters, younger or older, because both of those had been sold to wealthy landlords as concubines. It had become such a part of his character that he no longer even thought about it, no more so than with breathing or relieving his bowels or sleeping with his wife.

And so it had been on that morning when he'd found Crider Peel knifed to death in one of the low bunks at the rear of the warehouse. Lin Chow had held something back.

There had been an open jackknife beside Crider Peel's body, very gummy with drying blood. Before he sent one of his sons for Eldon Harvesty, Lin Chow had taken up the knife and cleaned it carefully and closed it and wrapped it in a red silk scarf and placed it in the little trunk that sat beside his sleeping mat in the living quarters, a little trunk that was as forbidden to his family as was the little lacquer box in his brain.

I am always keeping secrets in little boxes, he thought, and found it amusing.

Lin Chow could easily rationalize his action. He had just lost a customer through murder, and he reasoned that the knife might lead to another customer, who would certainly be hanged. Therefore, Lin Chow would lose not one smoker but two, in some kind of dispute he knew nothing about and in which he had no part. He was opposed to being victimized by events over which he had no control, so he held back the knife.

Lin Chow did not consider himself an accessory to murder. He thought of himself only as a good businessman trying to support a family, which meant keeping all the customers he could.

As the months went by, Lin Chow wondered more and more why the knife had been left. The work the blade had done on Crider Peel showed that the owner knew what he was doing, and Lin Chow could not understand why such a professional assassin would be so careless. Perhaps he had been frightened by sounds from the living quarters and, thinking someone was about to discover him, had dropped the knife in flight. Or perhaps the murderer had left the weapon intentionally, either to avoid having to carry such a terrible thing about, or else as a signature of his work. Lin Chow had heard of such things among Tong executioners.

But as the next New Year came, and then the spring, Lin Chow began to think that what this item held back was of no real value to either him or his ancestors. Perhaps it was of value to someone else. And this thought troubled Lin Chow greatly, because he had always been a man who did not cherish things that belonged to somebody else, and most especially to somebody else's ancestors.

It was almost a year after Crider Peel's demise when Mrs. Condon Murphy came into Lin Chow's laundry with her weekly bundle of clothes and lay them on the counter. Actually, she brought two bundles: a large one that contained the dirty shirts and underwear of all her clients except her young gentleman, as she called him. The young gentleman's laundry was carried separately, always in a pillowcase that had red and green cross-stitching around the hem.

Lin Chow knew that each week Mrs. Condon Murphy took the clean laundry of her regular boarders and opened it on the parlor table so that as each person arrived he had to find his own things. But the young gentleman's package she delivered to his room unopened, and left it square in the center of his bed. Lin Chow knew these things because Mrs. Murphy was a woman who enjoyed explaining the details of her routines in running such an establishment as a boarding-house, something incomprehensible to Lin Chow, for he believed that the less other people knew about his business, the better.

On that day Lin Chow himself was behind the counter, and he assumed that Mrs. Murphy had received her annual keg of bock beer and had been sampling it heavily. She smelled of malt and was more than normally garrulous, which, as Lin Chow knew, was very garrulous indeed.

"Now do them shirts in the young gentleman's laundry careful and neat," Mrs. Murphy said, her loud voice bringing two of Lin Chow's grandchildren from the living quarters to locate the source of the noise. Lin Chow turned and clucked sharply and the two grandchildren darted back out of sight like tiny, pigtailed foxes.

"Ah," said Lin Chow.

"Them's the best shirts money can buy, them shirts of my young gentleman. Likely not a one cost less than seventy-five cents."

"Ah."

"He's such a fine young gentleman," shouted Mrs. Murphy. "Why, just last month he donated a fine dray horse to the volunteer fire department. Yes, sir! And last year he helped that little girl, poor thing, when her daddy was killed. I only heard a little of it, right in my own kitchen, but I know enough to put two and two together. He was gone for a long time right after that, and no matter what the newspaper said, I think it was him took the little girl to her kin in Ohio, or wherever it was. I'd bet my life they didn't come here, but he took that child to them so she could have a nice home. Yes, sir! A fine gentleman."

"Ah."

"None of it's any of my affair," said Mrs. Murphy. "And I don't go about stickin' my nose in other people's business, you understand."

Lin Chow smiled a smile that betrayed neither mirth nor condescension. It was the smile to which citizens of Leavenworth referred when they spoke of Lin Chow's good manners.

"And he always pays his board on time," Mrs. Murphy said. "I can't say that for all my men. Take that Mr. Moffet. Right now he owes me for three weeks and still charged me regular price for my beer."

Lin Chow was no longer listening. He was thinking about that young gentleman of Mrs. Murphy's. In fact, he thought of little else for the next four days, finally concluding that Crider Peel must have been a Special Person to him. Why would anyone leave his business for a long time just for the purpose of seeing to the welfare of somebody else's girl child, unless there was a Special Person involved?

This revelation came as a mild shock to Lin Chow. He knew the reputation of Roman Hasford and he knew the reputation of Crider Peel, and the two were as different as circles and squares. Yet there it was; he had left his business to see after a girl child.

And he reasoned further. If there was this special thing between them, even if only a girl child, who better to have the knife than the one still living? He wasn't sure to what purpose. Except that perhaps he was tired of having the knife weigh so heavily on his mind, and now had an opportunity to get rid of it. He would never think of throwing a good knife into the river. Or of giving it to Eldon Harvesty, because the city marshal of Leavenworth would have some harsh things to say about Lin Chow's hiding it for so long. Besides, he didn't like Eldon Harvesty very much, and the knife had become a valued token in Lin Chow's mind and Eldon Harvesty didn't deserve to have it. He wasn't sure why it had value. Perhaps because it was now associated in his head with the fine young gentleman having a Special Person.

Special Person? Crider Peel? It was too confusing for Lin Chow to carry it any further.

That week, when Mrs. Condon Murphy returned for her laundry, her young gentleman's things separately wrapped and neatly tied, she was unaware that a knife inside the folds of a red scarf was among the shirts, each of which had cost at least seventy-five cents.

And with the knife was a note written with a brush and black ink on rice paper, laboriously written by Lin Chow himself, written in language that was not as good as he was capable of writing, but which he knew was in the style the whites expected from a heathen Chinaman.

The note read, "Young gentleman this special thing found at body Mr. Peel the morning his dying and very bloody."

It had begun to rain in midafternoon, and by the time Roman Hasford rode the sorrel to Mrs. Condon Murphy's boardinghouse, the skies were low and black and the wind was driving hard from the west, the rain blowing in sheets before it. That morning had been clear and cloudless, so his slicker was in the clothes closet at the boardinghouse, and by the time Roman arrived at the horse stall behind Mrs. Murphy's back porch, he was drenched to the skin.

"Mutton stew for supper," Mrs. Murphy called as Roman dripped across her kitchen.

This is a hell of a time for mutton stew, he thought, on a night when I'll get near drowned going downtown to eat something decent. But he said nothing.

In his room he stripped quickly, throwing his wet things

into the wicker basket Mrs. Murphy provided for dirty clothes. He saw the package of laundry in the exact center of his bed and sat down there, naked, and unwrapped the bundle. Beneath the first stiffly starched shirt was the red scarf with the knife and the note.

He stared at the knife for a long time before reading the note, and again afterward, holding it in his hand and feeling the rough texture of the brown-and-white bone handle. Then he opened it. The blade was six inches long and there were flecks of red rust along the cutting edge, where the tiny etchings of a whetstone had scored the metal long ago.

He read the rice-paper note again and then went to the cold stove in the corner of his room, opened it, and placed the note inside. He took a match from the top of the bureau and set fire to the note, and watched until it was consumed in a quick little burst of blue flame. Then he closed the stove door.

As he pulled on dry clothes, his eyes returned again and again to the open knife lying on Mrs. Condon Murphy's Joseph's-coat quilt. After he slipped into his slicker and took a dry hat from the closet shelf, he picked up the knife, closed it, and put it in a trousers pocket.

Bent against the driving rain, Roman Hasford walked to the Garrison Hotel. He ordered the chicken dinner but ate less than half of it. On the walk back to the boardinghouse he had to avoid a number of people on the sidewalks, out now because the rain had suddenly stopped. He stamped up to his room, wetting the stairs. The whole house smelled of mutton stew. Passing Mr. Moffet's room, he heard the low notes of a tentative voice singing, and it occurred to him that the little beer salesman was going to his mason jars earlier and earlier as time went along.

Locked in his room and in dry underwear once more, he sat at his desk with the bone-handled knife before him. Taking up the quill from its holder, he tried to bring forth the words that fit his mood, but could not.

God Almighty, he thought. I wonder if he killed Crider Peel partly for me. Partly because he knew how Crider Peel treated his own daughter and knew it would be a service to her and therefore to me. And knew that I'd even had thoughts of doing it myself, but could never build up to murder. Even for Catrina.

But surely not, he tried to reassure himself. Surely there were other reasons.

He looked at the knife and remembered, as he had all through his supper, as he had the instant he first saw that bone handle unraveling from the red silk scarf, remembered the first time he had seen it, going over and over the details like trying to recall a dream. The day in the buffalo carcass. The day they were hiding from the Cheyenne. The day of the snakebite. And the movement of that same bone-handled knife from the hand of one to the hand of the other, just before the sharp tip of the blade made its incisions into the fang punctures.

Finally he replaced the quill in its holder and closed the diary without writing a word in it, and snapped the knifeblade back into the handle. He blew out the lamp and crawled beneath the Joseph's-coat quilt because after the rain had stopped, it had turned unseasonably cold.

Well, he thought, whether he intended it or not, he did me a favor, and Catrina an even greater one.

But he knew these were thoughts that would never be committed to the pages of a diary or anything else. He would keep them locked in his head, along with the name of the man he now knew had killed Crider Peel.

I reckon, he thought, that it's a secret Tyne Fawley deserves to have kept. There have been enough counts against him without this, too.

He was still awake when it started to rain again, and somehow the sound of it on the shingle roof made him think of home and of his father and the old Jew at the Sugar Creek mill calling him "sprout" as far back as he could remember. The same thing Tyne Fawley had called him.

He tried to revive that terrible time when Tyne Fawley had carried him across the western high plains to Fort Wallace. It disturbed him that he could remember none of it coherently because of the snakebite sickness. And when that was gone, so was Tyne Fawley. And he hadn't seen him alive again, but only in that dismal funeral parlor, lying naked and with the pitiful blue wounds in his face and body.

It gave him some satisfaction that he knew something Jared Dane didn't. That Tyne Fawley had murdered Crider Peel. But that was mother to the next thought: Maybe Jared Dane had known all along.

It was three days before Roman Hasford made his decision, and this he did write in his diary.

> It has taken the better part of five years to show me that I was never meant for this Kansas border country. In that time I have had the agony of caring for a woman who thought I was beneath her station, and another who tried to trap me with her favors as though I were an old man randy for every opportunity. I have found female tenderness and affection and understanding only in the arms of a lady of the night who is old enough to be my mother. I have been shot at. I have been snakebit. I have lost one dear friend to the cholera; my life was saved by another who turned out to be an outlaw gunned down in the streets; and yet a third had his arm shot off. I've had frequent visits of what Mama calls the Green Apple Spurts, and almost died of a head cold during my first season here. I have frozen in winter, broiled in summer. I have been berated by army officers. I have been thrown into violent fits of temper. I was once thought capable only of emptying pisspots. I have seen great beasts slaughtered for the fun of it. I have witnessed corruption and been a part of it, the worst of this being that I came to regard such things as the normal way of doing business. I have made a lot of money, which thus far has offered me little of happiness. I have become addicted to strong drink.
>
> On the credit side of the ledger has been my discovery of the religion of Mr. Thomas Jefferson. And finding Catrina Peel, who in only a short time will be as old as Mama was when she got married.

One would assume that this is all a part of the process of becoming a man. But it appears to me that maybe there are places with a larger dose of peace and calm in which to do such things.

At least there are those two items on the credit side of the book that have made it worthwhile, I suppose. And besides that, I reckon Papa and I needed some distance between each other during the years it took him to get away from the war in his mind.

Now it is time for me to get away from things in my mind. Away from Mr. Hankins and Tyne Fawley and all the rest. And this is no place to do it because each way I turn, there I can see them.

Somehow, with all of that, I can't help but feel that maybe I was a better man when I came here than I will be when I leave.

Once it was decided, Roman moved swiftly to clean up his business so he could be in the Ozarks by the time the snow dusted Wire Road, along the valley of Little Sugar Creek.

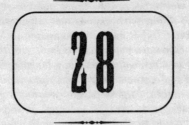

From the first, Mr. August Bainbridge had been an enigma to Roman. Everything about the railroad tycoon's methods of doing business was at least marginally repulsive to a hill boy whose only experience with economics had been the philosophy that a day's work deserved a day's pay—if not in money, then in kind.

Yet there was a fascination about such magnificent manipulations that was overpowering, perhaps more so because of Roman's initial innocence about how great financial achievements were given birth and nurtured to maturity in an age when the only restraints to free enterprise were laws that made outright robbery and extortion felonies but had little to say about bribery, monopoly, or the suppression of competition by whatever means.

It was a world of big dog eating small dog. And everyone seemed willing to let anything just short of fraud and embezzlement and extortion decide which dog would grow fastest. In such a pack, Mr. August Bainbridge had obviously always been a fast-growing dog.

Yet Roman Hasford liked him. He couldn't explain why. In all his experience with such things before Kansas, there had been only the merchant in Bentonville who charged more for calico cloth bolt goods and Boston-made shoes than they were really worth, because he knew nothing else like them was available within two hundred miles. Along with his father, Roman had hated that man. But compared to August Bainbridge, he had been a chicken mite.

Roman had often wondered about his affection for Bainbridge, and had come to the conclusion that despite his business practices, August Bainbridge was a genial, well-educated, caring man. At least he cared for those he placed on the credit side of *his* ledger, and somehow Roman had ended up on the credit side. Witness the gift of railroad-construction shares. Witness what Jared Dane had said about the Boss planning to put Roman in high parlors.

It had always been a pleasure to be in the company of August Bainbridge. The great man did not talk down to him, did not regard him as only fit to plow a hillside cornfield and nothing more. There had always been a certain warmth in their conversation, and mutual respect. At first this had impressed Roman beyond words, but later he had taken it for granted.

Well, Roman thought, when you get to know a man, I reckon there are always a few redeeming qualities, even with knaves.

Once he'd decided to leave Kansas, Roman felt conscience-bound to see August Bainbridge face to face and explain that the state legislature and the United States Senate were beyond his abilities and ambitions.

He sent a telegraph message to Topeka in the third week of September, and was delighted to have a response the very next day, inviting him for a visit to the capital of Kansas.

As he prepared for the short trip in one of Mr. Bainbridge's cars, dressed in a new suit and hat and patent leather and felt high-button shoes, he felt a little guilty. His real reason for wanting an audience with the Boss had nothing to do with a graceful withdrawal from political life. It had to do with business.

But who better to talk to about such things? Roman thought.

It was a measure of Roman's confidence in the friendship of Mr. August Bainbridge, a man more powerful, richer, and better known than the governors of Kansas and Arkansas combined. And just the thought of that puffed up Roman's pride.

Why, hell, he thought, positioning the diamond stickpin in the center of his necktie.

"Mr. Roman, have some roasted chestnuts," Fletcher said, placing a bowl of the steaming nuts on the dining table of Mr. August Bainbridge's private car. "And I got a whole load of St. Louis beer to go with it."

"Thank you," Roman said.

He was still a little awed at the opulence of this railroad car, where a person could spend his whole life without want.

"Mr. Jared gone off to Denver on business for the Boss," Fletcher said. "He gon' be sad he missed you. But the Boss, he said big supper right here tonight, him and you, and he'll be along in a while."

When the Boss arrived, Roman overcame the hard knot in his belly and came right out with it, after the oyster stew but before the lamb chops, and Mr. August Bainbridge smiled and said it was all right, so what did Roman want to do?

"Go to the Ozarks and raise good horses," Roman said.

"An exemplary ambition," Bainbridge said. "And how can I help?"

So Roman told him about the problems of liquidation, a word he had never used before to his knowledge, and then Mr. Bainbridge told him how.

"I am aware of your success in the meat-processing business," Mr. Bainbridge said, and Roman thought he looked rather saintly with the low sun's rays coming through the car's stained-glass windows, casting reds and blues and purples across his face. As Mr. Bainbridge puffed his cigar, the thick smoke was colored from the same source, floating like fired incense at some Oriental shrine, although Roman had never seen an Oriental shrine.

"There are a number of men in the meat-packing business who are more than a little interested in your venture. Kansas City men. Not unlike myself, they are interested in establishing their enterprise without serious competition. So I can tell you that there are serious people ready to pay serious prices for what you have in Leavenworth. I can apprise them of your intentions when you advise me to do so."

Mr. Bainbridge took a dainty sip from his brandy snifter and shook his head, frowning.

"Not completely satisfactory," he said, and placed the glass on the table and drew a deep breath.

"Now. First you must buy out that silent partner of yours, no matter what the cost. I'm sure she will sell. So that you are sole owner, and not merely two-thirds."

Roman was not in the least surprised that this man knew about Katie Rose Rouse.

"The Kansas City people will give almost anything to have what you've got in Leavenworth. So sell it to them, but only on the condition they'll take this garbage-disposal thing and the stockyard of the late, lamented Elisha Hankins. All in a bundle, you see?"

Roman saw. And knew that Katie Rose would sell her part in the business for some absurdly low price. And in that moment, watching August Bainbridge's face in a wreath of color, he could not avoid the knowledge that Katie Rose Rouse and this man sitting before him, the former a whore and the latter a merciless entrepreneur who could promote the useless slaughter of buffalo with no purpose other than the entertainment of politicians and business friends, had been largely responsible for his having become a modestly rich man, at least by the standards of Benton County, Arkansas, where there was so little hard cash that nobody had ever bothered to establish a bank there.

When he left, August Bainbridge took his hand and looked into his eyes.

"You have a quality, Roman. I wish you'd let me develop it."

"I reckon it's where it ought to be right now," Roman said.

Bainbridge laughed, a great, belly-shaking laugh.

"All right, son. When you're the biggest horse breeder in Arkansas, come back and see me."

"I hope to, sir."

When he took the train back to Lawrence, there to take the spur line to Leavenworth, Fletcher accompanied him to the passenger depot, and as Roman went up the steps to his car, Fletcher patted his back.

"I'll tell Mr. Jared you was here."

"Yes, thank you," said Roman. "Tell him I won't be back."

"It's a pity, sir," Fletcher said, grinning, his face almost blue-black in the station platform lamplight. "Him and the Boss think you kinda hung the moon."

It was stupid, but it kept Roman grinning to himself all the way back to Leavenworth.

Roman had become addicted to lists as surely as he had to rye whiskey. So now he made another to guide his steps through what he labeled "disengagement."

First was Katie Rose Rouse, and her reaction was exactly as Roman had expected. She sold him her share of hogs, buildings, wagons, mules, and collecting agency for three thousand dollars. With her property rights to the real estate at the hog ranch thrown in.

"That's not enough," Roman said.

"Roman, I'm tired of worryin' every time it rains about those damned hogs gettin' pneumonia," she said. "And I never fancied myself much of a garbageman."

"You've been a good friend, Katie Rose."

"It's been a hell of a good time, ain't it? You wanta come lay around in my bed for one last go-round?"

Roman laughed and was amazed that such a thing would have embarrassed him to tears only a few short years ago.

"No, thanks. Not that it hasn't been good before."

"Sure. What you remember of it."

With Elmer Scaggs, Roman came directly to the point.

"I'm leaving, Elmer."

"When you be back this time, boss?"

"I'm not coming back."

Elmer's eyes popped and he blinked and clenched his fists at the end of those long, fencepost arms. He seemed to sniff, as though he thought the stockyard office was on fire.

"Gawd damn, boss, what for?"

"To start a little farm in the hills," said Roman. "Raise some corn and garden truck and a few hogs and some fine horses."

"Well, Gawd damn, boss, I can do all those things."

"I was sort of reckoning to take you with me if you want to go."

Elmer jumped two feet in the air and howled, and suddenly Roman felt himself in the bear hug of Elmer's arms. But only for a moment, and then Elmer leaped back like a huge cat, and his face was red and his fists were clenched at his sides once more.

"There's no First Street saloons where we're going," Roman said.

"Hell, boss, I'm mostly weaned from that tit."

"We'll have to build a house and barns and outbuildings. The place I've got in mind was burned out during the war."

"You seen me build all that stuff at the hog ranch. I can build anything you want built."

"There's loose ends we've got to tie up here. So if you want to go, get yourself downtown and buy this stuff," Roman said, and handed Elmer a piece of paper. "And pick out our two best mules and the spring wagon and make a crate to carry three hogs—two brood sows and a young boar."

Elmer frowned, scanning the list.

"Fodder for the hogs and about twenty horses for two weeks," he mumbled. "Tack and grub for two weeks on the trail. Two new Winchester repeating rifles and ammunition. Some buckshot for my double-barrel."

"I'll be carrying considerable money," Roman said, to explain the guns. "And we'll have those horses."

Elmer laughed, a great burst of sound.

"Hell, boss, we'll keep all that stuff safe. Anybody else goin' with us?"

"Orvile Tucker, if he wants to."

"Gawd damn, I hoped you'd say that. This is gonna be a helluva lot of fun."

"I hope so."

Then Orvile.

"Mr. Roman, I never thought I'd get the chance to go back to where the snow ain't deep in the winter."

"Don't bother loading any of your heavy smithing stuff when Elmer brings the wagon around. Just your own truck. We'll buy all we need after we get there. Cut out about seventeen good mares and one stallion from the stock pens. We're gonna start us a herd in Arkansas."

"And Junior?"

"Of course Junior. But I've got to warn you. You're going to find a hoe in your hands a lot of the time. You can't stand around that forge all day, and we'll be farming."

"Mr. Roman, I growed the best sweet potatoes and squash in all of Tennessee and Kentucky. And I can lay rail fence a mile a day."

Then, remembering what he'd heard about the message sent over the wires when the last spike was driven in the first transcontinental railroad, Roman sent a one-word telegram to Mr. August Bainbridge in Topeka. "Done!"

And five days later, four men in stovepipe hats and clawhammer coats arrived from Kansas City to buy his holdings. They looked alike, with muttonchop whiskers and enlarged noses with burst blood vessels, and they came on the same railroad train. But they weren't friends, and each one fawned and winked and snickered and pleaded his case against the others.

Competition is a wonderful thing, Roman thought.

It was like an auction sale, each of the Kansas City men trying to outbid the others, and Roman carried it along for three days. Mrs. Condon Murphy had to control traffic in her parlor, three of the buyers sitting in horsehair chairs and glaring at one another while the fourth was upstairs in Roman's room, bargaining. Then they rotated. None left Mrs. Murphy's parlor until well past eleven each night, each afraid to turn his back on the others, each expecting and getting another chance.

At one point Mrs. Murphy, up beyond her bedtime and irritable as only she could be, charged into the parlor with a crock milk pitcher in her hand.

"Take them hats off indoors!" she shouted. "Don't you know how gentlemen is supposed to act? And if you've got to smoke those stogies, do it out on the porch. This house is gonna stink like a tobacco barn for a week."

When the deal was finally struck, Tallheimer Smith was called in, and now it really was done. After Spankin Hankins's money for the yards was deducted, Roman had a letter of transmittal for eleven thousand seven hundred dollars to deposit in his express-company account.

Roman wrote in his diary the last entry he would pen in Kansas: "Making money can be a great pleasure and even a lark. It was difficult to keep from laughing, watching those men push and shove and try to show off like a bunch of boys in the fourth grade out to impress the girls in the class. Papa won't believe it. All told, I'll be bringing home almost twenty thousand dollars. A fortune. Maybe I'll start a bank myself."

It was a sparkling clear morning, the sky almost painfully blue with nothing across its dome and only a few puffs of white to the west, where the early sun touched a scattering of cotton-ball clouds. The grass had withered and died in late September, and now, in the first week of October, it lay in a thick mantle, looking crisp and fresh, running down the slopes to the Kansas River like a golden carpet just brushed.

Along the many little draws that marked the tributary creeks and along the river itself, the timber had turned to autumn colors, the yellows of the sycamore and the burning browns of oak and the blood-reds of Chickasaw plum and sumac. In the dead grass and among the low brush that fringed the stream-line trees were the fall birds; some, like the brilliantly yellow warblers, on one stage of their migration south of the Rio Grande, and others, like the masked cardinals, not going anywhere because they would winter here.

Roman particularly liked the cardinals because of their flashing color and their clear call of *wha-cheer-cheer-cheer*, so sharp on the thin air. He knew he would be seeing them all the way to the hills of Arkansas, two hundred miles to the south. He had spent his childhood watching them in the low foliage of the dogwood trees behind the barn at his father's farm.

It was their second day out of Leavenworth, and now, having just broken camp, Elmer Scaggs sat on the spring-wagon seat with the mule lines in his hands, watching Roman for the signal to move. Nearby, Orvile Tucker had the little horse herd ready, riding a big buckskin stud and watching for the same signal. Roman looked across the land to the south and laughed because it felt so good. And Elmer laughed, too, and Orvile. Junior, catching the mood, whistled and stamped and seemed to laugh as well, his lips peeled back from ivory-colored teeth.

"All the fine colors and smells of fall have come out to bid us farewell," Roman said, and felt foolish for saying it.

But Elmer and Orvile both nodded, grinning widely, their faces shaded under new hats and Elmer's new beard showing black with streaks of gray and Orvile's cheeks a shining chocolate.

"Let's ford this old river and head south," Roman shouted.

"By Gawd, boss, Arkansas or bust!" Elmer howled, and slapped the reins across the mules' rumps, and they stepped out, drawing behind them the wagon with the hogs in their crates at the tailgate, bags of grain and travel tack and food piled just behind the seat, and under the seat Roman's money, some in gold, some in greenbacks. Almost twenty thousand dollars! And leaning against the seat, two shining new repeating rifles and the shotgun.

As they moved toward the river, the horse herd trailing the wagon because they knew that was where the grain lay, there was a sharp whistle from far off, back along the trail to Leavenworth. When Roman turned, he saw a single rider coming fast, and Elmer and Orville saw him, too. Orville rode up beside the wagon and Elmer passed him one of the rifles and then lay the shotgun across his lap.

Roman watched the horseman come nearer, growing larger in the sun, and then saw the empty left sleeve in the yellow duster the rider wore.

"It's all right," he said. "It's Jared Dane. Go on to the ford. I'll meet you on the other side."

As the herd and the wagon moved down to the crossing, Roman reined the sorrel back and rode to meet the oncoming rider. He couldn't recall that he'd ever seen Jared Dane on a horse, and saw that the one-armed man rode awkwardly. As they approached one another, Roman pulled in on Dane's right and held out his hand and Jared Dane took it in his own with the same cold, hard little grip that Roman remembered.

"Hello, Roman Hasford," said Jared Dane.

"How'd you find us?" Roman asked.

The tiny twitch of lip at the corner of the mouth was all the answer Roman got, and expected nothing more. Jared Dane looked around the countryside, as though surveying it. He's always looking for enemies, Roman thought. Dane was wearing his summer straw hat with the outlandishly wide brim, and Roman smiled.

"I've always liked that hat," he said.

Jared Dane's pale, pinched face showed no sign that he'd heard. Now he was watching Roman's little cavalcade going into the water of the river.

"A good day for traveling," Dane said.

"It's a nice sendoff."

Dane shifted in his saddle, his one hand holding the horn, but still his eyes did not meet Roman's. "I wanted to wish you well. Our last meeting was something less than pleasant. I didn't want that to be the final memory we had of one another."

"I thank you," Roman said, and suddenly there was a swelling in his throat and he hated it because it spoiled all the rest of this fine day. "I wanted to break clean. But you've been a treasured friend. I seem to be saying that to more people in this godforsaken place than I thought I ever would."

"It's been mutual," Dane said, and now the flat, expressionless eyes went to Roman's. "If you'd stayed out your whole string here, someday I would probably have been working for you."

Roman was glad he'd said it, true or not, because it effectively broke his quick little burst of melancholy.

"I can't imagine that."

"Stranger things have happened," said Jared Dane. "And now you're off to those hills of yours, and before long you'll be marrying that little black-eyed girl."

Roman had thought he could never again be amazed at what Jared Dane knew about the happenings on this wild border, but he was amazed now. How Dane knew, Roman refused to contemplate; he refused to get his mind involved in such mysteries, because now he was getting shed of Kansas and all it had meant, getting it all behind him. So he said nothing, but sat mute on the sorrel, and returned Jared Dane's cold stare.

"I never saw her," said Dane. And he looked away toward the ford again, where the horses were already across, the wagon coming close behind, Elmer Scaggs shouting and whipping the mules with the lines. "But I understand she's a beautiful child."

"I see her more as a young woman, now," Roman said, and despite his best efforts his words were sharp. It brought the little twitch to the corners of Jared Dane's mouth once more.

"Well, she will be soon enough," Dane said.

One of the cardinals in the willows along the river gave his sharp, liquid whistle, and Jared Dane's head cocked to one side.

"Redbird," he said. "I always liked redbirds."

"Yes," Roman said. "Me too."

"Well," said Jared Dane, reining away with his one good hand. "I wanted to tell you. When you're located, if you ever need me, get word up here and I'll come."

Roman laughed again, but it was a hollow laugh and he knew it. Because he knew Jared Dane meant what he said.

"Jared," Roman said, "where I'm going, now the war's past, men like you would scare the hell out of everybody. And I don't reckon I'll ever need you."

Roman thought Dane would ride off without another word, but Dane pulled in his horse and sat for a long while with his back to Roman, and finally turned and looked over his shoulder.

"God, Roman Hasford!" he said. "Don't you know that people like you are always needing people like me? Trouble is, you find problems with admitting it. Goodbye."

Roman watched Jared Dane's back grow smaller as he rode away, and only after a long moment did he say it, not loud enough for Dane to hear.

"Goodbye."

Roman didn't know whether to laugh or cry. He could have willed it either way. But there was one thing. When Dane had delivered himself of those last words, there had been on his lips the only true, cheek-creasing smile Roman had ever seen on the cold little face.

God Almighty, Roman thought. I'm gonna miss that son of a bitch!

And as the yellow-dustered, straw-hatted figure rode out of sight into a far draw, Roman Hasford turned the sorrel back toward the river, where the cock cardinal was giving his sweet call once more.

DOUGLAS C. JONES has written thirteen highly praised historical novels. He received the Friends of American Writers award for best novel of the year for *Elkhorn Tavern*, and was three times the recipient of the Golden Spur Award for Best Western Historical Novel. He lives in Fayetteville, Arkansas.